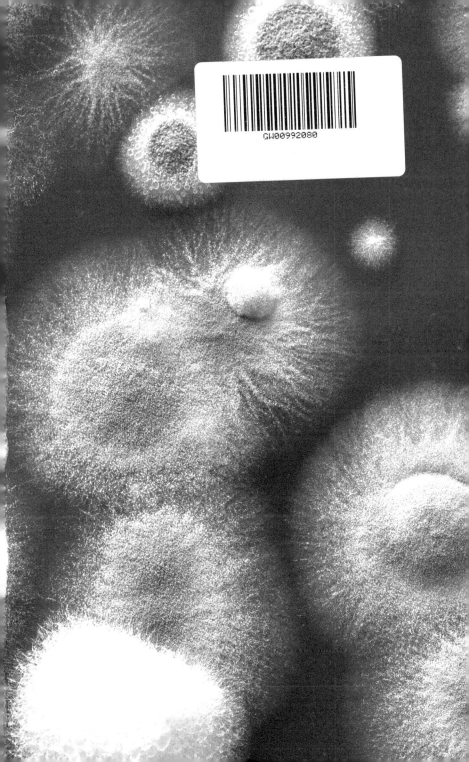

GW00992080

A STORY BY
ADRIAN M. GIBSON

A FUNGALVERSE NOVEL

MUSHROOM
BLUES

THE HOFMANN REPORT
BOOK ONE

Welcome to The Fungalverse

First edition March 2024

Cover Art: Felix Ortiz
Cover Design: Adrian M. Gibson
Interior Design & Graphics: Adrian M. Gibson

ISBN: 978-9942-45-320-4 (Paperback)
ISBN: 978-9942-45-319-8 (Hardcover)
ASIN: B0CTCF9TCF (eBook)

The Kinoko **XB** Book Co.

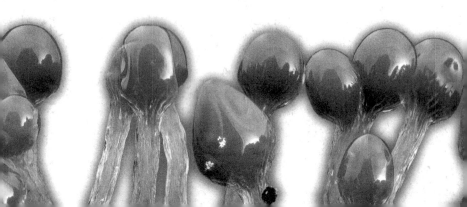

For mom and dad,
    the spores that bore me life
For Natalia,
    the mycelium to my mushroom
And for my sons,
    the most precious fungi

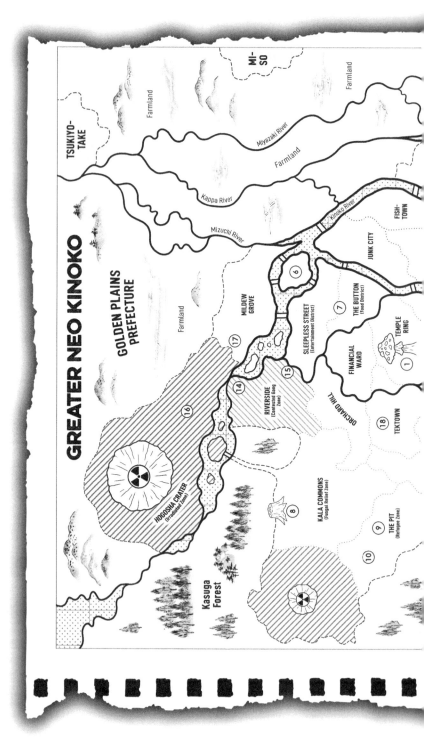

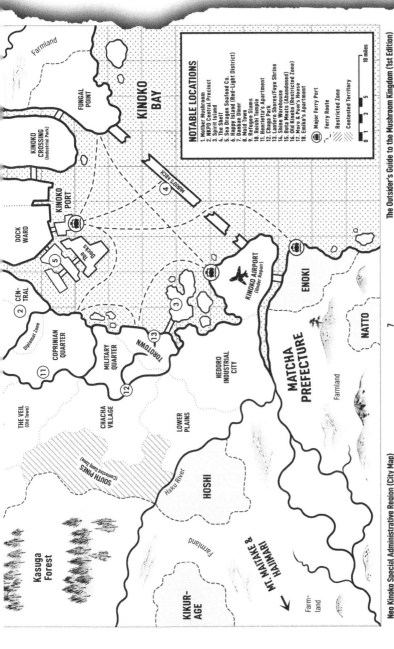

NOTABLE LOCATIONS

1. Mother Mushroom
2. NKPD Central Precinct
3. Spirit Island
4. The Shelf
5. Sea Dragon Seafood Co.
6. Happy Island (Red-Light District)
7. Daidoan Diner
8. Mold Town
9. Refugee Slums
10. Reishi Temple
11. Henrietta's Apartment
12. Chaga Park
13. Lantern Shores/Fuyu Shrine
14. Shii Warehouse
15. Buta Meats (Abandoned)
16. Old Kinoko (Restricted Zone)
17. Moro & Pom's House
18. Emiko's Apartment

⚓ Major Ferry Port
- - - Ferry Route
▨ Restricted Zone
▨ Contested Territory

0 1 3 5 10 miles

Farmland

KINOKO BAY

FUNGAL POINT

KINOKO CROSSING (Industrial Park)

KUMO'S ARCH
④

KINOKO PORT ⚓

DOCK WARD

The Docks

⑤

CEN-TRAL
②

Diplomat Zone

COPRINIAN QUARTER
⑪

THE VEIL (Old Town)

MILITARY QUARTER

TORIOTOWN
⑬

⑫

CHACHA VILLAGE

SPIRIT ISLAND
③

KINOKO AIRPORT (Under Repair) ✈

⚓

⚓

ENOKI

NATTO

MATCHA PREFECTURE

Farmland

HEDORO INDUSTRIAL CITY

LOWER PLAINS

SOUTH PINES (Contested Gang Zone)

HOSHI

Haku River

Farmland

Kasuga Forest

MT. MAITAKE & HAJIMARI

Farm-land

KIKUR-AGE

THE FUNGALVERSE: GLOSSARY

Fungal/Mycological Terminology

Fungus (pl. fungi): Any of a group of spore-producing organisms feeding on organic matter, including molds, yeast, and mushrooms.

Mushroom: An aboveground fruiting body of a fungus that typically consists of a stem and cap.

Mycelium: The part of a fungus that is usually underground, consisting of a network of fungal filaments or hyphae. Its main function is to extract nutrients from soil.

Hypha (pl. hyphae): The branching filaments that make up the mycelium of a fungus.

Spore: Microscopic, single-celled units produced by mushrooms in the process of sexual reproduction (roughly analogous to seeds).

Cap (or pileus): Top of the fruiting body that is seen above ground and supports a spore-bearing surface.

Gill: Fleshy plate-like or blade-like structures attached to the underside of the cap in many species of mushrooms.

Pores: Tiny tubes, or holes, on the underside of a variety of mushroom caps, used for spore dispersal.

Stem: The stalk-like feature supporting the cap of a mushroom.

Veil: A protective layer of tissue that may cover all or part of a mushroom.

Mold: One of the structures that certain fungi can form, resulting in a furry growth on the surface of organic matter, especially in the presence of dampness and decay.

Bioluminescent: The bio-chemical emission of light by living organisms.

Fruiting body: The spore-producing organ of a fungus, often seen as a mushroom or toadstool.

Polypore: A bracket fungus in which the spores are expelled through fine pores on the underside.

Translations of Common Hōpponese Phrases & Words

Haowa: Good morning/afternoon

Zaowa: Good evening

Haomi do: How are you?

Ariari do: Thank you

Yisima: Excuse me

Kaidono: I don't understand

Baebae: Child or loved one

Jiujiu: Brother/sister (friendly term for both friends and relatives)

Shushu: Uncle/auntie (age dependent--from young to old person)

Damigami nai: Bless the gods

Damitare: Godsdamnit

Shabi: Bitch

Bakira: Dirty or cheap

Kuta dai: Shut the hells up

Doredore: Out of my way!

Chikero: Oh, shit!/Oh, fuck!

Udarai: Pain in the ass

Zunoro: Curse/cursed

Gaikamu: Foreign scum

Gaigai: Coprinians

Shimin: Colonizer

Shinkin: Fungal Hōpponese

Common Slang & Slurs

Fungal: Colloquial term for native Hōpponese

Coppies: Slang for Coprinians

Blues: NKPD officers

Meatbag: Racial slur for humans

Hophead: Slang for Fungals

Buttons: Slang for Fungals

Sporesack: Racial slur for Fungals

Gillie: Racial slur for Fungals

Molder: Racial slur for Fungals

Half-breed: Mixed-race human/Fungal

Muties/Partials: Deroga-tory slur for half-breeds

The Long War/The Invasion: Refers to the Spore War

Shine: Bootleg rice wine

Hōpponese Honorifics

Shen: Used to address a person of higher rank or social status, mentors, guests, customers, seniors or someone unfamiliar.

Kato: A title of respect to address colleagues or a person of the same rank.

Jero: A title of respect to address a person of a lower rank.

Dari: Used to address children, friends or someone familiar, but can also be used in a demeaning manner.

Bae: An expression of endearment, especially towards a child or loved one.

Deities & Spirits of the Hōpponese Eien Religion
THE ETERNALS

Ame: *The Typhoon*; Goddess of Rain, Storms and Typhoons; daughter of Matsua and Murio; sister of Denki and Kazan.

Chaga: *The Timekeeper*; Goddess of Time and the Unseen; daughter of Yomi and Mother Chikyu; sister of Hogosha, Reishi, and Karu.

Denki: *The Lightbringer*; God of Thunder and Lightning; son of Matsua and Murio; brother of Ame and Kazan.

Heriko: *The Sentinel*; God of Passage, Clarity and Change and gatekeeper to the Great Beyond; born out of The Great Burst of spores that created the cosmos; brother of Yomi, Mother Chikyu, Murio, and Matsua.

Hogosha: *The Destroying Angel*; Goddess of War and Divine Protector of Hōppon; daughter of Yomi and Mother Chikyu; sister of Reishi, Chaga and Karu.

Karu: *The Shapeshifter*; God of Wind, Seasons, Agriculture, Harvest and the Spreading of Spores; son of Yomi and Mother Chakyu; brother of Hogosha, Chaga, and Reishi.

Kazan: *The Fiery One*; God of Volcanoes, Earthquakes and Fire; son of Matsua and Murio; brother of Ame and Denki.

Matsua: *The Brightness Above*; born out of The Great Burst of spores that created the cosmos; Goddess of the Sun and the Sky; wife and sister of Murio; sister of Yomi, Mother Chakyu, and Heriko; mother of Ame, Denki and Kazan.

Mother Chikyu: *The Great Mother*; born out of The Great Burst of spores that created the cosmos; Goddess of Creation, Life, Nature and Dawn; gave birth to the Islands of Hōppon and the cycles of life and death; mother of Hogosha, Reishi, Chaga, and Karu.

Murio: *The Guiding Star*; born out of The Great Burst of spores that created the cosmos; God of the Moon and the Stars and the ferryman of dead souls to The Great Beyond; husband and brother of Matsua; brother of Yomi, Mother Chikyu, and Heriko; father of Ame, Denki and Kazan.

Reishi: *The Healer*; Goddess of Fertility, Healing and Charity; daughter of Yomi and Mother Chakyu; sister of Hogosha, Chaga, and Karu.

Yomi: *The Great Persuader*; born out of The Great Burst of spores that created the cosmos; God of Creation, Death, Dusk and The Great Beyond; gave seed and spores to the Islands of Hoppon and the cycles of life and death; father of Hogosha, Reishi, Chaga, and Karu.

THE FOUR PROTECTORS, SERVANTS OF KARU

Haru: Spirit protector of spring and source of the east wind.

Natsu: Spirit protector of summer and source of the south wind.

Aki: Spirit protector of autumn and source of the west wind.

Fuyu: Spirit protector of winter and source of the north wind.

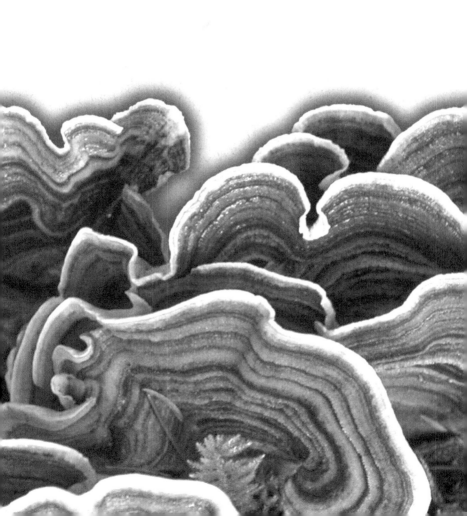

"Nature is not our enemy, to be raped and conquered.
Nature is ourselves, to be cherished and explored."
—Terence McKenna

"Snow:
years of anger following
hours that float idly down—"
—William Carlos Williams

MOLD & MUTILATION

[1] Case File #42-56
Spirit Island | 5:44 a.m.

- - - - - - - - -

NO GOOD DAY ever started with death before coffee.

I stood on the shoreline of Spirit Island, gazing upon a lumpy trash bag. It was nestled in an icy bed of seaweed, next to a rotting mycopaper lantern. A handful of bioluminescent motes floated above the water. Waves lapped against the bag where a large rip revealed a pale patch of hairless skin. Pungent saltiness rose up from algae and cold ocean spray, overpowering whatever I was about to find in there. I took out a face mask and put it on—NKPD protocol, and no way I would let anything contaminate me.

My feet crunched on gray sand as I adjusted my weight, heart beating faster. The bag was too small, especially for a body. But I knew what must be inside. Why else would dispatch have sent me a one-eight-seven code on my pager?

Before touching the crime scene, I took out my voice recorder: "Detective Henrietta Hofmann. Nineteenth of Twelfthmonth. Spirit Island. Black bag, suspected murder."

I sighed and put the recorder away, staring down into a brackish pool amidst the seaweed. There were puffy bags under my dull green eyes. My lips were chapped and my hair straggly. I hadn't had time to fix myself up, rolling out of bed to rush over here. Not that anyone would give a shit what the middle-aged female detective looked like, wrinkles and all.

Goddamn, I needed some caffeine.

Grey clouds threatened snow, and bitter wind rippled across Kinoko Bay, whipping my ponytail and sending stray strands of gray-blonde hair across my face. I pulled my trench coat tight with a shudder.

I yawned. Nightmares of a car on fire had kept me up last night. It was a miracle I'd even remembered mittens—anything to shield my skin from winter's frigid touch was welcome.

I put aside personal gripes to focus on why I was here: That bag.

Sticky sweat accumulated inside my mittens. It wasn't like the bag would come alive, finger-like fungi wriggling everywhere. This wasn't the first dead body I'd seen, either. Not even close.

But God, I fucking hated mushrooms and mold and the whole bloody mycological lot. Not a day would go by in Neo Kinoko where I wouldn't curse Frederick for exiling me here.

That prick.

I had to get my shit together. Focus. Forget about my bastard ex-husband—he could rot in a pile of fucking fungi for all I cared.

Reaching inside my jacket, I traded the warmth of my mittens for a pair of examination gloves. A shock of cold greeted my hands as I bent down. Both of my knees cracked with the weight of age.

Down at bag-level, I could already smell something foul. Hints of brine and decomposition invaded my nose. The scent memory of that foul combination lingered on my tongue.

Snapping on the gloves, I examined the bag. Seaweed draped across the black plastic, as if trying to pull it back into the sea. I spotted remnants of thick blue rope tucked between the green-brown fronds. Could have been tied to something to weigh it down. Bricks, or rocks?

There were small Hōpponese logograms on the rope. I couldn't read them, so I made a mental note to check with forensics and get them translated.

Nothing else was visible.

I pinched the ripped opening and lifted it. First to hit me was the stench: The brine was just a sample—nothing compared to the punch of putrid flesh now wafting from the opening.

Tiny red crabs with slime mold and fruiting bodies on their shells scuttled out of the bag. I sifted through the muck. And then I felt it, something round and bloated. I widened the opening, wincing as I stared into the eyeless cavities of a fungal child's human-like face.

Memories flooded my mind: Playing in the grassy backyard, sledding in winter, summertime visits to the cabin in southern Coprinia, jumping off the lakeside dock. Then, a memory-turned-nightmare.

Fire. Blood. Fear. Screaming.

I was haunted by the imagery of Elisabeth. Her face stared back at me, cold and empty, features that were a subtle blend of Frederick's and my own. I winced. Suppressed recollections bound by trauma, alcohol, and years of destructive behavior.

Bloody Hell, I had to focus.

I turned away from the bag and into the crisp ocean breeze, trying to escape the repulsive smell and taste. The thought of a dead kid chilled me. But deep down, I was more disgusted by the fact that the victim was a fungal. I could hardly stand to see mushrooms on a dinner plate, let alone be in the presence of *mushroom people*—even when they were a corpse.

This city was a purgatory—Frederick had made sure of that, exiling me to a place he knew would make me miserable. But I held a glimmer of hope that it could also be a chance to start anew. After years of drowning in a pool of booze and prescription antidepressants, anything was an improvement. But war and suffering lingered in this Hellhole.

And fungi were everywhere.

Hōppon, Neo Kinoko. These places had become wastelands wrought by the destroyer of worlds—my people. What the government had sold to Coprinians as the rebuilding of a liberated society was, in reality, the world's most public open-air prison.

A scam, a sham. Just like my being here.

Waves lapped rhythmically as the sun continued to rise. Seagulls squawked nearby. I returned to the small, decapitated head inside the bag. Sand dripped along decomposing skin, and my eyes began to water at thoughts of the past. The cool sting as tears trickled and pooled at the edges of my mask before starting to freeze.

I had to clear my head and prioritize. What happened to this child?

The neck appeared cleanly cut, but … I leaned closer. A thin patch of skin had been removed near the jugular. Strange.

Both eyes were removed or eaten post-mortem by sea lice, crabs, or fish. The skin was pockmarked and peeled away from water exposure. What remained had a waxy quality and a pallid discoloration. The nose had deformed and the lips were half-eaten, decayed. As well, the victim's hair was shaved and the mushroom cap atop their head was gone. Severed at the stem.

All that was left was the bruised and bloated base connected to the skull.

I burned with the impulse to look away, but my investigative instinct urged me onward. I searched inside the bag, through the sand slurry around the partially submerged head. A section of cut-off leg revealed bone amongst decaying muscle. I saw two more shapes: Distended limbs, the flesh puffy and peeling.

My optimism for an ID drew me to the child's partially opened mouth. White filaments of mycelium grew out from between the lips, draping down like a macabre curtain. My stomach churned. I ignored my gut feeling to stop and turn away.

I gently unlocked the stiff jaw, peering inside. The sight made me gag. A carpet of wet, white mold and mycelium coated the inside of the victim's mouth. Tongue, roof, gums. The parasitic growth continued all the way back to the throat, where it clumped like dense cotton balls.

Probing for teeth with my gloved finger, I cringed at the cushiony softness inside. Not a single tooth—just a rancid stench.

I pulled my finger from the victim's mouth. It was then that I saw the mold and mycelium quiver.

All of a sudden, the fungal threads began to shake. I fell backwards, startled. Half of my ass was submerged in freezing water and algae. The moist mycelium slithered out of the victim's maw. Then the woolly mass clogging their throat exploded in a burst of spores.

The minute particles ejected outward. They flew at me in a translucent mushroom cloud that I couldn't avoid. I scrambled back onto the damp sand on gloves and boots, feeling the spores enter into my eyes. I blinked furiously, desperate to rub them out. Part of me was considering rinsing them out with seawater—even if it stung, at least that might sterilize the spores.

"Fucking Hell," I cursed. How could I be so Goddamned careless?

My eyeballs were raw and watery. I massaged them with the sleeve of my jacket, praying I wouldn't get infected.

Ten years of the Spore War. Two years since it ended in Coprinian victory and occupation. And still, the only thing we had to fend off the fear of contagion were shitty masks and a dwindling supply of anti-fungal meds.

Angrily, I tore off my examination gloves and mask and threw them onto the sand. I shoved a hand into my jacket pocket and took out a small plastic bottle. Removing the cap, I shakily shoved two pills into my mouth and swallowed them dry.

Though I'd never heard of anyone actually getting infected, the anxiety of it kept me on edge, urging me to prevent a terrifying hypothetical. I stared at the head in the bag, mycophobia attempting to override my rational mind. My limbs trembled and my teeth ground together.

Goddamnit … I took a deep breath. I still had to do my bloody job. But there wasn't even a body left, just … parts.

I stood and stashed my pill bottle. Shoving the examination gloves and my mask into a disposable bag, I unclipped the radio from my belt. My ass was frozen, pants covered in sand—a small price to pay to get away from that fucking head.

Dialing in my radio, I spoke into the receiver: "NKPD dispatch, this is Detective Hofmann of the Homicide Division. Badge number 881. Do you read me?"

"We copy, Hofmann," a crackly female voice replied.

"One-eight-seven confirmed at Spirit Island. Send a forensics team over, ASAP."

"Copy, detective."

"Over and out."

I clipped my radio and returned to the dead child. Glaring at the rotten head, I felt a nagging unease that it might burst open and release more spores. The cavernous void of the child's lifeless face and empty eye sockets stared up at me, while frigid wind nipped at my exposed skin. Time stood still, and all I could do was grind my teeth beneath the aging contours of cold-reddened cheeks.

There was no way I could pass this case off to anyone else.

Captain Ridgeway would refuse, 'cause he'd been dumping all the shitty cases on me. Plus, no one in Homicide would care about a fungal kid, especially with all the protests over missing children the past few months. Cops were burnt out, pissed off, and I was the bottom rung on a ladder full of small men with big egos.

I sighed, praying this dead kid wouldn't be the death of me.

Mold and mutilation, a bag washed ashore—how the Hell was I going to solve this one?

RUBBLE
& RUIN

- - - - - - - - -

PATROLLED THE beach, clearing my head of irrational fears of fungi and spores. Pulling out my voice recorder, I noted the clues I'd picked up on: "Dismembered limbs and head. Cap cut off, bruising around edges. Heavy duty bag, black. Rope, blue and red, logograms in Hōpponese. Mycopaper lantern, rotten."

But questions tugged at me. "Who would chop up a fungal child? Where did this body come from?"

My mind raced with possibilities as I paced. The rope, the decay, and the location made me think of boats …

"Fishermen? Could they have dumped the body overboard?" I twisted my boots in the dark sand, *tap-tapping* my pen on my chin. Then again, the tides and waves in Kinoko Bay could've brought it in from any number of places.

Boat horns blared out on the bay. The black beach was riddled with kelp, mushroom colonies growing on their slimy surfaces.

Not far off, I heard shouts and chants—the kind of reverberation that accumulated in a crowd. I could make out the high and low pitches of Hōpponese, but at this distance it was too muffled for me to pinpoint what was being said.

I paused and followed the curve of urban sprawl as it hugged the vast bay, west of Spirit Island and northward toward Central and The

Docks. There, the Neo Kinoko skyline was cut through by the mouth of the Kinoko River.

I'd thought Morellum was huge—especially as Coprinia's capital city—but Neo Kinoko was monstrous. How did this backwards species manage such a feat of engineering?

Spirit Island was a rare case in that no one lived here. Who would? It was just rocks, sand, and trees. This place was a reminder of what Neo Kinoko must've been like before modernization.

Still, modernity made for a striking silhouette of rubble and ruin against the glow of the rising sun. A sprawl of fungi-speckled towers thrust into the sky. Some had been turned to dilapidated stumps by the war, untouched, even two years on. But nothing made an impression like that of the Mother Mushroom. The mile-high fungus was the tallest in the entire Hōpponese archipelago, overshadowing and dominating the metropolis—it loomed like a watchful matriarch.

I wondered how old that bloody thing must be.

I'd seen it from the NKPD central precinct, but not up close—I never wanted to. Maybe it was the warts peppering its bright red cap, or the ridges of its gills. Could have been the way its veil billowed on a windy day, enveloping the gargantuan stem like an undulating dress. It prickled my skin to see any kind of fungi up close, let alone one large enough to block out the sky.

I still couldn't wrap my head around them, these fungals and their city. Spores erupting in my face wouldn't help me develop a feeling of comfort in their presence, either.

My train of thought was cut off by choked cries. Nearby, a slim fungal patrol cop interviewed an elderly fungal—the one who'd found the bag. The old gillie sat on the sand, rocking and sobbing with his hands covering his face. The cop was crouched beside him. He had a shaggy, gray-and-black mushroom cap atop a short frame, with scruff on his face and teeth slightly yellowed from cigarettes. The bold yellow letters of the NKPD practically jumped off the blue police-issue jacket he wore.

"I was patrolling nearby in Hedoro Industrial City, and sensed something wrong," the patrol cop had told me when I'd arrived.

Sensed? I had no idea what he'd meant by that. What was he sensing? How had that led him here?

I hadn't even given him the chance to introduce himself—it would've meant me being close to him and his horrible mushroom cap head for far longer than I was okay with. He seemed diligent and attentive, sure, but also naïve. The type that was young enough to try and prove himself before the system broke him.

I'd decided to let him handle the interview: They were the same species, spoke the same language. Given how eager he was, he'd likely be able to get more out of the witness than I could. I wasn't exactly in the mood to talk to a blubbering old sporesack, either.

As I approached them, I still felt the spores from earlier scratching at my corneas. I slowed, taking a second to rub my eyes.

"*Haowa*," I said—good morning in their tongue. I motioned for the cop to continue as I observed, trying to hide my discomfort.

"I am sorry that your prayers were disturbed in such a terrible manner," the cop said in Hōpponese, consoling the old fungal in soft tones and massaging his hunched back. The hophead cop's unsettling mushroom head bobbed, gills flaring as if breathing. "Take your time and answer when you are ready."

Even after four months in Hōppon, I found their language tricky and their mushroom heads … off-putting.

"I-I am … I …" the elder trailed off.

"Please relax, *shushu-shen*," the cop urged him, using the word for uncle and the honorific for senior.

Now that I was close, I studied the old fungal. His wispy mycelial beard bent to gravity as much as the wrinkled, pale blue cap atop his head. Like every fungal, he had creepy colonies of mushrooms growing from each of his shoulders. The little fruiting bodies poked through the mycofabric of his plain, white Eien robes—the clothing of a religious fanatic and devout Hōpponese. Dressed like that, it seemed obvious why he'd be shivering from his brittle legs up to his puckered cap. But his eyes darted back and forth and he had a spooked expression on his furrowed face.

What was he afraid of?

Grayish spores flowed from his gills as he burst into tears again. I had to restrain myself from leaping backward in disgust at his spores. Instead, I put my mask back on.

"The … the t-temple," the old fungal stammered. His withered finger pointed away from the beach, toward a tall wall of evergreen trees. The forest dominated the center of Spirit Island.

"… festival … in two days," he muttered. "This island … this city … *zunoro*! Our people will know … they will come!"

My ears were still adapting to the peculiarities of Hōpponese speech. *Zunoro* … I struggled to remember the word. I clicked my voice recorder and repeated it several times—it was the only way I'd remember to ask for a translation later.

I looked at the tree line, dense with foliage, the rocky ground sprinkled with snow. Was there a temple up there in the forest? Who will come? And which festival was he talking about?

Then it clicked. Captain Ridgeway had told the Homicide department that the winter solstice was in couple of days. The locals would be celebrating a lantern festival, praying to one of their pagan gods.

Something I'd learned from human history was that if you took away a people's religion—their faith and foundations—you'd take away their hope.

That was the mistake we humans made when Coprinia invaded Hōppon: The government and military left the fungals' religion intact. With Eienism still present and practiced, hope persisted.

All of a sudden, the old sporesack screamed, his voice cracking and gills spasming: "They are here!"

"*Who* the bloody Hell is here?" I demanded.

The cop's gills twitched and his attention was torn away. He ran down the beach, waving his arms. I squinted in his direction and saw nothing of note. Then, from the far edges of the shore, I heard shouts growing louder. A rhythmic chant underscored it, adding an eerie atmosphere to the unfolding scene.

"They have come for the child," the witness murmured.

The skin beneath my jacket pricked with goosebumps. The dead body?

That's when I saw them over the low dunes: Hundreds of feet away, the tops of dozens of fungals' mushroom caps, swaying as they crossed a wooden bridge onto Spirit Island. The flaring red and blue of police lights strobed on the far side, where the densely packed houses and shrines of Torotown met with the walls of a great temple.

Shit … This couldn't be good.

I radioed dispatch: "Send backup. *Now!*"

CONTAINMENT

[3] Case File #42-56
Spirit Island | 6:38 a.m.

- - - - - - - - -

"STAND YER GROUND!" Commander Baird bellowed into a megaphone from beneath a black, disposable face mask. His distinct accent and rolling 'r's were evident of his northern Coprinian upbringing. "Do. Not. Engage!"

I stood behind the frontlines of a fungal protest with the riot squad's leader. Baird was in his fifties—pink-skinned, slim and muscular with bone white hair and pale orange stubble. He wore a black bulletproof vest over a matching blue jacket and pants. The sleeves on the thin jacket were rolled up, revealing faded military tattoos on his sinewy forearms.

"Not cold?" I asked him, rubbing my mittens together. My ass was still damp and the wind kept it properly chilled.

Baird chuckled. "Nae. Nothing warms the blood and the loins like the threat of danger."

I groaned. Men …

"WE WANT JUSTICE!" the protestors called out. "RETURN THE CHILD TO THEIR PEOPLE!"

I still couldn't understand how those bloody buttons had gotten here so fast. How did they know about the child? And why did they want them back?

Sprays of sand and pebbles showered a wide wall of riot police, skittering and bouncing off of their plastic shields. Planted behind metal crowd control barriers, more than forty armored officers were armed and ready: Shields and batons raised, pepper spray canisters hanging from their belts, rifles slung over their shoulders. The protestors pushed against the swaying barriers, throwing whatever they could get their hands on at the cops—rocks, sand, shells, kelp, and other pieces of ocean detritus. They were determined to get their hands on that dead kid.

Some diabolical gillies had even brought bags of mold. They lobbed fistfuls into the air. The particulate clouds caught on the swift breeze, spreading across dozens of officers at a time. They wore masks, as did I. Still, not one of them shied away, their sense of duty stronger than the risk of contamination.

Was I contaminated? I fiddled with the med bottle in my jacket pocket, imagining myself turning into a colonized corpse like that dead child. That cloud of spores had no doubt entered my body somehow …

I'd have to get a blood test as soon as I returned to the central precinct.

Shouts rang out from the mob, angry, dark spores pouring from their flared gills. Male and female fungals united in a scathing rallying call: "LET US THROUGH, *GAIKAMU!*"

Foreign scum.

I scoffed. Ironically, that's what both the Hōpponese and Coprinians thought of one another.

Winter wind howled across Kinoko Bay, stinging my still-itchy eyes. It smelled musty, like a library filled with timeworn books. What were the odds that the wind carried mold and spores with it?

"Steady, lads!" Baird boomed. "Defensive posture—only engage under clear and present danger!"

Outwardly, I was the lead investigator of this crime scene, and the simmering protest was threatening my control.

"Will they hold long enough for forensics to catalog and pack the crime scene?" I asked.

Baird lowered his megaphone and winked. Beneath his mask and around his eyes, I saw his skin wrinkle in what could only be an arrogant smile. "Aye, these are strange circumstances for an investigation, but it ain't our first protest like this. Children go missing and the gillies get all riled up."

"How many have you had to tamp down?" I asked.

"Around a dozen over the last few months," Baird said. "But don't ye worry, me officers are unwavering. We know how to handle them."

"Good. Keep it that way."

"Look, I know the lads in Homicide are always giving you a wee bit o' difficulty, but …" He gave me a once-over, lingering on my chest. "Not everyone is out to get ye."

Ugh … the whole force seemed to be brimming with self-righteous assholes and pompous pigs. How did I fit into all that? I had no fucking idea. But of course, Frederick had me exiled to a land of mushrooms and misogynistic men. Fungals, the NKPD could handle with an iron fist, but not the rampant sexism within its own ranks.

"Listen, Baird, my ass and tits are not your business. You just take care of things here."

"Uppity bitch," Baird muttered, diverting his gaze. "Can't yous take a joke?"

"Focus on the task at hand and less on your 'loins,'" I said. "Forensics will wrap up soon. After that, it's a matter of getting the evidence off the island—which means clearing out the fungals. If any of those spore-sacks step out of line, you know what to do."

Baird puffed his chest. "I don't need yous telling me how to do my job."

"Just get it done," I warned.

We watched the colony of fungals grow in number, Baird grumbling under his breath like a whiny schoolboy. What started with less than fifty had increased three-fold in under an hour. They were drawn to each other somehow, more hopheads trickling onto the sands by the minute. NKPD reinforcements had arrived in time to keep the protestors at bay—the crime scene was cordoned off with bright yellow police tape, and metal barriers stretched from the water to the forest's edge.

Things had gone relatively smooth. So far.

"HOW MANY OF OUR CHILDREN WILL DIE?" the protestors roared.

A female protestor banged on the shield of an officer. Determination was written across her pale face, despite her eyes being puffy and red from crying. Her orange, upcurved cap shook as she struck the shield over and over. Black spores streamed from her gills and her Hōpponese words echoed across the beach:

"That is one of our children!"

What the Hell? How did she know the victim was a kid?

Emboldened by the woman, showers of stones and debris rained on the riot soldiers' armored bodies, face shields, and helmets. I could see from their expressions that their patience was wearing thin. At some point, the bubble would burst—as it always did. It would start innocuous: Someone or something on the opposing side would spark the flame. Then it would catch fire, a mob forming like a colony of mushrooms from a web of mycelium.

The powerless and oppressed attempting to grasp a fleeting sense of power, violence trailing in its wake.

A CPAN helicopter circled above, maintaining a watchful eye. Ambulances and police vans were already parked on the other side of the bridge. Their sirens flashed in blinding reds, whites, and blues. More riot police had gathered there, forming a pincer around the protestors, and NKPD officers were on-site with cuffs and stretchers at the ready. A group of cops held back news crews, who'd already started capturing the unfolding events.

The fungals would deserve whatever came for them.

"Excuse me, Hofmann-*shen*," an accented voice called. Was he using that honorific because I had a higher rank?

The fungal beat cop approached Baird and I—the old gillie witness was with him, head lowered. The cop bowed, his posture perfect. It took a few seconds before he rose. He touched two fingers to the inky black rim of his cap: "May Matsua above shine bright upon you this day."

Matsua. Was that one of the fungals' gods?

"Spit it out," I demanded.

"The forensics team is ready for you."

I turned to the hophead cop, making sure to maintain some distance. "What's your name, officer?"

"Nameko, ma'am. Nameko Koji." He paused. "Or, as your people prefer it, Koji Nameko."

"Don't call me 'ma'am,'" I warned. "What do—"

Before I could finish, a knot of kelp landed on my left boot with a wet *slap*. Handfuls of sand followed, scattering over the defensive line. Some of it pattered against my chest, neck, and jaw. I flinched. Glaring at the roiling mass of incensed dissenters, I ground my teeth.

"Fucking molders."

I kicked the kelp off my boot and snatched the megaphone from Baird's grip. He didn't have a chance to object. "Neo Kinokan citizens, please cease and desist! This is an active NKPD crime scene, and you are required by Coprinian law to vacate these premises. Leave peacefully or we will be forced to take action. If you continue to resist, the Coprinian People's Army Navy will intervene."

And that's when it would become brutal.

In response, the protestors chanted, "*GAIKAMU! GAIKAMU! GAIKAMU!*"

They shoved the barrier and struck the soldiers' with fists and rocks. The riot police readied their batons or reached for pepper spray canisters. One cop took a swing and clocked a fungal man on his cap.

"Cease and desist!" I said, trying to keep my voice controlled and passive. "You are in violation of Coprinian law!"

Suddenly, the witness ran from Koji's side. Despite his frail form, he moved with lithe strides. I lunged for him, but he slipped from my grasp. Koji chased him. The old gillie pressed through the back row of riot cops, heading directly into the fray, toward the dividing line between police and protestors. Confusion spread, the police unsure of what was happening.

"*Jiujiu*, stop!" the witless old bastard cried out in his native language.

The protestors didn't care. They pushed against the barrier, rocking it back and forth. The metal frame pealed against the shield wall like a death knell.

"Please, stop this at once!" he continued. "Do not fall into the trap of violence! No one else need be hurt today!"

It was a fool's plea—the justice the fungals felt they deserved wouldn't be satiated.

The gillies crashed into the blockade. Koji grabbed the witness and rushed him back behind the frontlines as the soldiers braced to retaliate. Harder. Spores and sand hailed onto their helmets. Harder. Rifles were raised, fingers resting on triggers and hooked in the pins of pepper spray handles. Harder. A section of the barrier collapsed, and all Hell broke loose.

Baird grabbed the megaphone and yelled: "Bring them down!"

The protest had evolved into a riot. Fungals poured through the gap like spores from gills, ramming into riot shields. Pepper spray hissed in white plumes. A bitter aftertaste filled the air, resting in the back of my throat. Shouts and wails rang out amidst the pounding sounds of batons striking flesh and fungi.

I watched an officer shoot pepper spray directly at a sporesack's cap. They collapsed to the ground, thrashing around as the spicy spray clung to their gills.

Koji made his way back to Baird and I, his arm wrapped around the witness' hunched shoulders.

"Nameko," I scolded, "he was under your charge!"

"I apologize, detective," he said with a curt bow. "It will not happen again."

"It better not." I looked at Baird. "You and your men need to control those gillies. *Immediately*."

"What's our directive?"

"Containment. Put them in their place and get this mess cleaned up as quickly as possible."

The old gillie's body shook, his wide-eyed stare fixated upon me. "Do you mean with force?"

"Yes," I admitted.

Koji glared at me. "But our brothers and sisters could be killed!"

"Then let them. It was their choice to come here." I spat on the ground, trying to get the taste of pepper spray out of my mouth. "Now you two, come with me. And Nameko, don't let the witness out of your sight."

"No," Koji challenged.

Baird took out a pistol and cocked it. "You signed up to be one of us. Back out now, and I'll treat yous like the rest of them sporesacks."

Koji's nostrils and gills flared. After a moment, he slackened, hooking his arm around the witness. I led them down the beach to the sounds of baton-battered bones breaking, the crack of warning shots fired into the sky, and the tortured wails of fungal rioters.

CURSED

[4] Case File #42-56
Spirit Island | 6:57 a.m.

- - - - - - - - -

BRUSHED CLUMPS of sand from my coat. The angry clamor of clashing rioters and police was ever-present, but I didn't let it distract me from my duty.

A long forensics tent had been erected, surrounding the crime scene and rising onto the dry shore. It was the same navy-blue as the NKPD uniforms, with the department's acronym emblazoned on the side in yellow. Bursts of illumination leaked from the cracks, illuminating the black-sand beach. The forensics team announced their presence with every click of their camera.

"Wait outside," I told Koji. "And make sure he"—I waved at the old molder, who stood emotionless with his hands behind his back—"doesn't run off again."

"Yes, ma'am," Koji said, including the bloody "ma'am" to spite me.

The cop gave me a shallow bow and stepped aside. I lifted the flap of the tent, squinting as another flash of light nearly blinded me.

Amongst the forensics team were two male technicians, dressed in hooded full-body suits, masks, booties, and gloves. The third was the lead crime scene investigator, Francis Glessner.

I watched her direct the techs as they photographed the bag. Yellow numbered markers had been placed around the crime scene. The techs circled the dismembered child like vultures. The tent felt claustrophobic: Three people working fast and efficient, stacks of plastic boxes in one corner, a table along the side with trays on top—there was hardly room for anything else.

"Cissy?" I called.

The lead investigator was busy jotting notes down on a real paper notepad. When she looked up, her blue eyes shone like a clear Coprinian lake. Putting her pen and paper on the table, she waddled over to the entrance. She fit snugly into her body suit, and her wild mane of reddish-brown curls was tamed beneath its hood.

"Hen, darlin'!" Cissy's tone was chipper, given the hour and the occasion. "How are you, love?"

"Morning, Cissy. Tired, but surviving."

The portly woman winked, flashing a bright smile. "If only I had coffee to offer. Sounds like things are heating up out there, too …"

"It's a shit show. Somehow the fungals got wind of the body, but Baird and the riot squad are handling it." I stretched my arms and neck. "Do you have a minute to run me through what you've found so far?"

"O' course. Anything for another woman in uniform." She gestured at me and the gray trench coat I wore, my black mid-calf boots, and the wool scarf wrapped around my neck—none of which were standard-issue. "You know what I mean. Anyway, check this out, and put your mask on."

She ushered me inside the tent. I adjusted the straps on my mask and entered. Warmth washed over me—the kind that stank of sweat due to too many people in too small a space. Even worse, the wretched, rotten smell of death and brine permeated.

Cissy's team was in the process of transferring the bag and body parts onto the table. They laid the pieces on metal trays.

"Quick 'n' careful, boys," Cissy said in her lilting accent. "We don't want these parts exposed to too much air. Remember, photographs of each before you pack and send 'em off to the medical examiner."

"Yes, ma'am," the techs said in near unison.

One of them held back a glare when he caught me eying him. He had the glowering, emasculated look of someone who felt demeaned to be working under a woman. Served him right.

"Alright, Cissy, what have you got?" I asked, my hands perched on my hips.

She gestured for me to follow. "Look 'ere."

We stood behind the techs as they went about their business. "First impression: The decomposition is tricky to pinpoint, as water and sea critters do a number on dead bodies. But given the recent cold water in Kinoko Bay and the state of decay, I'd say it's been down there for, mmm, seven to ten days."

I cocked my head, leaning closer. "Seven to ten days? You sure?"

"We'll need to do further analysis back at the lab, but I've got a keen eye for this kinda thing."

"I believe you. What else?"

"Dental matches are off the table, seeing as every tooth was yanked. That mold and mycelium did a number on the mouth tissue as well. Bloody gnarly, pullin' that stuff out."

I trembled. The itch beneath my eyelids was back, taunting me with infection.

Cissy pointed at the top of the head. "See there? Cuttin' off the mushroom cap like that denies us any potential spore print. The murder-er damn well knew what they were doing."

"And the bruising around the edges of the cap and neck?"

"Bruisin' needs a full day to develop. Could indicate that the removal was done at least a day before the victim died."

The dismemberment, the planning—all of this had purpose. But for what? "Where could the rest of the body be?"

Cissy shrugged. "That's what you'll have to figure out, Hen."

"And the rope? Could any trace evidence be pulled from that?"

Cissy tapped her mask, eyes up. "We can run an analysis, and it might give us a profile. Slim chance, though, seein' as how it's been un-derwater."

"So, best bet, we get those logograms translated," I said. "We can match that with the manufacturer, find out who they sold it to."

"Manufacturers …" Cissy exhaled. "Here in Hōppon, that'll be a dead end before we even get started. Most of the stuff in this city comes from back home."

"And if it comes up with a positive DNA match?"

"Honestly, Hen, DNA records are even more of a mess." Cissy pursed her lips and crossed her arms. "Half the city is in ruins, most o' those starvin' fungals are undocumented, and the army and navy have been scramblin' to sort whatever records existed from before the war. The new government's still up to its ass in bureaucratic bullshit."

"Crap," I muttered, pinching my eyebrows. I felt a headache forming beneath my forehead. "Is there *any* way of IDing the victim?"

"Whoever did this, it was brutal and without mercy," Cissy said. "But they were also thorough. Freakin' psychopath, doin' this to anyone, let alone a kid. It's gonna be tough."

I peered at the techs. They were organizing the body parts, limbs and head laid out like some sick tableau, ready to be labeled and sorted into a forensics cooler.

"Thanks for the updates, Cissy. Inform me as soon as you have more information. You have my number."

Cissy gave my arm a sympathetic squeeze. "I've got your back, sister. Oh, I almost forgot!" She gave me a small stack of instant photographs.

I shuffled through them. They were photos of the crime scene and the key pieces of evidence.

"Thank you," I said. "Next time I see you, I want some answers and a coffee."

Cissy laughed, loud and unrestrained. The forensics techs were so startled they nearly toppled an evidence tray. "You got it, Hen. No sugar, two creams."

— — — — — —

THE BRISK WINTER air bit my exposed face as soon as I left the tent and removed my mask. But that fresh feeling went stale when my mind replayed the visual of the victim's rotting visage like a tape on rewind. The severed mushroom stump and the empty eye sockets.

"Fuck," I whispered.

I had multiple clues but no leads.

Putrid fishiness rose from the nearby lapping waves. The riotous din of police and sporesacks rang out across the beach. From this distance, I could see fungals being hauled off in handcuffs. Others were badly injured, laying bloodied in the sand. Led by Baird, the riot cops were relentless.

Turning to face Kinoko Bay, I noticed fishing boats and trawlers peppering the water, returning to the Docks from an early morning catch. Crisscrossing the boats were small ferries, private crafts and larger CPAN vessels—impromptu naval coast guard, established after the war.

I searched for Koji and the witness. They were up the beach, near the tree line. Koji was taking a final drag from a cigarette, dropping it onto the sand and grinding it down. He looked like a restless dog, expecting his owner to return home with toys and treats.

Why did that sporesack become a police officer? What good would it do to mire himself in a human institution?

I walked closer, but kept my distance. The witness was a few feet from Koji, sitting on his knees in prayer. His lips moved and he hummed in a low tone.

"Nameko," I said.

Koji flinched. His golden irises glowed, even under the shadow of his cap and narrowing gaze. Now that I saw him up close, I noticed the fibrous scales covering the large mushroom atop his head. Like a shaggy mane, the scales curled up into dark brown tips. And the black scruff on his face was … *actual mold*.

I recoiled, but pulled myself together before he noticed. There was at least one thing this cop could be useful for at the moment.

In cold Coprinian, I said, "I need you to translate some Hōpponese for me."

"And why should I help you?"

I closed the distance between us, my temper outweighing my aversion to fungals. I could smell his earthy musk and the stink of cheap tobacco. Pressing my forefinger against his chest, I said, "'Cause it's your *job*. You chose to wear blue. You chose to serve the Coprinian authority."

Koji worked his jaw. Trickles of darkening spores wafted from his gray gills, divulging his worsening mood.

"A quick translation," I said, "and then we'll be out of each other's lives."

He complied by holding his hand out. I passed him the photos Cissy had given me. Tangible evidence that might bring tangible leads.

Koji looked at the photos one by one, angling his head. His eyes perked up at one in particular. Eyebrows furrowed and body tensed, he said, "The logograms are faded and worn, but I can pick out a string of numbers. It is likely they are from the rope's production lot, but ... I recognize this."

"Recognize what?"

"The rope itself. The blue color, and the red threads running through it."

"Where have you seen it before?"

Koji pointed at the ocean. I followed his finger to the east, toward the collapsed skeleton of Murio's Arch. The remaining middle section of the bombed bridge was sprinkled with the twinkling lights of The Shelf: An ad hoc, off-the-grid fungal shantytown.

Soon after I'd arrived in Neo Kinoko, my training officer warned me that The Shelf was a symbol of defiance. The bridge was destroyed as a warning, a message from a dominant superpower to the rebels they sought to control. Instead, the gillies rebuilt—a big fuck you to Coprinia, where neither CPAN nor the NKPD had any jurisdiction.

"There?" I asked. "That's where we'll find answers?"

"I have a … contact there," Koji replied. "I hope he will provide clarity, yes."

Hope.

That notion was nothing but the fickle desire of fools. I didn't want to rely on this fungal, let alone bring him into my investigation, but I had nothing else to go on. The slow wheels of forensics would take time to draw their conclusions. Meanwhile, my clock was already ticking.

"Let's *hope* your contact is there," I said, "and willing to talk."

I nudged my thumb in the direction of the witness. "And what about *zunoro*? He kept repeating that word earlier."

"My elder's name is Keisuke Nariyoshi, and—"

"I prefer Nari," the old button said in Hōpponese. He rose from the sand, fine grains slipping from the fabric of his robe. "*Yisima*, Nameko-*jero*. Excuse me for interrupting."

Koji was about to speak, but Nariyoshi held up a wizened hand to stop him.

"Detective Hofmann," the gillie said. "I know you understand me. You have *sinned*. My people, those who have gathered on this beach, weep for the children they have lost. For the lands and livelihoods that they have lost. Containment, you said to your fellow human—your actions perpetuate a cycle of violence that need not exist."

"All I want is to solve this murder and move on with my life," I uttered through gritted teeth in Coprinian. I understood his language better than I could speak it, but I wouldn't satisfy him by letting those filthy words leave my mouth. "I don't need your bullshit sob story. Nameko, tell him what I said."

Koji interpreted my words begrudgingly.

"Yes, of course you want to be done with this," Nariyoshi mused. "Duty to one's country, appraisal from authority, yet also the desire to be left alone. Is it not ironic that we all want to be left alone and escape the shackles of our burdens?"

I glared at him. "*Zunoro*. What does it mean?"

"Cursed," Koji said.

"Cursed?"

Nariyoshi took a long breath. His thin mycelial beard billowed in the wind. "Yes, *zunoro* means cursed. I used that word because the spirits who reside here are no longer satiated. They have given up and will abandon us. They will abandon Spirit Island, and, soon enough, Neo Kinoko and Hōppon as a whole. How will our people survive without the spiritual bonds we share?"

"Mother Chikyu help us," Koji whispered.

"Mother Chi—" Another one of their gods? Was Koji an Eien religious fanatic, too?

Noriyoshi continued: "I found the bag washed up on shore. I sensed it, compelled to inspect it closely. This beach is where I meditate, after praying at the shrines in the forest."

I examined the edge of the woods, which rose to a hill at the center of the island. In a gap between the fragrant, towering pines stood a spirit gate. Its coat of crimson paint was dull and peeling, and one of the horizontal, wooden beams on top had partially caved in. Beyond the gate, a snow and moss-covered stone stairwell led up, into shadow.

"But now," Noriyoshi said, "Spirit Island is tainted with the death of an innocent—it is *cursed*. And yet, you condemn more fungals to a similar fate …"

"Thank you for the fable," I mocked, Koji interpreting my words.

Noriyoshi's pale blue cap quivered. "The gods will decide your fate."

"My God, or your gods?"

"Only time will tell."

Fuck this … the old molder was getting on my nerves, and I had a job to do.

"Nariyoshi, as soon as those rioters are cleared out, you're getting in a squad car and heading to the central precinct to give your official witness statement." Then I pointed at Koji. "And you, you're going to take me to The Shelf."

THE OUTSIDER

[5] Case File #42-56
Kinoko Bay | 8:31 a.m.

- - - - - - - - -

FREEZING, SALTY MIST sprayed over the railing of the refurbished ferry, sprinkling my face. I looked across Kinoko Bay at The Shelf, not daring to touch the railing—mycelium had almost entirely enveloped the corroded metal.

The depressing cloud cover from earlier had disappeared. Instead, the rich orange hues of the early morning sun bloomed along the horizon, daubed like brushstrokes across the sky. A brisk breeze whipped across the water and stirred up waves. The bay was busy with morning boat traffic and the smells of fresh-caught fish.

Koji stood off to my right, smoking another Goddamned cigarette. The smell made me gag. I kept a purposeful distance between him, myself, and his filthy habit.

How was he not freezing? I was bundled up as best I could manage, with a trench coat, sweater, scarf, a loose knit cap and mittens. He had nothing but a bloody windbreaker on.

A dozen little shrooms poked through the shoulders of his jacket. Mycofabric patches were stitched on, the blues not quite matching. The NKPD was too stingy for a small expense like that—more likely he "upgraded" it himself. Fungal biology was bloody confusing.

I pulled my coat tighter. As if that would better protect me against the cold.

The piece of crap ship Koji and I were on was a rickety ship named

Virosa's Strength. Ironically, its metal hull groaned with every movement, rivets ready to burst.

The old Coprinian craft would have fallen apart already, were it not for the sickening fungal growths that colonized it. Hairy blooms of mycelium covered every surface in a squishy blanket. Small fruiting bodies sprouted up all over, covered in beads of saltwater. There wasn't any proper seating, just multi-colored polypore mushrooms that grew from the floors or walls as makeshift chairs or benches.

I clenched my fists, palms trickling with sweat beneath my mittens—I was fine standing where I was, not touching any of it. In my periphery, I caught Koji flashing me a dirty look.

"What the Hell is your problem, Nameko?" I said in Coprinian, swiveling to face him. I lost my balance as the boat passed over a swell, but I held firm and planted my boots on the mycelial deck. "You've been looking at me like that since Spirit Island."

"It is nothing," Koji said. He side-eyed me and exhaled a plume of smoke.

"It's *not* nothing," I retorted. "If you've got something to say, say it."

The pause that followed was long and loaded. Koji burned his cigarette down to the filter and tossed it overboard. Finally, he said, "What you and your riot police did to my people … the prejudices of war do not simply disappear once peace has been declared."

"It was an active crime scene!" I spat, wanting to walk over and smack his insubordinate ass. "*They* crossed the line, *they* initiated force, so *they* forfeited their rights."

"Duty does not beget cruelty," Koji said. A second later, the blaring horn of a nearby CPAN coast guard ship drowned out our conversation.

After the ship passed, I continued: "My duty is to my country and the NKPD, and that means upholding the laws of this land."

"*This land*?" Koji scoffed. "What do you actually know of this land? Our laws and customs? Coprinians came here attempting to erase our identity, but it is an experiment doomed to fail."

That brought me to laugh, short and harsh. "You hold your people in high regard, Nameko. *We* won the Spore War!"

"Is that you talking or the NKPD? CPAN? General MacArthur? What does *your* heart tell you is the right thing, or are you so imprisoned by duty you are unable to think for yourself?"

"Go fuck yourself, Nameko."

"I will consider self-copulation, but that was not my point. Understand that The Long War was just the beginning—none of us need to be enslaved to cultural programming."

Just the beginning? Cultural programming?

I couldn't match the words coming out of his mouth with the fact that he was wearing an NKPD uniform. "Why the Hell did you join up to begin with? What good would it do a gillie like you to surround yourself with humans who hate you? You're the only fungal cop on the force."

Koji's eyebrows lowered, casting gloomy shadows over his face. I covered my mouth and nose as thin trails of gray spores escaped from between his gills. They were promptly rushed away by ocean winds.

No answer. He remained silent.

A bottle smashed behind me and I spun around. The pervasive punch of something like moonshine stung my nostrils—the ex-alcoholic in me knew the smell all too well.

Shards of wet glass spread outward from the open door of the boat's bridge, a pool of colorless liquor soaking into the cushioned deck of mycelium. The captain was a leather-faced fungal, with an equally leathery cap. He was far too broad to be crammed in that little room. Wobbling and singing a shanty in Hōpponese, he clutched the ship's wheel with one fist. The other was held out, fingers curled as if still holding onto the bottle he'd just dropped.

I'd had to bribe the drunken bastard. "Humans on board … is bad for … business," he'd slurred before we boarded.

But two bills of military scrip and a single rice ration card did the trick. Money and food were tight in a post-war colony, so everyone's opinions, scruples, and morals were subject to change—for the right price. Hell, even the coast guard and port officials took bribes for off-the-books boats like this one to cross the bay unmolested.

Most everyone in Neo Kinoko was corrupt to one degree or another.

A few minutes had passed when Koji finally answered. "I joined the NKPD because I thought I could help my people from the inside." He leaned his elbows on the railing. Running a finger along the fungal filaments, he took out another smoke. He stared across the bay as the ferry crested a wave. It landed with a splash, frigid droplets speckling my cheeks and mouth.

I licked my dry lips, tasting salt. The booze-soaked captain sang obnoxiously, his hand loose at the wheel. I glanced back every other second, worried he'd run us into another bloody ship.

"So, you thought learning Coprinian and 'integrating' yourself would allow you to do that?" I asked. "How'd that turn out?"

Koji peered down at the water, shaking his head and cap. He scratched at the moldy fuzz on his well-defined jawline. I wondered what lurked beneath this fungal's exterior—what demons he might be hiding. Was his mind scrambled from fighting in the Long War? Was I just another colonizer in his eyes? Was he as uncomfortable around me as I was around him?

I was the stranger in his strange land, after all.

"What do you know of The Shelf?" Koji said, changing the subject. He took a pull on his cigarette.

"Just the basics. NKPD and CPAN recommend that humans stay away—the authorities have no jurisdiction there."

"They are correct. The Shelf community is tight-knit, industrious, and fiercely anti-colonizer. It is unlikely you will receive a warm welcome—they may harass you from the moment we dock."

I chuckled and it came out a little dry. "Look at me: A divorced, female cop. I'm used to being unwelcome and harassed." I gestured to Koji. "Not like you won't stand out, either. In that outfit, you're essentially a coppie in blue with a cap for a costume."

Koji took a deep inhale of ocean air, thin cigarette fumes drifting into my face. I held my breath, and my temper.

"You are right—I wear this uniform and carry the weight of betrayal," he said. I caught a glimpse of regret in his expression. "But this investigation is an opportunity to do good for my people in a way I could not without it."

I rubbed my mittens together, the fabric tugging. What was I doing, putting my life in the hands of this hophead? "Who's your contact on The Shelf?"

Koji swallowed. "Someone I have known for a long time."

"What kind of bullshit answer is that?" Why was he being so cagey?

"You will have to trust me, and follow my lead."

Trust him? I could barely trust any human in this city, let alone a gillie. There was no way I was going to go into that Hellhole on my own, but that meant admitting I needed Koji's help. Crap …

"Whatever happens, we stay together," I said, my tone hard. "Now, put out that fucking cigarette. The wind is blowing that shit right into my eyes."

"Apologies, detective." He flicked his smoke into sea.

"And reverse that bloody jacket. I'll stand out enough for the both of us."

Unconsciously, I leaned down and propped my arms on the rail. I immediately pulled back from the mycelium, causing a couple of loose vertebrae to pop along my spine.

Bloody Hell …

The Shelf and the shattered remnants of Murio's Arch were only a mile out. Ramshackle layers of polypore-topped shacks stacked one on top of the other. Flocks of boats, trawlers, and junk haulers latched onto the makeshift framework like leeches on human flesh.

I sighed. Part of me regretted getting on this Goddamn ferry, but it was too late to back down now—this case had to move forward, and so did I. I breathed deep, preparing to step into unfamiliar territory.

— — — — — —

SALT, SEAFOOD, AND gull shit mixed to create an unholy stench. It hit me the moment Koji and I stepped onto the docks of The Shelf. My knees were sore after forty shaky minutes on that sad excuse for a ferry, but it felt good to be on somewhat solid ground again. Except …

I groaned. Of course, "solid ground" was actually damp, spongy docks made of Goddamn mycelium.

"Come," Koji said.

Soaking in my surroundings, my detective brain clicked into gear.

I followed him through the dockyard. It bustled with activity: Bronzed fungal fishers hauled crates brimming with silver-scaled mackerel and wriggling octopus, all of which were tainted with colorful patches of mold and fungal growths. Boats moored and unmoored, and sailors tied salt-crusted knots. Round cages full of spindly-legged crabs rattled as they were heaved across fibrous snow-sprinkled piers.

It was as though the outside world didn't exist, and the fungals could sustain themselves here.

Koji and I stepped off the pier onto a wide mycocrete boardwalk— actual solid ground. Extending beyond it was a main street, with alleys branching off like arteries. Spread farther back, the base of The Shelf was a maze of cramped buildings, street stalls, and shacks. All of the structures were made from mycelium, mushrooms, and mycocrete, intertwined in an organic mass with few straight lines or sharp angles.

I looked up. "Wow," I whispered.

Until now, I hadn't taken in the full breadth of The Shelf. From below, its immense structure was unsettling, lit by the orange glow of the morning sun. Hundreds of polypore mushroom shelves—striped with rippling bands of reds, grays, and creams—were stacked in colossal tiers. The tiered fungi climbed hundreds of feet up the towering remains of

Murio's Arch, clinging to the crumbled remains of the bridge.

On the main street, a colony of fungals conglomerated in a packed stream of foot traffic. They shuffled past each other with eerie fluidity, their mushroom caps oscillating. Disorderly fungal children zipped amongst the legs of the adult herd. I watched them dip in and out of the unrelenting throng with ease, only to scamper off down shadowy backstreets.

One thing was clear, though: Not a single human around.

"Where to now?" I asked, uneasy and wanting to move. I was an open target, standing here doing nothing. It was time to move and meet his contact so we could leave this Godforsaken place.

The corners of Koji's yellow eyes crinkled as he squinted. His cap and gills twitched. "I cannot sense her. She is obscured."

"Sense her? What does—"

"Koji-*dari*?" a gruff voice yelled. "Koji-*dari*!"

Koji peered around, his gills twitching again. He searched the street before replying in Hōpponese: "Roku-*shen*? Is that you?"

"Koji!" the voice called out. "It is you! Get over here and say hello!"

"What the fu—" Before I could protest, Koji grabbed my arm and pulled me past fishers, vendors, and hagglers until we were sucked into the thrum of the morning commute.

I did my best to keep my head down. The thick smell of earth tickled my nose as Koji cut a diagonal path across the crowd. I felt closed in, claustrophobic. I bumped into solid bodies, and disgusting slippery mushrooms smeared across my cheeks.

"Nameko," I urged.

A few stink eyes were cast, and slurs slipped from several strangers' mouths: *Gaikamu. Shimin.*

Foreign scum. Colonizer.

"Nameko, *get me out of here*." My head throbbed—I was starting to panic.

"Do not worry," Koji said, tugging hard on my forearm. "I sense an old friend."

I counted the seconds, each one lasting an eternity. My heart raced, sweat dripping down my spine. I lost track of time. What may have been a minute or an hour later and we were through … thank God.

I was bent over, holding my knees and panting. Each breath sucked in the stink of seafood.

"This way," Koji said in Coprinian, oblivious to my discomfort.

Gathering my composure, I followed him toward a street food stall. It was painted bright red with white banners hanging above the countertop, adorned with Hōpponese logograms. Behind the counter stood a pudgy cook, who dropped what looked like fish balls into a boiling vat of broth. A cluster of a dozen brown-capped fungi grew from his head, curling around each other like the petals of a flower. Mycopaper lanterns hung above his caps.

"Roku," Koji said.

The cook looked up and beamed, his flushed cheeks puffing. Sweat ran down his stems. Drops trailed down the top of his forehead before being absorbed by a stained white headband.

"Koji, my brother! *Haomi do?*"

Deep-fried scents enveloped me as we approached. Koji leaned over the side of the stall—both he and Roku touched caps. They were still for a second, then they clasped forearms, laughing and smiling.

"I am well, Roku. And you?"

Roku kept cooking while he spoke. "Same old, same old. You know how it is. I thought I sensed you." A thick-bladed knife came down with a *thwack* on a wood cutting board. With swift motions, Roku smacked the flat side of his blade on a group of mold-spotted squid before scoring and skewering them. He quickly tossed them atop a charcoal grill. "It's been a while since I last saw you on The Shelf."

Koji rubbed the back of his pale neck. "I have been … occupied."

The wrinkles around the cook's mouth creased with contempt. "With that *gaigai?*" He pointed the tip of his knife at me.

"I'm not a bloody colonizer," I hissed in Coprinian.

"NKPD detective," Koji finished in Hōpponese. "She is investigating the murder of a fungal child."

Roku put down his knife. He wiped his hands on the towel slung across his shoulder, then rolled up his sleeves. The sinewy muscles beneath glistened from the glow of the grill. He picked up his knife, furiously scaling some hand-sized fish.

"Blues shouldn't be coming around here," Roku mumbled. He gestured to the crowd with his blade. "You think the folks won't notice?"

I looked around. Sitting on a bench nearby, a pair of old, bright-capped female fungals wearing floral robes drank steaming cups of tea. A few boys argued in front of a vendor selling handmade mycopaper lanterns. At the entrance to the adjacent alley, a group of young girls juggled homemade bean bags, their caps bouncing.

Not a single fungal was focused on me.

"I know," Koji replied, "but it is urgent, and we must see Iroh and Hana."

Who the Hell were Iroh and Hana? His contact—or *contacts*?

"You know, a lot's changed since you left," Roku said, "You abandoned us, boy."

"Where are they?" Koji asked, ignoring the slight.

Roku paused, pursing his lips. "Skinner's. Hana's been spending a lot of time there lately, especially after …"

"After what?"

Roku tilted his head, sending streams of sweat sliding down his temple. "You don't know?"

Koji shook his head.

"Best go talk to her yourself," Roku said.

Something landed at my feet: A shoddy bean bag, its stitches frayed and the fabric faded. I picked it up and brushed off the dirt, then looked over at the fungal girls playing. They stood in a semi-circle at the entrance to a dark alleyway covered in mycelium and green, glowing shrooms.

There were five of them, wearing raggedy dresses and coats. Each had a bean bag that they tossed into the air and caught on the backs of their hands.

Except one.

The shortest girl—her face round, topped by a creamy white cap flecked with brown spots—walked up to me. Her yellow irises shone. Even with her unsettling fungal appendages, the girl had a luminous expression that brought me back to a simpler time, when Elisabeth's giggle or grin was enough to get me through a day.

I squeezed the bean bag. It was a handmade motley of cheap scrap cloth filled with grains of rice. The other girls looked at me with curiosity. Their small caps bobbed back and forth, as if questioning what the Hell a human was doing on The Shelf.

The sweet-faced girl held out a dirt-covered palm. I reached out, the bean bag touching both our hands like a doorway between disparate worlds. Her friends began sputtering rapidly in Hōpponese. Suddenly, they stiffened, eyes going wide as their caps trembled.

"Amaya, *baebae*! What are you doing?" a woman screamed in Hōpponese. "Get away from my little girl!"

Amaya snatched the bean bag from my hand and ran to her friends. I spun on my heel to see a short fungal woman in a bright purple robe hurrying toward me. Anger was plastered on her face, making her pale, plain features scrunch up and wrinkle. Her mycelial sandals slapped the mycocrete with every exaggerated footstep. Black spores spilled from her gills, blending with her fluffy, moldy hair.

"Idiot," one of Amaya's friends jeered at her. The five girls stepped away, nearer to the alleyway.

"Back off, *gaigai*! Away from my child!" The mother waved a flour-coated rolling pin at me.

"Stand down!" I ordered in Coprinian. She kept waving the bloody thing at me, so I repeated my demand in Hōpponese.

Koji stepped in, placing his hands on the woman's mushroom-speckled shoulders. "*Jiujiu*, please calm. This human means no harm." He grabbed the rolling pin and lowered it. "Put it away, sister. You are threatening an officer of the law."

"*Their* law doesn't hold power here!" she spat.

Except if they harmed a cop. Then, the full weight of the NKPD—maybe even CPAN—would come crashing down on their rebellious fucking caps.

"*Gaikamu*!" someone yelled from the busy street. "Leave us alone."

Glancing around the docks, I noticed the entire fungal crowd had stopped. A handful of them were staring at me, then a few more. Every gillie around was looking at me.

Hundreds of them.

I wanted to hide away. To get the fuck out of here and not have all those yellow eyes focused on me.

More curses and words of ill intent were hurled my way. Something flew out of the throng. A fresh squid came hurtling toward me—slimy, dripping, and peppered with brain-like fruiting bodies as it soared through the air. I stepped aside just in time. The wet cephalopod splattered on the ground where I'd previously stood.

I whipped out the SIG P26 pistol holstered on my hip.

My heart pounded. The colony was silent. Their yellow eyes pierced with mixed expressions: Anger, anguish, agitation. These fucking molders wanted to throw shit at me? I was ready to strike back, to put a bullet in one of their caps as an example to the rest of them.

I pointed my gun at the fungals, noting positions and distances, categorizing threat levels. The woman with the rolling pin stood with her arms spread in front of the five girls. Her tense appearance displayed a mix of terror and determination. Koji stood frozen in place a few feet from me. Roku held his knife up.

"Leave, both of you," Roku warned. "You shouldn't have brought her here, Koji."

Did they think I was a threat to them? To their children? *They* were the ones who agitated the situation.

But ultimately, it didn't matter. I was a human—a colonizer—entering protected territory, like a virus targeted by white blood cells.

Dozens of fungals edged closer to me. Warm sweat beaded on my forehead, tingling as it met cold air. I switched off my gun's safety. None of the bastards said a word, but their body language was similar. The way they looked at me, heads and caps tilted, as if they were connected somehow. They muttered in unison, bodies tensed and aggressive. Their glares glowed with hostility, and the mutterings rose to a chant.

"Outsider. Outsider. Outsider."

I shouldn't have come.

Bloody Hell, I should've bribed the ferry captain to wait for us. If I moved now, I could run to the docks and steal a boat. Or was it more feasible to jump into the freezing water and swim? Would hypothermia be worse than facing these fucking fungals?

"Outsider."

They closed in around me. I fired a warning shot, attempting to scare them off. The deafening *bang* of my pistol's report echoed off the walls and water. Fungals screamed and the crowd erupted into disarray. Amaya, her mother, and her friends had disappeared. Dozens of hands reached out to grab me. Roku lunged with his kitchen knife.

Next thing I knew, a hand snagged my wrist. I stumbled through the shadows of a narrow corridor. A familiar voice and the smell of cigarettes pulled me back to reality.

"Stay with me," Koji said. "They *sense* you as a threat. Now the whole Shelf knows you're here."

CRACKS

- - - - - - - - -

MY SHOULDERS HEAVED, leg muscles aching, my flushed face drenched with sweat. I panted and ran after Koji through tight, mold-ridden alleyways made of mycelium. Shouts echoed nearby. My once-athletic lungs struggled to pull in air. Nauseating scents of ocean brine and musk settled on my palate and made me gag.

The whole Shelf knew I was here … They *sensed* me. And now they were after us.

Stumbling around a damp, algae- and mushroom-infested corner, I stopped to catch my breath. I didn't want to touch anything, didn't want to be here. But deep down, I knew I had to keep going—to push through the discomfort and revulsion. If anything, just to live and see another day.

"Run faster, detective!" Koji shouted from ahead in Coprinian.

"I—" That was all I could manage between knackered exhalations. "I-I can't … keep up."

Koji came to a standstill. His breathing was even. His eyes found mine, filled with a seriousness that seemed to pierce my soul. "You are strong and capable, but I can sense them closing in. We must move!"

Sense. Sensing. Those bloody words kept coming up, but what the Hell did they mean?

I took a long breath through my nose, exhaling through my mouth. That was a question for another time. I stood straight and forced my legs to move.

Yells echoed in the corridors behind us, a frenzied slurry of angry Hōpponese curses. Windows opened. Fungals flung household objects and spat at us we ran. I barely ducked out of the way of a plate as it shattered on the wall beside me. I fired blind warning shots above and behind me, hearing frightened screams in response.

"You dare threaten our children?" the plate-thrower accused from overhead. "You dare use your gun here, in our *home*?" Her vitriolic voice faded into garbled vulgarities as Koji and I kept up our escape.

The relentless stomping of our fungal pursuers began to consume my mind. But the image of that decapitated head was burned into my mind. A child, mutilated in a manner so horrific. What if this were to happen again, to another innocent child? Even if it was a fungal, even if it put my life in danger, I couldn't let another kid fall prey to that horror.

I had to pursue this case to its end. To exhaust every lead.

Cold air dried out my throat as I pushed my body to its limits. My legs cramped, feet throbbing. Sweat dripped down my back and from my armpits, my trench coat feeling heavier and heavier by the second.

Koji was only a few feet ahead. I knew he was slowing so I wouldn't lag behind and get lost.

Fungals continued to lob objects at us from above. Showers of spores rained down. I coughed and choked, covering my mouth. I felt the motes landing on my skin and floating into my eyes. Blinking madly, I trailed Koji through alley after alley. The Shelf was a dark, dank maze that I would never comprehend, punctuated by a hail of pottery shards, spores, and rotting food.

The taunts of our pursuers increased in volume and density. They were so close. It was as if a swarm of bees had amassed, furious and ready to defend their hive.

Ahead, the mycelium on a wall slithered and retracted. A hulking fungal man emerged through the opening, blocking our path with hundreds of pounds of muscle. His wide, caramel mushroom cap pulsated, and black spores surged from his gills as he charged.

"Leave our home, *shimin*!" he roared.

Upon seeing the other fungal, a trace of recognition dawned on Koji's face. "Don't slow down. Don't use your weapon."

Koji tore threads of mycelium from the walls, sprinting full tilt toward the massive molder. As he neared, Koji dropped to the ground and slid between the attacker's legs. Mid-motion, he looped the threads around the giant's ankle, then reached the other side and pulled hard.

I heard Koji whisper, "I am sorry, *jiujiu*."

The colossal sporesack's expression went from fury to surprise. His momentum and weight caused him to topple, smashing face-first into the ground. Even with the mycelium to soften his fall, I still heard the *crunch* of his nose breaking.

Koji rose to his feet. "He will not stay down for long. Come."

I followed, stepping around the moaning, squirming fungal who Koji had felled like a lumberjack does a tree.

We swerved left. Then right. Left again, and again. My brain couldn't handle the baffling layout of this labyrinth. The stairwells and ladders that went up to who knew where, disappearing behind overlapping layers of enormous, flat mushrooms. The passageways that widened and thinned, or overflowed with growths of foul fruiting bodies that I had to force my way past.

But Koji seemed to know these passageways, leading us—

Right into a colony of fungals.

Fuck.

The gillies closed in, blocking off the far end of the alley. They were armed with clubs, wood beams, knives, and fish hooks—whatever makeshift weapons they'd found. Standing shoulder-to-shoulder, their bright, golden eyes ablaze with a hatred.

Every one of them was unique—different heights, different caps, different faces and features—but together they bellowed in perfect synchronicity:

"Outsider! Colonizer! Invader!"

One of the fungals hurled a wood beam. I ducked as it connected with the wall beside me and shattered into splinters. Needle-like projectiles shot out, cutting my cheek and the hand I raised to block my eyes.

Immediately, I raised my pistol, but Koji saw and urged me to lower it.

He lifted his hands in a placative gesture. His gills quivered, sending out submissive pale spores that flowed toward the colony like a white flag. "We do not mean harm to anyone on The Shelf," he said, then pointed to me. "She did not intend to hurt the children. She is only here to solve the murder of one of our own."

The burly fungal with the broken face stepped forward. Rivers of blood ran down from his mangled nose and into his mouth. His thick arms flexed, ready for round two. He grinned, huge and terrifying, ichor staining his crooked nose red.

"You are no longer one of us, Nameko Koji." His voice rumbled the mycelium on the walls. "You are no longer my *jiujiu*. And you know how we treat outsiders on The Shelf, don't you?"

Koji stepped forward, hands spread in an attempt to mollify the crowd. "Oze-*kato*, please. We are investigating the murder of a fungal child!"

"Why must humans always interfere?" Oze cracked his knuckles, each *pop* echoing. He scowled. "Were your people not satisfied enough when they burned our cities? Raped our women and killed our children? When will they keep their filthy *gaikamu* hands *off of us*?"

His final words boomed through the alley like the shockwave from a bomb.

Raped? What kind of twisted human would risk contamination in that way? I'd heard of half-breeds, but the thought sickened me.

Oze stepped forward. Ink-colored spores flowed from his gills, as did all the other fungals in the colony. Their spores coalesced like a cloud of mosquitoes. I swatted them away as they swarmed around me.

Koji grabbed my arms. He spun me around and shoved me down

the corridor. "Run!"

Rancorous cries snapped me out of my stupor. Koji urged me along and I forced my legs to move, hard and fast. My muscles throbbed. The furious howls of our fungal pursuers followed us like a fever dream. Projectiles clattered and shattered, sending fragments that struck my back and lacerated my skin. Doorways unraveled like yarn in the mesh of mycelium that held The Shelf together. Gillies burst from their homes, lunging and clawing, forcing me to dodge or slow down. I let loose a few blind shots, knowing they would hit someone.

"Leave us alone!" a hophead woman shrieked from a window.

The mycelial walls closed in around us. Tighter and tighter, the air became balmy, moist, and sickening. The space ahead was choked with dense tendrils and mushrooms that reached out, wriggling and wet.

I stopped. Koji collided with me, both of us nearly tumbling to the ground.

The path ahead was blocked … A thick bloom of ghostly white mycelium had grown into an impassable lattice that stretched from wall to wall.

Koji pulled out a short knife and hacked at the tangled mass. "Go through, Hofmann!"

There was no way I was going in there—no way I'd succumb to that claustrophobic doom. Droplets of sweat poured down my forehead and into my eyes. I winced from the salty sting. "I … I …"

"Hofmann, *move*!" Koji screamed, still slicing at the filaments.

But it was too late. I couldn't force myself to do it, to crawl through that musty tunnel, smothered by fungi until the life was sucked out of me. But I could make a last stand. If I were to die, here and now, I could kill a few of those sporesack fuckers before I departed for Heaven.

I stood and lifted my gun. Gripping its cold metal shape, I ejected the magazine and checked how many rounds I had left: Seven shots.

That would do.

The fungals pressed toward us—dozens of bodies that seemed to clog the corridor. They waited, knowing we were trapped, forming a mass of oppressive bodies and mushroom caps that reeked of sweat and decaying earth. I raised my pistol, finger on the trigger, prepared to pull.

I took a deep breath. Steadied my grip. Three. Two. One—

"Hofmann, don't!"

Koji smacked the gun from my hands as soon as I fired. My weapon flew across the alley, halfway between me and the gillies. The bullet went wide, striking Oze in the shoulder and sending a spray of blood into the air. Behind Oze, a fungal fell from the glancing shot.

"Did Nariyoshi's words fly over your cap?" Koji said, the knife gripped firmly in his fingers. "Enough slaughter!"

"Too late for that, Nameko."

There was no way I could get to my gun before they got to me.

He rushed in, followed by a disorienting number of hopheads. Within moments, a heavy fist hit the side of my head, knocking me to the ground and sending my knit cap flying. Dirty hands smothered my face. I smacked away flailing limbs and digits. Fingers raked at my eyes and nostrils, hooking my lips and thrashing me around. The foul taste of soil and filth made me gag. I screamed, but it was cut off by the bile that escaped my esophagus.

I spat out vomit. A violent motion jerked me backward, almost ripping off my trench coat. I heard Koji growl and someone wail. A solid object clubbed the back of my skull, making my vision go black.

Blows rained down on my back and shoulders. Blood blended with bruises.

I went wild in retaliation, fighting with a fierceness I thought I'd abandoned ages ago. I hadn't felt this invigorated since my all-too-frequent drunken bar brawls back in Coprinia—except this time, I was sober.

Even with the pummeling I'd received, I kept going. The alley was crowded with fungals, so I threw haphazard punches. Some bastard plunged a fish hook into my thigh, but I plucked it out and gouged his chest with it. I hit random fungals left and right, even as I was tossed around like that little girl's bean bag. I almost struck Oze on his broken nose, but he somehow anticipated my fist and dodged at the last second.

I wouldn't stop until my heart gave out.

But the buttons were just so Goddamn fast, moving with the fluidity of dancers, never touching and always knowing where the others were. Technology and firepower were the only way the Coprinians could've beaten these bloody bastards in the Spore War. Hand-to-hand, humans were just no match.

Oze pounced. His broad hands dug into my upper arms and he slammed me into the ground. Up close, I could see his dirt-smudged, pockmarked skin. Feel the warmth of his breath and smell the fish he'd eaten earlier.

Bloody drool drizzled down his lips as he said, "You will regret ever coming to The Shelf, *bakira shabi*."

"Who you call dirty bitch?" I replied in sloppy Hōpponese, launching my skull at his. The top of my forehead connected with his already smashed nose—Oze roared in response. Gore gushed out, dripping all over me.

He picked me up and threw me against the ground again and again. My mind went woozy and my vision blurred. More fungals surrounded me. Koji was to the side, held back by three of his kin. A look of torment made his face seem sunken and aged.

"I do not want to do this, Koji, but you brought it upon us," Oze lamented. "Upon her."

Oze sat on me, forcing the air from my lungs. He held down my arms. A group of gillies surrounded me, crouching and chanting—a low hum that rose and fell in harmony.

Slowly, they crept toward me, half a dozen hopheads touching my torso, shoulders, face, and hair. Their eyes rolled back to reveal whites, as if they were in a collective trance. Their mouths moved as a low hum turned into a chant. Suddenly, the fungals began to twitch, and thin filaments wriggled from their gills.

"Cousin, please!" Koji cried, his voice hoarse and rattling. "Stop!"

Cousin?

And then I felt it.

My skin tickled at first, making my hair stand on end. Light grazes gave me goosebumps. It was like rediscovering an old lover—that awkwardness of intimate exploration. But those nostalgic sense memories deformed into something sinister and abominable.

The chant grew louder, more omnipresent. In concert with the incantation, slimy strands writhed across my arms and cheeks. I felt them wriggle through the holes of my clothing, slinking along my stomach and up toward my chest. Up my arms and around my back. Toward my neck.

Mycelium.

I screamed. The sound pierced my ears and echoed through the alleyway. Koji begged and cried as mycelium enveloped me like a cocoon.

My throat burned, my cries only adding to the power of the chant. Mycelium crawled across me like a moist blanket, reaching my collarbone and the top of my spine. Tears poured down my face as I heaved and wept.

"P-P-Please …" I begged. Saliva spilled over my lip and the rest of the sentence wouldn't form.

Fungal tendrils wormed up my neck.

"You forced our hand, human, so I am compelled to do this," Oze whispered, his white eyes quivering. "You and your kind bring nothing but pain."

The chant rose in a crescendo, as if signaling to the mycelium—

To strike.

My mouth and throat filled with hairy filaments, blocking off the path to my lungs. I twitched and gasped, my body fighting hopelessly for air. Mycelium flooded into cracks and orifices: My ear canals and up my nostrils, even the corners of my eyes. I tried to yell, to beg, but I couldn't tell if the sounds escaped—all noise drowned out. Every one of my senses suffocated.

This was it—how I would die.

Whether I went to Heaven or Hell, all I wanted was to see Elisabeth one more time along the way.

I jerked, the last gasps of my failing body. My heartbeat slowed. My lungs were deflated and convulsing. Fungal fibers filled my esophagus and worked their way into my organs. They squirmed around my eyeballs into the socket, working deeper toward my brain—probing my grey matter, the mycelium searched for something.

I couldn't comprehend what was happening to me. My body was being invaded and there was nothing I could do. I felt … helpless.

Memories trickled to the forefront of my mind, as if drawn forth by the mycelial dissection. A car engulfed in flames. Blood smeared across my hands. Elisabeth's voice called out to me from the void, faint and ephemeral:

"Mum … Mum …. Mum …"

I wanted so desperately to hold her again, but she faded before I could.

The mycelium continued to probe my insides—there was no way I could defend myself against this assault. All I could do was spasm and gaze listlessly at Oze's strangely meditative expression, at the wispy clouds floating by overhead, and the flecks of spores that fell like snowflakes.

"Enough!"

It all came rushing back.

My head pulsated and an agonizing rush of air flowed through my exposed throat. I coughed and sputtered, rolling onto my side. My heart pumped wildly in a desperate restart. Voices argued around me in Hōpponese and the mycelium that had so thoroughly invaded me was sucked back out. I screamed at the shock of that retraction. My vision went black, and all of my orifices burned.

My vision was still hazy, the edges of my eyes raw and violated. I searched for the unfamiliar, gravelly female voice.

"Enough!" thundered the voice again. "Is this how family treats one another? Is this how we treat our guests?"

"*Shushu*?" I heard Koji say. Sifting through my brain, I tried to remember what that meant in Hōpponese.

Auntie.

From my position on the ground, I saw a short, stocky, sixty-something fungal woman standing in the middle of the fungals. Gray strands of mold hung to her shoulders beneath a bulbous, brown mushroom cap. Her mouth was curled in a wrinkly scowl, and she wore a apron wrapped around the waist of a high-neck gray robe.

She approached me. I tried to move, but couldn't.

Crouching next to me, she said, "Do not worry, they will harm you no longer. My name is Hana."

DEATH COMES FOR US

[7] Case File #42-56
The Shelf | 10:04 a.m.

- - - - - - - - -

"GIVE ME THE bottle," I demanded.

Koji handed me a clear bottle with no label. I stood with my pants down in the middle of an empty bar, soaking a cloth with the sharp-smelling alcohol. I dabbed the hook wound on my thigh with it—

"Argh!" I gritted my teeth. "Goddamnit ..."

It stung. Worse, it stank like the basement moonshine Coprinian farmers were particularly fond of—the kind I'd get blackout drunk on just a few years back. It took everything in me not to take a swig.

"Nameko, pass me some bandages." I motioned him to hurry, staunching the bleeding with painful pressure. He gave me a roll of bandages, fine white hairs poking out of its surface. Its texture was soft, and it had a sickly-sweet scent.

"Mycelium? Are you kidding me?"

"It was just a puncture, so it should heal quickly," Oze said. The giant gillie piece of shit stood across the room with his arms crossed, a bloodstained bandage over the gunshot graze on his shoulder. He leaned against a bar top made of wide, flat mushrooms crammed together in a line, massaging his nose. He'd shoved tubes of mycelium up his broad nostrils.

"'Just a puncture,'" I mocked with a sour expression.

"Welcome to Skinner's Room, detective," Koji said.

"Not the warmest of welcomes," I grumbled in Coprinian, wiping blood from my wound, "and tell your cousin he can bloody well fuck off."

"*Jiujiu*—"

"I understood her, Koji." Oze cut him off, then paused. "I am sorry … about before."

I growled like a caged animal.

"You must understand," Oze continued, "I sensed the colony, our children, were in danger. I took action to protect them."

"*Compelled*, wasn't it?" I pressed. "That's what you said before you and the other molders invaded my body!"

Koji and Oze recoiled at my use of the slur.

Oze glowered at me. "When the community is in danger, when the children are threatened, it is difficult to resist the drive to protect."

"Eat shit," I said to Oze. "'Compelled,' 'driven to protect.' All excuses. And who or what compelled you, hm? The only reason I'm not dead and being eaten by mycelium is because of *her*."

Hana walked out of a back room with four ceramic shot glasses in her hands. "What compelled him—compels us—is none of your concern, human." She plopped the glasses on the shroom bar. Bioluminescent bulbs grew from the mycelial wall behind her, forming logograms that cast a greenish glow around the edges of her body.

The bar went quiet.

I fiddled with the bandage roll in my hand—I could care less about their feelings or Oze's remorse.

My hands shook as I unraveled the dressings. I wrapped it around my thigh, the memory of the hairy filaments slithering across my skin making me queasy. After tying off the bandage, I pulled my pants up and bound my scraped knuckles.

"Who are you?" I asked Hana. "You must have some authority here on The Shelf, if everyone listens to your word without question."

I searched for a place to sit or something to lean against. Skinner's Room was a long, narrow bar lit by bulbous fungal growths that hung from above and glowed with soft bioluminescence. Every surface was made of mycelium: The ceiling, the walls, the floor. The mushroom-top bar ran along one whole wall, with fruiting bodies growing in front of it—their stiff stems and cushioned caps acted as barstools. The floor had standing mushroom tables scattered around, and a moving mountain landscape mural made of colorful molds adorned the back wall. A small, wooden Eien shrine sat atop a shroom in the far corner of the room.

No such luck. It was all fungal.

"'Authority' is a colonizer's word," Hana scoffed.

"She was a resistance leader in the Spore War," Oze said, "as well as one of the original founders of The Shelf. Though she is too humble to admit it, the community here reveres her."

"They consider her one of their leaders," Koji added.

Hana laughed at that.

I rubbed the bandages beneath my trousers. Remembering how it felt when the filaments clogged my throat—the way the hairs made me itch—I wanted to tear the dressings off. "So, it's 'cause of you that this mycelial monstrosity of an island exists."

"It is because of myself and the other founders that desperate Hōpponese have a *home*," Hana snapped, "away from the machinations of humans."

What a fucking joke. Nothing could keep the fungals safe from human greed and malice.

I couldn't stop grimacing at my surroundings. After what Oze and the other sporesacks did to me—that nightmarish, mycelial intrusion—I wanted nothing more than to burn The Shelf into the sea. To kill them all. There was no forgiving what he did ... what they did. I shuddered. Not even time could heal that affront to nature.

But my rational mind prevailed. I was alive and I had a case to solve.

Koji walked across the room and patted Oze on his broad back. He helped his cousin clean his wound and reapply bandages. In his native language, Koji said, "I am sorry I broke your nose."

"I'm not sorry I shot you," I muttered.

Taking the pill bottle from my jacket, I watched this dysfunctional reunion unfold. I popped two anti-fungal meds in my mouth, desperate to cleanse my system before a blood test could confirm my state. I had no doubt I was infected to some degree.

Hana whistled. "All of you, *kuta dai*." Shut the hells up. "Koji, you disappeared for a year—a year—and then you come back with a coppie? What were you thinking?"

"*Shushu*," he said, sounding like a chastised child.

"Don't call me 'auntie,'" Hana spat. "You never reached out, never visited. You could have been dead for all we knew."

Koji went to the bar and placed his hands on his aunt's. He let out a strained breath. "I am sorry, Hana-*shen*. You deserved better." He nodded in Oze's direction. "You all did."

"Why in the hells did you go and become a blue?" Oze asked.

"The missing children," Koji said. Though I saw in his sullen expression that something dark lingered beneath the surface—a reason he was hesitant to admit, even to family.

Hana piped in: "Our whole community is in uproar," she glared at me with her golden eyes, "but her kind do nothing about it. Report after report, investigation after investigation, ignored or delayed. Other bodies have been found, but the police just ignore it—not a *single* child has come back to us."

More dead bodies? How could I not have heard of this?

Koji massaged Hana's wrinkled, bulging knuckles. "I joined so I could *find them*. What had I accomplished before? Being a fisherman and slaving away to satisfy CPAN quotas, only to scrounge for the scraps that they left us?"

Hana tore her hand from her nephew. She struck his cheek in an open-palmed slap that resounded across the room. Black spores flew from her gills like angry bees.

"You are a disgrace!" she cried. "Can you not see that they are using you?"

Koji cupped his reddened face, mouth agape—I could see the truth had hurt him more than his aunt's hand.

Question was, what would the NKPD be "using" him for?

"I have made my choices," Koji said.

Oze's fists were clenched, looking more like clubs with his stocky forearms. "Correct, cousin, *your choices*. Do you think I slave away? That I waste my life working on those boats and helping my family? Those are *my* choices, following in the footsteps of my forebears. What do your words say about my fath—"

The huge hophead choked up midsentence. He breathed heavily through his wide mouth, holding back tears.

"Oze …" Koji whispered. "Where is Iroh? Where is your father?"

Oze looked at the floor, hugging his hulking midsection.

"You. Human." Hana waved me over. "Bring the bottle."

I walked over and placed the booze on the bar. Hana picked it up and quickly poured four shots, the clear liquid reaching right to the rim of each. The sharpness ignited my nostrils—it smelled like it would strip my esophagus the way paint thinner stripped walls.

"It is too early for that," Koji noted.

"Drink," Hana insisted. She slid one glass to Koji, another toward Oze. She picked up a third and offered it to me. "It is *somake* rice wine, albeit a bit stronger than normal."

"I no drink," I said in Hōpponese. Correction: I didn't drink anymore.

Hana's yellow irises pierced me like an eagle eying its prey. She threw back the glass she'd offered me without a perceptible shift in her sour expression, then picked up the next. She glanced at me: "You can thank your cursed CPAN government for this swill. All alcohol production goes through them. Nothing is left for us but bootleg rice wine. The stronger, the better."

"Where is Iroh?" Koji repeated, cradling the cup.

Hana fidgeted. Her brown cap twitched. She brushed the ridges from her apron with tiny motions.

"He is dead," she finally admitted, her voice cracking on the last syllable.

Koji shook and put his drink down. "When? How?"

"Almost two months ago," Oze said. "A bad storm, out in the Fungal Depths. The whole crew was lost, and the ship sank. CPAN sent a small recovery operation, but … there were no survivors."

Koji's posture slackened and he dropped to his knees. Pain smeared its ugly form across his features, dragging him down like gravity. No tears were shed, but I saw bursts of gray spores flowing from beneath his cap. Oze crouched next to Koji and whispered something in his ear.

Minutes passed before Oze helped his cousin to his feet.

Koji turned to his aunt. Sadness seeped from the deepened lines on his face. His lips quivered, and teardrops pooled on his eyelashes.

"It is okay, Koji. Drink," Hana reiterated, "for him."

The three buttons threw back their drinks, as if this kind of hardship was commonplace.

"Now," Hana said, pointing a pale, bony finger at me, "tell me about *her*. I felt her presence ripple across the network. But why, in the name of Mother Chikyu, would you bring a human to The Shelf?"

Koji picked at the skin around his fingernails. "I am aiding her with an investigation. Evidence suggested that Iroh could be of service."

Oze scoffed. "Of service? You only return when you need something?"

"Investigation or not," Hana said, "I didn't think *you* would be the idiot responsible for bringing a human here." Hana poured herself another cup of the acrid alcohol and threw it back without hesitation. She glared at her nephew, gesturing at his police uniform. "Just look at yourself. You think turning that jacket inside out will hide who you've become? That you've joined the *enemy*?"

That last word bled with venom.

I slammed my hands down on the mushroom bartop, feeling the urge to, bloody Hell … defend Koji. The impact was softened by the bouncy, pillow-like caps. "Enough!" I said in their tongue.

Hana laughed. "Sit down, blondie. You'll loosen your bandages."

"*Shushu*, please," Koji said. "We are not here to argue. These days, we do what we must to survive, but Detective Hofmann is not here to hurt anyone. She is investigating the murder of a fungal child, and we need your help."

Hana closed her eyes and let out an exasperated sigh. She turned to me, her face shadowed by her cap. "So, detective, I take it you understand all that we are saying?"

"Yes, understand, but spoken Hōpponese no good." I hated the way my brain clogged up over their stupid language. "Speak Coprinian instead?"

That triggered a harsh titter from Hana. The old gillie folded her arms. "Typical colonizer mindset. Speak *your* native tongue, make everything easier for *you*. My nephew may say you are investigating a fungal murder—and I don't want you dead like most of The Shelf—but I do not trust you."

"Will you do this?" Koji pleaded.

Oze shook his head and cap. "It's a waste of time, mama."

"*I* did not say it was," Hana replied, weariness in her tone.

"Please," I said in Coprinian. All the translating was giving me a headache. "Look at these." I drew the crime scene photos from my inner jacket pocket and set them in a line across the mushroom cap counter.

With a groan and squinted eyes, Hana leaned in to examine them. Oze inched closer and did the same. Their faces washed over with a flurry of emotions: Horror, disgust, confusion, and finally, recognition.

"Who could have done such a thing?" Hana asked, a fragile quiver in her gruff voice.

"That is what we want to figure out," Koji said.

Hana tapped on the fourth photo. I turned it around, seeing the same rope Koji had reacted to on the beach at Shrine Island.

"I have seen this before," she said.

"As have I," Oze added. "CPAN supplies licensed fishing boats with standard-issue equipment. If we try and use any of our own materials, they burden us with fines. It is yet another way for the *gaikamu* to control us."

"Power and authority through bureaucracy," I said. The true Coprinian way—red tape and bullshit paperwork being the real reason nothing ever got fucking done.

Oze chewed his lip. "Yes, and these are the ropes that your bureaucracy provides us."

"If we follow the rope," Koji said, "we might be able to find the killer."

"Or at least more clues to point us in the right direction," I concluded. "Oze, write a list of all the fishing companies contracted by CPAN."

"Do *not* tell me what to do. You have no right, and I will not betray my kin."

Koji pressed his palms together. "Please, cousin. Think of the children."

Oze tapped his fingers on the bar top, making the big flat mushroom jiggle. "No."

"Oze, those missing and dead children deserve justice!"

"And what have the *gaikamu* done to prove that anything will change? How can justice ever be served for the crimes against our people?"

"Because it is *me*," Koji whispered. "I have faith that the work I am doing is bringing about change. However small."

"*Damitare* …," Oze groused. "Fine."

He went behind the bar and reached toward the mycelium wall. A cubby opened, as if it recognized his touch. He reached inside and withdrew a textured mycopaper sheet and a charcoal pencil.

"There are only a dozen companies operating out of Neo Kinoko. CPAN keeps a tight leash on them, tracking their catches and shipments." In practiced strokes, he wrote down elegant swoops and lines—logograms. Then he slid the paper toward me. "There's a list of names and locations. I work for Hōppon Fisheries."

"And Iroh?" I asked.

"Sea Dragon Seafood Co."

I picked up the paper, my eyes tracing the strange alphabet. Pausing, I ran my tongue along the inside of my cheek. "Nameko, take this—I can't read it."

Koji snatched the list without a word.

"That is not all," Hana said, her tone turning even more graven. "Koji, come with me."

Koji followed his aunt to the shrine in the back of the room. She held the clear bottle in one hand. I gathered the photos and walked closer, but Oze stopped me with fingers pressed against my shoulder. His stiff demeanor and the slight shake of his head said, *Leave them be.*

"Don't touch me," I hissed.

I smacked Oze's hand away but heeded his body language and waited in the space between fruiting tables.

While shuffling and reviewing the photos, I listened to Koji and Hana.

"Pray with me," Hana said softly. "Pray for Iroh."

The two clapped their hands three times. They placed their fingers to the rims of their caps and bowed deep, almost touching the floor. Swirls of fragrant sandalwood smoke rose to the mycelium ceiling from incense Hana had lit.

They stuck the incense sticks into notched holes on either side of the small house-like shrine, then laid offerings into three ceramic bowls at its base. Grains of rice, which Hana pulled from a mycelium satchel at the base of the shrine. Spores, which both fungals took from their own gills. And drops of alcohol, poured from the bottle that Hana held.

Koji caressed the edges of a faded mycopaper photo that was propped against the shrine.

In the photo, two young fungals stood with their fingers intertwined. Hana, I recognized, meaning the other must've been Iroh. They were dressed in plain clothing, and young Hana held a single flower up to her chest. The two beamed brightly. Dried, moldy rose petals were strewn about beneath the photo, as if that very flower had lived and died on the shrine.

Another picture rested on the shrine, less faded than the first. This one featured a family: A father, mother, and son, but any sense of happiness was absent from the scene.

Hana and Koji began chanting. Next to me, Oze muttered along amidst the strange, ethereal sounds of their lament:

"Murio, guide my papa along his journey into the afterlife. Heriko, open the doors of The Great Beyond to him. Mother Chikyu, provide him safe haven. Yomi, watch over his soul in the spirit realm."

Hana and Koji finished their recitation until the words faded into a stillness that only grief could bring.

"Death comes for us," Hana, Koji, and Oze said in concert, "and to the soil we return."

Memories of Elisabeth encroached. I felt goose bumps rise on my skin.

Were the fungals really so different—so *alien*—that my people could subjugate them as they had? That I could treat them like monsters and ignore the truth: Even though our religions were different, we still believed in the same fundamental principles of the universe. In life and death.

"Auntie," Koji said, "your senses are clouded. What are you hiding from me?"

Hana swiveled and rested the brim of her cap against her nephew's. "Daigoro … he is missing. Shikaku left to look for him, but he has not returned. That was weeks ago."

Koji took a deep breath, followed by a pregnant pause. "And you believe it could have something to do with this dead body and the children that have vanished?"

"Daigoro's disappearance is similar to what has happened all over the city—children vanishing."

Hana nodded. She took the newer photo from the shrine and place it in Koji's palm. "Daigoro's mother, Emiko, volunteers at the Reishi Temple in the Pit. Seek her out. Find Daigoro and Shikaku."

Could Shikaku have run away with the boy? Did he kidnap him?

"I will," Koji said. "I promise."

"You abandoned us once already. Do not make a promise you cannot keep."

"I will not break it." Koji's golden eyes watered, his free hand caressing his aunt's forearm. "It is my duty, auntie."

"And next time you decide to visit," she replied, glancing at me, "come alone."

Koji and Hana came towards me, standing around a small mushroom table. Oze joined.

"Hofmann?" Koji said. By the way he said my name, I knew how loaded it was with expectation.

"I can't guarantee anything. My case is the body we found on the beach, and this—your cousin and his kid—is personal." I clicked my tongue. "Get me to the Docks so we can conduct interviews, and then we'll talk."

Koji blinked, mulling it over. "Agreed. But I doubt we'll get back to the ferries without stirring up more trouble. How will we leave The Shelf?"

"I may have a solution," Oze added in his heavily accented Coprinian. He inclined his chin toward me. "So long as 'blondie' is okay with being around me for a while longer."

"Not like I have much of a choice," I growled, narrowing my eyes. "But keep your fucking hands to yourself."

FLOAT ON

- - - - - - - - -

AM *NOT* getting in that piece of crap," I told Oze. Beneath the vast, skeletal shadow of Murio's Arch, a small fishing boat bobbed in the ocean swell.

Koji, Oze, and I stood on the edge of a mycelial pier, crystallized with ice and piled with tangles of fishing nets. It was tucked between warehouses, workshops, and a sea-battered boathouse. A pale winter sun hung high over the horizon, causing reflected light to glisten on the sprawling surface of the Fungal Depths to the south-east. Stabbing winds blew across the ocean, stinging my tired eyes and sending loose hair across my face. I pulled my cap down. Tucked in as many untamed strands as I could manage, too.

"Is that uncle's boat?" Koji asked.

"It is," Oze said. "*Skinner's Skiff*, in all her glory."

"It looks like it'll fall apart the moment we set foot in it," I said.

Oze tsked. "I take her out daily," he said. "Well-maintained, sturdy, and seaworthy. Believe me."

I didn't believe him, but neither did I have a choice. I just had to keep a watchful eye. To get back across the bay and never return to the fucking Shelf again.

He led us down the dark pier toward the craft. This part of The Shelf was blanketed in near-constant twilight by the gargantuan bridge above. It brought a deeper bitterness to the air that sent a chill through my aging bones.

Up close, *Skinner's Skiff* was even less impressive. It was a tightly woven mesh of sun-bleached mycelium, about fifteen feet long. A tall cover grew out of the sides, arching over the back half of the boat. Its only "modern" upgrade was a diesel motor at the back, with a handle and seat for the driver.

"After you," Oze said.

He offered a hand, but I slapped it aside and stepped inside. "Piss off."

The boat wobbled. I found my balance and sat on the mycelium floor—there was nowhere else to sit. This morning alone had been a shock to my mycophobic system. I was ready to down a whole bottle of anti-fungal meds—if only the NKPD provided more than a strict monthly allowance of the stuff.

Rubbing the bridge of my nose, I waited for Koji and Oze to unmoor the craft. I craned my neck to see how The Shelf—along with barnacles, slime, and algae—clung to the massive mycocrete pillars that supported Murio's Arch. Attached to the base of the pillars were hundreds of thick mycelial cables that held the island in place. Docks, shacks, and warehouses were constructed at sea level, organically melding upwards into the cramped, towering colony of The Shelf itself.

And all of it was built on a foundation of Goddamn mycelium.

From here, I could see its gritty truths laid bare—and the disturbing-yet-ingenious living architecture of the fungals.

"Did y'all sense that meatsack who got loose?" someone said in Hōpponese.

A group of gillie fishermen strolled out onto a jetty some ways down the edge of The Shelf. They stumbled around and laughed, likely drunk on bootleg rice wine.

"*Gaikamu*!" another said. "What do the humans think they're doing coming here?"

The sporesack bastards kept gossiping, about food shortages, and children who'd run away or disappeared. One of them unzipped his pants and pissed into the sea.

"Oze!" a croaky fungal shouted across the docks. "That you?"

"Get down!" Oze warned. He walked off, acting casual. "Botan, *hao-mi do*?"

I threw myself onto the hull, hearing the sloshing of the water beneath. The hairy filaments on the boat's surface tickled my skin and tangled in my hair. I squirmed, sweat pooling under my armpits. Flashbacks to the alleyway. Mycelium entering my body. Thoughts of death and crossing over.

Elisabeth. My sweet Liz …

"It will be okay," Koji assured me with cigarette-tinged breath. "You will be okay."

I realized my pulse and breathing were racing. I was so close to leaving this cursed place. I needed to control myself, to focus and relax.

Oze, Botan, and the other fishermen talked. They complained about CPAN cracking down with stricter permits and licenses—life in war-torn Neo Kinoko wasn't easy for anyone.

Koji held my head, and I didn't have it in me to tell him to stop or move away. "Calm, Hofmann," he repeated. "Calm."

Oze popped his head into the boat. "All clear. They're …" He must've noticed my state. "Is she alright?"

"She will be fine," Koji assured his cousin. "Let us leave."

In less than a minute, Oze had us unmoored and the boat was jostling with the Kinoko Bay current. I sniffed, perhaps from the cold. My sinuses were raw, and the air reeked of rotten fish, algae, and plankton. I was never one for the sea, but at least this was better than being on The Shelf.

Anything was, after what I'd experienced. I glanced around, making sure Oze remained as far from me as possible in this shitty skiff.

I looked up at Koji. "You said you used to be a fisherman? Did you live on The Shelf?" I needed a distraction to divert my thoughts.

Looking in the direction of Murio's Arch, he said, "This bridge was a symbol for one our gods: The Guiding Star. He is the god of the moon and stars and the ferryman of dead souls to the Great Beyond."

"And so, when my people destroyed it during the war …"

Koji bowed his head and cap. "It was a desecration of our faith, our history, and our meaning." He paused, biting his lip. "After our defeat, this was where I lived. It felt strange to lie beneath the shadow of Murio's Arch, knowing that we had survived and so many of our brethren's souls had passed into The Great Beyond. But the Hōpponese are resilient, and we've banded together anywhere we could: The Shelf, The Pit, Mold Town, Kala Commons. Whatever slums your government afforded us, we made it work."

I didn't know what to say. Instead, I remained silent, surprised by Koji's openness. A sliver of trust given to someone he could have easily demonized, as I'd so readily demonized him.

"And where did the name 'Skinner' come from?"

"Have you ever caught and prepared a fish?" Koji replied, still cradling me as the boat swayed. I rolled my head from side to side to say "no."

"My uncle fishes … fished. I did not know anyone who could gut, scale, and skin a fish as fast as he could."

"Maybe that's why your aunt fell for him," I joked. "'A man who provides is a man you can depend on.' That's the bullshit my dad always tried to sell me on, anyway. Too bad life never ends up the way we expect."

Koji smirked, showing his yellowing teeth. "Very true, Hofmann."

Drifting farther from The Shelf, the boat rocked with the force of the waves. Life steered us in directions we were often oblivious to. I'd faced death many times, and knew the toll it wrought upon the soul. Elisabeth was not the first, but hers was the death that broke me.

Years passed after she died before I realized that time stops for no one. Not if you were a drunken wreck. Not if you had your shit together. Time would just float on. If you were too stupid or naïve or careless to pay attention, you'd inch closer to the end without even realizing it.

I'd ruined so much of mine, wasting years wallowing in self-pity and empty bottles. How close was I to my end?

I turned and laid on my back, sinking into the spongy deck. Koji's hands slipped away, and he leaned against the side of the boat. A briny breeze blew across the water. Staring up at the underside of Murio's Arch—its dark underbelly giving way to silver, clouded skies—my mind returned to the rotting countenance of a fungal child.

"A storm is coming in," Oze said. "I will pick up the pace." The boat jerked as it increased in speed.

I had leads: A rope and a list of fishing companies, written in Oze's handwriting. But there were still so many unanswered questions.

"Nameko? Read the list to me."

Koji took it out of his pocket, and began translating the names and locations. "Do you mind if I smoke while we do this?"

"Go for it," I said. "Just don't blow any of that shit in my face."

I fished the voice recorder from my coat. Preparing my already stiff back for a choppy ride across Kinoko Bay, I began parroting Koji's words into the microphone.

"Hōppon Fisheries, Dock F32. Ame Ocean Co., Dock H23. Tsuri Commercial Union, Dock F15 …"

CLEAN BUSINESS

- - - - - - - - -

DEEP IN THE warehouse network of the Docks, Koji and I rounded the corner of a metal-sided depot. Light snowfall trickled down from low cloud cover. It fell to the mycocrete beneath our feet, mixing with dirt and mold in a gray slurry.

"That was the eleventh bloody business on Oze's list," I said, devouring a plain rice cake. My throat ached with each swallow, knowing my body needed nourishment after what the mycelium had done. "Still nothing, though."

"At least the manager offered us tea," Koji noted, "but you did not have to deny her in such an offensive manner."

"Hōpponese tea tastes like dirt. What I need is a coffee." I took a final bite of the sweet, chewy cake and brushed flour from my fingers. "At least they had snacks, 'cause I was starving."

We continued, crisscrossing corridors until exiting onto a vehicle road. CPAN trucks rolled past. Armed soldiers sat in the passenger seats, and dozens more patrolled the docks. There was a palpable tension in the frigid air, with fungal dockworkers warily avoiding the sentries and their rifles.

I took out my voice recorder and listened: "Sea Dragon Seafood Co.," past me said. "Dock E13."

"Iroh …" Koji said, trailing off.

"Keep your emotions in check and your gills zipped, got it? I can't have you spooking a potential lead."

Koji flashed me a glare.

"I'm bloody serious, Nameko," I said. "Do you understand?"

He worked his jaw but complied with a single, "Yes."

"Good."

I was relieved to have gotten off The Shelf, but now I faced the realities of every homicide investigation: Interviews, following clues to dead ends, paperwork, and an ongoing grind until the puzzle pieces started to fit.

The real question was, what would I do with Nameko after this? He was competent, sure, but also a liability. In the heart of Neo Kinoko, a fungal cop would bring more trouble than a human on The Shelf.

Plus, this business with Iroh, Shikaku, and Daigoro was far too personal.

Repressed memories of my stupid, drunken ass flashed through my mind. How my inebriated anger had led to countless confrontations. The occasional set of handcuffs. Bar fights and misplaced blame.

Nothing good ever came from vendettas.

I pushed the thought aside and pinpointed the nearest quay. A supply ship was moored there, guarded by gray-clad soldiers. A group of fungals unloaded small crates by hand, carrying them into a nearby warehouse.

"We're at dock D27, so it shouldn't be far. This way."

Koji and I followed the road. Trucks rumbled by, spewing exhaust in our faces and stirring up grimy slush. Koji lit up one of his stinky cigarettes—how many of those nasty death-sticks did he smoke each day?

I coughed from all the noxious shit around me, counting the docks and warehouses as we passed: "D30, D31, D32, E01, E02, E03."

The road continued toward a bridge that crossed into the Dock Ward. A sprawl of low-lying warehouses and boatyards filled the distance, with radio towers jutting out at intervals. CPAN invested plenty of money and resources into rebuilding the docks and setting up a radio network, but they sure as Hell didn't care that half of Neo Kinoko still lay in ruins.

CPAN was resourceful and efficient—when it wanted to be.

I began to count again. Koji pulled out another cigarette and lit it. As my boots slopped in the wet snow, a gnawing thought came back to me.

"Nameko? What does it mean when your people 'sense?'"

Koji took a lengthy pull, then exhaled through his nose in long plumes of smoke. "We are connected," he said.

"Connected how? When Oze and the other fungals attacked me, I felt the mycelium inside me, like it was …" I cringed, trying to understand what the Hell Oze and the other sporesacks had tried to do to me.

"Oze and the others were protecting their community," Koji said. "The connections that my people have is deeper than any human can perceive."

"But that doesn't excuse what they did! I felt them inside my head, searching … It was barbaric."

"I do not disagree with you." His face sank, as if he was reliving things that he couldn't unsee. "But this is a deeply rooted function of our biology and culture. What is ironic is a Coprinian criticizing anyone or anything for being *barbaric*, especially in a land your people invaded and conquered."

"*I* didn't fight in the war, Nameko, but your cousin and his cronies did violate my mind. Why would they do that to me?"

The tip of Koji's cigarette glowed as he inhaled. "Memories."

"What is that supposed to mean?"

"By parsing your memories, they could determine what could hurt you most. To trap and torture you until you went mad."

I shuddered at the thought of those gillies imprisoning me in my mind and how close I was to reliving the traumas of my past … "The mycelium, how would it allow them to do that?"

"How easily can you explain your own biology? How do you breathe?

How does your brain form thoughts? The mycelium—even the spores in the air around us—are interconnected loci. We Hōpponese are natural extensions of that network. It gives us the ability to communicate with one another through emotional states, to reach into the experiences and memories of our kin, if we choose to open ourselves."

I couldn't grasp what Koji was saying. Interconnected loci, natural network extensions, emotional states—

"You two, halt!"

Ahead and to my left, a scrawny CPAN soldier stood between a pair of warehouses made of corrugated metal walls. His finger lingered on the trigger of his black, army-issue S14 rifle. With squinty blue eyes, he took in Koji and me. White flakes fell onto his gray uniform, replete with a matching helmet, black shoulder pads, and body armor that bulked up his measly torso.

"What can we help you with, soldier," I called as we approached.

"Papers, now!" he demanded, his voice sounding purposefully altered to come across deeper and more masculine. "What is your business in the Docks?"

"Let me handle this, Nameko." I took out my badge and showed it to the soldier. "Detective Henrietta Hofmann, NKPD Homicide Division, and this is Officer Koji Nameko. We're on an official investigation."

"'We'?" The guard pitched his head and looked at Koji, bemused. "What the Hell is a *gillie* doing in uniform? And put that out while I'm talking to you!"

Koji tensed. He crushed his cigarette in the snow. I wondered how often he'd had to deal with dickheads like this.

I got closer to the man, intentionally breathing in his face. "That's none of your business, *soldier*. Do you want to take it up with your superior officer, or shall I get my captain involved?"

The soldier's nostrils flared. "As you were," he conceded. Then his thin, pink lips cinched like a drawstring coinpurse.

"Thank you," I said. "Now kindly fuck off and bother someone else.

Let's go, Nameko."

"What just happened?" Koji asked, nonplussed.

"Small men with big egos," I quipped, leaving the soldier to deal with his self-esteem. "I've never had the patience for people like that, and I never will."

— — — — — —

FIVE MINUTES LATER, we found Sea Dragon Seafood Co.

It was a tall metal warehouse, fairly new but battered by saltwater and wind. One side of the warehouse was in-line with the dock—a straight drop into the freezing ocean. I motioned to Koji and we continued to the other side. Turning the corner, we entered into an open, covered loading bay. It extended down the dock, with space for a large boat to moor on the right. A faint odor of whatever spoiled seafood had gone to the dumpsters hung in the crisp air.

Around fifteen fungal dockworkers hauled wooden crates onto wheeled carts. They wore bright orange safety vests, lightweight jackets and heavy boots—they were clearly underdressed for the weather, but none of them seemed to give a shit.

Was this a genetic thing? Some kind of temperature regulation?

I peered at Koji. He'd finished his cigarette and billows of condensed vapor left his mouth with every controlled breath. It looked as though he was craving another one, the way his mouth twitched. Did the cold not bother him, either?

All I wanted was to curl up next to a fire, and here these molders were working in the winter like it was bloody autumn.

We continued into the loading bay. Raised, concrete abutments stuck out from the warehouse where two cargo trucks were being filled with dozens of crates. The crates appeared nondescript. I caught sight of one of the drivers in the cab, a shady looking hophead with tattoos.

The workers took notice of Koji and me. Their yellow-eyed gazes took me in with skepticism. Worse, their expressions turned severe upon seeing Koji dressed in a police uniform.

We were off to a good start.

Across the loading bay, a gillie woman stood next to a red door at the top of a ramp. She directed workers, a scowl permanently etched on her angular face. The colony of small, cream-colored fruiting bodies atop her head shook with every stern movement of her slender frame.

"Come on," I said, pointing at the woman.

I approached the fungal with my NKPD badge held at chest height. Koji followed behind, showing his as well. "Good afternoon," I said in Coprinian.

I inspected the button with a quick once-over. Her moldy, black hair was slicked back, tied up in a tight bun beneath her mushroom-topped head. She wore a safety vest, but beneath was a well-cut pantsuit that spoke of an administrative position. At the top of her pearlescent chest— mostly obscured by her buttoned shirt—I noticed the dark edges of a tattoo. Its lines moved slightly, as if agitated by my presence.

Our eyes met.

She gave me a disagreeable glare through squinted, custard-colored eyes. "You look pretty beat up for a detective," she jibed in Hōpponese, examining my bruised face and torn trousers. "What can I do for you?"

Bloody Hell, these fucking buttons … "I'm Detective Hofmann," I persisted in Coprinian. "We're here on official NKPD business."

No response. The sporesack just crossed her arms.

Koji placed his hands at his side and bowed—the bitch returned the gesture. In the confident tones of his mother tongue, he said, "*Jiujiu*, I am Officer Nameko Koji. Would you mind if we asked you some questions?"

The hophead's eyes narrowed again, darting from Koji to me. "Nameko-*shen*, I am Nikuya Yuki, floor manager of Sea Dragon Seafood Co. What business do you have with us?"

Of course, she'd respond to one of her own kind. But I wasn't about to bow down to every Goddamn fungal by speaking their language.

"We are conducting inquiries with local businesses," Koji replied. "If we could please speak to your superior."

Yuki pinched her thin, red lips and flared her flat nose. She spat on the ground at my feet.

I spat back. "You Goddamned mold—"

Koji stepped between us, his arms spread. "It is just an act of super-stition," he said in Coprinian. "Your people already stole our country, our city—many wonder what else might you take from us. Please, let the offense slide."

I growled and clenched my fists. One hand drifted to my pistol, but I stopped myself. It wasn't worth the trouble, and Yuki didn't deserve any response other than silence.

"This way, please," Yuki said in Coprinian with a lopsided smile. Turning, she pushed open the heavy red door.

We followed Yuki onto Sea Dragon's main floor. I was struck by the blinding fluorescent light tubes hanging from the high ceiling. The harsh sting of the warehouse's chilling air prickled my exposed skin. I popped my jacket collar and slipped on my mittens. Puddles glistened on con-crete floors, and the space smelled of strong antiseptic chemicals. Large freezers lined the left wall.

"This is quite the operation," Koji said. "How long has it been in business?"

The warehouse was lined with dozens of high-shelved rows. Each shelf was filled with stacked pallets, crates, containers, and plastic-wrapped boxes. I wondered what could be inside, beyond just seafood.

"One year, two months," Yuki replied.

She led us past more workers who were busy packing a large freezer container with frozen, thick-bodied fish. Stiff, bulbous mushrooms grew from their spines. The sight of fungi ruining something as delicious as fish left me feeling ill.

One of the workers caught my eye, exuding disdain then … fear?

He took a swig from a mycoleather bladder, but whatever was inside was pungent: Alcohol. But not just any alcohol. It stank of the swill Hana had poured at Skinner's Room that morning.

This moonshine was making its way across Neo Kinoko.

"Back to work!" Yuki yelled.

The gillie returned to his duties, but his expression and the stink of booze bothered me.

After a minute, we were near the back of the building. Yuki stopped at a red door with a square sign covered in logograms. She knocked on it in a notable manner. A code? A warning?

The office door clicked and opened. Yuki held out a hand.

Koji and I entered a square white-walled room. It was minimally decorated, furnished with a plastic desk and four beige filing cabinets. Somehow, the tiny space was much warmer than the warehouse, and a short, stout button with a round purple mushroom cap awaited us.

"Good day," he said in fluent, accented Coprinian. He bowed, but only Koji returned the formality. "My sincere apologies for Yuki—she can be quite forthright. I am Konno Iwashi, supervisor of Sea Dragon Seafood Co. How may I be of service?"

I flashed my badge, and Iwashi's pupils dilated. "Please, sit," he said, offering seats in front of the desk.

We sat, and Iwashi circled around to the opposite side. He cleared his throat, brushing the lapels of his loose brown suit jacket. The motion released a scent of cheap perfume into the air.

"I'm Detective Hofmann of the NKPD, and this"—I nodded toward Koji—"is Officer Nameko. We're here regarding an investigation and would like to ask you a few questions."

Iwashi coughed and scratched his chest beneath a pinstripe tie. He ran his thick fingers through thinning moldy hair. "Of course, of course. Anything you need, Hofmann-*shen*. Though I would offer you tea, unfortunately, it is hard to come by these days."

Anabuki Fishing seemed to have found a tea supplier, even if it smelled like mud and leaves. The rice cakes were delicious, at least. But that meant business for Sea Dragon must not be going so well—or funds were being diverted elsewhere.

"It is quite alright," Koji said.

I leaned forward. "Your Coprinian is quite good. How much of your business dealings are with the Coprinian People's Army Navy?"

"Oh, the majority," Iwashi replied. His demeanor loosened, calm settling on his plump face. "CPAN controls the port, but we act as a base of operations for various local captains and fishermen. A union or collective, as it were."

Koji wrung his fingers. "And what of a boat that—"

I dug my nails into Koji's thigh. The bloody idiot was about to press Iwashi on Iroh or the dead fishermen. His expression went from shock to frown, before settling on pensive.

"Excuse Officer Nameko. He's fascinated by boats, but now isn't the time to indulge in private passions." I played Iwashi harder. "So, no knowledge of black-market smuggling, trafficking, dumping? Any gossip of illegal activities?"

Iwashi took a deep breath, his rotund frame rising and falling. A faint trail of spores flowed from beneath his cap, and the small office began to smell of sweat and soil.

"Is that yes, or no?" I pressured.

"I have not heard anything for s-s-some time, as CPAN has been cracking down on such activity, nor would I debase my r-r-reputation like that." Then Iwashi looked at Koji. "Nor should we fungals disgrace ourselves as such, even in troublesome times."

He was closing up. It was time to change the angle.

I took out the photo of the rope from the crime scene. I placed it on Iwashi's desk.

"What is this, detective?" he asked.

"Rope," Koji answered. "The same rope that CPAN issues to all of its contracted fishing companies."

I tapped the photograph. "Have you seen rope like that?"

That elicited an anxious laugh from Iwashi. "Y-Yes, of course. All of our b-boats are stocked with them. We tried replacing them with myco-fiber ropes once, but inspectors fined us. Never again."

"And would you happen to have records of the inventory that CPAN provides you?" I inquired. "That includes lot numbers and any other relevant details."

"Of c-course." Iwashi began readjusting his tie. "But ... are we s-s-suspected of something? Where was this picture taken?"

I ran my tongue along my upper teeth. "At the moment, that is confidential. The investigation is ongoing and not all evidence has been cataloged."

"Right, right," Iwashi muttered, scratching his chest again. "So do you believe we might have some involvement in ... whatever happened?"

"We are simply following protocol and exploring every lead," Koji said. "The rope led us to reason that one of the local fishing companies might be able to steer us in the right direction."

"I assure you that I manage a c-clean business here."

"Of course, and that's not in question," I reassured Iwashi, playing him along. "But we're going to need detailed accounts of your company's dealings—thorough accounts."

Iwashi tilted his double chin down. Tiny beads of sweat trailed along his temples. "Yes, detective. I will s-s-send physical copies of our financial records and inventories to the NKPD by the end of the work day."

"Make sure it's sent to the central precinct," I requested.

I heard Iwashi swallow from across the desk. "Yes, detective," he said.

The pager rumbled inside my jacket. I pulled it out and read the message: *Meet Captain Ridgeway. ASAP. Bring Nameko—Hodges.*

Shit ... that couldn't be good.

Theo Hodges was the captain's assistant, and forever the bearer of bad news.

I rose, picking up the photo. "Sorry, Iwashi, but we have urgent business to attend to. Send over the paperwork as soon as you can, and thank you for your cooperation."

Koji rose as well. He bowed to the now sweat-stained supervisor.

Iwashi took leave of his chair, bowed in return, and walked to the door. "If there is anything else I can do to aid your investigation, detective, please do not hesitate to ask."

"I appreciate that," I said.

We left the office and made our way across the freezing warehouse. I shivered, reaching for my mittens.

"Is everything okay?" Koji asked.

I tried to decide what I could tell him. Where did we stand, and what the Hell was Ridgeway going to dump on my lap? My mind churned. Off to the side, I noticed two workers shooting us skittish glances. Yuki appeared out of nowhere and scolded them.

Iwashi was guilty of something, I just didn't what know yet. And Yuki … What part did she have to play in this?

"Detective?" Koji said.

"We're going to NKPD headquarters, Nameko." And if Hodges' message was any indication, there was going to be a reckoning.

MILK & SUGAR

[10] Case File #42-56
NKPD Central Precinct | 2:49 p.m.

- - - - - - - - -

MY GAZE WANDERED across the busy Homicide division bullpen, light bouncing off the windows of Captain Matias Ridgeway's office. I landed on Koji: He sat at my desk on the far side of the room, hands folded in his lap. Every human in the bullpen stared daggers at him. Dozens of officers and detectives roiled with disdain, all of their negativity focused on one unfortunate fungal.

"Hofmann!"

I startled in my seat. A fist slammed on the faux-wood desk in front of me, nearly knocking over a stack of papers. Ridgeway sat across from me, his face furious and hard-lined. A book shelf, liquor cabinet, and neatly arranged file boxes hugged the wall behind him, framing his square torso. His unpleasant musk filled the room—it was the smell of someone overworked, trying to mask it with heady perfume as opposed to a daily shower.

"Are you paying attention, detective?" he asked.

"Yes, sir." I cleared my throat, sitting straight. Upright posture, feet flat like those ruler-wielding tyrants taught me at boarding school decades ago.

Ridgeway glowered. He stood and removed circular reading glasses from his eagle-like eyes. Towering over his desk, he revealed a sturdy, six-foot frame and a freshly pressed navy-blue uniform. "Good," he replied, "because you and that *sporesack* out there caused quite a Goddamn mess!"

I eyed Ridgeway's well-stocked liquor cabinet. He'd imported the high-quality stuff: Lowland Park malt whisky, Isle of Glen dry gin, even a couple bottles of Gribnian Standard vodka. I did my best not to scratch the backs of my hands—a stress-induced habit that started when I gave alcohol the boot.

"I apologize, sir," I said with my most sincere tone.

"Apologies won't cut it!" Ridgeway yelled. A pause, followed by a sigh. He went to the windows and closed the blinds. "You know how those bloody idiots out there love to gossip."

Gossip and sexist remarks were all too common in my day-to-day. Koji wouldn't help my shit reputation, either. "I'm well aware, sir."

"Right, right. I'd offer you a drink, but, well"—he waved two fingers in my direction—"recovery and all that. Tea? I can tell Theo to make some."

"No, thank you, sir. I prefer coffee, although it's hard to come by a decent cup in this city."

Ridgeway chuckled. "It's for the best. Most of the coffee around here is that utter rubbish the military brings over. Real bottom of the bag stuff. And the tea—ugh, don't get me started on the tea." He blew out an exasperated breath. "These fucking gillies get it all wrong! No milk, no sugar, just … leaves. Tastes like ass."

I smiled. "I'm well aware of that, too, sir. But I'm fine."

"Alright, alright."

Ridgeway paced, coughing into the nook of his arm. His balding head wasn't far from the newly-installed ceiling tiles. The space was fairly small—twenty feet or so from end to end—and smelled of fresh paint.

"How're the renovations coming?" I asked.

"Doesn't matter how often they replace the ceiling, that mold keeps creeping in." Ridgeway cleared his throat. "Shoddy construction, choked supply lines, factory strikes back home—it's all a Goddamned mess, isn't it? Plus, this chronic cough doesn't fucking go away, and the anti-fungal meds are only doing so much. Speaking of which, did you get tested for infection?"

"I did. Even after my … incident this morning at the crime scene, the riot, and my time at The Shelf, my blood came through clean."

I'd only been in Neo Kinoko for a few months. Ridgeway had been here for years. Did he have an allergy, or was that what infection looked like? Slow and menacing, only making itself known through small symptoms before worsening.

Then I remembered what Koji had mentioned: *Spores in the air.*

"You're bloody lucky, Hofmann," Ridgeway said. "But you're even more lucky that I'm not tossing your wrinkly ass out after what you did."

"Sir, if you'll let me explain. Officer Nameko and I—"

"Went to The Shelf, unauthorized!" he interrupted. His bushy eyebrows twitched. "You know humans are discouraged from going there— police and military, especially. That island is anarchy."

"I agree with you," I said. "An entire island made of mycelium—it's Hell made manifest. But we *need* to retaliate, after what they did to me. They attacked an officer of the law, and we can't let them go unpunished."

"Even if she brought it on herself, eh?" Ridgeway sat down, looking deflated. "Politics, Hofmann."

"What is that supposed to mean?"

"It means I have to deal with the Goddamned Coprinian Military Governor, asking me why one of my detectives decided to stir up that hornet's nest." Ridgeway pinched the bridge of his large nose. "MacArthur has already been hounding me about the city's security, what with that fucking Fuyu Lantern Festival fast approaching. Neo Kinoko is on edge—you can sense it, can't you?"

"I can, sir." I tapped my fingers on my thighs, still wanting some recompense for what happened to me. Even if Oze was Koji's cousin, it didn't negate his actions.

"You saw what happened at Spirit Island, how worked up those protesting hopheads got over a *single dead child*." Ridgeway held up his pointer finger. "Striking them now would send the city into chaos."

"If I may ask, why is the festival such a big deal? And why is Governor MacArthur allowing it to take place?"

Ridgeway's gaze was shadowy beneath his prominent brow. "Why, indeed? The bloody government has requested the distribution of extra security across the city, and for what? To placate this inferior race?"

"Are they trying to ease tensions with the fungals?" I asked.

"Fuck if I know. Tensions have been high since the Spore War. Even if this festival is important to them, I doubt it'll do anything to lessen our hatred for one another." Ridgeway snorted. "If anything, they'll think we're playing them, just like we've done before. Why not just give them some bags of Goddamned rice and be done with it?"

My focus was drawn to the window facing the sprawl of Neo Kinoko. The bomb-battered husk of a once-great city. So many buildings, temples and homes still lay in ruin. But the unsettling Mother Mushroom stood tall, its presence a symbol of fungal resistance.

"Which brings me to a certain officer: Nameko." Ridgeway fidgeted with a ringbound book on his desk. It was a copy of *The Outsider's Guide to the Mushroom Kingdom*—a popular guidebook written over a year ago by some anonymous author. "This business on The Shelf can be tamped down, forgotten, another piece of paperwork to add to the pile."

"And the catch?"

"I'm assigning Nameko to your case."

"*What*?" I hissed.

"He'll be assisting you on this case, Hofmann."

Hell no. One morning with that Goddamn gillie was enough to inundate my mycophobic capacity.

"Sir, I have to object. Nameko chose to help me, and yes, it panned out. *This time*. But I can't take him with me on an investigation. You know this city. He'll be more of an impediment than a benefit."

Captain Ridgeway bellowed with laughter. "Do you think you have a bloody choice in the matter?" His expression returned to normal, all hardened wrinkles and that sharp stare. "How well do you know this city? You're investigating the murder of a fungal child, and Nameko knows Neo Kinoko and his community better than anyone on the force. He'll garner more trust from his people than you ever could."

"Pass this case off to someone else, then."

"No one will accept it," Ridgeway said. "Especially not if Nameko is involved."

"Then dismiss the case!" I was desperate. I knew that I couldn't let the child's death go unresolved. But the thought of Koji being at my side made me cringe.

"You know, Hofmann, you were brought from Coprinia because you chose to accept the deal your ex-husband offered. Do you believe any of us really want to be in this shithole country? Away from the homeland?

"Your chaotic ass landed on my desk four months ago. You know why? 'Cause I owed a friend in Coprinia a favor. Some piece of shit cop made a mess of things back home, and now I have to babysit her. How do you think that makes me feel? If I could hand this case off to anyone else, anyone, I *would*. If I could dismiss it, I *would*. But MacArthur and CPAN are up my ass and we're running a broken engine here as it is. If you prefer, I can just as readily send you back to Coprinia. What would be worse for you: Exile or imprisonment?"

I ground my teeth, both at Ridgeway's callousness and the choice Frederick had forced upon me. I steered the subject away from myself: "Why is *this murder* so important?"

"Because it got the fungals' attention," Ridgeway admitted. He turned away and hacked, the sound short and dry. "They're furious and now it's got MacArthur's attention, too. The governor doesn't want this to become more public than it already is."

"But Baird told me there have been previous protests. Why did those not garnered the same reaction?"

"*Those protests* were suppressed before they caught the public's attention," Ridgeway said. "Before the bloody journalists swooped in and spread the word. Now, I need you and Nameko to solve this murder and get everyone off my back. By any means necessary."

"What's our timeframe?" I asked, dreading the answer.

"Two days," Ridgeway said. "I want it wrapped up before the festival, before MacArthur and his fucking politicians start pestering me. *And* before the molders start rioting in the streets. Got it?"

"Bloody Hell, captain, that's no small task."

"You've got Nameko," Ridgeway teased, rubbed the stubble on his jawline. "He has his uses, things that no human is capable of. Plus, he has no choice but to follow our orders and join you on this case."

"What kinds of uses?" I asked, confused.

"Need to know, Hofmann. Now, what other leads do you have?"

Ridgeway was usually candid. This newfound secrecy bothered me.

"Hofmann?"

"I'm waiting on Glessner and her team to deliver their forensic report," I said, wringing my hands beneath the desk. "As well, Sea Dragon Seafood Co. could be involved, but I'm uncertain. The supervisor is sending over their records, so I'll comb through and see what I can find. I'd also like a search warrant."

"Good, good." Ridgeway coughed into his fist. "I'll take care of it."

"There's one more thing, sir." I was about to continue but paused. Would he find this angle worthwhile? "There are rumors of missing children. And others who've shown up dead."

"Human children?" he replied.

"No, sir. Fungal."

Ridgeway let out a sigh. "We have the reports, but our resources are spread thin."

"Has anyone followed up on those reports?" I asked.

"The majority have gone unanswered," Ridgeway admitted. "Both in Missing Persons and here in Homicide."

"Why?" I asked, my frustration building.

"We can't go investigating every Goddamned fungal murder or disappearance!" Ridgeway snapped.

"Except the one that went public," I said in a derisive tone.

"*Enough*," Ridgeway warned.

But I wasn't done. They couldn't keep brushing these crimes under the rug.

I leaned forward and placed my hands on the desk, looking him square in the eyes. "What if my victim is one of those children? One of the missing or dead." What if Daigoro was one of those children? "I have a hunch about this. If I'm right, it'll bring me one step closer to uncovering the truth—and getting MacArthur off your ass."

Ridgeway massaged his wrinkled forehead. With a gruff exhale, he said, "I fucking hate hunches, you know that? That shit is for amateurs and private eyes."

"If it doesn't pan out, what do we have to lose?"

He paused, staring at the intimidating stack of papers on his desk. "We lose time, Hofmann … We're always losing time."

Before I could respond, Ridgeway said, "You have two days. Take Nameko with you, ask Theo for the files, and don't cause more fucking problems. As it is, this cough and that damned Fuyu Lantern Festival are giving me enough of a headache—I don't need rogue detectives running amok, too."

"Understood, sir. Thank you."

"Don't thank me yet," Ridgeway said, waving me off. "Now, get out of here."

I saluted the captain and left his office. The entire bullpen was now looking at me—desk after desk, my colleagues shot me sour stares. All men, all with big egos to compensate for their meager cocks.

"Hey, gillfucker," Detective Windsor called from across the room. The blonde-haired asshole had his arms crossed and his feet on his desk. "How does it feel being fucked by fungi?"

I wanted to tell each and every one of them to eat a bag of moldy shit. To tell Windsor that he could shove a fruiting body into *his* body. It wasn't like I asked to drag that mushroom-capped cop along with me.

Instead, I ignored Windsor's ploy. Time was of the essence and I had to focus. All I had on my mind was a dead child's face, a handful of clues that made no sense, and a fucking fungal dragging me down.

Koji had better bloody deliver.

"Theo," I said, stopping in front of the assistant's desk. He was young, half my age and too damned fresh-faced to be this far from the homeland. His light brown hair was neatly parted, and freckles dotted his pale cheeks.

"Yes, detective?" he asked, hands cupped on top of a manila folder.

"I need you to pull some records for me: Any kids missing or dead in the last year—fungal, half-breed, or otherwise."

"Of course." He hid dental braces behind a closed-mouth smile. "When do you need those?"

"As soon as possible."

I turned and walked to my desk. There were piles of paperwork stacked on one side, unfinished and awaiting filing. Other than that, my desktop was empty—no photos, no attachments, nothing sentimental.

"We're leaving," I said to Koji.

He craned his neck and looked at me. "What did Ridgeway say?"

"You're officially on the case. Now get the fuck out of my chair."

"I am at your service." Koji stood so fast he almost knocked the chair over. "Where are we going?"

I thought back to Hana and the plea she made to her nephew in Skinner's Room. Her son and grandson were missing. Chances were, if we looked into Daigoro's and Shikaku's disappearances, they could provide clues for the other missing children—maybe even the dead kid on the beach.

The Pit. Hana had said that was where Daigoro's mother volunteered, and my gut told me it was the place to start.

"I thought we could benefit from some prayer and guidance," I replied, "so we're going to pay a visit to Reishi Temple."

RUBICON

- - - - - - - - -

KOJI AND I crammed into my crappy Albany Metro RT, the proximity claustrophobic. His cloying smell filled the car, like wet mulch after an autumn rain. The windows of the NKPD loaner fogged up from his errant breath, whereas mine was trapped beneath a sweaty face mask.

I tapped my fingers on the smooth plastic steering wheel. I couldn't stop myself from dwelling on the thought that his Goddamned spores were somehow getting through the covering. Entering into my lungs. Wreaking havoc from within.

How many anti-fungal meds did I have left in my bottle?

The fog on the front windshield got worse—I had to tilt my head to see through clear patches. I turned the heat up to max, then rolled my window down a crack. Stray flakes of snow drifted in, along with scents of fire smoke and grilled foods.

"Nameko, roll yours down, too."

He bobbed his mushroom-capped cranium in affirmation and complied. After thirty seconds or so, visibility cleared up. Only a few other cars were out driving, and the street was mostly empty, save for homeless gillies roasting mushroom skewers over a barrel fire. I looked ahead across the cheap dashboard: The Metro RT's royal blue hood had white splatters of bird shit on it.

Nothing like a good contrast.

I drove through the northwestern strip of The Veil, one of the city's oldest neighborhoods. None of its buildings were over three stories, most built from mycobricks and slanted mushroom-tile roofs. Others were made entirely of tightly packed mycelium, like the white shrines and temples that sprouted up on every block.

Somehow, this ward had been spared much of the bombing during the Spore War.

The light snowstorm from earlier had mostly died down, making way for piles of gray slush to form on the shoddy roads. I swerved to avoid a slight depression, but the left wheel snagged on something solid, landing with a *splash*. The stiff suspension sent a jolt through my uncomfortable seat and up my spine.

"Bloody Hell," I cursed. "How did you people get around before we arrived?"

"We walked," Koji said.

I glanced at the fungal. "Are you serious?"

Koji's thin lips spread in a smirk. "Yes, but the wealthy could often afford to take horse-drawn carriages, or sail. We are a nation of islands, after all."

"*Horse-drawn carriages*?" I couldn't believe it. It made sense, though: The human-occupied neighborhoods had been paved by the military, consistently maintained after the war. But most of Neo Kinoko was still cobblestones and packed dirt. "How backwards was your country before we arrived?"

"We lived in a way that fulfilled our needs," Koji reflected. "Coprinians are always rushing, without thought for what it is that they are doing. No journey is worth undertaking if the destination is not clear, and walking allows for an unparalleled depth of clarity and purpose. We fungals live longer than the average human, therefore patience is a virtue."

"It sounds ridiculous to me."

My knees ached just thinking about it, but driving wasn't my cup of coffee, either. Speaking of which, I still hadn't had a bloody cup of brew today.

I gripped the steering wheel, fingers trembling. A cold breeze permeated throughout the car, yet my palms were slick with sweat—all these years after the accident, and I was still a bit shaky every time I drove.

Koji peered over at my hands. Before he could comment, I said, "Roll up your window."

He did as I asked, but didn't respond. Simply stared out at this depressing city as it passed us by. I needed something to ease the tension, then I had to lay some ground rules with Koji.

Music.

"Open the glovebox," I demanded. "Grab the cassette from the top of the pile."

"What is a cassette?" Koji asked innocently.

I groaned. "The fucking plastic rectangles with two holes in the middle."

Koji popped open the glovebox and grabbed a transparent tape. "This one?"

I nodded and gestured for him to give it to me. Its label was worn out, but I knew exactly which one it was. A pilzrock favorite, one that always brought me back to simpler times, when life wasn't such a fucking mess. I slid it into the tape deck, basking in the rough clicks of mechanisms moving into place.

Then I pressed play.

"Rubicon" by Orange Nightmare began, drawing me in with its sweeping strings, airy flutes, and ghostly electronic effects. My hands relaxed. I regulated my breath in time to the song's ambient soundscape.

The pace of the music picked up as The Veil transitioned into the outskirts of The Pit, a guarded slum for fungal refugees from nearby regions of Hōppon.

Pockets of spindly fungals huddled around smoky burn barrels, beneath large mushroom growths that lined the street. Some molders sipped steaming tea. Others took ravenous bites of charred fungi, causing me to shudder. The thought of mushroom people eating mushrooms made me gag—it couldn't be normal. A group of ragged children threw dirty snowballs at one another, likely unaware of what "normal" even was.

Suddenly, a boy bolted across the street. I veered to avoid hitting him, narrowly missing his tiny hophead body by a few feet. The Metro's tires lost grip on the mucky ground, but I pumped the brakes softly, straightened out, stopped. I thought about opening the window and berating the stupid kid, but I opted for aggressive honking instead.

The child glimpsed back at me as if nothing happened, his expression neutral and his face covered in filth. He ran into a rundown home, out of sight.

What was the point of yelling at someone who had so little?

"Are you alright, Hofmann?" Koji asked.

Clenching my teeth, I put the car into gear and accelerated. "Yeah … fine."

The deeper I drove into the area, the more I noticed how many buildings and houses were collapsed. Nearly every one of them was broken or scarred—husks being consumed by large blooms of mold and mycelium. Thin layers of frost clung to any exposed surface, much like these poor gillies clung to existence with their homes destroyed.

This was hard living, and winter made it even harder.

Bloody Hell … What was going on? Was I starting to feel bad for these sporesacks?

I returned to the rhythms of "Rubicon," the thirty-four-minute track shifting into a dark and spectral symphony. I slowed the Metro RT to a stop at a four-way intersection with no lights or signs. The road here was covered in slick mud, and one whole section of street was blocked off by piles of rubble and colonies of fruiting bodies.

"Your music is …" Koji paused. "Interesting."

"Depending on how long this investigation takes, you'll be hearing much more of it," I said. Not that I wanted to have him around at all, let alone for an entire case.

"What is it called?

"Pilzrock," I replied. "Do you like it?"

"I am curious to hear more."

"The tapes were my father's," I said, remembering my old man's crooked smile and washed-out tattoos. "Even though I was born in Coprinia, he came from Pilzland. Grew up during a particularly rebellious era, too—pilzrock was the soundtrack for young punks and rebels. He gave me all these tapes before he passed away."

"The music has meaning beyond itself, transcending sound to become a symbol for the people." Koji looked wistfully out the windshield.

I was slightly impressed.

"I want to say thank you," Koji said.

Turning right, I eased the Metro RT onto a main thoroughfare. In the rearview mirror, I noticed a car mimicking my turn and hanging back at a controlled speed. "For what?"

"I am aware that I am not liked at NKPD. Despised even. The detectives, the officers, the receptionists—everyone looks at me as if I am … a disease. Yet you brought me with you on this investigation and—"

"You think *I* did that?" I spat in response.

"Then who did?" he shot back, a hint of attitude creeping into his tone.

Ridgeway.

The bitter truth lingered on my tongue like an anti-fungal pill. I didn't want Koji here with me, but I had no choice—I was forced into this.

"Listen closely, Nameko," I said. "You're with me 'cause Ridgeway wants this murder solved quick. You understand your people, your city, better than I do. The rules are simple: Don't step on my fucking toes and play your part. Got it?"

Koji worked his jaw. Speckles of dark spores drifted from his gills. I squeezed the steering wheel uncomfortably hard, adjusting my mask. My eyes darted across the car, to the side mirrors, before finally landing on the rearview mirror.

"We are being followed," Koji said.

That same Goddamned car was behind us, maintaining the same Goddamned distance. Son of a spore was right.

I sped up, just a smidge. "Tell me every detail you can about that car."

Koji swiveled slightly to get a better view. "Silver sedan. Good condition, and relatively new. The manufacturer is Derby. I cannot make out the model, but I've noted down the license plate number."

"Derby …" I muttered. "Only a human could afford that, or have the connections to bring in such an expensive import." Was it someone from CPAN? Could someone from the NKPD have tipped them off?

"They are not human," Koji corrected. "I can sense two of my people, but their emotions and intentions are clouded."

Bloody fucking great—we were being followed by fungals. Who the Hell were they? And why were they following us?

I was eager to lose this tail, so I turned at the next intersection. A minute later, the car followed suit. I kept this up a few more times, randomizing where I turned and how often. Still, they kept the same distance.

As if matching my growing anxiety, "Rubicon" had morphed into a pulse-pounding wave of synthesizers. Each throbbing chord and sweeping pad amplified my emotions.

I turned off the tape player.

The car was filled with a lingering silence and echoes of pilzrock in my eardrums. I had to focus, and I hated to admit that Orange Nightmare wasn't helping.

Abruptly, the Derby sedan roared to life behind us, closing the gap in seconds. Its windows were tinted, so I couldn't see who was inside—the shadowy outlines of mushroom caps were obvious, though. The car edged closer and closer to my rear bumper. A little bump nudged the Metro forward.

What were they playing at?

The car bumped against us again. Then again. And again.

"Nameko," I said. "What the Hell are they doing? Can you sense anything?"

"They are still blurred," he responded, "but I can sense anger, determination. No more."

"Show them your badge," I exclaimed.

Koji opened his window and leaned out, badge in hand. "You are intentionally damaging an NKPD vehicle! If you do not cease your actions immediately, we will be bound by law to arrest—" He slumped low into his seat the moment a handgun poked out of the sedan's passenger window. "Get down!"

Shots rang out. I ducked, attempting to keep an eye on the road.

The bullets hadn't struck us—it was a warning. I glanced back: They were still after us. Time to lose them.

I flipped on the light bar atop the car, pressing my foot into the gas pedal. The Metro's engine growled alongside the screeching wail and strobing reds and blues of the sirens. My whole body rattled as the rubbish Metro flew over wet, uneven ground. Changing gear, I increased my speed. Seeing an intersection ahead, I drifted, maintaining practiced stability with the steering wheel. My little loaner careened around the corner. Koji gripped his door as gravity pulled him toward the middle of the car.

Frantic honks sounded as I nearly grazed an oncoming vehicle. This street was busier, pockets of traffic flowing in either direction. Mostly human, 'cause few gillies could afford a car.

An idea popped into my head.

It wasn't going to work to play cat-and-mouse across The Pit until our gas tanks ran dry. Koji and I were already headed into the CPAN-guarded zone, so why not take advantage of the extra firepower?

The Derby continued its chase, firing low shots that splashed into the snow or ricocheted off the bottom of the car's chassis. Horns blared, and a stray shot sparked off the side of a delivery truck.

I just prayed they didn't puncture a tire or any of the Metro's vital parts.

"Nameko, give me an update," I demanded.

"I believe they are trying to scare us. For what purpose, I do not know."

"Well, radio for backup! Fire your fucking gun! Just do something!"

Koji withdrew his pistol and fired out the window. One bullet struck the Derby's left headlight. He fired again. The effect disoriented me, the deafening blasts sucked away as fast as they came.

"Dispatch, this is Officer Koji Nameko! Requesting backup. We are under fire in—"

Barreling through a junction, a vehicle coming from the right nearly collided with us. Koji dropped his radio. The car careened toward a small colony of fungals on the side of the street. Terrified and screaming, the pedestrians dove out of the way just in time. They narrowly avoided the mass of metal and glass that crashed into a heap of rubble and trash.

In all the confusion and chaos, the silver sedan had caught up to us—our fungal pursuers were now parallel to the Metro. They curved toward the center of the street before rushing back and slamming into my side of the car.

The force of the impact shook me. It left dents in the door and almost snapped off the sideview mirror. My mind flashed through a series of traumatic memories: A car on fire, twisted metal, the stink of coppery blood and gasoline.

Focus.

Out of my periphery, I saw that the sporesack bastards were going to try it again, so I planted both my feet into the brake pedal and pushed. My car swerved, sliding on slush until it finally stopped—the engine stalled out and died. Koji scrambled to pick up his radio. Ahead of us, the Derby spun and lost control. The rear of the vehicle collided with a tall street mushroom in a spray of glass and spores.

Its windows were shattered, and I saw a massive fungal sitting in the driver's seat. Speckles of blood bloomed on his wide face. He grinned, revealing several gold-capped teeth. He brushed glass from the shoulders of his crisp black suit and made to exit the car.

Bloody Hell.

We had to get out of here. Now. Those molders were armed, and Koji and I were not in a position to start a gunfight in a populated area.

I turned the key in the ignition and the Metro grumbled back to life. Bringing the car around, I took off in the direction we'd come from. That's when I saw another car hurtling toward us.

"Fuck me," I said. "Nameko, hold on!"

Pressing the gas pedal to the floor, I shifted from first to second gear. Second to third. Third to fourth. Faster and faster, directly toward the sporesack pieces of shit in the second car. I was sucked into my seat, as was Koji beside me. Every instant brought us closer, and closer, and closer.

Until the other vehicle veered away at the last moment.

In the rearview, I saw them whip around. They sent a wave of slush onto a handful of parked cars, then came in pursuit of us.

"Did you see that big bastard, Nameko? Who are they?"

"I cannot say with any certainty." Koji leaned out the window and discharged a couple of rounds.

"Where is the nearest military checkpoint?" I asked Koji.

He closed his eyes, as if plucking the details of a map from his mind. "Checkpoint Chappel. One mile west."

"Tell me how to get there. And fast."

Following Koji's directions, I tore through the streets of the outer Pit. Koji kept our pursuers busy, firing off intentional misses that sent them swerving and slowing down. They shot back at us. I heard one bullet pierce the Metro RT's rear end with a metallic *clunk*.

Going faster, I drove through an intersection with a rare traffic light. It shone green before shifting to yellow as soon as I passed. Our tail sped up to make it through.

"Turn left here," Koji said.

There it was, blocking off the entire street: Checkpoint Chappel—only one way in or out.

Not just anyone could get into The Pit. Koji and I had reason to be there, along with NKPD papers to back us up. Sure, there were smuggling routes in and out of the refugee zone. Bribes were common business, too, even at checkpoints. But I had a gut feeling that whoever was following us would turn tail and run at the sight of CPAN guns.

The checkpoint was a compact, square building placed in the middle of the road. Boom gates blocked the road on either side of it. Surrounding the checkpoint were sandbag barriers, with more than two dozen heavily-armed CPAN soldiers guarding the perimeter. They snapped to attention when they noticed two cars speeding toward them.

The soldiers raised their rifles, stepping forward into a line that spanned the width of the street. A scrawny blonde man left the building with a megaphone raised.

"This is a CPAN checkpoint!" his voice reverberated. "Slow down, immediately, or we will open fire!"

I drove with my right hand, waving my badge out the window with my left. "NKPD! Do. Not. Shoot!"

Glancing in my rearview mirror, I saw the second car turn off at the last junction. It disappeared from sight.

My gut had always served me well.

"Who could that have been?" Koji asked.

"I don't know." And *that's* what bothered me.

But now we had the miltary to deal with. I slowed down, continuing to wave my badge. Beyond this checkpoint was the heart of The Pit.

I'd seen the maps: The zone was closed off, hemmed in by bombed-out buildings, two-layered sections of barbed wire fences, and Kasuga Forest to the west. Guard towers lined the long perimeter, and rotations of CPAN soldiers patrolled around the clock—not to keep anyone out, but to keep the gillie refugees in.

Under watch and under control.

"State your business!" the man with the megaphone called out.

I rolled the Metro forward. Upon closer inspection, he was a young, pimple-faced officer. His blonde crew cut sat beneath a gray wool side cap. Even with his square jaw, he hadn't outgrown his infantile features.

Handing him my badge and the paperwork from Ridgeway, I said, "Official NKPD investigation. And apologies for the commotion. Do you mind calling for backup and arresting those sons of bitches? They fired on two officers of the law, after all."

The officer scoffed at me. He gave Koji a stink-eyed look, then shoved the badge and papers through the car window. In return, I gave him a piece of paper with the license plate number on it.

"Let them through!" he shouted. Then: "We'll take care of them, but next time, don't bring your shit onto our doorstep."

"Cheers, officer." I offered him a mocking salute.

As I rolled up my window, I heard him mutter under his breath, "Best leave that sporesack amongst his filthy kind before you leave."

I guided the Metro through checkpoint, around potholes and past bullet holes, into the grimy slush and rubble of The Pit. But my heart was still racing. This investigation had taken on a whole new level of danger. Koji and I were after a murderer, and now some mysterious fungals were after us.

What was the likelihood the two were connected?

SUBDUED

[12] Case File #42-56
The Pit (Refugee Zone) | 4:39 p.m.

- - - - - - - - -

SPARE SOME SCRIP?" A homeless gillie proffered his grimy hand toward me. I recoiled, almost smacking it away on instinct. The bastard had followed Koji and I for half a block, and wouldn't bloody leave us alone.

It had taken a while to find a safe place to park the Metro RT. Streets were blocked off by CPAN military trucks, and most were impassable except on foot. This area was hit hard during the Spore War. Ironic, then, that all the refugees from ruined neighboring towns were corralled into this pit of collapsed buildings, mud, and mold.

Even then, I hadn't expected it to be this much of a shithole.

"C'mon, *gaigai*," the fungal persisted, stumbling beside us. "How 'bout a ration card?"

"Fuck off," I said from behind my mask.

Even with the heavy CPAN presence here, I kept looking over my shoulder. Part of me was annoyed by this relentless beggar, but I also feared that golden-toothed sporesack to lunge out of the shadows at any moment.

Koji took a few bills from his pocket and placed them onto the beggar's palm. "A gift, *jiujiu*."

The homeless fungal stopped. He bowed so low that his cap grazed the filthy ground. "*Ariari do*. May Matsua shine bright upon you!"

As if on cue, a soldier appeared and snatched the bills from the molder's hands. Another soldier came in from the side, striking him in the ribs with the butt of his rifle. The gillie crumpled into a fetal position. Sad sputters of spores fell out of his dirty gills as the two soldiers kicked him again and again.

I kept walking. "You shouldn't have wasted your money, Nameko."

The muscles in his jaw bunched up. He glanced back at the brutal, senseless beating.

"Leave it," I said. "That's not why we're here. Where's Reishi Temple?"

Koji sighed. "This way. It is not far."

We continued down the narrow road, surrounded by destitution. Fungals were passed out on the ground, lying in dirty snow and puddles crusted with ice—it was hard to determine who was sleeping and who was dead. The air reeked of urine, shit, and acrid alcohol. A chill crept through my bones and the foul smells clung to my nostrils. I pinched the metal strip on my mask, securing it to my nose. As we walked, I picked out several rail-thin mums attempting to feed their crying babies from near-empty breasts.

The distinct squeals and hiccups of the infants dredged up remembrances that I hadn't realized I missed—sounds that once satisfied my motherly instincts. Now, on a putrid street in The Pit, all it did was cause painful memories to resurface.

I clenched my mittened fists. Like fragile flotsam in rough seas, I drowned out those thoughts. The self-loathing, anger, and ego that I bathed in booze for years …

I had to concentrate. Koji and I had one goal here: Find Daigoro's mum at Reishi Temple.

We followed the piss-stained street, making our way past the dilapidated remains of mold-covered buildings. Mycobricks and debris were strewn about. Rusted bomb shells and bullet casings littered the ground—few solid structures remained in this wasteland.

"Have you been to the slums before?" Koji asked. He pulled out his pack of cigarettes and lit one of those mushroom-tipped cancer sticks.

I shook my head. "Most of my cases have been in human wards, dealing with human problems. The CCTV network makes things a lot easier, too, but that doesn't extend beyond the Coprinian Quarter, Central, or the Temple Ring. A lot more difficult to catch criminals without video evidence."

In reality, so much of this city was still a mystery to me—most of it unfriendly toward humans.

"The slums stink of contempt and abandonment," Koji observed. "Fungal refugees are the ones who suffer at the hands of Coprinian negligence, despite being the victims of a war they did not start."

"Out of sight, out of mind."

"And easier to control," Koji mused sullenly, taking a drag.

Somehow, though, there was life here.

Fruiting bodies sprouted from the collapsed ruins, creeping through cracks and bullet holes. Refugees had lined the street with tents, stalls, and communal spaces, using bombed buildings and wrecked pillars as structural supports. I heard unfamiliar Hōpponese dialects coming from various colonies of fungals. Most were dressed in rags and blankets, huddled around burn barrels to warm their extremities. Shroom skewers charred atop the fires of makeshift grills. Icy winds pulled smoke along the street, clouding the air.

I wondered what these streets may have looked like before the war—before humans arrived. The Pit was a ramshackle mess, but it was also survival born from the necessity to live. Even a species as alien as the fungals were born of the same basic, biological instincts.

But as foreign as they were to me, I was once again an invader in their world: Most every molder we passed gave me a loathsome look.

One old gillie woman spat on my boots and cursed, "*Shimin shabi*." Colonizer bitch.

I moved to act—a desire to punish her flaring up—but Koji stopped me. The wrinkled old sporesack saw my death stare and went back to constructing a lantern, attaching thin paper to a rectangular wooden frame. I noticed dozens of people along the street, adults and children alike, in different stages of assembling lanterns. Cutting mycopaper, building frames, painting logograms onto the sides with a charcoal and water paste.

After a moment, it clicked. "The Fuyu Lantern Festival," I said.

"Despite the destruction wrought upon us," Koji exhaled a puff of smoke, "we have been given a chance to celebrate. Whatever scarce resources we have, this holds meaning for us."

This city, the war, the *aftermath*. It was like stumbling through the gates of Hell and seeing humanity's worst nightmares come to life.

"Will you celebrate the festival?" I asked.

Koji stared intently at a nearby wall. He crushed his cigarette butt into the ground. "For many, the festival will serve as a distraction from the truth. But that is not something I can avoid."

I followed his gaze: A thick sheet of white mycelium crept up the remains of a mycocrete structure. Strange colorful mold grew from the mycelium, forming into detailed portraits of children and logograms beneath.

Missing posters.

One after another, I counted young fungal faces. Twenty-two in all. The final portrait was of a little girl whose features were mostly human, save for a handful of fungi sprouting through her hair—a half-breed. My skin prickled at the thought, remembering what Oze had said about gillie women being raped during the war.

"Everything I do," Koji said, "I do for them."

"Is Daigoro here?"

Koji pointed to a poster of a small boy. The moldy depiction showed Daigoro with a serious expression, lips pinched and eyes withdrawn. He had tousled black hair below a plump brown cap.

"I can see the family resemblance," I said, noting the shapes of Daigoro's button nose and round ears.

"Something is happening nearby," he whispered. His gills shook.

"We must go."

— — — — — —

ANGRY SHOUTS ROSE above the din of the crowded corridor. Koji and I hurried past fungal vendors, drunks, scurrying kids, and dozens of CPAN troops. Most had their rifles at the ready—fingers hovering over the safeties—and they wore black body armor over gray wool military fatigues.

These soldiers weren't here to keep the peace. They were aching for a fight, whatever form that took.

"This way," Koji urged. "I can sense a perturbed colony of considerable size close by."

How big was "considerable"?

We slipped into a dank alley, mycelium snaking across the ground and fungal growths sprouting from the walls. Up ahead, a tall, well-built soldier was pissing into the bowl-shaped cap of a mushroom. Another laughed nearby as he stomped on a couple of crumpled lanterns. A middle-aged gillie was on his knees next to the lanterns.

"Please, stop," the fungal pleaded in Hōpponese, tears streaming from his quivering yellow eyes. "I have done nothing wrong."

"I don't know what the fuck you're sayin'," the peeing soldier taunted over his shoulder. "Nobody gives a shit about your stupid festival anyways."

The stomping soldier stopped with his leg mid-air, eying Koji and I as we approached. He cocked a brown, bristly eyebrow. "A sporesack and a coppie, eh? What the Hell do you two want?"

"None of your business, spanner," I warned. "But if you think messing with an NKPD officer is a good idea, then go ahead."

He stepped back with his hands held high, allowing Koji and I to proceed. While his tormentors were occupied, the fungal gathered up his crushed lanterns and ran away.

"A molder cop," the pissing soldier mocked with a barking laugh. He took a quick look at Koji. "Want me to piss on your cap too? Won't cost you a scrip."

Koji chuckled. "If it is anything like the sad spectacle that is your penis, I am afraid I would be quite disappointed."

The pissing soldier lunged at Koji, his minuscule cock still hanging out. I instinctively stepped between them, launching the base of my palm into the soldier's neck, right below his chin. His head snapped back. He fell to the ground, coughing, wheezing, and clawing at his throat.

I opened my trench coat and ran my fingers along my pistol's grip. "I warned you, you fucking pissants. Take your useless asses, leave this alley, and go do whatever it is CPAN has paid you to do. Understood?"

They both nodded with contemptible scowls. The stomping soldier lifted his croaking friend off the ground, hauling him in the opposite direction.

"Thank—" Koji began.

I cut him off with a firm, "Shut up."

Shouts and chants flared up ahead as a Coprinian voice echoed through the alleyway. I led Koji to the exit, out into a muddy intersection filled with hundreds of fungals. Another Goddamned protest.

More gillies trickled in around the margins. Dozens of protestors held up large signs made from mycelium and mold. One read, BRING BACK OUR BABIES. Another had COLONIZE US, KIDNAP OUR KIDS emblazoned across it in fuzzy mold.

The missing children.

Clearly, Ridgeway and everyone at the NKPD had underestimated the gravity of the situation. This was a red line for the fungals—a powder keg waiting to blow.

The protestors faced a two-story building where a bomb from the Spore War had left a gaping hole on its corner. Black spores flowed from their gills, filling the air like gnats at a bog. I tightened my mask, not daring to edge any closer to that crowd. My gaze was drawn upwards.

Holy shit.

Up on the second floor, where the floorboards still held strong, stood a man donning the fineries of CPAN command: Duncan MacArthur, Coprinian Military Governor and Commander for the Liberation of Hōppon.

MacArthur wore an ornate peaked cap that rested above aviator glasses. The skin on his face sagged with age, but the man still held himself tall. The breasts of his thick, gray winter jacket were draped with colorful medals, adding to his already grand presence. He smoked from a large pipe, casually holding both hands in his jacket pockets while surrounded by several armed guards on either side.

In fluent Hōpponese, MacArthur spoke into a megaphone: "Calm down, my dear fungals." His words immediately silenced the restless colony below. "Rest assured that we are working as hard as possible to assuage your many ails. Winter is upon us, yes, but we are receiving daily shipments of rations and supplies for the entire city. That includes—"

A gruff male voice interrupted the governor's speech. "We haven't been given anything! We're eating *mushrooms* to survive, and there you stand, lying to us again!"

I scoped out the agitator: A gillie with ragged clothing and a flat mustard-colored mushroom cap speckled with jagged warts. He raised a fist into the air, revealing a forearm sleeve of writhing, moldy tattoos.

Another fungal broke in. "Your soldiers abuse us and you expect us to trust you? Winter is already here!"

MacArthur, exuding confidence and calm, said, "Do not fret. The homeland has been preparing a full-fledged investment into the restructuring of Neo Kinoko—and soon Hōppon as a whole. The betterment of this nation is at hand. Change is coming!"

"Who cares about change when all you Coprinians do is take!" a female fungal yelled in hoarse Hōpponese. "Someone has stolen our children and no one will do anything about it!"

Another woman cried out: "And what of the dead child your police found this morning? My son has been missing for weeks!"

"Please, calm," MacArthur said. "I assure you—"

"How many of our kids have to die before you do something?" a male molder cut in. "More than a dozen of our little ones have been *murdered*—why aren't their deaths being investigated? Dead or alive, we want them returned to us!"

More than a dozen ... I recalled what Baird had said on the beach, the protests that he'd been called in to shut down.

MacArthur leaned to the side and murmured something to one of his guards. He returned to his megaphone. "Our top officers are investigating these disappearances and murders as we speak. We will not allow your children to fade into memory."

That was a fat fucking lie. Missing Persons wasn't doing shit about this.

News programs back home always framed MacArthur as a hero during the war—now he was the liberator of a ruined nation. But in truth, he was just another advantageous prick, exploiting his position of power and leaving scraps for the rest of us. It was obvious: These fungals meant nothing to MacArthur, CPAN, or the NKPD.

They were pawns in a complex geopolitical game that I didn't fully understand.

Still, a pang of pity plagued me, for them and their dire situation. I knew what it was like to be tossed aside, exiled and forgotten. The feeling sunk into the pit of my stomach like a bad meal.

Out of the corners of my eyes, I tracked purposeful movements—soldiers. MacArthur and CPAN held all the power here, and they weren't afraid to show it.

Scanning the crowd, I quickly realized that all of the fungals had their eyes closed. Koji's were, too.

"*Gaikamu … Gaikamu … Gaikamu …*"

The criticisms accrued, palpable frustration compounding in the dense mob of refugees and protestors. MacArthur responded with pacifying platitudes that were unlikely to convince them.

"It is happening," Koji whispered, his lips barely moving.

A cry rang out across the crowd. Something flew through the air, exploding in a shower of glass and flames on the wall below MacArthur's makeshift stage. His guards immediately raised their weapons, pulling MacArthur away from the building's edge.

"Death to *shimin*!"

"For the lost and forgotten!"

Two more explosive cocktails were thrown, erupting in shattering conflagrations beneath MacArthur and his cohort. Soldiers fired into air, a warning to the throng not to step out of line any further.

I spun and grabbed Koji. "We need to leave. Now."

"I must stay and help," Koji insisted, resisting my grip.

I snagged the collar of his jacket. "Don't be so Goddamned stupid," I hissed. "You stay here, you're more than likely to die with a bullet in your cap. *Where is the temple?*"

Koji pointed up the street to our left, away from the protest. Mushroom-roofed walls met a crimson spirit gate. "There."

"Cease your aggression at once," MacArthur ordered, "or suffer the consequences!"

I dragged Koji's ass away. He didn't fight back, nor did he make it easy for me. Likely it was a small attempt at moral resistance—stubborn bastard.

The clamor of angry fungals grew until a blood-curdling scream consumed the air itself, as if in a vacuum. The sporadic *pop-pop-pop* of rifle fire, followed by more pained howls. I ran faster, my boots splashing in puddles of slush and slime. Forcing Koji in front of me, I pushed him along until the gravity of the situation settled inside his stupid fucking cap. A mass of fungals hastened alongside us, almost knocking me over. Koji held my arm as they shoved and bumped hysterically, heading for safety in a suffocating cloud of dark spores.

MacArthur's steely voice blared across the intersection with a direct order for his troops: "Subdue them."

The soldiers obeyed, unleashing crackling waves of gunfire. Each shot made me flinch.

How easily I had told Baird to "contain" the protestors on the beach … Was I just a reflection of MacArthur and Coprinia, programmed by my culture to think a certain way? Were my thoughts even my own?

Nariyoshi's words repeated in my mind.

The gods will decide your fate.

Koji and I neared Reishi Temple. Pressed against weeping fungals, we squeezed through the temple's main gate like water rushing down a sluice. My mask was torn from my face. I had no time to react as I was prodded forward.

Amidst the acrid smell of gunpowder and the terrified screams of protestors, I wondered how my God would judge me.

BLOODY ROSES

[13] Case File #42-56
Reishi Temple | 5:14 p.m.

- - - - - - - - -

THE SCENE INSIDE the Reishi Temple's grounds was chaos. Protestors and terrified refugees continued to pour in. Their cries of agony and anger clashed in a dissonant elegy. Colonies of distressed fungals huddled together for warmth and comfort, but the persistent stench of copper unnerved the atmosphere.

A handful of dead fungals had been laid in the middle of the temple's open plaza, trails of blood in the snow demarcating the path to their final resting place. It was too late for them.

This sacred site was tainted by the fallout of a shapeshifting forever war.

I trembled as I reached for my pill bottle—the anti-fungal meds rattled inside. I popped two onto my palm and swallowed them dry. My mask had been torn off, and I didn't have a spare. What were the chances I got infected now? Did I even give a shit anymore?

Bloody Hell … I was a mess. This *place* was a mess.

A slew of volunteers helped injured fungals, laying them atop mycofabric stretchers. They were taken into a long building, its slanted polypore roofs glistening with stippled snow and hanging icicles. The volunteers repeatedly shouted "Doctor! Nurse!" in Hōpponese, desperation evident in their cracking voices.

Koji was rooted to the snow beside me, looking exhausted and sullen. He fiddled with a cigarette between his fingers.

"Move, Nameko," I said. "We have to find Daigoro's mum."

"I am compelled to assist my people, Hofmann. My duty is to them."

"Right now, your duty is to me, to this investigation, and to the NKPD!" I calmed myself, exhaling slowly. "Humans did this, so my help means nothing to them. But you and I have the capacity to find those missing children—to find Daigoro."

Koji's gills twitched furiously, as if overstimulated. "I cannot ignore them! There is too much pain and emotion. It …" He choked up, swallowed. "During The Long War, the sensory overload was constant. For years, I did not have time to breathe without being reminded of my brothers and sisters dying around me. Day after day …"

I couldn't even begin to imagine what he'd gone through. The psychological scars he'd experienced. But the emotional burden of someone you cared about dying was one I was all too familiar with.

Scores more gillies entered into the plaza, bearing the signs of rough beatings: Gashes on their caps, faces, and bodies, broken bones, swollen bruises, and bullet wounds. The pleas for help were relentless, the entire temple swathed in a shroud of dark stress spores.

"Mother Chikyu, why have you cursed me?" a frail old fungal bemoaned, burying his bloodied hands in the snow.

These were brutal reminders that CPAN was in control—that MacArthur wasn't afraid to crush dissent.

"Look, Nameko, I understand. But we've got a job to do." Time was ticking on this bloody case. "Where is his mum?"

Koji stared blankly at his blood-and-mud-stained boots. "Her name is Emiko, and she is a shrine maiden."

He gestured to the far edge of the plaza. An icy stone path led to a steep set of stairs, rising into a copse of black-barked pines. Water droplets rained down from a wobbling branch as a bird took flight. Above the snow-covered canopy, a stunning crimson tower stood tall and bright against the overcast sky.

"That is the main temple," Koji said. He brought his palms together at the brim of his cap in silent prayer to the resident pagan deity.

Gunfire rang out from several blocks away. Nearby, a young boy began to cry, wrapped tight in his dad's arms.

"C'mon, Nameko," I said, "There's nothing more we can do here."

He put the cigarette between his lips. It hung there for a second before he lit it. "You are right."

I took Koji's limp arm and pulled him along, our footsteps crunching in the crispy snow. Halfway to the temple stairs, I saw a yellow slip lying on top of the snow—a ration card. I leaned over, back aching, and picked it up. One half was soggy, but I could still read the Coprinian: VALID FOR ONE RATION PACK AT OFFICIAL CPAN FOOD BANKS.

The illusion of generosity—passive-aggressive Coprinians had always done that so well.

"C-c-can I … have it?" a timid voice asked in Hōpponese.

I took my eyes off the card and met the yellow gaze of a half-breed boy—his features were an unsettling mix of fungal and human. Six red mushrooms grew from his greasy brown hair, and his round face was marred with dirt. He couldn't have been more than five. He offered me an awkward baby-toothed smile, swaying his underfed body beneath a saggy threadbare sweater.

The sight of the child filled me with unease. He was a physical manifestation of a heinous act, one that I still couldn't comprehend—both from a moral standpoint, and a biological one.

How had those soldiers who'd raped not been infected? How could humans and fungals successfully *breed*?

"Careful," Koji warned. "The fungalnet is already alight with activity."

The ration card was pinched between my forefinger and thumb, but I was hesitant to get near the boy. Koji was right to be wary: I remembered what had happened on The Shelf. The fungals were unafraid to defend their own, especially a child.

I flicked the card toward the half-breed. It landed in the snow at his feet. He lowered his head timidly, his cranial fruiting bodies bouncing. As he bent over to pick it up, I saw the fuzzy, black edge of a mold tattoo etched into his neck.

Why the Hell would a child have a tattoo?

The boy snatched the card off the ground, his eyes darting left and right. He took off. Without looking back at us, he said in squeaky Hōpponese: "*Ariari do.*"

Watching him sprint across the plaza, the ration card waving in his little hand, a thin grin graced my face—a rare occurrence these days.

But that feeling dissipated the instant I saw a short, paunchy man sitting on a bench, tracking the boy through beady eyes. His puffy lips stirred in minute movements, and a facial tick made the mole below his right eye twitch. Even more unusual and distinct were his deformities: His cap was partially inverted and cracked, sections splitting off to reveal puckered pink gills. Laid atop his lap, his normal left hand massaged an elongated, slender right hand.

"That was a kind gesture, Hofmann," Koji said, snapping my attention away from the man on the bench. He blew out a plume of curling white smoke.

"I didn't do it out of kindness." More like pity.

I glanced at the bench, but the gillie was gone. The hairs on my arms stood on end beneath my jacket—seeing him had triggered the overprotective instincts I'd had when Liz was younger.

The instinct that warned of danger.

"Let's go." I pulled out my voice recorder and made a note about the strange fungal. About the boy's tattoo. "Those stairs look like they're going to kick my middle-aged ass, and I want to get it over with."

We hiked up the temple stairs, me in front. There was no bloody railing, so I went slow and steady. On either side of the stairs were stone lanterns, frosty shrubs, and fungi with icicles hanging from their caps. Evergreen branches arched overhead, keeping the stone steps relatively free of ice.

Fucking Hell.

Reaching the top, I paused and caught my breath. My knees were on fire, and ninety-nine steps weren't going to do my weak joints any favors.

Reishi Temple was even taller and more impressive up close. Surrounded by trees and the white winter sky, the structure had an ethereal quality about it. The tower had four floors, each wider than the tier above. Mycelium trailed up the red wooden walls, and polypore mushrooms dusted with snow hung down from every floor like fungal awnings.

The moment Koji and I neared the temple, its crimson front doors creaked open. Four male gillies in heavy jackets exited. They fanned outwards, two on each side, severe countenances beneath the shadows of their mushroom caps. Their steady breaths were visible in the frigid air.

They said nothing. Just stood, waited. I was sure that these spore-sacks had weapons on them

"*Haowa*," I said. Still no response. "Yeah, good fucking afternoon to you, too."

I heard the shuffling approach of slippers on wood. A young woman in a white, loose-sleeved robe and a scarlet skirt appeared in the entryway. Her smooth violet cap was the color of a fresh bruise, curling inward at the top in a shallow dimple. She bowed at the waist, her eyes lowered. "Welcome to Reishi Temple. I am Aoki Emiko."

"Allow me," Koji whispered to me in Coprinian. He bowed in return. "Greetings, Emiko-*kato*, I am Officer Nameko Koji, and this is Detective Henrietta Hofmann of the Neo Kinoko Police Department."

Emiko stood straight, a brief jolt of recognition visible in the stiffness of her lips and the slight bulging in her eyes. "Follow me."

One of the guards neared Koji and I. He smelled of burnt wood and cheap alcohol. "No shoes."

Koji and I removed our boots and left them on a shelf next to the entrance. The bitter cold enveloped my soles through my socks, and I remembered again why I hated winter.

I stepped up onto the raised wooden floor of the temple. Behind me, Koji whispered a prayer to Reishi and Heriko before crossing the threshold, his eyes closed in a moment of respect.

"This way," Emiko called back to us in a soft timbre.

We followed her through the breathtaking temple interior. A tall foyer was lined with thick mycelial pillars the color of carmine. Several shrine maidens swept the open spaces, their yellow eyes fixated on their task. Another maiden was on her knees polishing a section of flooring— the soft bioluminescent glow from red ceiling lanterns reflected off the shiny wood surface. On one side of the room were ornate mycoleather drums, resting atop mushroom stands. On the other was a polypore table filled with candles, bottles of rice wine, and lit incense. Trails of smoke drifted in the air, the scent of herbal sandalwood permeating the room.

"You should not be here, Koji-*kato*," Emiko scolded quietly in Hōp-ponese.

"What do you mean?" Koji asked.

"You do not know who you are dealing with." Emiko stared back at us, her stare lingering on me. "These roses are stained with blood."

Roses?

"But we are here to help *you*," Koji said. "We want to find Daigoro."

Emiko's shuffling feet came to a halt. "I do not want her help." A stillness settled in the already tranquil temple. She nodded and continued her sliding walk. "And regardless, it is too late—you have entered their domain, and must pay respects."

Their domain? She spoke as if Reishi was here, in the flesh.

Emiko led us through the foyer, toward a dais. At its rear was a simple shrine with vibrant green latticed doors and a stone statue in the center. Weak light crept in through gridded windows, catching on motes of dust and spores.

But my focus became fixated on a fungal woman hunched over on the floor beneath the shrine. She sat cross-legged, her back exposed and her front wrapped in a bundle of robes. Her bare skin was like porcelain, standing in stark contrast to the rich blackness of her moldy locks. Beneath a red bulb-shaped cap dotted with white spots, her sharp eyes and buttery irises tightened at our arrival.

Kneeling behind her was a stocky male molder with a gray conical cap, its thin ribs covered in fine hairs. He was shirtless, showing off a torso covered in colorful ink, with an empty strip from sternum to waist. His velvety mold tattoos swirled across his trunk-like torso, creating a surreal tapestry of flowers, fishes, demons, and dragons. A single colorless rose occupied the space between his collarbones.

"Stay still, Airi," he said softly.

One of his hands stretched out a small section of the woman's pale back. The other firmly held a slender wooden handle, with tightly-packed needles attached at the end. Ghostly spores flowed from his gills, twisting around the needles and merging with the black ink on their tips. With practiced precision, he skillfully sunk them into her skin.

He was *tattooing her*. Except this felt private—almost intimate.

The hunched woman winced through gritted teeth. "Please, proceed."

Emiko held out an arm, ushering Koji and I forward. We stood before the dais. "Yaegiri-*shen*," Emiko said, "may I present Nameko Koji and Henrietta Hofmann of the NKPD."

The woman gave the tattooist a tender look. "That is enough for now, Horiyoshi-*bae*."

Horiyoshi cleaned his needles in a cup of alcohol. He dried and placed them on a mycoleather roll alongside different-sized needle groupings. With a cloth, he wiped ink and blood from the woman's back. Then he gathered the woman's robes and caressed her shoulder, then helped her to her feet.

"My name is Yaegiri Airi," she said, "the leader of this temple, and all who call this particular community home." Standing tall, she revealed her shapely nude torso, gently cupping her round belly—she was pregnant. Vivid tattoos embraced her growing child on either side, rising up to her shoulders and down her arms. Like Horiyoshi, she had a simple rose carved into the top of her chest. "To what do I owe this visit?"

Koji gestured at the room around us. "It is a miracle that this temple remains in such pristine condition, Airi-*kato*."

Horiyoshi draped the robes over Airi's torso, and she closed them around herself like a curtain. She sat cross-legged on a floor cushion at the foot of the shrine. "It was not always so," Airi said. "As a fellow walker of The Eternal Path, Koji-*jero*, you would know the importance of revitalizing such revered sites."

I noticed Airi used the honorific for a person of lower rank.

"I do," Koji agreed. "I myself found solace in the old gods, as many of us did during The Long War. Healing is what we needed, and so that is what we have sought."

"Indeed," Airi said. "Now, sit."

Koji and I settled down on the floor before Airi. I looked at the statue in the shrine: The flowing hair of a mushroom-capped goddess, hands spread, open to all. Stone fungi grew from her shoulders and back, reaching upwards as if toward Heaven. An offering of dried rose petals laid at its base.

Airi's gaze narrowed. "Pleasantries aside, officers, why are you here?"

"Missing children," I said in Hōpponese.

Koji took my bluntness and rolled with it. "It has come to our attention the staggering number of children that have disappeared—fungals and half-breeds. As the leader of this temple, you must know something. Are the rumors true?"

"I have—it is impossible to ignore the collective outcries of our brothers and sisters. I sense their mourning and confusion every day. But allow me to tell you both a story. I have a sordid past, one that I am not ashamed to share." Airi's hands massaged the soft curves of her midsection, hidden beneath her robe. "During the war, I was a comfort woman. It was the only means by which I could survive, so I slept with Hōpponese and Coprinian soldiers alike—whoever was willing to pay."

She sighed wearily. "Do you know how many abandoned children were born as a result of the war? Hundreds, if not thousands. Fungal and half-breed children of sex workers and soldiers, abandoned to the unfortunate fates of back-alley abortions or destitute lives on the streets.

"I have been toyed with and abused, but also underestimated. That is the failing of the powerful: They underestimate those beneath them. The formal war is over, yes, but the struggle for control is not. This temple is a home, a foothold, and a chance to rebuild."

What hypocritical bullshit.

Here she was talking about rebellion and rebuilding, even though she was safe from danger in her tower, indulging in a tattoo session with her lover. Meanwhile, fungals—*her people*—suffered down below.

My gut told me that she was hiding something, concealing key information with misdirection.

"So, the missing children mean nothing?" Koji asked. His gills flared, tiny gray spores trickling out. Could he sense that she was lying, too?

Airi scoffed, and I saw Emiko suppress a grimace. "What is one child in comparison to the generation of lost souls that this war has cost us? We must face the future, head on, as Hōpponese … regardless of the necessary sacrifices." She intertwined her fingers on her lap. "So, officers, why are you *really* here?"

"Clarity," Koji replied.

Throwing her head back, Airi cackled. Her demeanor took on a needle-sharp edge. "Neither of you truly understands what you seek. Now, I would kindly ask that you leave, as I have more important matters to attend to. Emiko-*jero*, show them out."

"Thank you for your time, Airi-*kato*." Koji smiled and bowed. "It has been … clarifying."

"Good luck to you and the father," I said to Airi in Coprinian. The woman's face twisted in a vicious scowl, a stream of angry black spores hissing from beneath her cap.

Koji and I both stood, following Emiko out of the temple before Airi or her goons caused us any trouble. We put on our boots and I stepped out into the bitterness of Neo Kinoko winter.

"Blessings upon you, Koji-*kato*." Emiko said. All she offered me was a sour stare.

"Emiko …" Koji whispered.

Tears crept along her eyelids, but she held them back. "I cannot speak any further without drawing suspicion, but you must find Shikaku. He will lead you to my *baebae*." Emiko bowed, then took one of Koji's hands in her own. She slipped something onto his palm. "A farewell token."

She let go, retreating back into the temple. I took in a chilling breath and slipped on my mittens. Koji and I descended the stairs to the plaza below.

"What did she give you?" I asked.

Koji unfolded a piece of mycopaper and read: "Happy Island redlight district. The Moldy Rose." He sighed, replacing the note with a cigarette.

"The Moldy Rose?"

"It's an underground club owned by the Kinoko Rose gang."

Kinoko Rose.

The imagery of Airi and Horiyoshi's tattooed roses inked their way into my brain: Who else was a part of this? And what game were they playing?

"Go home, Nameko," I said. "Clean yourself up, get something to eat. After that, you and I are going to have a night on the town."

Koji slipped a cigarette between his lips. "You will need to put on something nice, then." He winked. "There's a dress code."

ALMOST BLUE

- - - - - - - - -

YOU'VE GOT TO be bloody joking," I snapped. My fist was clenched, moments away from clocking the gillie cockhead. "Is that why you had me dress up?"

Koji and I strode through a gloomy alley a block from The Moldy Rose. The walls on either side dripped with moist mold and mushroom colonies. I was reminded of the chase through The Shelf, and the fear of fungi closing in around me.

I cursed Captain Ridgeway for assigning Koji to this investigation.

Koji glanced over at me. His shaven face took years off his formerly scruffy appearance, revealing defined cheeks and jawline. He wore a gray mycowool jacket over a well-fitted suit, his little shoulder mushrooms poking through the fabric. Even the shaggy scales on his mushroom cap were combed down.

"You look good," he said, lighting a cigarette with practiced precision. "It will work."

I scoffed—I didn't *feel* good. Dressed in a fur-lined leather jacket, white sweater, light blue jeans, and black boots, I felt fucking ridiculous. "It's one thing to dress nice, but it's another for me to be your God-damned escort."

A freezing breeze blew in from the Kinoko River, turning the alleyway into a wind tunnel. It carried with it the stench of musty earth and river trash, which made the name Happy Island seem like a cruel joke.

"I am sorry, Hofmann," Koji said after a long drag, "but they will only let a human in if they believe that … that I am paying for you."

Fucking disgusting. "You could've told me beforehand that I'd be part of your kink show." I crossed my arms and ground my teeth. "Let's just get this over with."

We continued past a dingy restaurant, a hole-in-the-wall bar, and a smoky tea shop. A sketchy dealer hawked illicit substances to two destitute fungals in a dark alleyway. Red lanterns hung from the wires across the street, and moldy signs flashed with colorful bioluminescence. A pair of glassy-eyed fungal prostitutes posed in front of a spore-lit sex shop.

There were no cops around. No soldiers. No order.

Happy Island was nestled in the middle of the river and didn't allow cars to enter, which made its tight streets and corridors the perfect place for illegal activities to breed. And in this northern section of Neo Kinoko, police and military presence was sparse—save for raids, there was little else they could do to keep a place like this in check.

"The Moldy Rose is around the corner," Koji said under his breath. "Pretend you are drunk."

He started swaying, hooking one arm through mine. He leaned so close to me that his gills ran along my loose hair. I suppressed a shudder, but played along.

We turned onto a narrow side street, cramped even more with piles of rotting garbage and mushroom-speckled rats. Koji led me toward a nondescript corridor—it was tucked between two boarded up businesses covered in bullet holes, blooms of ghostly mycelium, and mold graffiti that said KILL ALL COPPIES in Coprinian letters.

On the wall next to the passage entrance was a patch of glowing mold in the shape of a rose.

We entered the corridor. Two hulking fungals stood in front of a red door, dressed in black suits with muscles and guns bulging beneath. Fuzzy ink was visible on the edges of their necks and wrists. One of the bouncers had a caramel cap with upturned gills, and the other had a tan, flat-topped cap that extended out to the sides.

The two big buttons barely moved as we approached. I could smell their mulchy musk more strongly with each step. Koji held me close and greeted them. "*Zoawa.*" Good evening in Hōpponese.

Flat-Top gave us a confused look. "Ugh, you with that *gaikamu*?" His voice grated like sandpaper.

Koji slipped his arm loose and held my hand—the sweat on his palm was cold. He intertwined his fingers in mine in an unexpectedly intimate moment. "I am."

"He my boyfriend," I said in Hōpponese with a lopsided grin.

"Ha, ain't that somethin'. Isn't she a bit old for you?" Caramel Cap asked Koji. He snickered, the gills of his mushroom cap flexing.

"That is how I like my women." Koji winked at the guards. "More experienced."

Both of the huge fungals burst out into heavy laughter, their broad chests convulsing. Caramel Cap pulled a silver flask from inside his jacket and took a swig—it smelled sharply of moonshine.

"You're fuckin' weird, know that?" Flat-Top finally said.

"We go in?" I said in Hōpponese, feigning an unsteady stance.

Caramel Cap put his flask away and folded his arms. "What's the password?"

Koji squeezed my hand, his clammy grip firm but gentle—I wanted to tear myself away. After a pregnant pause, Koji said, "A rose by any other name would smell as sweet."

How the Hell did he know that?

Caramel Cap stepped forward. "Arms up." He patted both of us down. I'd hidden my small pistol in a bra holster, and a knife in my right boot. Lucky he didn't check either spot.

The bouncers stepped aside. Flat-Top opened the red door. He leaned in close and clapped Koji on the shoulder, causing the little fungi there to twitch. "Have fun, lover boy. He-he."

We bowed. I pretended to almost fall over. Koji lifted me up, carrying me through the entrance into a hallway. The door closed behind us, and we were instantly enveloped in near-darkness.

"Now to find Shikaku," I said softly.

The only thing that gave me any sense of direction was faint green illumination emanating from up ahead. I flung Koji's sweaty hand aside, heading toward the light.

"How the Hell did you know the password?"

"It's a long story," he replied.

"Oh, do tell."

"Shikaku …" He paused. "Shikaku is a member of Kinoko Rose. He brought me here a couple of times."

"*What*?" I hissed. This was getting better and better. "How much do you know about Kinoko Rose? Are you secretly a member?"

As I neared the green glow, I realized it was a stairwell—its walls and steps were coated in a woolly bioluminescent carpet with fruiting bodies sprouting up. The low bass rhythms of music vibrated from below, making the moldy hairs and mushrooms quiver.

Son of a bitch.

My fingers shook. Fear and disgust could not control me, I repeated in my head. My job and my duty superseded my aversion. I could overcome it.

I descended, one step at a time.

Koji spoke up from behind: "I am not a member, Hofmann. Kinoko Rose have existed for over a decade. No one knows who founded them, but the war emboldened their violent behavior. They have since thrived in the aftermath."

"And your cousin?" I jerked away from a low-hanging shroom. "What else haven't you told me?"

"He joined them during the final years of the war. We have … grown apart since then."

"Nothing more?"

"That is all."

The music got louder as I reached the bottom of the stairs. I hurried through a hanging mycelium curtain, entering into The Moldy Rose. Then I was struck by a full sensory onslaught.

The club was built into a long, arched bomb shelter made of mycelium. Its claustrophobic confines heightened the sweaty humidity and smells of pungent booze. Cloying cigarette smoke hung in the hazy air. I had to remove my jacket, feeling the heat of at least a hundred accumulated bodies. But the density of fungi everywhere left me on edge.

There was a mushroom-top bar in one corner, where a cramped colony of fungals were conversing and drinking over crooning jazz. Mushroom cap tables and polypore booths were packed with well-dressed molders, lit by flickering mushroom bulb fixtures that hung from the ceiling by their stems.

"Let us find a place to sit," Koji suggested.

I nodded and he led me to a set of mushroom stools in a dark corner. I sat down. It was a decent spot to scope out the club.

"Go get us something to drink," I ordered Koji.

"But you do not drink," he replied, setting his jacket and cigarette pack down on his stool.

"Soda water," I said. "If they don't have that, don't bother asking for an alternative."

Now that Koji was gone, I let out a deep breath—a moment to exhale out all of my anxiety. I needed something to ground me.

Music.

At the far end of the room was a raised mycelial stage. It extended from the back wall, where a crimson sheet of mold clung there like a backdrop. Bioluminescent lamps dangled above the stage, casting soft yellow light on a group of gillie musicians: A pianist, a drummer, a bassist, and a singer.

They played a slow jazz number that crept into my soul, one note at a time in a caressing melody.

Front and center, the singer stood in front of a microphone stand.

Dressed in a fitted red dress, her pale skin reflected the warmth of the fungal lamps. Despite her short stature, she commanded attention and carried herself with grace. Her salmon-pink cap was plump, her moldy black hair fluttered as a steady wave of white spores flowed from white gills. Her blood-red lips kissed the microphone:

"Darling, you and I, our hearts intertwined. Strands of mycelium course through my mind. War tears us apart, but what can we do? Gathered in the darkness, our bond remains true. Almost blue, darling, I love you."

My feet tapped along to the subtle beat and sultry lyrics.

There was a strange synchronicity between the bandmates. Their limbs and digits moved as if pulled by an invisible force. Streams of spores drifted from their caps and swirled together in time with the music, almost like a visual effect in a film. It was nauseating and alluring at the same time.

My thoughts drifted back to what Koji said at The Docks: *The mycelium—even the spores in the air around us—are interconnected loci.*

Were these musicians connecting through the mycelium network? Did it also affect the crowd?

The singer continued to croon: "In this city full of sinners, it's just a matter of time. The fruiting bodies that feed where we lie."

I surveyed The Moldy Rose, the jazz coursing through my ears. I spotted two other humans—females whose arms were wrapped around stylish sporesacks. Even if we were all "escorts," at least I wasn't the only human here.

Dozens of gangsters dotted the room. Black jackets, open-collared shirts, busy fingers trying to fondle scantily-clad whores, cigars and cigarettes and bottles of contraband booze. And on every single one of them, a rose tattooed on their upper chest.

These gangsters would kill me before they ratted on their brother. I had to find information on Shikaku another way. The staff, perhaps?

The song began to slow down, easing into its denouement. "Descending into the unknown, trust in me and you," the woman sang. "We soak up the pain of these mushroom blues."

I watched her expression turn solemn, likely for dramatic effect. She stood on the stage with her eyes closed. The instruments faded into silence and the lamps dimmed. The whole club hushed for a brief moment, then erupted into applause. Bright white spores poured from the gills of the audience, filling the room with the physical embodiment of sonic ecstasy.

Instinctively, I covered my mouth and nose, slowing my breathing. I didn't have a mask here—that would be far too conspicuous.

Goddamnit … I'd forgotten my anti-fungal meds.

The singer bowed. "*Ariari do*. We are Faye and The Valentines, and we will return after a short break."

Faye.

The sounds of conversation filled the club again. My eyes tracked Faye as she stepped off the stage, strutting toward the nearest booth. She sat atop the mushroom cap table, one leg tucked under the other in a suggestive stance, then leaned in and kissed a lean, clean-cut gillie on the cheek. The possessive bastard pulled her close, leaning his angular face and brown cap with conical warts against her chest. Faye rolled her eyes and playfully shoved him away.

But I wasn't paying attention to them anymore. I was drawn to someone seated at the rear of the table: A big fucking button with gold-capped teeth.

"Bloody Hell," I muttered.

Gold Teeth slammed his fists down on the table, knocking over several bottles. He had a similar cap to Faye's, but it was a darker shade of pink, veering towards red. His gills curved up around the brim, revealing scarred edges. The big bastard burst into body shaking belly laughter, his open-collared shirt showing off his rose tattoo. The lean fungal with Faye laughed along, picking up a toppled bottle—he also had a rose tattoo on his chest.

"Shit …" I rubbed my forehead.

Kinoko Rose was after us. Which also meant we were on the right trail.

Faye snatched a package of smokes from Gold Teeth's blazer, taking out a single cigarette. Her lips moved as she said something I couldn't hear. She picked up a mold-fur jacket and walked across the room, ducking through a side door.

The gangsters wouldn't talk, but she might.

I snatched Koji's cigarette pack and took one out. Then I followed after Faye.

— — — — — —

A SMALL SPARKLE of orange flame lit up the rooftop's edge above The Moldy Rose. I'd stalked Faye up four flights of stairs and my knees had already cramped. I gazed out at Neo Kinoko as I walked toward the singer. To the south, the Mother Mushroom cast a staggering silhouette across the overcast sky.

Faye had brushed snow off the mycobrick ledge, sitting there without a care. I'd put my jacket back on, but I was freezing. And here she was in nothing but mold-fur coat with her bare fucking legs dangling over the side of the building.

"Have light?" I asked in Hōpponese.

The singer turned to me, her amber eyes bright. "Your Hōpponese is atrocious," she replied in Coprinian, tossing me her lighter. She brushed away more snow from the ledge. "Sit."

I lit Koji's cigarette and inhaled very slowly, just enough for the tip to glow. My gag reflex was triggered, and I bit back bile—bloody death stick tasted like a sweaty sock smelled. How did Koji smoke these vile things?

Sitting down on the ledge next to Faye, the cold spread across my bum.

"You have a beautiful voice," I said, staring down at the street below.

Drunken shouts and laughter rose up on a chill wind. "Where did you and your band learn to play jazz?"

"Not all that the *gaigai* brought here was terrible." The fungal blew smoke and smiled. A bit of lipstick was smudged on her tooth. "There is charm to your culture, despite it being overshadowed by greed and death and war. Many of my brothers and sisters wouldn't dare defile themselves with anything foreign—it is all tainted by proxy. But my friends and I found solace in jazz. It spoke to our broken hearts."

I faked a drag, exhaling a tiny puff. "I was surprised at how you made it your own, though. Jazz isn't easy to pick up."

"Music is truth. If the rhythms connect with that truth, learning the instruments and the chords, all of that comes naturally as a result."

It reminded me of how my dad talked about pilzrock. The rebellious attitude of him and the punk movement in Pilzland was amplified by the music. Truth amplifying truth.

"Why did you follow me?" Faye asked. She tapped ash over the edge. "No one ever joins me on the roof, and you have the hunger for something in your eyes."

She was good.

"I'm looking for someone."

The gillie's left eyebrow lifted. "This is not a desirable place to go looking for anyone."

"Because of those men you were with?" I guessed.

"If you do not know their names already, then you are better off leaving it that way. Move on."

The singer flicked her cigarette butt over the edge. It cartwheeled through the air, leaving flecks of ash in its wake. She spun her legs around and stood to leave, but I seized the hem of her red dress.

"Not so fast, Faye," I said, warning her with a tug on the fabric.

The molder snickered, smacked my hand away and made for the rooftop access. I shot up, tossing my smoke. Faye had a head start, but was stupidly wearing heels—I reached her before she got to the door. I clasped the fruiting bodies on her shoulders, causing her to gasp. Pulling hard, I whirled her around and slammed her into the snowy roof. In a matter of seconds, I whipped the knife out of my boot, pinned her down, and had the blade's edge pressed against her throat.

"Don't fucking move," I snarled. "Now, I'll repeat: *I'm looking for someone.*"

Faye grinned. "Straight to business and no foreplay? What a shame."

I dug the knife into the pale skin of her neck, right below a mold-like mole. "You're going to make this fun, aren't you?"

She spat in my face, the glob striking me below my eye. "Touch me, do *anything* to me, and Sumi and Dikku will cut off your head."

"Now we're making progress," I said with a fierce smile. "Who's the big fucker with the gold teeth? Sumi or Dikku?"

The singer's teardrop-shaped face scrunched up. Dark spores poured from her gills.

"I know they're Kinoko Rose, and I know you're connected with them." I made mocking kisses. "Lucky for you, I'm NKPD, which means I can arrest your pearlescent, angel-voiced ass for a number of reasons before they ever find out what happened."

"NKPD …," Faye said. She licked her scarlet lips, her eyes narrowed—I could see the gears churning beneath her cap. "You coppies are so fond of bending the rules to your whims. No recourse, no accountability. Benefits of the colonizer, correct?"

Captain Ridgeway's words echoed in my mind: *By any means necessary.*

The knife still held to her throat, I raised my free hand in a fist, ready to knock this mouthy sporesack out cold.

"Get off of her!"

I was dragged away from the singer. My knife fell to the ground, the snow deafening its landing. A thin trickle of blood dripped from its blade. I reached beneath my shirt and pulled the STOHL .357 pocket pistol from my bra holster. Throwing my weight into the person behind me, I slammed them into the ground, got up and took aim.

The barrel of my gun was lined up with Koji's shocked face. He lay in the snow, palms out and pale spores flowing in surrender.

"Goddamnit, Nameko." I turned the pistol on Faye instead.

She waved a porcelain-skinned hand at me and cackled. "Go ahead. Shoot me. What have I got to live for? All I want is out, and, in all honesty, death is on my list of options."

"Lower the weapon, Hofmann," Koji urged.

He was up on his feet now, approaching slowly. Placing his hand on the gun, he brought it down inch by inch. I didn't resist him—that fungal didn't deserve to die, even if she was in bed with gangster scum.

"Nameko, that's enough." I looked at Faye again. "What do you mean 'out?'"

"Like everyone in this hellish city, I am a struggling fool. But my curse is family. Where does talent get you when a rose is constantly piercing your side with its thorns?"

Rose? Thorns? Family?

It clicked into place, like the mechanisms in a cassette player before the tape begins to spin.

"You're related to Gold Teeth," I said, "and you want out of Kinoko Rose."

"You are sharp." Faye grinned, wagging a finger at me. "And you two are NKPD, which means you have the resources I need."

I laughed and holstered the pistol beneath my sweater. "There it is. Now we're useful because we have the resources. Who the Hell are you?"

"You saw me on stage, so you already know who I *pretend* to be: Faye and The Valentines!" she said sardonically. The woman twirled the long, jet-black curls of mold beneath her cap. "But my real name is Ryo, and Dikku … he is my brother. I would gladly be rid of him, though I wouldn't resort to anything too drastic."

"What do you want, Ryo?"

"As I said before, I want out." Step by step, she neared Koji and I.

"To be free from Kinoko Rose, my brother, Sumi, *all of it*—and you two are going to help me."

"Why do you think we'll help you?"

Ryo crossed her arms, smirking. "Because I know Kinoko Rose's operations, its members. You said you were looking for someone, so give me a name."

I paused, grinding my jaw. It couldn't be this easy. What game was she playing? "Then what would you need from us? From the NKPD?"

"You and that cute fungal cop"—she regarded Koji—"are going to guarantee me NKPD protection from Kinoko Rose: A new identity and a ticket out of town. Now, tell me who you want to find."

Goddamn … no bullshit. *She* was the sharp one.

"Shikaku," Koji said.

Ryo's face frowned in recognition. "I know where he is. Bring the paperwork and meet me in Kala Commons."

"Any more requests, Miss Ryo?" I asked jokingly.

"That's all. For now." The cunning gillie winked, playing me like the crowd she sang to downstairs. "There's a market on the south side of Mold Town, between the tent city and the base of the tree. Be there at midnight." Ryo elegantly spun around, brushing snow from her dress and jacket. She walked toward the roof access, then disappeared down the stairwell.

"Fuck me," I muttered.

"Godsdamnit, Hofmann …," Koji growled. Black spores flowed from his gills and blew out into the wind, "Next time, do not leave me out of the plan."

"I don't need you to lecture me," I grumbled. Wasn't much of a plan, anyways. "Now, Let's go. We have preparations to make."

THE DESCENT

[15] Case File #42-56
Kala Commons | 12:24 a.m.

- - - - - - - - -

WHERE THE HELL was that Goddamned gillie? I tapped my foot and glanced down at the cracked face of my wristwatch. "She told us midnight."

We waited for Ryo at the edge of the empty market near Mold Town. Shoddy stalls were packed up for the night, awaiting the return of early morning vendors. The place smelled of old fish and stale blood. Stray dogs and cats roamed the slush-covered space, licking at dirty puddles and riffling through piles of unsorted garbage. Mushrooms grew from their backs and the tips of their tails, as if everything in this cursed country decided to merge with fucking fungi.

"Patience, Hofmann," Koji said. "She is not here to do our bidding."

"And what's that supposed to mean?"

Koji leaned against a stall, arms crossed. "You know very well what it means. What you did to Ryo on the rooftop … it was unjust. What is the purpose of carrying your badge if that is how you treat innocent people?"

"She had *information* and I wasn't about to let her get away."

"Not everyone is a mushroom for you to crush beneath your feet!" Koji was standing now, his body stiff. "No investigation is worth sacrificing your soul."

I laughed, a raspy, pitiful sound. "I lost my soul long ago." It had been chipped away over years. Day by day, case by case. But the moment my Liz died was the moment my soul faded into nothingness. "I—" I bit my lower lip. What was I doing, even considering saying sorry to Koji? A fungal, for fuck's sake. "I'm the lead on this case, so keep your opinions to yourself."

A job was a job, and Ridgeway gave me a deadline—I wouldn't let Koji or anyone else get in the way of that.

I ignored Koji's silent glare and looked toward the south. Several miles of tent city sprawled: The Kala Commons, a relief zone for fungals. It was home to over a hundred thousand Hōpponese, the destitute and dispossessed whose homes were destroyed during the war.

To the west, the tent city sloped down toward a large crater, formed during a Coprinian bombing campaign in the final year of The Long War. The bomb zone was blocked off by layers of razor-wired fences, CPAN guard towers, and spotlights.

The gillies survived the war and came here seeking refuge. Instead, they'd found themselves in a prison.

I hugged myself to stop my body from shivering. "It's freezing out here. Five more minutes, then we leave."

"She will come, I am sure," Koji said, "though I do not sense her."

"There's that bloody word again: Sense." I sniffled. "You said at The Docks that fungals are extensions of a network. Ryo and her bandmates, their spores blended together." As if they were communicating.

Slivers of moonlight shone down through a cloudy night sky. Wind blew across the taut mycelium tents like ocean waves.

Koji rubbed his bare hands together and took a deep breath of subzero air. "The fungalnet. That is what we call it, what connects my people."

The fungalnet.

"So, what, Ryo and the others were connecting while playing music?"

"Yes," Koji confirmed. "They were tapping into one another's emotional and creative states of being, as well as those of the audience."

Goddamn.

It was like being partaking in a collective drug trip, with spores being the mode of ingestion. I shivered at the thought of what else spores could do to the mind …

I craned my neck to take in the hulking trunk of Mold Town—its ancient stump rose from the rubble of Neo Kinoko like a leviathan from the sea. It stood hundreds of feet high, an immense inky silhouette in the calm gray of night. Colonies of wide shelf mushrooms grew from the stump's sides, their undersides peppered with the faint lights of fungal homes.

"It's not natural, being that connected," I said. "Reading someone else so openly."

"It is to us," Koji countered.

"Though it is not all it is hyped up to be," a warm, smooth voice called out.

Ryo emerged from the shadows between two stalls. A pair of emaciated rats ran off at her presence. Despite her change in appearance—a loose mycofabric sweater and black pants as opposed to her flashy red dress—she still exuded an uncanny charisma.

Maybe the memory of her singing was still ringing in my head …

Ryo continued: "Even with all the intimacy our biology offers us, it is a farce. The universal language isn't love, nor is it music or connection … it is loneliness. Eienism and the old gods be damned—we are born alone, and we die alone."

This caused Koji to visibly cringe. He mumbled under his breath to Mother Chikyu about Ryo's transgression, his fingers on the brim of his cap in prayer.

Cynicism or piety. Connection or solitude. We didn't have time for this.

"Enough with the philosophy discussion," I said. "Where have you been?"

Ryo clicked her tongue. "Roses and thorns, as usual. I apologize for my tardiness." Her expression shifted to a sudden hungry desperation. "Do you have what I asked for?"

I slipped off a mitten, the bite of night air nipping at my skin. Unzipping my jacket, I took out a sealed envelope and held it out to Ryo.

"From my superior, Captain Ridgeway of the NKPD," I said, "confirming your request for protection, relocation, and a new identity."

Ryo tried to snatch the envelope, but I jerked it away—my middle-age reflexes held up.

"Only under the condition that your information proves useful," I said.

That got a derisive snort from Ryo. "Of course, it's *useful*! I wouldn't be risking my stem if it weren't. Do you think turning on Kinoko Rose is a trivial decision?"

Koji spoke up: "Why are you turning on them?" He played with a cigarette between his fingers, having quickly shifted from the habit of prayer to that of smoking. "Have they done something to you?"

"That is an understatement," Ryo said, her usually smooth features wrinkling up in disgust. "I am forced to perform for the public, singing at Sumi's and Dikku's whim, and—and …"

"And what?" I asked.

"T-To perform for … for Sumi … Look, I want out, okay? I-I need to get out."

Bloody Hell … What were they doing to her?

"I want *out*," Ryo repeated, her eyes and lips trembling. "Can we help each other or not?"

I approached Ryo, fighting against my mycophobic willpower. Her gills flared each time she inhaled, and tears ran down her smooth cheeks. She smelled of roses, ironically enough. Staring into her watery golden eyes, I placed the envelope onto her palm. "You show us where to go, how to find Shikaku, and I will get you free."

This investigation needed a breakthrough, and she was our way in—even if I had to use her to get there.

"As will I," Koji added.

Ryo managed a thin smile, droplets rolling across her lips. She bowed, then folded the envelope and shoved it into her pants pocket.

"Thank you. Now, follow me."

"Where, exactly?" I asked, still skeptical of Ryo. Could she be trusted? "You haven't told us anything."

Ryo gestured at Mold Town's gargantuan form.

"We're going *into* Mold Town?" I asked.

"No," Ryo's face turned serious. "We are going *under*."

Fuck me. I ground my teeth, trying not to imagine what kinds of horrors lived below the roots of that giant tree. I put my mitten back on and cracked my knuckles.

"Now, you two do exactly as I say," Ryo said. "Do you understand?"

"Yes," I muttered.

Koji stepped forward. "Show us the way, Ryo-*kato*."

– – – – – –

RYO GUIDED US through Mold Town's labyrinth of roots, alleys, homes, and businesses. In a matter of years, the stump had transformed into a miniature city all its own. Mycelium laid the foundation for roads, pathways, bridges, and stairwells. Fungal structures grew from that, eventually clinging to the tree's wooden skeleton in high-reaching polypore shelves.

We skirted the open-air plaza at the heart of the ad hoc settlement. From this angle, I couldn't even see where the atrium broke through the top of the stump and met the night sky.

"You would attract too much attention here," Ryo warned, motioning for us to follow her down a thin corridor between houses. "Humans do not venture into Mold Town often. Sensing your presence might send the whole colony into alert."

By "you" she meant me. This place was fungal territory, and Kinoko Rose had used that to their advantage.

"How do we know you're not leading us into a trap, Ryo?" I questioned.

"We do not have any other leads," Koji replied. "Her emotional intentions are clear to me. She does not desire to harm us."

Ryo glanced back at me, her lips pressed in a thin line. "Neither of you has to trust me, but believe me when I say, I am *done* with Kinoko Rose."

Goddamnit … That would have to do. For now.

The gradual downward slope of our path meant we were descending beneath the base. My nose was taunted with the smells of mulch and mildew the further we plunged into the bowels of Mold Town. The cold, clammy air became more concentrated and slightly warmer.

A pair of gillie kids tore around a corner, almost colliding with us. They each had folded papers in their hands and wore thick sweaters that bunched up at the neck. They were gone as fast as they'd arrived.

"Tell us what you know about Kinoko Rose," Koji said.

With a deep sigh, Ryo looked down at the floor. "I will, but we must continue moving."

We wound through a twisted network of subterranean passages, plagued by gnarled roots and blooms of white mycelium. Along the way, I noticed empty dirt hollows, communal meeting spaces, and homeless encampments with bedrolls laid out and fires burning. Scents of grilled mushrooms wafted through the tunnels.

It struck me as perverse—almost cannibalistic—that gillies would actually eat other mushrooms. Was that what MacArthur and CPAN had driven them to? The only way to survive the food shortages?

"My brother is Waru Dikku, the big one," Ryo said, swiveling to take in a two-way tunnel. She took the left path. "The other man you saw is Washizu Sumi. Together, they head Kinoko Rose's operations."

"Are they the leaders of the gang?" I stubbed my toe on something hard. "Son of a bitch!"

The way grew dimmer, and I kept tripping over roots that snaked across our path. Koji and Ryo somehow avoided them with ease, like she was passing information along to him, or they could somehow see in the bloody dark.

I scanned the ground to avoid tripping again.

Ryo shook her head. "Dikku is The Stem and Sumi is The Veil," she said. "There is another above them, The Cap, but I have never met them nor heard their real name."

The Stem, The Veil, The Cap? Were those codenames or something?

"How did you become involved with Kinoko Rose?" Koji asked.

"After the war, Dikku started bringing me to parties, and I—" She hesitated, then laughed softly. "I met Sumi. We fell in love."

"What I saw in The Moldy Rose didn't look like love. What happened?" I ducked below a low hanging tangle of roots and mycelium.

"Sumi and Dikku's power and influence grew. Kinoko Rose expanded. After the war and the occupation, Sumi changed—he became angrier, more determined."

"Determined to do what?" I probed.

"I do not know. He has stopped talking to me, trading tenderness for abuse and silence. I know he loved me once, but that has faded and our relationship has become one of convenience. I am ..." I could hear Ryo hold back a sob. "I feel like I am just a toy for him to fuck and lash out at."

Koji snarled. "How could Dikku allow this to happen to his own sister?"

"My brother is weak. He would never stand up to Sumi. That bastard has threatened me, forced me to stay quiet and conceal my bruises. He flaunts me on stage, but no one knows what he does behind the veil of privacy."

That sick gillie piece of shit. No one deserved that kind of treatment—especially from family.

"I need to be rid of them," Ryo said, her voice breaking.

"And we will do our best to get you out safely," Koji reassured.

The tunnels tightened, feeling narrower and shorter. Slimy fruiting bodies emerged from every direction, forcing me to brush past them—

either that or crawl on all fours.

All sounds were muted, save the crunching of footsteps in dirt and my increasingly heavy breathing. I braced myself on a large root, its texture rough on my hands. My chest heaved. I'd never done well with tight spaces, but I needed to persist. To keep going and get to the bottom of this Goddamned case.

"How far?" I asked. "Where is Shikaku?"

"We are close," Ryo said, her breath steady. She turned right at a junction with a tangled knot of roots and mycelium burrowing into the ground at the center. "This way."

The deeper we descended, the warmer it got. We weaved through damp tunnels, walls covered in dewy blankets of mold, networks of mycelium, and glowing fruiting bodies. Incandescent spores trickled in the air, increasing in concentration. I wanted to hold my breath, or slam down a whole bottle of anti-fungal meds. It felt as though Ryo was leading us to our deaths. And now she was avoiding questions.

"Where the Hell are you taking us?" I hated the ambiguity of our destination. "No more stalling."

The farther down we went, the more I realized this was somewhere no human was ever meant to be. The roots of Mold Town bore deep into the earth, and I was finding it harder to breathe. The air was dense and humid, even though the tunnel had widened. A stifling scent of decay permeated.

"He operates one of Kinoko Rose's di—" Ryo's gills twitched. "Get back!"

She herded us into a tangled wall of roots, gathering a floor-to-ceiling mesh of mycelium and rhizomes to conceal us. Fine filaments tickled my neck and head. I cringed, flattening myself against soil and trying not to squirm. Something swollen and round was pressed against my hair. The stink of Koji's cigarette breath brushed across my skin, and I heard the sticky sound of his perspiring gills contracting.

"Did you sense something?" Or *someone*?

"A patrol," Koji said in a hushed tone.

Bloody Hell.

I clenched my jaw tight, wanting anything other than to be here. But I couldn't stay still with all these fungi around. I fidgeted, causing the bulbous shape behind me to spasm. It popped, releasing a cloud of spores that engulfed my head. I coughed and jerked away, squeezing my eyes shut.

"Fuck, fuck, fuck," I cursed under my breath.

All of a sudden, hands burst through the mesh that concealed us and seized me. I was thrown to the slime-covered dirt floor, rolling until a mass of hairy mushrooms stopped me.

Ryo gasped. The sounds of fists meeting flesh echoed in the passage. I scrambled to my feet but was struck in the back of the head with something blunt and solid. Stars danced in my vision. Koji grunted amidst the sounds of scuffles.

I was dragged to my feet, face-to-face with a puffy-cheeked fungal holding a wooden club. He snarled, baring yellow teeth that stank of fish and … moonshine. Without hesitation, I swung an arm up, clapping him on the ear with an open palm.

"*Shabi*!" he howled, throwing me aside and holding the side of his head.

I fell hard on my back, the wind rushing from my lungs. Gasping for air, I sat up, but the sporesack was already pointing a strange-looking pistol at me. Then Koji appeared behind him, mycelium extending from beneath his fingernails. I gaped in horror as he quickly wrapped the fungal threads around the gangster's neck and tightened his grip. The gangster's eyes bulged, his swollen face turning red. His gun fell to the dirt as he clawed desperately at Koji's hands. Koji just stared blankly—no emotion.

My mind flashed with the sensations of what Oze and the others did to me on The Shelf. The suffocating filaments boring into my body. The fear I felt as I approached death's door.

And Elisabeth, her voice calling out to me.

Stomach acid stung the back of my throat, but I stopped myself from retching. To witness this, the demons inside Koji—how mycelium grew from his own body. He was capable of the same violation his cousin had committed. Every fungal was capable of invading another person …

What else had Koji done? What other secrets was he hiding?

"Ryo," Koji called out.

I scanned for her in the tunnel's bioluminescent glow. She was nowhere to be seen—she'd abandoned us. Another gangster lay unconscious a few feet behind Koji and the sporesack he'd choked out. Still wheezing, I got onto all fours. With a shaky hand, I reached under my sweater for my pocket pistol.

"Don't move, *gaikamu*," a man said in low-pitched Hōpponese. "Hands up, or I'll blow your fucking head off."

UNDER PRESSURE

[16] Case File #42-56
Mold Town | 1:22 a.m.

- - - - - - - - -

OUR CAPTORS SHOVED us along a series of corridors. They'd bound my wrists with mycelium and taken away my pistol—they'd done the same for Koji. Balls of mycofabric had been shoved into our mouths to shut us up. I tried desperately to spit mine out, to no avail.

Ryo's betrayal stung, and I felt like a fucking fool for falling for it. That bitch had hooked us, and led us right into a trap. But then why play the game of hiding from the patrol? Why reveal her personal life to us?

She'd said she wanted out. Unless it was just lie after lie …

I was bloody confused, tired, and fed up of dealing with fungals.

We passed another patrol, two greasy-faced gillies who grinned viciously. "What's a coppie doin' below ground?" one of them said in Hōpponese. The other snickered. "Boss is gonna fancy himself a *gaigai*, he-he-he."

I still had the knife tucked away in my boot—I thanked God for that small blessing. None of these sporesack bastards had thought to check there, and I would gut them the moment any of them let their guard down.

The two patrol gangsters stopped, their eyes lingering behind me: Koji. They spat at him and walked off, continuing their rounds.

I was just glad I didn't have to look at Koji right now. The sight of mycelium growing from his fucking fingers was seared into my memory. What demons lurked in the darkness of his mind? And if he was willing to do that to one of his own people, what line would I have to cross to fall prey to that corruption of nature? Oze had done it so easily …

But now wasn't the time to dwell on fear. We were captive. I had to concentrate on the present moment, my present surroundings.

I could smell the booze before we even arrived wherever we were going. There was a sweet nuttiness that lingered in the tunnel, but it was soured by the burning sting of ethanol. What the Hell was going on here?

The closer we got to the source of that stench, the hotter and more humid it became. Wriggling slime mold membranes and moist mushrooms smothered the dirt walls. Spores and faint steam choked the air. I blinked furiously, hating the prickle of particles on my eyes and the sweat dripping down my forehead.

One of the gangsters pulled aside a veil of mycelium and roots to reveal a narrow side shaft. I was prodded through the entrance and along a dark, muggy path.

The odor of alcohol was unbearable, creeping into the depths of my addictive psyche. It taunted and enticed me. I couldn't even remember how long it'd been since my last drink, and the thought of just a taste—

I stumbled forward. My captor pushed me again, poking me with a gun that felt more like flesh than metal. "Move it, *shabi*."

Piece of shit. When I got free, I was going to make him pay.

A minute later, the tunnel opened up, and my jaw dropped: It was a Goddamned distillery. We stepped out onto a raised dirt platform, and I took in the overwhelming nature of Kinoko Rose's operation.

A gaping cavern had been carved into the earth, with gnarled roots the width of a person curving along the ceiling thirty feet above. Mycelium clung to the roots. Large, luminescent colonies of fungi hung from the ceiling, casting a yellow glow throughout the chamber. The gangsters had reshaped the space into a rectangular pit, providing stable ground for them to cobble together a bootleg factory. Dozens of hunched, shoeless buttons worked tirelessly, their filthy skin was slick with sweat, while gangsters drank and berated them.

"No slacking, you lazy fucking *shinkin*!" one gang member shouted. "*Udarai*." Pain in the ass.

Down below to my right, several fungals polished, washed, and soaked rice by hand in tubs. Next to that, wide wooden vats were perched atop steamers. Sheets of mycofabric were draped across the vats, bulging as clouds of vapor billowed out. More workers shoveled steamed rice onto fabric laid across slats—they spread out the scalding rice with raw hands to cool it down.

There was no love for the craft. The gillies looked exhausted, their movements robotic and their eyes listless.

This was a bloody sweatshop.

My captor's fleshy gun jabbed me in my back, pressing into a painful knot of muscles. "Keep walkin', *gaikamu*," he said.

We continued along the raised earth platform, where the gangsters had set up a lounge and a kitchen. In the lounge, mycelium couches grew from the ground. Kinoko Rose members sat around, playing dice games and swigging from bottles.

The cooking area was alight with activity, an older male and two female fungals hurrying about their stations. A whole fish sizzled in a frying pan with butter and garlic. One woman charred skewered shrimp over an open flame. Six mycofuel tanks were lined up along the wall, providing gas for the stovetop burners, where noodles boiled.

I hadn't eaten in hours, and the savory scents of seafood made my mouth water. But how did they get their hands on all this? On ingredients like that?

Another forceful nudge sent me stumbling toward a set of dirt stairs. I descended, passing five rows of stacked wood casks—there had to be hundreds of barrels here. There were also areas for bottling, maturing, pressing, and fermenting. My weakness for alcohol was overwhelmed, tested with every penetrating whiff of rice spirits.

But that compulsion went away as soon as we approached an area walled off by folding mycopaper partitions. A thickset gangster awaited us, his wide jaw set as he aimed his pistol at Koji and me. The gun looked organic, like it was made of fungal flesh—I'd never seen anything like it before.

"Both of you, through there," he said, gesturing to an opening in the dividers.

We did as he ordered, entering into a makeshift office space. Mushroom tables lined the partitions to my right, covered in paperwork. A spongy fungal growth grew out of the wall ahead like a living corkboard. Maps and blueprints made of mold sprouted from it, showing different areas of Neo Kinoko, Kinoko Bay, and … Fuyu Temple?

I willed my memory to remember everything I was witnessing.

To the left, in the middle of the office, a wide-brimmed shroom served as a desk for a gillie gangster with his polished mycoleather shoes propped up. His mushroom cap was slate gray, with shriveled ridges like a sun-warped leather saddle. Beneath that was buzzed black hair, a round face, and a pencil mustache. A scar ran across his lip, and two missing teeth spoke of someone used to violence. He wore a loose-fitting gray suit and a black button-up shirt, opened at the collar to reveal his sweaty chest and the roiling edges of a rose tattoo.

Papers were sprawled across the flat mushroom's surface. The papers were covered in rows and columns—delivery orders or shipping manifests. What were these bloody bastards planning?

I had to get my hands on that evidence. Something. Anything.

Koji and I were shoved forward. Two gang members stood on either side of the desk, their guns trained on us. The two who'd brought us in stood behind us, pistols pressed into the backs of our skulls. We were cornered, but I couldn't give up on finding a way out. I scanned the office for a potential escape route. There: Behind the desk, a small doorway partially obscured by roots and draping mycelium.

Another tunnel? Where did it lead?

The sporesack at the desk chuckled and licked his teeth. He glanced at Koji. "I thought I sensed you, cousin. It's been too long."

Shikaku.

"Let 'em speak," Shikaku demanded, flicking his fingers at us.

The gags were ripped from our mouths. I coughed and spat on the floor. "Molder motherfuckers," I cursed in Coprinian, tugging at my wrist bindings. "Do you have any idea who you've kidnapped?"

Shikaku scoffed. "Of course, I do," he replied in my language, his accent heavy. "Don't think so highly of yourself, Detective Hofmann. You've been very troublesome for us. How convenient that you walked right into our clutches."

One of the other gangsters spoke up: "There was someone else with them. A *shinkin*."

A fungal. Ryo.

Shikaku clicked his tongue. "No matter. We have these two, and that'll be enough for Sumi and Dikku."

Ryo hadn't betrayed us … If that was the case, I prayed that she'd already left Mold Town and was long gone.

"*Jiujiu*," Koji said, "you do not have to do this."

Shikaku stood and stepped around the desk. With an exaggerated stance straight out of a cliche crime flick, the fungal waved his gun in our faces and switched to Hōpponese. "What're you doing here, cousin?"

"Daigoro," Koji said bluntly.

"Ha! Did my mother send you? Oh, how she misses her little grandson. But that brat is safe. For now."

"Where is he?" Koji hissed. "What have you done with him?"

Spittle flew from Shikaku's mouth as he said, "*Kuta dai!*" Shut the hells up. He lunged at Koji, planting the tip of his fungal pistol under his chin. I saw how it was organically grown from woven mycelium. Ad hoc weapons for down-and-out survivors, when Coprinia put a ban on firearms for fungals.

Shikaku stood slightly shorter than Koji, glaring up into his cousin's eyes. "Daigoro is *my son*! What happens to him doesn't concern you."

"And what of your father?" Koji tilted his head down, leaning into the gun barrel. "Was his death not my concern? Why did no one tell me?"

"You smell like them, *traitor*." An ink-colored cloud streamed from Shikaku's gills and spread outward. I held my breath—like that would even help protect me from that sporesack's sullied spores. Shikaku continued: "You became a blue when we needed you most. My father was a fool who brought his death upon himself, and you made your choice to abandon us ... my mother should never have sent you to find me."

Koji growled and inched closer to his cousin. "Whatever it is you are doing here, I will put a stop to it. Wherever Daigoro is, I will find him."

Shikaku gripped his gun tight, stretching his neck side-to-side and scowling. The petals of his rose tattoo crept above his shirt collar. "You talk a big game for someone who is about to die." The gangster lowered his weapon and returned to the opposite side of the desk. He grabbed a bottle from the floor and waved it back and forth. "How about a drink before you pass into The Great Beyond? The finest *somake* shine in all of Neo Kinoko."

Somake shine ...

My mind fluttered with recollections of pungent, clear booze: The ferry captain, Skinner's Room, The Pit, The Moldy Rose.

"At least I make an honest living," Koji replied, his fists curled and white-knuckled. "All of this is drowning our people in despair. Does it do us any good to forget what happened? To forget our pride as fungals?"

Kinoko Rose was dousing the city in their bootleg *somake* rice wine—a powerful concoction to dull the masses. And I knew all too well how alcohol could ruin a person's life.

Shikaku cackled. "You think I give a shit? If the people want it, Kinoko Rose is here to provide." He looked at me, grinning. "In the world that her people made for us, we do what we gotta do to survive. The *shinkin* veil their pain, and we earn from it."

"You are a disgrace," Koji said.

Shikaku opened his mouth to retort. But before he could get his next word in, a shadowy shape emerged from the dark tunnel behind him. Shikaku's gills spread, sensing danger. He spun around just as Ryo thrust a short blade at his head.

The following moments played out in slow motion.

Shikaku dodged to the side as Ryo's blade sliced through the edge of his cap. He dropped his weapon, crying out in pain. Ryo whipped out her own pistol and fired four times. Two of those bullets whizzed past my head, and I flung myself to the ground. Both my guard and Koji's collapsed in pools of bloody viscera. Two more gangsters were bleeding out on the floor from fatal abdominal wounds.

"Reinforcements!" Shikaku screamed, dark spores jettisoning from his trembling gills. "I want the human alive!"

Shouts of confusion rang out. Next thing I knew, the entire distillery erupted in pandemonium. Workers scattered and ran for the upper exit. Gillie gangsters dropped their bottles and their dice, looking eager to join the fight.

Shit … we were vastly outnumbered.

Shikaku bolted out of the office in retreat, away from the pissed off singer and her trigger finger.

Ryo broke the mushroom desk at its stem, knocking it over for cover. She continued to fire. Several more gangsters tried to enter, but Ryo held them off with continuous gunfire. That momentary distraction gave me enough time to scrunch my legs up and pull the knife from my boots. I clumsily turned the blade around in my bound hands. Sticking the handle between my thighs, I sawed the mycelium restraints until they frayed and snapped.

Koji was nearby, squirming on the ground. A gangster held him down, the barrel of his fungal pistol digging into Koji's cheek.

"Nameko!" I yelled.

The gillie fucker looked up at me in surprise. In rapid succession, I sliced my blade across his neck and tore the fungal gun from his hand. He gurgled and fell backward as blood gushed from his throat.

I cut through Koji's bonds. "Get yourself a gun!"

Ryo kept up her covering fire, slipping back into the tunnel entrance. "Hofmann, Nameko, this way."

Koji and I ran behind the toppled shroom desk. Papers were strewn across the floor. Fungal bullets ripped through the paper partitions, embedding into our cover with muffled *thuds*. Shikaku and a crew of gangsters were unloading on us. A stench like metallic sulfur and musty earth mixed with smells of steaming rice and acrid shine.

Koji fired off a series of blind shots. Shikaku shouted, other voices blending with his in a chaotic cacophony. Machinery clanked and bottles smashed—the distillery was in upheaval.

"Come to me, now," Ryo urged from the tunnel. "Hurry!"

I poked my head above the desk but was met with a salvo of gunfire. Chunks of cap rained onto my hair. It was a good ten feet to the entrance—plenty of room to get hit, especially at the rate Shikaku and his gangsters were barraging us.

"We're pretty well screwed, Nameko," I admitted. I turned to Ryo. "We need a diversion."

Holding two fingers to the brim of his cap, Koji muttered a prayer. As if this was the time to waste on faith. "Outnumbered does not mean hopeless."

"Blind optimism isn't going to help us right now! We're cornered and we have to move."

Koji sent a determined volley overtop the desk, ducking as a projectile struck the edge. We were showered with fungal particulates. Angry, muffled shouts echoed across the distillery.

Koji inhaled. His cap and gills quivered. "I will follow your lead, detective."

I wracked my brain for an idea. Anything that would serve as a distraction, enough for us to make our escape. The alcohol was flammable, but not explosive. Then it hit me.

The kitchen. The mycofuel tanks.

"Close in!" Shikaku bellowed. "Bring me the *gaigai*!"

"Ryo, Nameko, give me covering fire," I ordered.

The two sprayed random shots through the paper partitions. A gangster wailed in agony. Two more gillies ran into the office, guns blazing. Koji tightened his fingers around the chitinous grip of his pistol and pulled the trigger. He fired two bullets that struck each of the gangsters between the eyes, their faces and heads erupting in a spray of blood and spores.

It was now or never.

With the gangsters occupied, I crept to the corner of our cover and looked out. The raised dirt platform was a few hundred feet away. Six tanks. All I had to do was hit one—I could make the shot.

I took aim and fired. Once. Twice. Three times.

In a split second, I heard the faint hiss of pressurized gas, followed by a ball of fire and a succession of concussive blasts. The searing shockwave knocked me onto my ass. Shrapnel flew overheard, puncturing the walls and the corkboard fungus. I smelled smoke and sulfur. The cavern shook and dirt sprinkled onto my face. Then larger and larger clumps fell down.

Fuck … This whole place was going to collapse.

I struggled to my feet, my bones and joints aching. Koji was on his side, covered in dust and spores. He moaned, his eyelids half-closed. I helped him up, only now realizing that sections of the distillery were being consumed by the blaze. Barrels burst into flames, releasing noxious plumes of black smoke. Gangsters groaned and screamed.

"Nameko, get up!" I tugged on him. He was heavier than he looked. "We have to get out here!"

"I am fine," Koji reassured. "I am fine."

I saw the dusty papers scattered across the floor. This was the evidence we needed.

"Go to Ryo," I said. "I'll be there in a moment."

Chunks of dirt and mold and mushrooms fell from the ceiling, hitting my hair and torso. I scooped up as many of the documents as I could, cramming them into the pockets of my leather jacket. Then I ran to the tunnel.

Oh, no …

Koji held Ryo in his arms. Her cheek was gouged out. Shrapnel was lodged into the left side of her torso, blood pooling on the fabric of her sweater.

"She is breathing," Koji said, stricken with worry, "and I can still sense her pulse."

Sweat dripped down my face. "Can you carry her?"

He nodded. Cradling her, he rose to his feet. The shouts of gangsters reverberated through the tight tunnel. The cavern quaked again, causing a deluge of dirt and mold to collapse near the entrance.

"Go," I pleaded. "Go."

Koji took off into the darkness beneath Mold Town, Ryo fading away in his arms. I followed, destruction unfolding behind us.

AFTERMATH

- - - - - - - - -

A TURBULENT PILLAR of gray smoke poured from the monstrous trunk of Mold Town, where a section of the tree's foundations had collapsed. The moon, flames, and flashing sirens illuminated the night. Ash flakes fell to the ground, adding to layers of icy snow. The air reeked of burnt wood, like the wildfire smoke that drifted up to Coprinia from eastern Setero every summer.

I sat on the hood of a police cruiser, not far from the entrance Ryo had led Koji and me into earlier. The small plaza I was in strobed with blue and red lights. I watched the practiced motions of a CPAN firefighter detachment as they unraveled a hose from their fire truck.

A handful of gangsters and sweatshop workers had been caught—they were cuffed and being escorted to an armored van by NKPD officers. Dozens more cops had cordoned off the area with tape and barriers. They stood at attention, ready to repel any aggressive onlookers.

Ambulances were on the scene, too. Paramedics escorted soot-covered fungals out of Mold Town—some were injured, scorched, unconscious. Those who were awake groaned and shrieked and wept, racked by smoke-induced coughs.

Crowds of impoverished gillies had emerged from the surrounding slums and tents. A mix of curiosity and terror emanated from their worried faces. Angry outcries and choking sobs at the pain being inflicted upon their people. If the blaze spread, the entirety of Mold Town could burn, not to mention the tent city that sprawled for miles around.

"Please, stop the fire …," an old fungal woman pleaded in Hōpponese from the other side of the barrier. "My family is in there."

"Stay back," an officer replied to her in Coprinian. "No one goes in."

A younger gillie man tried to jump over the barricade. He was grabbed by two cops, slammed to the ground, and handcuffed.

"Fuck you, coppies!" he spat as he squirmed. "Let me … through!"

All of this, because Koji and I had followed Ryo. Because we'd gotten ourselves caught. Because I blew up those bloody tanks …

What a fucking mess.

A disaster like this would be big news—neither MacArthur nor Coprinian top brass would want the scandal of a fire and burnt bodies dumped at their feet. And Captain Ridgeway would surely drag me over the coals of Mold Town for this one. But that was nothing compared to the crippling realization that I'd torched these fungals' homes to save myself.

I shivered, staring up at the plume of smoke. My ass froze on the metal hood, and the sticky layer of sweat that clung to my skin was now uncomfortably cold. Koji walked over with a foil thermal blanket bundled under one arm.

"Here," he said, draping the blanket over my shoulders.

I flinched and withdrew, snatching it from his hands. He huffed, a slow despairing sound. I put the blanket on myself, though it didn't help much—the weather was still as bitter as a bottle of gin.

"What is wrong?" Koji asked in Coprinian, breaking the uneasy stillness between us. His cap was covered in bruises. Bags hung under his golden eyes, which he rubbed with a raw knuckle.

"Your …" I trailed off. How would I say this? "The mycelium that grew from your fingers—what Oze and the other fungals did to me … is that how?"

Koji's nose and brow scrunched, his upper face cloaked in shadow. "Yes."

"In the tunnel, the way you choked that gangster …" I paused, rubbing my hands together. "That wasn't the first time you've done that, was it?"

"I do not want to discuss this," Koji said. He withdrew a cigarette from its pack and slipped it between pressed lips.

I swiveled on the hood to face him. "Nameko, look at me. What the Hell is going on?"

"It is none of your concern," he replied, his voice sharp.

"You're on my case," I spat, slamming a fist on the car. "Of course, it's my Goddamned concern. You sprouting fucking threads from your hands is bloody well my concern!"

"If you are so troubled, take it up with Ridgeway," he retorted, his gills twitching and releasing trickles of dark spores. He lit his smoke and exhaled through flared nostrils.

I gaped at him, shocked at the harshness in his tone. The deflection and the attitude. What did Ridgeway have to do with this?

It bothered me to admit it, but I needed this fungal on my side. More conflict between us would just spell disaster. "Nameko, if we're going to work this investigation together, we can't hold back stuff like that. There needs to be a basic level of trust."

Koji scoffed. His cigarette hung limp from his mouth. "You talk about trust, but do you even trust yourself? I did not choose to be assigned to this case—"

"Neither did I, you ungrateful fucking molder!" I snapped. I hadn't chosen any of this.

"*Do not speak to me like that.*" Koji delivered each word with animosity. He worked his jaw. The faint shadow of moldy stubble was already growing back.

But … Goddamnit, he was right.

I didn't trust myself. I was a walking catastrophe, dragging my emotional and psychological baggage behind me like a sad fucking tourist at an airport. Alcoholism and abuse. A marriage ruined. Elisabeth's death … And now exiled in a city I despised, one full of fungi, a culture I couldn't comprehend, and a language I struggled to understand.

So many things weighed on me, haunting my conscious and subconscious mind.

I barely knew Koji, so of course I couldn't reveal everything about myself. But I couldn't continue like this, either. Ridgeway did this to us, not Koji. The least I could do was save myself the headache and accept the hophead's help.

"I … I'm sorry," I admitted. "I freaked out. I don't do well with fungi, okay? Especially after Oze …"

Koji blew out a relieved breath and a lungful of smoke. "You do not say? One day with you, Hofmann, and that fact has been plainly obvious."

I snorted. Laying back on the hood, I gazed up at the sky. The moon shone bright and clear. Sprinkles of stars were visible behind daubs of dark clouds.

Frederick would be so bloody pleased to see how my banishment in Neo Kinoko had panned out so far.

"This investigation is far more complicated than I'd imagined," I confessed, "so let's make a deal. We don't have to spill our guts to each other, but at the very least I need to know that you'll have my back."

"Have I not had your back all day?" Koji snapped.

"It wasn't—" I stopped myself from saying that it wasn't enough. "Look, we're in this together, okay?"

Out of the corner of my vision, I saw Koji take another drag, his expression dour. He blew a column of smoke into the already smoky air. "Okay," he agreed, "so long as we look out for *each other*."

"Deal." I instinctively lifted a hand to seal our agreement with a shake, but pulled it back. "Just don't go sprouting fucking filaments on me."

Koji's face turned somber. His hooded eyes were sunken. "For the record, what my cousin did, it was not deserved—no human can survive that kind of invasion, and Oze knew this. He acted out of collective impulse, and he and the others took it too far."

I almost said, "So did you," but bit back the words.

The memory of Koji's blank expression wouldn't leave me alone. He was hiding something, I knew, but it would take a lot of digging to get that out of him. Question was, would we really have each other's backs when shit hit the fan?

We sat in there in silence for a few minutes. Finally, I asked, "Was Shikaku found amongst the dead?"

"Thirteen bodies have been recovered from the distillery, but no definite evidence that he was among them."

And that meant he could be dead or alive. "That cousin of yours is a real asshole. Honestly, I'm not a big fan of your family."

"Neither am I," Koji admitted with a subdued smile.

"Were you able to sense anything from Shikaku? Emotions, intentions?"

"He was obscuring himself," Koji said, fiddling with his half-burnt cigarette, "but one feeling came through: Vengeance."

"Vengeance." I pondered on that, trying to decipher what Kinoko Rose could be plotting.

"Do you think she will be okay?" Koji asked, tilting his chin toward an ambulance.

Ryo was out cold, pale, laid on top of a stretcher. A blanket was draped across her legs and torso, and a bandage covered the gaping wound on her face. Two paramedics hurriedly loaded her into the back box of the ambulance, their conversation terse and tense.

There were a few field hospitals in Kala Commons, so likely Ryo would be taken to one of those—no way CPAN would allow a fungal in a human hospital.

"I believe she will," I said after a minute. "She came back for us. However long it takes for her to heal, I'll honor our agreement."

Trust was a tricky thing.

It turned out Ryo didn't screw us over, and I wasn't going to back down from my end of the bargain. I'd get her that new identity, and then I'd help her escape this cursed city—even if I was bound to remain.

"As will I." Koji placed his palms together and prayed. "Hogosha, The Destroying Angel, divine protector, thank you for lending us your strength."

At least someone still had faith, 'cause mine was waning, fast. I needed a sign that this investigation wasn't dead in the water like that child on the beach. I sat up, and the papers from the distillery crinkled inside my jacket. I prayed to God something in there would reveal a much-needed clue.

A pair of humans—a man and a woman—walked toward us from across the plaza, wearing matching navy-blue NKPD jackets. The male made a quip that elicited a laugh from his partner. From their comfortable body language and banter, it was clear they'd worked together for a while.

Pangs of jealousy plagued my mind—it had been so long since I'd had someone who I could confide in.

The female had a pretty face. Dark-skinned, short and round, with gray locks hanging down. Despite the frown now gracing her face, she had full cheeks that had perked up when she laughed. She approached with the upright posture and surety of someone who rode horses.

Her partner, on the other hand, had a slouch that screamed desk jockey. He was fairly tall, with a balding head and squinty eyes beneath oval glasses. His approachable-yet-introverted demeanor came across as someone destined for insurance—he'd probably stumbled into police-work.

"Morning," the man said with a salute. "I'm Detective Hartog, and this is Detective Jackson."

Detective Jackson eyed us warily. "Vice squad."

"About damn time," I said.

"Just be happy we're not dragging your asses to the precinct for a whipping," Jackson scolded. "You two made one Hell of a mess, and you woke me up in the middle of the Goddamned night."

Hartog cleared his throat, pushing his glasses up his pointed nose. "In all seriousness, we're taking over from here. We've been pursuing Kinoko Rose for months. We located several of their distilleries around town, but haven't been able to pin anything directly on them."

"And then you two decided to stroll in here and screw it all up." Jackson swept an arm toward the fire, the smoke, and the burning bark of Mold Town. She placed her hands on her hips and cocked her head. "Isn't that right?"

"I apologize for our error," Koji said, lowering his head in a placating bow.

"Not you, I. I want to hear it from her." Jackson glowered at me. "Months of work, down the drain. Kinoko Rose will go deeper underground. They'll disappear and cover their tracks more carefully than before."

I clenched my teeth, feeling the pressure in my molars. "You want me to say sorry? We're not bloody schoolchildren."

"Come on, Detective Hofmann," Jackson said. "Ain't that hard to own up to your mistakes."

Hartog placed a hand on Jackson's shoulder. "It's not that important. We've got more pressing matters to attend—"

"It's the *principle*," Jackson snapped. "We uphold the law, even in Neo Kinoko. No one is above it, and the NKPD doesn't need any one-woman armies."

If curbing addiction had taught me anything, it was that admission was the first step. But I wasn't about to apologize to this uppity officer. We scowled at each other for a minute or so, neither of us breaking eye contact.

"Come on, Jackson," Hartog interjected. "Don't push it. We've got a lot to clean up. Plenty of paperwork to fill out, too."

With a grunt, Detective Jackson gave me a top-to-bottom glare. "Were you able to save any evidence?"

Koji glanced at me. I refrained from moving, so the papers in my jacket wouldn't make any noise. Ridgeway had given me two days, and time was ticking. But I wasn't about to fuck over my own team—NKPD was NKPD, even if first impressions didn't go well.

"Here." I took out the documents, feeling the winter air nip at the bare skin under my sweater. "I grabbed as much as I could before the distillery collapsed." Then I recounted what I'd seen. The mold maps of the city, the bay, and Fuyu Temple. Blueprints for buildings I couldn't pinpoint.

"If only you didn't blow the place to Hell," Jackson grumbled.

Detective Hartog stepped in before Jackson could say anything more. He took the papers from me. "Much appreciated, Hofmann."

"Of course, detective," I said, stretching my sore back. "A favor, though: Please send copies of those to the secretary in Homicide. I'd like them on my desk tonight."

"I will take care of it." He placed a hand on Jackson's back and not-so-gently urged her away from us. "And we will contact you if we require any further information. Thank you for your cooperation."

"Yeah, yeah, I get it. We're leaving," Jackson said. "My knees are fucking sore, anyways."

She turned and left. No farewell, no bullshit. At the very least, I could empathize with her about achy joints.

"Good night, detective," Hartog said. He looked at Koji. "Officer."

I gave him a curt nod before he ran and caught up with Jackson.

"Suck up," Jackson chastised as she and Hartog ambled away. "Next time, I'll unleash my inner eight-year-old on your ass."

Their voices faded amidst the commotion of the plaza. The constant crackle and smoky stench of the raging conflagration. Desperate fungals begged the police to let them search for their injured relatives.

So much destruction. And solving one murder seemed only to cause more.

I stood up and rolled my sore neck. There was a lot of work to do.

Clues and evidence raced through my mind—I doubted I would sleep much tonight, if at all. A quick nap and some coffee would do me good. At least I had decent brew at home.

"Go and get some rest," I said. "I'll see you at the precinct in the morning. Be there at nine a.m."

Koji looked as if he would protest, but my icy stare stopped him. He got up off the hood. The car's suspension squeaked.

With a deep bow, he said, "*Zoawa*, Hofmann."

"Good night to you, too, Nameko."

CONNECTIONS

- - - - - - - - -

I HOVERED ABOVE a kaleidoscope of photos and paperwork laid out on the checkered linoleum floor of my apartment. Hours spent poring over all of the evidence, and still this case confounded me.

Who killed that child, and why? What did Kinoko Rose and their distillery have to do with all of it?

Lifting my mug of freshly brewed coffee, I took a sip and breathed in its earthy nuttiness—it was scalding, even with a hefty addition of cream. But I kept drinking, savoring the warmth in my throat and the bitter acidity that lingered on my tongue.

Without my longtime vice of alcohol, all-nighters were bloody rough. After a quick stop at my desk in the central precinct, I'd returned home and forced myself to nap. Twenty minutes of eyes closed was all my racing mind could sustain.

And that's where coffee came in to save the day, even if the taste of this military ration brand was bland and acidic.

I wandered around my barebones studio apartment, letting the steam from the coffee waft into my nostrils. The place had been swiftly assembled by CPAN after the war—part of the packed human tenements that comprised the Coprinian Quarter—so it wasn't much to look at to begin with. My mattress remained unmade across the room, plopped atop a low slat frame. The walls were white, with no pictures or paintings. Emptiness was the only way I could describe the gaping vacancy of furnishings between my bed and a modest kitchenette.

Frederick had always been the one with an eye for interior design. I'd let him do what he pleased with our home. But in my mind, a home was about functionality, food, and sleep—the essentials. Anything more than that was an extravagance.

Since I rarely spent time in this apartment, what was the point of decorating it?

I sat cross-legged in front of the tapestry of evidence on the floor. My case files were the most adornment this apartment ever saw, yet this one was more complex than anything I'd dealt with in Neo Kinoko. I leaned forward and scanned photos, manifests, and police reports. Potential clues. Potential answers.

That was the hope, at least.

Iwashi had also sent the paperwork from Sea Dragon Seafood Co., which was piled in two large stacks on the floor. Financial records, transportation deliveries, inventories—the whole deal. A whole year of meticulous documentation.

I chugged the rest of my coffee, craving the caffeine boost it would offer my worn-out mind.

Rolling my head in circles, I stretched my sore neck. My eyes landed on small speckles of black growing around a light fixture on the ceiling … Mold.

My throat constricted. I forced myself to swallow.

Nowhere in this Godforsaken country was safe from the creeping contamination of fungi. This fucking apartment, this building, this city—it was all cursed. Colonized and infected by spores and mold and whatever other repellant shit these fungals found to be normal.

Frederick knew damn well how to punish me, exiling me to this Hellhole. Jail time, or this purgatory—that was the ultimatum he'd given me. Part of me regretted choosing Neo Kinoko. In reality, which was more of a prison?

I picked my voice recorder up off the floor. "Tell super about mold growth," I reminded myself. Honestly, if it was in my flat, surely the whole building was infested. I had no bloody idea how he'd rid the place of it.

I went to the kitchen and filled up a glass of water. Taking two anti-fungal pills eased my mind some. A copy of *The Outsider's Guide to the Mushroom Kingdom* lay on the counter. I picked it up, knowing its maps might prove useful.

Immediately after, I returned to the evidence, immersing myself in the grisly dissections that had plagued my thoughts for a day now. The dead child on Spirit Island had sent me on a journey that was already too much to handle. But deep down, the mother in me wouldn't let it rest.

Sobriety solidified my understanding that I couldn't just drink away the pain and the guilt of what I'd done to Elisabeth. Duty was what drove me now, knowing that someone in this city was harming children. I'd done it once myself … I regretted it every day since.

Whoever was responsible for *this*, I was going to find them.

"Ask Cissy about updates on the autopsy," I said into my recorder, "and visit the morgue as soon as possible." I hoped she would have some clues as to the child's identity.

Something. Anything.

The photo of the rope lay next to those of the body. Koji had convinced me to go to The Shelf—it had paid off, even if Oze almost broke my brain. Ultimately, Koji had proven himself useful, despite being a pain in the ass sometimes.

I tapped the photo. Sea Dragon Seafood Co. was involved somehow. None of the inventory listings showed that any rope had gone missing, but the lot numbers matched up—the rope on the bag had come from Sea Dragon.

Now, the problem was how it had gotten on the bag and why it was still listed on Iwashi's records.

Turning on my recorder, I said: "Iwashi and Yuki are concealing something. Rope is listed in records. Positive number match. Are they manipulating records? Need warrant to investigate Sea Dragon any further."

Still, it didn't make sense … What would they gain from this?

This investigation brought up so many more questions than answers. Everything was happening too fast to properly understand, like a puzzle dumped out of its box, pieces sprawled out on the table in an incomprehensible mess.

I glanced to the side, where my portable cassette player and a pair of over-ear headphones lay on the floor. Pilzrock had gotten me through dozens of cases—this time was no different. I slipped the headphones on and pressed play. Caffeine flowed through my system and "White Night" by The Dresdens blasted into my eardrums.

Bobbing my head along to the melodic psychedelic rhythms of the song, I continued to wring my brain like a wet towel.

Gut instinct told me that there was a connection between Sea Dragon and Kinoko Rose, but I couldn't pinpoint it. The rose tattoos on the gangsters' chests. The Moldy Rose. The shine being distributed around Neo Kinoko.

Reishi Temple and Airi certainly had a part to play, too, but who was pulling the strings? Sumi and Dikku? Even with her relationship to Sumi, and Dikku being her brother, I still couldn't trust Ryo. Once she recovered, Koji and I would have to pay her a visit.

One thought nagged at me. Ryo had said there was someone above Sumi and Dikku. The Cap. Who was this mysterious leader?

I shuffled through the paperwork from the distillery. Detective Hartog had been true to his word, promptly sending translated copies to the Homicide bullpen. Most of them were shipping manifests and delivery reports. It wasn't a lot to go on, but after careful examination I picked up on something: References to boat shipments between The Docks and The Shelf. Which docks or boats, I couldn't decipher—the names and specifics were masked through numbered codes.

There were also a series of coded deliveries made to various locations in a neighborhood called Riverside. I flipped through *The Outsider's*

Guide, finding a map of the city. Riverside was in the north, right across the Kinoko River from Old Kinoko, an irradiated zone that CPAN had bombed to Hell years back.

I scoffed. Riverside was contested gang territory—NKPD and the military had no jurisdiction there, unless they wanted to engage in urban warfare. It was an ideal place for Kinoko Rose to operate in.

After noting all of that in my voice recorder, I spied a folder off to the side. I reached over, picking up the thick set of files that Hodges had compiled. It contained reports of missing and dead children, as well as locations for the increasingly frequent protests and riots. After what I saw yesterday—the fungals going to Spirit Island specifically for the child—I had a hunch that they were connected somehow.

Was yesterday the first occurrence, or could there have been more?

I didn't even know how long it took me to connect the dots. I was absorbed, reading each report, ensuring their validity, pinpointing the positions of events, reviewing the names and photos of those missing or dead. I color coded the exact placements in *The Outsider's Guide*. By the end, I had a map of Neo Kinoko peppered with dots.

"Death Mask" now blasted through my headphones, entering into a dramatic buildup of pounding percussion and wailing guitars. I sat back and absorbed the information.

Bloody fucking Hell.

I breathed out, my cheeks ballooning. All of the missing children reports originated in The Pit, The Shelf, or Kala Commons. There were fifty-three in total. But the dead kids, that numbered at fourteen. Every death except three coincided with the site of a protest or a riot. I remembered the fungals in The Pit, their cries for justice.

With the map in front of me, the connections were so obvious—how could this have been ignored, not a single case solved? What else was the NKPD sweeping under the rug?

I had to tell Koji about what I'd discovered. "Fuck," I muttered. Looking at my wristwatch, I realized the time: 9:09 a.m.

Koji must've already showed up at the precinct. I gathered all the evidence into two boxes and headed out the door.

— — — — — —

THE NOISE IN the bullpen was unbearable, confirming why I never did any work here. Detectives drank steaming cups of mediocre coffee, trading stories and bragging about investigations solved. The room smelled of stale sweat and must—the mold on the ceiling was spreading. Sampson, the desk sergeant, listened to a Coprinian football match on his portable radio. Every Goddamned goal was met with a full-throated cheer, and each missed shot resulted in him pounding on his desktop.

That obnoxious prick. I wanted to shove the radio up his pudgy ass.

Heading toward my own desk, I saw Koji. He sat in my chair, hands folded on his lap. As I passed my colleagues, they gave me dirty stares. They whispered to each other, as if I couldn't hear them gossiping about me and my new fungal "lover."

Immature bastards.

"Sorry I'm late," I said to Koji as I approached. I dropped the two boxes in front of him.

A ball of paper flew past me and hit Koji in the cheek—he barely even flinched. "*Hoawa*, Hofmann," he said in Hōpponese-tinged Coprinian. He stood and continued: "It is quite alright. They have been pestering me for the better part of twenty minutes. Would you like your seat back?"

"No, it's fine," I replied. "We won't be staying long. Look—"

"Did you sleep at all last night?" Koji interrupted, motioning to my face.

I hadn't cleaned myself up at all. What difference would it make to conceal my eye bags and wrinkles when our time was limited and I didn't much care?

"No, well, I took a nap, but … look, shut up and listen." I placed a hand atop one of the boxes. "I found—"

Before I finished my sentence, a nasally voice called out from across the bullpen. "Hey, Hofmann, your molder boyfriend has been spreading his spores all over the place. Get him out of here, will you?"

Windsor. That blonde, blue-eyed son of a bitch just wouldn't leave us the fuck alone. A few seconds later, he and his lapdogs Morris and Hughes surrounded my desk. Koji didn't budge.

I groaned. "Please, gentlemen, kindly piss off from our general vicinity."

Morris cut in, sounding and looking like a squealing pig wrapped in a suit: "Are you really going to stick up for this gillie garbage?"

Windsor and Hughes laughed, haughty and uptight. Hughes placed his petite fists on the desktop. "Hofmann clearly loves bathing her cunt in spores, eh?" The scrawny bastard tried to appear tough, but it was impossible when his face was as sharp as a chicken's and his slender body barely filled out his off-the-rack suit. "Nothing like the feeling of moist gills in the morning, right, boys?"

As if I did anything more than *tolerate* Koji's presence, but in no way could I stand these three human turds.

"I'm not screwing the fungal"—I nodded toward Koji—"but neither is my business any of your fucking business. So again, *piss off.*"

Windsor puckered his lips, jutting out his protruding chin and square jaw. He feigned a punch, as if trying to scare Koji. To his credit, the hophead didn't so much as blink, even though Windsor was half a foot taller and more muscular.

In a calm tenor, Koji said, "Apologies, detective. Though I do not understand what I have done to upset you."

"Forget your apology," Windsor spat. "It's you. Your very presence in this bullpen. In this building."

"Watch it, Windsor," I warned.

"Or what?" He shoved Koji, knocking him onto the floor. Koji did nothing. He sat on the floor, his yellow eyes burning with a hatred that his body didn't betray. "What are either of you going to do? You and this sporesack are a disgrace to this precinct." Windsor raised a thick-handed fist above Koji. "A disgrace to Coprinia."

"*What is going on?*" Captain Ridgeway boomed. His deep voice filled the room as he stomped toward us from his office.

Instinctively, I saluted to Ridgeway. Windsor, Morris, and Hughes did the same. Koji remained still and seated on the floor.

"Detectives, explain yourselves," Ridgeway said, his hulking frame trembling. He removed his small glasses and cleaned them with a cloth.

Windsor responded first. "Officer Nameko …"

"Officer Nameko, what? I couldn't hear you," Ridgeway mocked. "Does his existence bother you? Do we all need to cater to your bloody fucking sensitivities, Windsor?"

"W-We were just playing around," Hughes stuttered. "Friendly chat, nothing more."

Ridgeway snorted and then coughed. "Is that right? More like a few racist idiots trying to boost their egos, hmm?"

I grinned. Windsor, Morris, and Hughes glowered.

"You know," Ridgeway continued, "I'm not fond of fungals either. This country, it makes me anxious. And this Goddamned cough doesn't go away. But you know what I always remember? I am here because I have a *duty*—a duty to serve our nation and do what is asked of me."

Morris and Hughes looked down at their feet, defeated. Windsor fumed and his heavy brow furrowed. Koji remained stoic. I didn't say anything, knowing Ridgeway would effectively belittle these idiots.

Ridgeway briefly made eye contact with me. "It was on my orders that Officer Nameko accompany Hofmann during her investigation. As such, you," he jabbed a finger at the three detectives, "keep your fucking mouths shut. As far as this case is concerned, he is your equal. Understood?"

Equal. I'd never heard the word uttered in regards to a fungal.

Windsor snapped: "How can you even say something so monumentally stupid? Equal. *Equal!* We are superior to *them*. We invaded their lands, and they lost! Hōppon is ours now, and we still have to go around treating one of them like a peer? They're filth, not worthy of life let alone—"

Ridgeway moved so fast that no one was able to react before his thick hand was gripping Windsor's collar. A gasp escaped Windsor's mouth as Ridgeway lifted him off his feet.

The whole bullpen went silent. Dozens of detectives watched, dumbfounded. Morris and Hughes scuttled backwards.

"Do not talk back to me, boy," Ridgeway threatened. "Ever. I said equal and I fucking meant it. Do *not* get in the way of Hofmann's investigation. Do *not* question my orders. Do *not* jeopardize our standing with CPAN all because you can't keep your head out of your own egotistical ass. Do. You. Hear. Me?"

Windsor nodded, his eyes wide with a mix of terror, surprise, and anger.

"Good." Ridgeway let go Windsor, who immediately readjusted his collar and tie. Morris and Hughes rushed over to help him, then led him out of the bullpen.

"Sir," I started, but Ridgeway's scowl stopped me from saying anything more.

He spun on me. "Do not *sir* me. You are on thin fucking ice, Hofmann. You're lucky that fire in Mold Town was contained, but four hundred buttons had to be evacuated. And that bloody car chase in The Pit? What the Hell were you thinking?"

"That was Kinoko Rose," I retorted. "They tailed us and tried to take us out!"

"Yes, well, your little escapade caused quite a bit of property damage. At least it was in an area that nobody gives a crap about." Ridgeway closed his eyes and worked his jaw. "No more fuck ups."

"I'll do my best," I said with a cheeky salute.

Ridgeway sneered. "That's a shit answer, Hofmann. How about next time, you choose the option that pisses me off the least and doesn't bring the wrath of MacArthur down upon me." He massaged his large nose. "Just get Nameko and his Goddamned cap out of here. Get fresh air, food, I don't care. Leave until things cool down, then go solve this bloody thing before tomorrow."

"Yes, captain," I said.

Ridgeway marched back to his office without another word to me. He stood at the door and stared around the bullpen at everyone pretending not to have witnessed the altercation. "Back to work!" He walked inside, his office windows rattling as he slammed the door shut.

I leaned down, my knees popping as I bent. With a grunt, I lifted Koji up by the arm. He peered at me, his mouth and gills quivering. Suppressed pain and rage lingered beneath the surface of his watery, yellow eyes.

"Thank you," he whispered. Brushing his jacket, he straightened himself out.

"No need. That was all Ridgeway."

"And yet …"

"Don't say another word about it." I grabbed my jacket and slipped it on. "We've got a lot to talk about, so let's find somewhere with less … assholes."

"Have you eaten breakfast?" he asked.

I shook my head. Four cups of coffee and anti-fungal meds sure as Hell didn't count as food.

"I know just the place," Koji said.

"What kind of food?"

Koji smiled. "Do not worry. It will be my treat."

HARD TRUTHS

- - - - - - - - -

PARK OVER THERE," Koji said to me from the passenger seat of the Metro RT, pointing at a half-collapsed property up the street. This ward was a mess—boarded up windows, piles of bombed mycobrick buildings, mycelium and mold reclaiming surfaces. Just a scattering of businesses remained, and a handful of fungals wandering about.

The Button bore the scars of war and a general sense of abandonment, and there didn't appear to be much *food* in the food district.

I pulled over just before a tall street mushroom. I'd learned my lesson in the past, how those fucking fungi could leave a dusting of spores all over a car—it was a pain in the ass to clean that stuff off.

The Metro's heaters rattled, but the warm air was welcome. I pressed stop on the tape deck, "Brick & Bone" by Tashué still ringing in my ears.

"How far is this restaurant?" I asked. "I'm starving."

"Through there." Koji gestured to an alleyway, nestled between two ruined structures. They were partially collapsed, mycelium snaking through crevices. Floors and sections of walls were missing. Colorful mushroom colonies bloomed in damp corners. A pair of squatters in rags peered down at us from the second floor.

Koji grinned. "And, well, 'restaurant' is a loose term."

"What the bloody Hell does that mean?" I turned off the car. The engine cooled down with a series of metallic clicks, and residual warmth from the heaters lingered in the interior. I jangled the keys at Koji in warning. "After last night, I'm done with surprises."

Koji placed a hand on his chest, mocking a Coprinian mannerism. "I cannot promise anything."

"Bloody Hell, Nameko …" What did he have in store for me?

As soon as I opened the door, I was hit with a blast of frosty wind. I stuck my foot out, hesitating. Was I really that hungry? I sighed. Yes, I was.

I locked the car and slipped on mittens and a knit cap. An overcast sky dampened the day's already gloomy atmosphere. Damaged cobblestones below my feet were lined with ice and mold—I had to watch my footing to avoid slipping or tripping. I hurried into the alley, Koji following behind me.

The broken brick walls were overgrown with bioluminescent mold patches. Spores pulsated and glowed in the choking shadows, colonies of fungi blocking out light from above. I hunched, feeling constricted and exposed at the same time.

I patted my jacket—I'd forgotten a mask again, but my bottle of antifungal meds was there.

"Not much farther," Koji said, as if reading my body language.

A minute later, the corridor opened up into a small courtyard of packed dirt covered with patches of grimy snow. Three of the walls were bare brick, but the one at the opposite end of the enclosure had a rusty door in the middle. Above it, two glowing mold logograms grew from the wall. Off to the side, a few old fungals sat on stout brown toadstools that sprouted from the ground. They smoked hand-rolled cigarettes. A stink of loam, leaves, and clover clung to the crisp air.

The old molders looked up, eying Koji and scowling at me. Their gills twitched beneath faded, creased caps. My heart sped up. Adrenaline flowed.

One of them gave Koji a quizzical stare. A bushy eyebrow raised near to where gills and skin merged at the top of his wrinkly forehead. "Koji-*dari*!" he exclaimed in Hōpponese, exhaling a plume of smoke from cracked lips. "It's been ages—you look different but you sense the same. Wanna puff?" The short man held out his cigarette with a liver-spotted hand.

"No, thank you, Takashi-*shen*," Koji answered. Him saying no to a cigarette? That was a miracle.

Koji approached the men and gave them a deep bow. "You lot look to be in good health, uncles. Are you keeping well?"

"As well as them coppies allow us," Takashi said. He and the other Fungals laughed heartily, then returned Koji's bow. Takashi spat, a brownish glob landing on the snow. He lifted his patchy mycowool sweater, scratching the folds of fat under his round belly. "Speakin' of which, why you got a *gaigai* with you?"

Koji rubbed the rim of his shaggy cap. "This is Detective Hofmann of the NKPD. I'm assisting her on a case, but this, well, we can call it a lesson in her cultural education."

"What?" I interjected in Coprinian. "All I agreed to was breakfast."

"And that is what we are here for," Koji said. "Partly. Welcome to Danban Diner."

Takashi chuckled, showing missing and rotting teeth. He stroked the white strands of mold that grew from his chin. "Dunno what you two just said in that devil tongue, but if she's with you, she's welcome to eat here."

"*Ariari do*," Koji said with a curt bow.

Takashi snapped his gangly fingers. One of the other fungals stood, heaving the rusty door open with fingerless mitts. It creaked and complained, but finally relented. A blast of balmy air followed, filling the courtyard with smells of rich broth and steamed rice.

"Happy eating," Takashi said. He slipped his cigarette between his lips.

Koji pressed his hands to his cap and prayed to Murio. A moment later, he walked through the door. I paused next to the three men, their bodies reeking of smoke, earth, and body odor. In an experiment in cordiality, I bowed to them. "*Ariari do.*"

That elicited a toothy grin from Takashi. He chortled and patted one of his buddies on the stomach. "Told you they ain't all demons."

The old buttons broke out into raspy laughter. One of them laughed so hard he started to hack up his smoker's lung.

I didn't know how to react to that. Should I have smiled? Or were these gillies taking the piss? Instead of making a fool of myself any further, I ignored them and entered into the humid heat of Danban Diner.

— — — — — —

KOJI AND I sat at a mushroom-top table pressed against the diner's back wall. The bloody seat was a shroom, too. I scratched my sweaty hands, then dried them on my trousers. I couldn't stop tapping my feet, as if they had a life of their own. Every movement I made, I was afraid I'd touch the table, or brush my legs against the gills on its underside.

"Relax, Hofmann. No one here is going to hurt you." Koji stood up. "I will return soon with our food."

"What're you going to order?"

Koji ambled away. "Cultural education," he said over his shoulder with a smirk.

Cheeky bastard.

I scanned the room. At first glance, it reminded me of the soup kitchens in Morellum's ghettos: A line of folks looking for a bite to eat, shuffling alongside a service counter or crammed around communal tables. I'd became familiar with those kinds of places while doing court-mandated community service.

But there was a hint of something different here.

Instead of worn-down faces and a melancholic atmosphere, Danban Diner was filled with dozens of lively fungals—male and female, young and old, disfigured and destitute. Their conversations, laughter, and the slurping of noodles and broth permeated the space. Drinks spilled across polypore bars and shroom tables. A pudgy hophead with facial scars and a missing arm served food to customers. Koji spoke with him, their rapport friendly and personal.

I'd gotten used to emotional breakdowns and drug-fueled manias at the kitchens I'd worked in, but these gillies seemed spirited.

I settled back into my mushroom chair. Breathing slow, I attempted to relax. Next to our table, mold pictures grew from the wall. They depicted friends and families, with big smiles and full bellies. The one-armed fungal was in most of them, except … whenever the photos were taken, he still had his missing limb.

Despite all the pain and abuse these people experienced day-to-day, this gathering space offered a sense of genuine community and connection—a momentary glimpse of positivity amidst the general shittiness of Neo Kinoko.

Koji returned to the table, two ceramic bowls stacked up one arm and utensils in his opposite hand. With precise motions, he laid down napkins with chopsticks on top. Then he placed the bowls on the table. Straight away, my nostrils were struck by a wave of savory smells.

He sat down. "So, detective, what did you discover during your night of … research?"

I filled him in on what I'd learned that morning. The rope coming from Sea Dragon Seafood Co., the deliveries to The Shelf and Riverside, the connection between the children's deaths and the protests.

"This is troubling," Koji murmured.

"Troubling is putting it mildly."

"For now, let us eat and replenish our spirits. Only then can we properly focus on the case."

I peered down at my dish. The base was a mound of white steamed rice, cooked to fluffy perfection. On top were thin strips of dried seaweed and … mushrooms. Thick caps, sliced and glazed with a glistening brown sauce.

"Nameko …" I scratched the back of my hand. Admittedly, it

smelled incredible, but—

"Is something wrong?" Koji asked, but his face betrayed an ulterior motive.

I took in the room, my eyes darting from fungal to fungal. But not just them—their bowls. Images flashed through my mind of desperate hopheads roasting mushrooms over burn barrels in The Pit, or in a hollow beneath Mold Town. Every *thump* of my heart vibrated across my chest. Fungals consumed fungi, their teeth digging into cooked mushroom flesh.

"They are all … eating …," I stuttered.

My gag reflex triggered and I held back rising bile. Sweat beaded on the edge of my hairline, in my armpits, on my back. I couldn't eat this.

"Hofmann," Koji said in a reassuring tone. "You can do this."

"Fuck you, Nameko …"

All sounds faded and warbled as my hearing distorted.

The information entering my brain was unfocused, unfiltered. I caught the elated tones of morning conversations: Talk of the Fuyu Festival, another dead child, the fire in Mold Town. One of the cooks yelled "More rice!" as a radio emitted on high volume from the kitchen. The host spouted off in Hōpponese, something about a cold front coming west across the ocean—a large winter storm was headed to Neo Kinoko. Would the festival be postponed or canceled? Was it a grim omen? A sign from the gods? Would there be more protests? Riots? Food shortages? Deaths?

My skull throbbed. I gripped the fleshy brim of the fungal table and, and, and—

"Henrietta." Koji's hands were on top of mine, holding me tight. "Breathe."

Sweat dripped down my face. I pulled my hands away, dabbing myself dry with a napkin.

"Relax your mind," Koji said calmly.

"Piss off …" I took deep breaths, counting to sixty like they taught me in rehab. Feeling myself ease into calm, I had the wherewithal to whisper, "Why the Hell did you bring me here, Nameko? Was this some kind of joke to you?"

"Hōppon is not for the weak of constitution." He picked up his cheap wooden chopsticks and rubbed them together. Fine splinters fell off. "I understand that you detest fungi, but I see how strong you are. To live among us is to live *like us*."

"I never wanted to come here in the first place," I spat under my breath. "Me being here, it's a *punishment*! Does that get through your thick fucking cap?"

"Whatever the reason for you being here," Koji said, "that does not mean you have to treat it like a prison. The burdens you carry, they are all in your mind."

"It's not just—" Elisabeth's death was not *just* in my mind. My drinking, the blackouts, the abuse, the fights, the divorce—all of that had become far too real. "Since when did breakfast become therapy?"

"Since the captain teamed us up for this investigation," Koji replied bluntly.

"Well played."

"Now," he continued, "Danban Diner happens to be one of my favorite establishments in this city. Danban"—he gestured to his bowl—"is a Neo Kinokan specialty, and …" He glanced at a picture on the wall. Etched in mold, a small full-faced boy stood between a middle-aged man and … Hana. I recognized her from the photo in Skinner's Room.

"Is that your dad?" I asked.

"He used to bring me here when I was growing up. We would travel up to the capital from my hometown, Hajimari, to visit my aunt and her family." Koji's face lit up with nostalgia. "This was our favorite table."

"Is he still alive?"

"Still alive. Still farming." Koji straightened his posture. "Now, time to eat."

He'd distracted me from the food, but my palms were still soaked with sweat. "Isn't there any … any meat on the menu? I mean, how can you fungals eat the same thing that you're made of?"

Koji's face grew serious. His eyes narrowed. "Meat is a luxury only humans can afford. My people scrape by on scraps, on the things we can scrounge together or grow ourselves. Most of the nation's rice goes to CPAN. Sheep, pigs, cows, fish—CPAN. What do you think remains for us?" Koji jabbed a finger at my dish. "*That* is all cultivated and cooked by fungals who are barely holding on. We eat mushrooms because they are a part of us. We eat mushrooms because what goes into every fungal is given back to the earth. But now, with what your country has done to us—with so little else—we eat mushrooms to survive."

"Nameko, I …"

Koji's seriousness shifted to a more empathetic demeanor. "I believe, deep down, that you are a good person. But how would you know what we are really like if you are only basing your judgments on perceived truths? Truths told to you by the very government that invaded us."

I sat there, dumbfounded.

Koji wasn't pulling any Goddamned punches today—his hard truths sunk into me. What did I actually believe? Even after a single day with him, I could feel my perceptions shifting.

Deep down, there were plenty of similarities between our species. Flashbacks to wartime propaganda flipped through my mind like a film reel. Commercials and posters and government addresses, all projecting the concept of the savage gillies—islands full of uncivilized warring tribes, spores and mold that crept and colonized.

I was beginning to see it for what it was: Indoctrination by way of fear and disgust.

Without giving me a chance to respond, Koji said, "Please, eat. It is rude for a guest to decline the food offered to them."

I stared at the chopsticks, not knowing how the Hell to use them. "I … Is there a fork I could use?"

"You are in Hōppon, so no," Koji said with a smile. He showed me how to hold them between forefinger and thumb. "If you cannot figure it out, use them to shovel the food into your mouth. That is what we teach our babies."

"Smartass," I grumbled.

I gave up after several embarrassing attempts with the chopsticks, opting to hold them in a closed fist. Lifting the bowl to my mouth, I paused, closing my eyes—not seeing the mushrooms was the only thing that could help.

Again and again, I hesitated.

My fingers trembled at childhood memories of bland fungi. The rubbery feel on my tongue as I'd spat out or thrown up the mushrooms my mum and dad had forced upon me. How many bloody times had they threatened me when I wouldn't eat? And how many bloody times had I sat at the table for hours, refusing to comply?

I tried once more, but gagged. A mouthful of vomit rose up. I swallowed it and gagged a second time. My aversion to fungi was engrained at this point. Every synapse in my brain was firing, urging me not to eat it.

"You can do this," Koji encouraged.

"Fuck you, Nameko."

I could do this. Gripping the chopsticks, I went for it, scooping the food into my mouth—

—and the first bite was delicious.

I focused on everything but the fungi in an attempt to override my phobia. The rice was soft-yet-firm, melting on my tongue and sticking to my teeth. The seaweed delivered a salty punch and a satisfying crunch. But the mushrooms … my God. They were savory and tender, bursting with rich meatiness. The glaze was sweet, with a hint of bitterness at the end.

"How is there so much flavor with so little?" I asked.

Koji beamed at me. "Simplicity is resolved complexity. When the intricacies of ingredients are understood, their expression becomes simple." He dipped his cap in prayer. "Karu, The Shapeshifter, thank you for this harvest—I receive this food." After a second, he tore into his bowl.

We both devoured our danban, much to Koji's satisfaction. White spores trickled from his gills. He sat back, placing his chopsticks across the brim of his bowl.

I finished with a satisfied groan, not even dwelling on the fact that my stomach was full of fungi. "Any chance they have coffee?"

Koji chuckled. "Green tea, if that will suffice?"

"It most certainly won't." I felt a vibration in my jacket pocket. "Hold that thought." I pulled out my pager—there was a message from dispatch. All of the positivity I felt melted away in an instant.

"Is everything alright?" Koji asked.

"There's another one …"

"Another what?" Koji titled his cap, his forehead scrunched up in confusion.

"Another dead child."

COLD
AS ICE

[20] Case File #42-56
Temple Ring | 11:53 a.m.

- - - - - - - - -

KOJI AND I stood around the edge of a rough hole, cracked open in the opaque ice of the canal. Floating in the middle of the breach was a torn piece of black plastic.

Around us, the wide canal's surface was entirely frozen over. Tall mycelial walls crept up either side, covered in rimy fruiting bodies. Cherry trees lined the top, their skeletal branches coated with frost.

My face prickled as a chilly gust swept through the waterway. I couldn't wait for winter to be over.

"Karu's wind is strong today," Koji said offhandedly in Coprinian. "Here."

He pulled a length of mycofabric from his jacket, passing it to me. A handmade gray scarf. I nodded in thanks and wrapped it around my numbing neck. The material was a bit itchy and smelled of Koji's musk— like dirt and cigarettes after a rainstorm.

Koji's gills quivered. "A storm is coming," he stated assuredly. "And I sense disturbances nearby."

"Let's focus on this first." I gestured to the hole. "Notice anything?"

A light snowfall picked up. I tiptoed around the hole, unsure of where the ice could support my weight. Koji was just as precarious in his heavy boots. We were like a couple of fledgling Sveppurian fishermen out for their first catch.

"The ice is thick," Koji said. He knelt down and peered into the opening, submerging half of his bare hand in the water. How he could endure the subzero water was beyond me. "About four inches or so."

He shook his wrist, spraying droplets all around. A few frigid beads landed on my forehead and cheeks. I squatted down next to him. My knees croaked and I feebly rubbed my mittens together.

"There hasn't been a day above freezing the last week," I noted. "Seems like a lot of trouble to do this."

"Whoever hacked the ice did it for a reason." Koji ran his palm along the frozen surface, tracing the jagged cracks. His gills tensed up beneath his cap. "See here: They used a tool to do it."

I got closer. Flecks of rust dotted the ice around the hole. Son of a bitch …

"Can you sense anything?" I asked.

"Nothing clear, but I can sense trace emotions." He pursed his lips, eyes closed. "The weight of death remains. Hopelessness, fear … and contentment."

"Someone planted the bag here," I muttered.

"And they themself broke through the ice."

"But why?" That was the burning question.

My gaze lingered on the hole. On the thin piece of plastic that bobbed in the water. The canal was eerily quiet, sounds absorbed by the falling snow.

Koji worked his jaw, specks of snow now clinging to his clothes. He stood and brushed himself off. His mouth opened to speak, but a strange tension took over him—his eyes and gills fluttered.

A high-pitched scream rang out, echoing across the canal.

"*Up above*," Koji warned.

We left the hole behind, careful not to crack the ice. Nearing the edge, Koji broke into a run. He lunged up a natural stairwell formed from mycelium. I hurried after him. With every exhausted step I took, the Mother Mushroom came into view above me, washed out by a snowy fog. I saw the fringes of its mountainous cap consumed by clouds. The deep gills wider than streets lining its underside. By the time I got to the top of the ladder, only the upper third of its tremendous stem was visible.

It was like standing beneath the skyscrapers in Morellum—only once you lingered in a thing's shadow could you comprehend its size.

I reached the top of the stairs, my feet crunching on snow and gravel. The path was covered in a fine blanket of white, hemmed in by the canal and a stone wall. The Temple Ring was opposite the wall. I'd never been so close to the Mother Mushroom, separated only by the patchwork of temples and shrines that surrounded it.

Koji was already down the path, running toward two cops and a fungal woman with a purple cap.

Police cordons blocked off the footpath in either direction. Barricades had been set up, each one manned by handfuls of human officers accompanied by Pilzland Shepherd police dogs. I'd made sure we were prepared this time.

I jogged in Koji's direction. The two cops wore masks and stood back from the button, giving her a noticeable amount of space. Meanwhile, Koji was consoling the purple-capped hophead. Further ahead, Cissy and two technicians—the same pale pair from Spirit Island—had set up a forensics tent. The three of them slipped inside.

As I got closer to the fungal, I registered who it was: Emiko, the shrine maiden from Reishi Temple.

She was on her knees now, her body heaving with wracking sobs. She wore a simple white robe, its hem smeared with dirt and wettened by snow. A thick flow of dark spores poured from her dimpled cap. The officers visibly cringed and inched further away from her. At my arrival, they straightened up and saluted.

"Officers," I said. "What are your names?"

"Harrison," said one. The other was Dudley.

"Who called this in?" I asked.

"I did," Dudley replied, looking unnecessarily proud. "Harrison and I saw a hophead run screaming from the path. They disappeared before we could question them, but we came down here and found …"

"Right. Good work. Stand to attention, gentlemen." I went to Koji and Emiko.

"I've been searching for him … searching, searching, searching …" Emiko craned her neck, finally taking notice of Koji and me. "Why haven't you found him? Where is Daigoro?"

"We found Shikaku," Koji said, "but we are still looking for your son."

I knelt down beside Emiko. She flinched and glared at me. "What are you doing here?" I asked.

"I sensed it," Emiko said with a blank stare. Her attention was drawn somewhere else, up in the sky.

"Sensed what?"

"I … I cannot explain …" Her gaze returned to Koji. "She would not understand—she is not one of us."

"Emiko, please." Koji cupped his hands around her face. "What did you sense?"

"A signal," she whispered.

I wanted to grab her by the mushrooms on her shoulders and shake a straight answer out of her. But Emiko's emotional state was delicate. Patience was key.

"Hen!" A twangy voice called. Cissy poked her head out of the forensics tent. "Get over 'ere."

"Nameko, stay here with Emiko," I said. The two cops gave me cautious looks. "Fucking Hell … you don't have to be right next to her, but keep an eye on them. Radio me if anything comes up."

"Yes, ma'am," said Dudley in a rumbling baritone.

They saluted me again before I headed toward the tent. Flashes of light burst inside, reflecting off of the surrounding snow. Cissy waited for me at the entrance.

"Good morning," I said, approaching the portly crime scene investigator. She was dressed in her full-body suit, booties, gloves and all. Her brown curls were loose and knotted. "Long time, no see."

"Duty calls, am I right?" Cissy laughed. She peeped down the path at Koji. "That must be the gillie you got stuck with."

"Officer Koji Nameko," I said.

"Na-may-ko." Cissy played with the phonetics a few more times. "Goddamn Hōpponese—I never can get the pronunciations right."

I clapped my hands together to get Cissy's attention. "Hey, focus. What have you got?"

"Right, sorry Hen." Cissy lifted up the flap and led me into the tent. My nose was hit with an antiseptic smell. Cissy requested that I stay near the entrance.

The two technicians frowned when they saw me. I waved and smiled. "Hello, gentlemen." They immediately returned to their work.

Laid out on a plastic-lined table in front of the grumpy techs were body parts. Yellow numbered triangles were propped next to each piece of the victim. The techs photographed and cataloged the bodily fragments.

"Well, you already saw that hole down there," Cissy said. "This bag had been ripped open already. The kid's head was floatin' near the surface of the ice, for all to see."

"Bloody Hell," I said.

Cissy pointed to the table. "Just like Spirit Island: A decapitated head, eyes and teeth removed. Two forearms and two calves, cut at the joints. No hands, no feet. Strange thing, though—this child ain't fungal."

Not fungal?

I examined the head more closely, eyes drawn to the neck. Unlike the first victim, there was no patch of skin removed near the jugular. I continued. The rest of the shaved head looked human. No cranial mushroom cap, but ... small, severed stems stuck out across the skull. Ten in total.

"A half-breed."

"That's right," Cissy reaffirmed.

"The spore print," I said, scratching my jawline with my soft mitten.

"Does it work the same way for muties?"

Cissy nodded. "Once again, no ID. But given the size of the limbs, skull and facial structure, it's another child. Six or seven, I'd say."

"What else?" I asked.

"Well," Cissy said, nibbling at her lip, "this is the bit that bloody stumped me. The body is fresh."

"*What*?" I shouted.

Cissy scratched the back of her wild mane. "There're few signs of decomposition, and the skin ain't bloated."

My eyes went wide. "Which means it hasn't spent any time underwater."

This confirmed what Koji and I had concluded on the canal: The killer planted the body here, on purpose.

"Two bodies, same manner of murder," Cissy stated.

"A serial killer," I said. All of the facts from this morning flooded into my brain. The sites where bodies had been found. The protests and riots that occurred in those same places. A pattern had emerged.

Emiko's words drifted across my agitated consciousness: *A signal.*

My radio crackled to life. "Hofmann!" Harrison exclaimed. "We need you."

I seized Cissy's bicep. "Pack all of this up. *Now*! Take it to the morgue, get it cataloged and ready for autopsy."

"Hen, what's going on?" Cissy yelled. "I don't understand—"

"Something's going on. I can't explain—just page me when the bodies are ready for examination. Now, move!"

I burst through the tent flap, hit with a wave of cold. I quickly scanned the path. The eastern cordon was clear. The west … shit.

A colony of fungals had amassed at the western barricade. More than a hundred, at least. Chants of "*Shimin! Shimin! Shimin!*" and "*Gaikamu! Gaikamu! Gaikamu!*" drifted down the path.

I sprinted in the opposite direction, toward Koji, Emiko, Harrison, and Dudley. My boots almost lost purchase on the snow-covered gravel.

I righted myself and kept on moving. Harrison waved at me, both arms swinging above his head. Koji hugged Emiko, who thrashed in his grasp.

"Harrison … Dudley," I said, catching my breath. "Call backup … then make sure Francis Glessner and her team make it out here. Go!"

They nodded in unison and took off to the forensics tent.

Emiko wailed in Hōpponese. "Let them come! Let them come!"

I crouched beside Koji, who struggled to contain Emiko's wild movements. "Nameko, we need to leave. Emiko isn't safe here."

In reality, no one was safe here. I'd been partly responsible for what happened at Spirit Island yesterday, and I regretted it. This was guaranteed to end in a similarly brutal fashion—with or without me.

"Safe?" Emiko cackled through tears and trickles of snot. Inky spores gushed from her gills. "How will we ever be safe if we can't even take care of our own *children*? Daigoro is lost …"

"He is *not* lost," Koji reassured her. "We will find him, but we must go."

"Go where?" Emiko spat.

"To the central precinct." I reached out to Emiko in an attempt to calm her. She snarled in response. "We'll bring you in for questioning, nothing more. Surely your story can provide more clues for what happened to Daigoro and the others."

Emiko flailed her arms, striking Koji in the cheek. "I will not go there with you! I would rather stay here with my people than go to the NKPD and never be free again. An interrogation room is one step away from prison."

"We are not arresting you, Emiko," Koji said, grunting as he gripped Emiko tighter. "You know Shikaku. You are a *witness*."

Emiko shook her head over and over. I looked down the path, where the protestors grew in number. They carried mycelium signs and threw clumps of snow at the cops blocking their way.

"The child!" a man screeched, his cry raw and pained. "Is it my child?"

I leaned closer to Emiko, my buttocks nearly touching the ground. In Hōpponese, I said, "We find your son. Need help first."

"Oh, that's rich!" Emiko turned to Koji. "Do you believe this coppie crone? As if I would believe any word that comes out of her *gaikamu* mouth! Her people have plagued us."

"I care. *We* care." Koji held her close. "We will report what happened here, but we do not need to go to the precinct. Where would you feel safe talking to us?"

Emiko's body trembled, then slackened—her energy was waning. "My apartment, in Tektown." She stared daggers at me, the bitterness in her eyes as cold as ice. "But she does not step foot inside."

"Done," I said. I grabbed Emiko's arm and shot to my feet, tearing her from Koji. A lingering pain in my knees throbbed. I ignored it, hauling Emiko's stubborn ass down the path, away from the swelling protest.

"Hofmann, that is enough!" Koji yelled from behind me.

I turned a deaf ear to his pleas. Emiko began to sob again, repeating her son's name like a broken cassette playing on a loop. "He is dead," she cried—her grief had unhinged her.

I knew what that was like. How it felt to actually lose a child.

Fear could do that to us. Fear of the unknown and the truths we wished we could prove. Those were the insidious paranoias that dug into us like parasites, festering and rotting the mind—corrupting us from the inside out.

Snow drifted across my face as I escorted Emiko to my Metro RT. I shoved her in the back of the car, Koji objecting to my rough treatment. Fuck his nice guy tactics—I was determined to deliver Daigoro to her, regardless of how much she hated me and my people.

I fired up the engine, blaring the sirens, and flicking on the light bar. The images of two dead children were frostbitten into my brain. This case confounded me, begged for answers, and I was Hell bent on figuring it out.

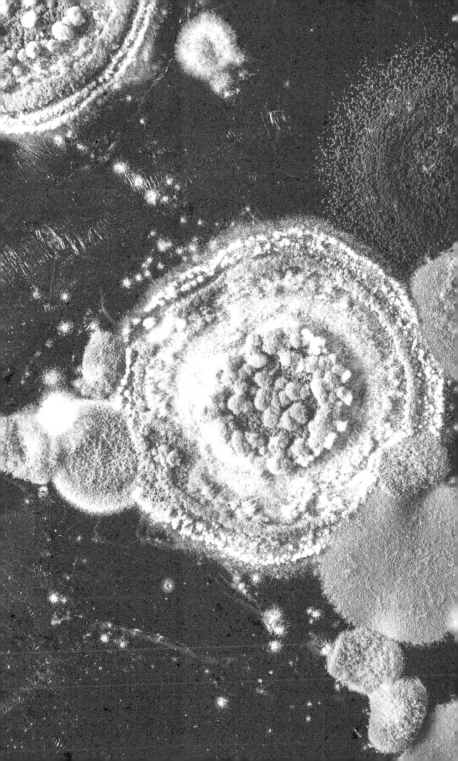

EMPTY PROMISES

- - - - - - - - -

WAITED DOWN the hallway from Emiko and Koji. They were having a tense conversation outside of her apartment—clearly about me. Emiko gave me scornful looks, and Koji made animated gestures with his hands and arms.

This hall and the whole building were made of mycelium. Floor-to-wall filaments had been fused together in the fungals' rushed attempt at post-war reconstruction. Apartments like this weren't substantial, but they filled up fast—all of the public housing projects did, from Tektown to the Kala Commons.

Koji waved me over. I pinched my nostrils, walking warily as my footsteps kicked up spores from a carpet of mold.

"You can enter," Koji said, "but Emiko has asked that you remain at the entrance."

I ran my tongue along the inside of my cheek. This was a big compromise on Emiko's part, especially after the way I'd treated her, but Koji insisted I be present. "Okay. Anything else?"

The muscles on Koji's jawline tightened. "I would request that you apologize, but Emiko does not particularly care to hear one. In her words: 'An apology from Hofmann would be as empty as the promises you have made regarding my son.'"

Cold.

Emiko crossed her arms, her youthful face twisted in a severe scowl.

She turned and placed her right palm on a mycelium door. The dense white threads tremored at her touch. For a moment, they crawled across her skin—examining her. A second later, the mycelium retracted into the surrounding wall, revealing an open doorway.

Without uttering a word, Emiko walked through. Koji and I followed, but I remained at the entrance, as requested. The mycelium grew back behind me, causing me to jump. Its tendrils slithered and susurrated as they reconnected.

How the Hell could anyone stand living here?

Emiko's dwelling was a single-room that stunk of grassy tea and mildew. To the right of the door, two mold mattresses grew from the floor, laying side-by-side. At the back corner, a wide mushroom table and toadstool seats sprouted up in an organic dining set. Next to that was a mycelial kitchenette that extended from the wall, a single mycofuel tank leaning against the cabinet. Bulbous fungi hung from above, shedding a pallid yellow light across the space.

The home was small, sparse, depressing—much like Emiko. But it was better than most hopheads in Neo Kinoko could afford.

The problem for me was, there was no bloody heating in here. I blew warm breath into my hands, still unable to understand how the fungals weren't bothered by the cold. That'd be the only bit of their biology that I'd steal from them.

Emiko prepared tea in the kitchenette. She drew water from a mycoplastic faucet and boiled it on a stovetop. The counters were nearly bare, only a few containers of rations stacked on top, and a miniature garden of edible fruiting bodies at one end.

Koji sat at the table, the apartment's sole window beside him. It offered a frosted glimpse of a curtain of snowfall. The calm beginnings of a winter storm were lit with greens and yellows by the bioluminescent lights of neighboring businesses.

Tektown was true to its name: Music and advertisements blasted outside, hyping up the latest deals on Coprinian tech imports, pirated films translated into Hōpponese, and appliances that would revolution-ize the home.

As if anyone in this city could indulge in crap like that.

"*Ariari do*, Emiko-*kato*," Koji said, "for inviting us into your home."

"Enough with the formalities," Emiko replied, not bothering to look at him.

She poured water from two ceramic cups into a matching teapot. After a minute of steeping, she refilled the cups with brewed tea. She gently tapped the teapot and left it on the counter, then took the cups to the table and set them down—one for her, one for Koji.

Emiko stole a quick glance at me, contempt in her icy expression. I felt like a voyeur.

Rising slightly from his seat, Koji made a shallow bow. "Thank you for the tea. You have a lovely home."

"*Damitare*, Koji …" Emiko sat across from him. "My home is woe-ful. Imagine raising a child here."

"That's not what I—"

"I know what you *meant*," Emiko snapped. "Please, drink. It is not much, but it is the best I can offer."

Koji took a sip. "This tastes like the leaves from the slopes of Mount Maitake."

"They are." Emiko's face lifted in a fleeting moment of brightness. "It was a gift."

While Koji and Emiko spoke over tea, I looked around the apart-ment for potential clues—not that there was much to see. Patches of black mold bloomed along the edges of the ceiling. There was a closet with a hole in the floor that I supposed was a bathroom. Beside the bed, a few toys lined the wall. They looked handmade, spun from mycelium. A collection of mold photos grew above the beds, showing a smiling Emiko and Daigoro at various stages of their lives together.

"Can you tell me about this signal that you sensed?" Koji asked. "The one that brought you to the canal?"

Emiko hunched over her tea, breathing in the steam but not drinking. Her eyes began to water. "It is not the first one—it has been happening often as of late. A powerful surge of emotion that would overwhelm my senses with … with waves of suffering and confusion." She sobbed, trails of tears making her face glisten. Spores drifted from her gills and floated around the table. "At first, I thought they were nightmares—remnants of memories from past kin. But then … the voices started. The signals returned stronger, with children calling out for help. Dissonant, desperate, dying … I swear, I could hear Daigoro's voice amidst the cacophony."

Not memories of the dead … Experiences of the living.

Koji placed a hand atop Emiko's. She shrunk, but ultimately accepted the gesture. He continued: "What did the signals compel you to do?"

"To wander until the voices became clearer, more distinct. Only when I heard the voice of a single child would I know that I had arrived."

I perked up, scrutinizing Emiko's words and body language. Her gills were tight. She swallowed loudly.

"Arrived where?" Koji pressed.

"The sites where the dead bodies were found," I answered.

Emiko's attention snapped to me, as if the sound of my voice was a knife to the throat. "The detective is correct. Myself and others would descend upon these signals. More often than not, it would result in protests, then chaos at the hands of Hofmann's human brethren."

Koji leaned back on his toadstool, bringing both hands to rest on his thighs. "Why have I not felt these signals on the fungalnet?"

Emiko tilted her head, seeming puzzled. "I do not know … Perhaps they are targeted."

"Targeted at specific segments of the fungal population," I guessed.

"But why? Who would benefit from this?" Koji pondered. He rubbed his moldy stubble, then took a final sip of tea.

That was the question that nagged at me: Who would benefit from protests and dead children? And *why*?

"Shikaku," Emiko said. "You mentioned he knows where Daigoro is. That my boy's life is in peril. Where is he?"

"We found Shikaku operating an illegal distillery beneath Mold Town," Koji replied. "There was a fire. His remains were not found."

Emiko fidgeted with her fingers. Her expression appeared sunken and troubled. "He is still out there …," she whispered.

"We believe so." Koji's cap twitched, his gills puffing and contracting like respiring lungs. "For what purpose could he have taken Daigoro?"

Emiko drank. Her eyes darted from Koji to her cup.

"He …" She cleared her throat. "He left me, just before Daigoro was born, saying he was destined to fight for our people against the invaders. I … I was forced to raise Daigoro alone, in the middle of a war. I found refuge in a woman's shelter, twenty-two of us taking care of one another and our babies.

"After the Spore War ended, I had heard that Shikaku was still alive. The rumor was, he had joined a gang or some kind of resistance movement. I found him and demanded he help me raise Daigoro. Money, care, *anything*! But …" Emiko paused. Koji gave her an encouraging nod. "He swore he had gone straight, working on a fishing boat with his brother. Of course, he had nothing to offer. Over a year passed, and no word. Then, six months ago, he reappeared as if from The Great Beyond. He wanted to see Daigoro, to get to know him better. Naive as I was, I embraced the change, thinking we could turn a new cap and finally be a family." She sniffled and wiped away fresh tears. "One day, we were here in this very room. Shikaku sat down next to Daigoro and said, 'I need your help with something very important, Daigoro-*bae*. Will you help me?'"

"How did Daigoro respond?" Koji asked.

Emiko smiled weakly. "He obliged, of course—you know boys can admire their fathers. Shikaku said he had a new job, that the men he worked for were going to make Neo Kinoko a better place, and wouldn't Daigoro like to help? My little boy couldn't have been more pleased …

This was last month."

Koji exhaled. "And not long after that, Shikaku disappeared with Daigoro."

"Yes." Emiko wiped away tears with her sleeve. "But you two saw him: Shikaku is alive, so Daigoro must be, too."

"For now," I muttered.

Parents were like fortresses of guarded memories. But over time, the seemingly strong foundations could rot from hope, crumbling from within.

My head rushed with thoughts of Elisabeth.

When she was thirteen, we'd gotten into an argument, her, Frederick and I. Something so inconsequential I couldn't even remember. That night, Elisabeth was gone.

She'd disappeared for a whole day. Turned out, she'd snuck into her friend Charlotte's house. Charlotte's parents were completely unaware that Elisabeth was upstairs. We arrived at their house, frantic and exhausted. The two girls were watching a movie, as if nothing had happened. Liz had the gall to smile at us when we arrived to pick her up: "Hello mum and dad!" she'd said. Stupid girl.

My fists were clenched and shaking. The realization sunk in that those kinds of moments—those feelings—were long gone. Distant echoes that could only haunt me, like an infected wound festering in the depths of my subconscious. All those years we hurt each other—venomous words, flaring emotions, clashing egos.

But none of it compared to what I did …

I prayed that Daigoro was alive. Emiko still had a chance to watch him grow up and experience the joys, heartaches, and frustrations of being a parent. She deserved that, but she didn't deserve to be strung along.

"We will find your son," Koji said, repeating his words from earlier. "I promise."

Emiko sat motionless, staring silently at her empty teacup. I'd been in her position before, where a promise unfulfilled could break you.

I felt my pager rumble. Pulling it out, I read a message from Cissy: *We made it out. Back at the morgue. Autopsy ready in an hour.*

"Nameko," I said, "We have a date with the medical examiner. Wrap it up."

Koji tensed at the mention of the medical examiner. Strange. He quickly stood and bowed to Emiko. "*Ariari do*, for the tea and for your time. I—"

Emiko raised her head. "Please, Koji-*kato*, do not burden me again with fantasies. Find my boy or do not, but the next time we see each other, I pray to Mother Chikyu that we will have more answers than questions."

Koji bowed again. He crossed the apartment, pressing his palm into the mycelium door. It unfurled and he left. I glanced back at Emiko, who remained on her toadstool, unmoving. There was nothing more I could do for her except find her boy. I exited the apartment.

Koji was waiting for me. We walked down the hallway.

"Kinoko Rose is planning something," I said to him. "That Goddamned distillery, the disappearances and deaths, the *signals*. Your cousin is involved, somehow, and Daigoro is in danger."

"Agreed," Koji replied, "but the path ahead is uncertain."

"Bloody uncertain is right. Which is why you can't go making promises you aren't guaranteed to keep."

Koji scoffed. "You believe offering someone hope is a bad thing?"

"The truth is a harsh pill," I said. "It tastes bitter in the beginning, and sweeter at the end. Time heals the truth, but lies linger like parasites. They wait for the right moment to manifest and devour their host. What Emiko needs is pragmatic facts, not blind falsehoods."

Koji ground his teeth, but held his tongue—he'd dug us a fucking hole with his optimism.

There was no telling what Cissy and the coroner could offer us, so until the evidence became clearer, all we had to go on were Koji's empty promises. Here's hoping we wouldn't bury ourselves in that hole.

FRAGMENTED MEMORIES

[22] Case File #42-56
NKPD Central Precinct | 2:50 p.m.

- - - - - - - - -

THE CHIEF MEDICAL examiner did a final review of the children's body parts, with Cissy observing at his side. Two chopped-up bodies, their pieces arranged on separate steel slabs in the NKPD morgue—the fluorescent light tubes above shone spotlights on the victims.

Koji and I stood back, allowing the experts a moment to finish. I wrung my hands, feeling the room's cold creep up beneath my clothes.

The irritating scent of formaldehyde filled the room, prickling my nose and clinging to the back of my throat. This morgue was like every other one I'd ever been in: Sterile and lifeless. I'd never liked them. Whether it was Morellum or Neo Kinoko, morgues turned something as organic and natural as death into a scientific experiment.

Still, this was a necessary and valuable part of the process. Even the green chalkboard that hung on the wall, dispassionately detailing the weights of victim's various organs.

I caught Koji picking at his fingernails in my periphery—he'd been on edge ever since I told him about the autopsy. "You okay, Nameko?"

"I am fine," he replied brusquely under his breath.

Bloody Hell. As if this investigation wasn't proving difficult enough, but now I had to deal with Koji's moods.

Cissy beckoned us over with a gloved hand. "C'mon, we're ready." Her voice was muffled by a mask. She donned a surgical gown, and a cap wrangled her brown curls. "Thanks for the warnin' back at the canal.

Things got a bit messy, but we got outta there with everything cataloged and intact."

"Of course, Cissy," I said, then gave the chief medical examiner a two-finger salute. "Afternoon, Jeremy."

Even beneath his medical outfit, Jeremy Cooper couldn't conceal his awkwardness. Hunched posture, droopy ears, and deep creases visible around squinty eyes—he hid himself away amongst the dead, where he was most comfortable. He was bloody brilliant at his job, although I'd no idea how a man in his early sixties willingly ended up in Hōppon.

"H-Hello, Henrietta," Jeremy responded in his timid stutter. "How are y-y-you?"

"Just fine, thanks." I pointed to Koji. "Jeremy, Cissy, this is my partner for this investigation: Koji—"

"N-N-Nameko-*jero*. Yes, yes." Jeremy bowed to Koji, who returned the gesture. "We are acquainted."

"When the Hell have you two met?" I asked, sawing my tongue along my upper teeth.

Jeremy opened his mouth, but didn't say anything. Then he squeezed his lips together, sending wrinkles sprawling across his skin. The idiot had clearly said something he shouldn't have. He slipped on his own mask, covering half of his flushed face.

"That is not important right now," Koji said dismissively. He faced Cissy and bowed. "Glessner-*shen*, it is an honor."

Not important? How did a *beat cop* know the chief medical examiner? That Goddamned gillie was hiding something.

"No formalities with me." Cissy waved Koji off playfully. "It's just Francis to you, Mr. Na-may-ko."

Koji smiled thinly. "Understood … Francis."

"Now, I'll let you get to business," Cissy said with a resounding clap. "Jeremy had the honor of performin' the autopsy on the first victim. The second hasn't been given a proper top-to-bottom, so we figured you three could run through his conclusions. Alright, gloves on!" She handed Koji and me each a pair, along with masks.

"Are you off, Cissy?" I asked.

Cissy huffed. "I am. Ridgeway's got me workin' my ass off this week. Take care, you lot."

I thanked Cissy. She removed her garments, disposing of them in a medical waste bin before leaving.

Putting on my protective equipment, I noticed Koji had tucked his away in a pocket. Jeremy led us to the space between the two slabs. Even through the mask, I was suffocated by antiseptic smells.

Koji lagged behind. He whispered: "Murio, guide these young spirits on their journey to The Great Beyond."

Jeremy stepped closer to one of the slabs, the one with the fungal on it. His hand hovered over the head. The top section of the skull was removed, revealing the victim's decomposing brain. I almost vomited— fuzzy white mold and strands of mycelium coated the cerebrum, slipping between the pale folds.

Was that how every fungal's brain looked? Enveloped in fungi?

"G-g-given the skull and facial structure," Jeremy said, "as well as the size of the limbs, it is indeed a child. Between six or s-s-seven years old. The half-breed, on the other hand, is b-b-between five and six."

"Toxicology reports?"

"Nothing as of yet. They are still being processed, b-b-but we are hoping to get them soon." He pointed to the body parts, laid caringly atop the metal surfaces. "Both murders, same m-m-method: Decapitated head, eyes and teeth removed, two forearms and two calves cut at the joints, and no hands or f-f-feet."

I swiveled from one slab to the other. Different children, their bodies defiled. Identical in how they were dismembered. But …

Leaning forward, I examined the half-breed's head. "So why would the killer switch from fungal to mutie? And the neck—the victim from Spirit Island had a patch of skin removed, but the half-breed doesn't."

Jeremy bent down and ran his finger along the severed edge of the child's neck. "Yes, I n-n-noticed that. The cut on the second victim was done a few inches higher than the first."

Koji narrowed his eyes. "The killer is learning from their mistakes."

"But it is most c-c-curious as to *why* would they have removed a patch to begin with," Jeremy said.

Brands? Tattoos?

"I don't know …," I admitted. "What else?"

Jeremy sucked in a breath. "I have concluded that the half-breed v-v-victim was dismembered *alive*, then dumped within hours of dying."

"Matsua above …," Koji murmured.

"How can you be sure?" I asked, still skeptical.

Jeremy stroked his masked chin. "The p-p-parts from the first victim show signs of rigor mortis—stiffening of the muscles in the face and limbs, specifically—as well as the uniform discoloration of livor mortis. This suggests that they were killed first, then dismembered after a period of at least twelve hours before being dumped into the ocean. But …" He trailed off.

I rolled my hand. "Out with it."

"The second does not. It is, well … it is c-c-consistent with what I experienced as a field doctor during the Spore War. Um, soldiers who required … amputation."

Crossing my arms, I pressed him. "Elaborate, Jeremy."

"Amputations often result in significant b-b-blood loss, and that blood accumulates at the site of dismemberment. In the case of the half-breed, there is no bruising … rather, I encountered signs of s-s-severe hemorrhaging."

I ground my teeth. "So, the murderer *meant* to dismember this child alive?"

"I believe so."

"Why change their method?" Koji asked.

"I do not know," Jeremy admitted, "but I *have* d-d-determined the manner by which the body parts were, um, removed." His thick eyebrows perked up in consternation. "The excisions from the canal victim match those from Spirit Island, and the form of the cuts indicates a specific t-t-tool."

"What kind of tool?"

"Well, the killer favored their l-l-left hand," Jeremy noted, "judging by the angle of the cuts. And the action itself was p-p-performed using a hacksaw or similar instrument."

"How can you tell?" asked Koji.

Jeremy pointed at the base of the neck and around its circumference. "Notice the subtle ridges and t-t-tears along the bone, in comparison to the precise cuts through skin and the muscle. This is indicative of a serrated blade on the former, and a knife on the latter."

"Bloody Hell," I said.

Jeremy stretched his neck, accentuating the hunch in his upper back. "It appears the dismemberment was d-d-done with the skill and precision of, um, a professional."

"A serial killer," I corrected.

"Now, now, we must not j-j-jump to conclusions," Jeremy said. I heard his foot tapping under the slabs.

"Don't be a fool, Jeremy. Two deaths following a consistent pattern—those are the beginning signs of a serial killer. In this case, a butcher seems more likely. They knew how to bleed these children, how to expertly cut them up." I pinched the bridge of my nose. "It still doesn't make sense, though. Why kill a fungal and a half-breed child? And why dispose of the bodies this way? Clearly, they didn't *intend* to get caught—"

The signal.

The killer didn't want to get caught, but they did want the bodies to be found.

I thought about the other dead children and the protests. Had this murderer been responsible for those as well? What kind of a panic would that unleash upon this city's fragile foundations?

"Nameko-*jero*," Jeremy said. "I believe I have d-d-done as much as I can for today. Would you mind?"

"Mind what?" I asked.

On the opposite side of the slab, I saw Koji nearing the fungal victim. He reached out to the head, examining it with a dead look in his eyes, like he was doing this against his will. Fine filaments grew from his fingers and trailed toward … the exposed brain.

"Nameko!" I lunged at him, but Jeremy held me back.

It was too late. Koji's mycelium had intertwined with that of the brain. Dread coursed through my mind. My body shook, heartbeat racing. I wriggled from Jeremy's grasp, sending him tumbling back into the half-breed's slab.

"Enough, Hofmann!" Jeremy shouted. "That is what we p-p-pay him to do!"

"The child," Koji whispered, "I sense … fragmented memories. Cannot … resist."

I rushed around the table and seized Koji. I tugged at the fungi growing from his shoulders—he didn't react. His golden eyes fluttered. My thoughts raced with flashbacks to Oze and that alleyway on The Shelf. "Nameko, what are you *doing*?"

"Do not force me to c-c-call security," Jeremy yelled. "You are interrupting Officer Nameko's p-p-process. It is in his contract!"

All of a sudden, Koji threw his head back, causing me to lose balance. I collapsed to the floor. White spores flowed from Koji's gills and swarmed around the victim's brain. His lips moved—he muttered in Hōpponese, but I couldn't hear or decipher it.

The spores from Koji's gills turned black. His mutterings sped up. Then his face contorted into an expression of shock. Tears rolled down his cheeks, and spores swirled around the room. Time seemed to slow as Koji convulsed. He twitched and writhed, his mycelium disconnecting from the head. The threads retracted into his hand, then he fell to the floor beside me.

I crawled over to Koji. Cradling him, I removed my jacket, rolled it up and slid it under his cap. His body spasmed—I felt for breath and found nothing. His pulse was slowing, and his skin was turning blue. Yet somehow his mouth still moved, mumbling as if possessed.

"He will be f-f-fine, Hofmann," Jeremy urged, trying again to tear me away from Koji. "This is not his first t-t-time."

But I wasn't about to listen to Jeremy—that hunched bastard had done this to Koji. I tore off my mask and gloves. A pressure pounded in my head. Disgust welled up inside me, but I forced it down.

I had to help him.

Placing one hand over the other on his chest, I counted compressions—all the way up to thirty. Taking a deep breath, I placed my mouth over his. He tasted like mulch and tobacco, and I had to suppress a gag.

Pinching his nose, I exhaled. Once, twice.

Thirty more compressions. Two more breaths. Time became a blur. Nothing else mattered except for Koji to wake the fuck up again. Not Jeremy's whining about protocols and contracts. Not the cut-up remains resting on slabs.

"Nameko, *wake up*!" I pleaded.

Koji gasped and I stumbled backward onto my ass. His eyes shot open—bright, yellow, and bloodshot. He sputtered and hacked, then rolled into a fetal position. I returned to his side: "I'm here. You're okay."

"Just g-g-give him a glass of water," Jeremy said, "and he will be fine."

"Then *you* bring him one," I snapped.

Jeremy walked off, grumbling about how Ridgeway would hear about this.

Through wheezes and dry-heaves, Koji whispered, "I … I know."

"You know what, Nameko?"

"I know …," he coughed, "where this child died."

GAME PLAN

[23] Case File #42-56
NKPD Central Precinct | 3:39 p.m.

- - - - - - - - -

KOJI PACED FROM one side of the smoky meeting room to the other. "How many times do I have to repeat? I will *not* tell you."

I slapped a handful of documents down on the cluttered surface of a plastic table, almost knocking over my paper cup of coffee. "And that's the bloody problem! You're holding back on me. All this"—I gestured to the maps, the stacks of zoning and property records from city archives—"is us *working together*. You said to me that we'd have each other's backs. We're supposed to be a team, but you can't even honest about what the Hell happened in the morgue."

"It is not for me to decide," Koji said, exasperated. He rolled up the sleeves of his white button-up shirt. "My contract will not—"

"Yeah, yeah, your Goddamned contract and its a non-disclosure agreement. You've said that half a dozen times." I rubbed my clammy forehead, glaring at a to-go container with only a single rice ball left. "Look, Nameko, I don't know what Ridgeway and the NKPD have you doing for them, but ..." I grabbed my coffee and took a sip. "It doesn't seem right, okay? What you did, it reminded me of ..."

"Oze," Koji finished.

Fucking Oze.

I twisted the cup around, staring at the swirling brown liquid. Koji lit up another one of his cigarettes. He pulled the ashtray closer, where seven butts had piled up—I regretted allowing him to smoke while we brainstormed. We'd commandeered a small meeting room in the central precinct for our research. A bare affair with white walls, brown wood trim, and panel floors. Table, chairs, and a rolling chalkboard. No windows, just colonies of black mold spreading from the ceiling corners and an ever thickening tobacco fog.

"Nameko, I know what it feels like—the violation. But these are *dead people* we're talking about."

"Please, let it go." Koji took a long drag. As he exhaled, his eyes fell. Droplets of condensation dripped from his gills and onto the floor. "Please …"

I couldn't let it go.

Like this case, it was the kind of thing that would fester in my mind and grow into a foul tumor. Only once I knew the truth could I excise it. Koji was capable of terrifying things, and the NKPD was using him. For what purpose, I didn't know exactly, but Ridgeway did.

I was stalling, wasting time when we needed to focus on the evidence in front of us. Finally, we had solid clues, so I would appease Koji. For now.

"Tell me again what you sensed from the child," I said.

Koji narrowed his eyes, knowing I was deflecting. "Aching hunger and desperation. A dark space with glowing fungi and rattling chains. The smell of fish on someone's breath. Oppressive fear. Finally, hanging upside down in a room with blood-stained walls."

"Hunger …," I mumbled. "Could the killer be starving his victims?" I took off my jumper, sweat rolling down my chest—the NKPD sure as Hell liked to overdo it with the central heating. I'd stripped down to a plain black undershirt, but Koji kept puffing away and ventilating through his gills like it was no big deal.

"That is the most likely scenario," he replied. "Isolate and deprive them—that would make death a welcome reprieve."

I scratched at the back of my hands. "Jeremy said the dismemberments were done with the precision of a professional. Who could have that skill set?"

"A surgeon," Koji suggested.

"All the surgeons in Neo Kinoko are employed by CPAN—the humans at least. Do fungals even have surgeons?"

Koji shook his head, releasing a cloud of fumes. "Mycelium is nature's surgeon."

That made me shudder, the thought of what the gillies subjected themselves to. "Alright, surgeons are out. But you mentioned fish—what about butchers?"

"My people are very fond of meats—pigs, sheep, cows." Koji smiled. "It has been some time since I enjoyed the taste of meat, but CPAN was very thorough in killing off our local livestock."

"That's 'cause—" I stopped myself. The Coprinian government had slaughtered millions of animals during and after the Spore War. Propaganda portrayed them as mutants—sacrilegious animals that had merged with fungi, just like the barbaric Hōpponese. "Rattling chains and blood-stained walls. Butcher shops or slaughterhouses are a decent starting point."

"I concur."

So, we needed to find a butcher shop or a slaughterhouse. But which one? I eyed the stack of zoning and property records warily. "Let's get to it."

— — — — — —

AN HOUR HAD passed, and we'd combed through countless documents. Koji and I stood on opposite sides of the table, consumed by research in a steamy room. Years of paperwork was getting us nowhere—CPAN records from after the war, Hōpponese records from before, mycopaper covered in logograms that I couldn't read. It also didn't help that there were hundreds of butcher shops and slaughterhouses across Neo Kinoko.

This situation felt hopeless. Threads of truth dangled from the suffocating blanket of bureaucracy, like searching for a single spore in an entire cloud.

I wiped stinging sweat from my eyes. "Anything, Nameko?"

"There is too much," he lamented. "We must narrow it down somehow."

I pored over the documents we'd collected—there had to be a way to pinpoint the location. Records showed that more than sixty of these businesses had been shut down during the Spore War, or taken over by new enterprises. Many more were commandeered by CPAN for control of the city's food production.

Strangely, a sizable number had dropped off the radar entirely in the last few years—no records of closure, no transfer of ownership. Nothing. They were scattered around town in a haphazard way, with no discernible pattern.

My brain throbbed.

I shoved the last morsel of a seaweed-wrapped rice ball into my mouth. After I finished chewing, I said, "You know, fungal food is growing on me."

"Only yesterday you were so quick to judge my people," Koji said, a grin plastered on his face. "Now look at you: Eating Hōpponese food, learning about our culture and customs—"

"Don't bloody push it. I said I like your *food*, not you or your country." I wiped my mouth with a mycopaper napkin.

Koji hovered across from me, hands placed atop the maps. His lips were pinched in a thin line. "And yet you helped me save Ryo in the distillery—you could have left her behind to die."

"A life is a life," I grumbled. "Plus, you were the one who carried her."

"Nonetheless, you made a choice." Koji inclined his chin, as if pondering my words. "A life is a life … Would you believe, that is very much in line with Eien thinking? Whether it takes the form of a human, a fungal, a tree, or a river, all life is precious and all things are imbued with spirit."

Life was indeed precious. Even if it took the form of a fungal or half-breed child, no one deserved to die—especially not the way they did. But Koji's philosophical musings were going over my head.

"No more religious talk," I said. "What are we looking at with all this bloody paperwork?"

Koji leaned across the table. He had dark circles under his eyes, but his countenance was resolute. "There are large concentrations of slaughterhouses in The Button, Fishtown, Hedoro Industrial City, and Dock Ward. But there are also some sprinkled throughout Kala Commons, Kinoko Crossing, and Riverside."

I pulled my chair closer to the table. Its legs scraped and screeched across the floor. I slid a map across the table, tracing my forefinger across its textured surface.

Riverside … Where had I heard that before?

"Hofmann, what is it?"

"Give me a moment." I found Riverside—a contested gang zone.

Then it clicked.

I grabbed the translated scans from the distillery and shuffled through them. "Where is that delivery report?" There. I slid it across the tabletop. "Nameko, take a look."

He spun the paper around. Tilting his cap back and forth, he said, "I am confused."

"Kinoko Rose deliveries," I said, "going to *Riverside*."

Koji scratched at his moldy stubble. "The deliveries are in code. I do not know how to decipher it."

"We don't need to decipher it." Excitement built up inside me—my gut told me I was close to cracking this. "Pass me the property records."

Koji handed them to me. I flipped through dozens of documents, cross-referencing them with the map. "Here." I pointed at four property records. "These are the only slaughterhouses in Riverside. The first was destroyed during the war. The second and third were demolished and replaced with warehouses. But, the final one, it's *abandoned*."

Koji snatched the page. His eyes darted back and forth as he read out loud: "Buta Meats. It closed down last year. There is no property title to determine ownership, but there is a signature. I can make out the name Bue, but the rest is too messy."

"Could that be where Kinoko Rose had been making deliveries?"

"It is possible," Koji acknowledged.

I grinned. "Then it's worth checking out."

- - - - - -

SNOW DRIFTED LAZILIY across the windshield of the Metro RT. I barreled through Orchard Hill, down sloping streets and past dilapidated estates. The ward was a literal hill, located northwest of the Mother Mushroom. I could picture the wealth its opulent properties once held, but those decadent days were long gone—bombs had blemished the landscape, chasing the affluent out of their homes.

A darkening overcast sky hung low above the city. Riverside sprawled out to the north, hugging the Kinoko River. Its streets were packed with warehouses, offices, and factories. Across the river was the ruined patchwork of Old Kinoko, along with a gaping, irradiated basin more than five miles across.

Hogosha Crater.

"Do you mind if I smoke a cigarette?" Koji asked from the passenger seat.

"Savor it," I said. "Just roll your window down."

Koji slipped a smoke between his lips and lit it. The interior glowed from his lighter's dancing flame. He opened his window a crack, blowing a plume through the gap.

Crisp air filled the car—it was a welcome change to Koji's earthy musk. I had "Children of Time" by Portia playing on cassette. It was one of those long pilzrock jams that evolved into psychedelic, atmospheric mania—the kind of song Frederick hated, but my dad and I would enjoy together over beers on late nights.

Koji examined a map of Riverside, flicking ash out the window. "One of these days, you will have to share more of your music with me."

I laughed. Did he expect that I was going to make him a mixtape, like we were in high school? "We'll see … Now, what's our game plan? Get in there and scout the place out?"

A low growl rumbled in Koji's throat. "You do not know Riverside. These contested gang zones are nearly impossible to predict. The moment we enter, one or more of the gangs will know. Plus, there is a light bar on top of your car, and decals of POLICE on either side—no matter what, we will stand out like fruiting bodies after a fresh rain."

I squeezed the steering wheel. "What do you suggest, then?"

He pointed to the map, his finger tracing a line from Orchard Hill up into Riverside. "Buta Meats is on the eastern side of the zone, next to the canal bordering Sleepless Street. My recommendation is that we enter from the south—there are two avenues that can best serve our approach. We choose one, proceed with haste, then hide the car a couple of blocks from our destination. After that, we continue on foot."

I scratched the back of my head. My ponytail was loose, so I took off the elastic and let my unwashed hair down. "You think the gangs won't notice us speeding into their territory?"

Koji crushed his cigarette butt in the ashtray. "There are four gangs here, all vying for control. New ones crop up, whereas others are subsumed into more powerful entities. I pray they will be too preoccupied with each other to take notice of us. The less time we give them to react and track our location, the better."

That was bloody reassuring. "And Kinoko Rose? Are they in play here?"

"I believe so."

I downshifted, easing the Metro down a steep incline. "It's risky."

"If The Long War taught me anything, it is the necessity of adaptability. To analyze your situation and decide upon the best course of action."

The hophead was right—not that I wanted to admit that to him. There was a moment of silence, punctuated by pilzrock and the squeaky swish of the windshield wipers.

Koji took out another cigarette. The car soon filled with acrid smoke. "Well? What is our course of action?"

"We go with your plan," I said, tapping my fingers along to the beat. "Go in fast, search Buta Meats, then get the Hell out."

The tip of Koji's cigarette radiated orange, his cheeks puckering as he inhaled. He gave me a side-eyed look, one eyebrow raised. "You agree with my plan?"

He knew the city better than I did—its politics and its intricacies. Rushing in didn't sit well with me. But if our goal was in the middle of a Goddamned gang zone, what choice did I have?

Patience wouldn't apply here. The necessity of adaptability—that's what we needed.

"You're right …," I admitted. "Now, show me the route." I cranked the volume on "Children of Time."

All that mattered right now was solving these murders and arresting whoever did it.

Koji smirked. He bobbed his head and hairy cap to the music, his smoke perched between two fingers. He laid the map on the dashboard, drawing a path into Riverside—our path to Buta Meats.

"Follow this road for one mile," Koji said. "I will tell you when to turn."

"Got it."

We were headed straight into the heart of darkness. The troubling question was, what would we even find there?

HOOKS & CHAINS

[24] Case File #42-56
Riverside (Contested Gang Zone) | 5:24 p.m.

- - - - - - - - -

EASED MY foot off of the accelerator, guiding the Metro toward a gloomy alley sandwiched between two deteriorating factories. My grip steady on the steering wheel, I eyed the road warily. Snow coated its surface, piling up in huge potholes.

Thankfully, we hadn't come across any signs of gangs. Yet.

I turned the tape deck off, wishing I could hear the raucous conclusion to "Nightmare Country" by Anaba.

But now was the time to focus. I parked the car and killed the engine. The crumbling factory walls were covered in frosted mold and faded graffiti. Tangled mushroom growths arched over the alley, hung with hundreds of pointed icicles.

"Buta Meats is two blocks to the northeast," Koji said. "I will be able to sense the presence of nearby fungals, so long as they are not purposefully obscuring themselves."

I gave him a two-fingered salute. "After you."

We got out of the car. The subzero air nipped at my face as I did my hairup in a ponytail. I slipped on a wool cap and leather gloves, then wrapped Koji's scarf around my neck—he hadn't asked for it back, so it was mine for the time being.

A *crack* echoed nearby. I instinctively dove for cover behind the Metro's trunk. More gunfire sounded, muffled by the weather and the distance.

Koji looked at me, the cold bringing a flush to his face. He held up his hand for me to wait. His gills convulsed in time with his fluttering eyelids—he was sensing.

"We are clear," he said. "They are not close."

Fucking Hell … Of course, our best lead was in a Goddamned war zone.

I got up and popped the trunk. Its rusting hinges complained as it creaked open. I reached in and unzipped a duffel bag. I laid out flashlights, handcuffs, a sheathed hunting knife, a Tremblay MKIV revolver, and two boxes of ammunition. Grabbing two flashlights, I handed one to Koji.

"You got handcuffs?" I asked.

"I do."

"Good. Check your ammo, too."

I strapped the hunting knife to my belt, but left the revolver—I had my trusted SIG P26, after I'd lost the STOHL .357 in Mold Town. Koji took out his own SIG P26 and removed the magazine. He examined it, popped the magazine back in with a *click*, then racked the slide. We both holstered our weapons.

"Ready?" I asked.

Koji nodded. He gazed up at the sky. "The sun has almost set—the cover of night will benefit us, but we should not linger."

We approached the alley entrance. I checked around one corner, and Koji the other. Honking cars sounded in the distance, but there was no one around. Koji waved for me to follow.

Keeping close to the factory's mold-speckled walls, we snuck along the rundown street. There were several empty lots, filled with naked shrubs and sheets of snow. Most of the buildings here were worn-down warehouses, boarded-up businesses overgrown with fungi, and crumbling mounds of mycelium-infested mycobricks.

There wasn't a soul in sight in this frigid wasteland.

I couldn't understand why the gangs would fight over Riverside—

only in Neo Kinoko would someone gut you for scraps.

"Cross the street," Koji commanded. "Now."

More shooting rang out. Farther up the road, I saw the flare of muzzle fire coming from windows in two opposing buildings. Gangsters unloaded upon one another, shouting incoherently in Hōpponese.

We left the skirmish behind. Passing through a series of cramped corridors, we exited onto a parallel street. Half of a tower block had been leveled by bombs. All that remained was a collapsed husk of rubble strewn across the road.

"It is not much farther," Koji said, stealing a glance in my direction.

We approached Buta Meats from the west. It was a long, squat structure. Bullet holes riddled its brick walls, and mycelial webs stretched across the front windows and entrance.

Next to the slaughterhouse was an abandoned property, now an overgrown field blanketed in white. I noticed an animal lot behind Buta Meats. It was fenced off, but sections were broken or missing—no animals had been here for years.

"Let's check the perimeter," I whispered.

We rushed across patches of icy snow toward the main entrance. Dogs barked close by, as if sensing our presence. Koji tore away the mycelium, but the door was locked. No signs of obvious activity. No clear points of entry, either.

"The back," I said.

We made our way around the building. A service entrance on the side was also locked. Continuing toward the back, we came across a small loading bay—it wasn't even spacious enough for trucks to enter. Clearly this was a pre-war business, when Neo Kinokans were dealing with horses and carts.

A brick wall bordered the loading bay, its middle section destroyed. Just beyond the opening, a broad snow-filled cavity had been carved into the earth by an artillery shell.

Koji tapped my back and pointed to the rear of the slaughterhouse.

"There."

A doorway.

I tried to open it, but it was rusted shut. Koji attempted and failed, as well. Above the door was a broken window. Glass shards clung to its frame.

"Do you think you could fit through?" Koji asked.

Bloody Hell.

The window was wider than my shoulders, but I wasn't eager to climb up. Still, we didn't have many options.

I unfurled Koji's scarf, wrapping it around my fist. "Boost me."

Koji cupped his hands and squatted. I placed a boot on his palms, my knee popping as it bent. He heaved me upward, until my face was level with the window. Using the scarf, I knocked the glass free, then pulled myself through.

I floundered, trying to turn myself around. In an awkward motion, I spun and landed on my feet—my arms ached from the effort. I shouldered the door until it budged, cringing at all the noise I was making.

Son of a bitch … If anyone was here, they would've heard that.

Koji unholstered his gun and took out his flashlight. I did the same. We flicked our lights on and entered. The sun was already setting, and without windows the room was consumed by darkness. It was fucking freezing, too. The beam from my flashlight pierced the shadows as I swept across the space.

It was a locker room.

Mold and mycelium coated most every surface, and the air stank of decaying wood. Filaments trailed through stagnant puddles. Against one wall, rotten cubbies provided pulp for a colony of orange antler-like fungi. Decomposing mycoleather boots lined another wall, consumed by fuzzy patches of green mold.

"I sense nothing here," Koji muttered.

What the Hell did that mean?

We crossed the room, toward an open door. To the right, a communal shower was overrun with blooms of white fungal threads. They crawled from drains and shower heads, creeping across the tiles in thick bundles.

Koji waved me through, into a long corridor. There was only one way forward. I took each step with tact, sweeping the space with my light. But the pervasive silence penetrated my mind, unsettling me.

There was a door to my left.

"Nameko, cover me." I lifted my gun and flashlight, counting down. Three. Two. One.

Sweeping around the corner, I checked left, then right. No contacts. It was an office space, with a flat mushroom desk that had sprouted younger fruiting bodies around its stem. Polypore shelves lined the walls, their caps tattooed with dust.

I noticed something on the desk: A plaque of some sort, made from mycelium. Several moldy logograms grew from it.

"Nameko," I whispered. "What does this say?"

Koji neared the plaque. "Owner." He paused. "Nikuya Bue."

The name from the property record. But Nikuya …. That family name rang a bell.

"Yuki," Koji said in a hushed tone.

"Fuck me …" Sea Dragon Seafood Co. I scratched the back of my head and … held my breath.

A mold-cushion bed was in the corner, budding from the floor. Filthy mycofiber blankets were strewn about, and a dirty patchwork doll lay discarded next to the bed.

It looked as if a child had been here.

"Hofmann …"

A chain clinked in Koji's quaking hand, as if reliving the experiences he'd witnessed in the morgue. In the other, he held a shackle. The chain ran along the floor until it reached a hook drilled into the wall. My heart clenched. A child had been here—chained and imprisoned. I clenched my gun and flashlight. What kind of fucking monster would do this?

"We should proceed," Koji suggested.

"Yeah …" I inhaled, trapping the air in my lungs. After a few seconds, I exhaled. "You're right. Let's keep going."

We proceeded down the hallway. Another office, followed by an open room on the left. Mushroom stools and tables occupied one side of the space, with a mycelium kitchenette on the other. Coils of blue CPAN-issued rope were stacked in one corner.

"It is a lunch area," Koji said.

I shone my flashlight on the kitchenette—edible mushroom colonies rose from its threadlike countertops. I opened cabinets but found nothing of note. A subtle smell like the sea began to seep into my nostrils.

Searching frantically, I came across salted fish stashed inside a cupboard—there were dozens of them, all wrapped in cloth.

"What the Hell?"

Koji came over and ran his fingers along their dehydrated spines. The heads had been removed, leaving only the bodies and tails. "The smell of fish on someone's breath."

All of a sudden, dogs barked and snarled close by. Their cries resounded through the hallway—they were *inside* the slaughterhouse. A high-pitched scream came right after, piercing my eardrums.

I turned to Koji. He stood motionless, his eyes twitching. He squeezed them shut, holding his cap as his gills vibrated violently. "The child is alive …," he murmured. "I sense them."

Another scream echoed, followed by reverberating sobs and canine howls.

I bolted from the room, leaving Koji behind—there was no time to lose. I rounded a corner at the end of the hall, straight into a space devoid of illumination. A foul stench invaded my senses. I gagged on a combination of decayed flesh, sour milk, and ammonia.

More pained shrieks.

I shined my light in every direction, trying desperately to find the source of the anguished cries. Three sets of chain tracks trailed along the ceiling, with dozens upon dozens of large oxidized hooks hanging from them. Flies choked the air and the carrion stench of rotten meat was suffocating—at least fifteen or twenty putrid pig carcasses were still snared, suspended by their decomposed legs. Chunks had fallen off, littering the floor, where cockroaches and insects nibbled at the flesh.

Yet another scream. More barks.

My feet splashed on wet concrete floor as I ran. I glanced down, horrified to realize that the puddles were a dark shade of crimson. Looking back up, I noticed chunks of fresher meat hanging from several of the hooks. Flies swarmed and buzzed, feasting on the remains of …

I didn't even want to think about it. My mind reeled and my heart raced. Where the Hell was Koji?

Far across the killing floor, I saw a faint glow around the fringes of a door. I turned off my flashlight and stepped toward it. As the darkness returned, bioluminescent mushrooms began to pulsate. They colonized half of the room, burgeoning in the damp crevices and devouring the rancid remains of swine. The fungi twitched in reaction to my movements.

I slowed down, inching closer. I heard faint whimpers, a muffled voice, and guttural growls. Closer. A man hummed a tune, his deep tone accompanied by strange tinny sounds. Closer. I raised my gun, switching off the safety. Closer.

The dogs barked and snarled.

Up ahead was a sliding metal door covered with rust and scratches. It was slightly ajar and lit up my path. I rushed to the wall next to it, pressing my shoulder against cold mycocrete. An overpowering odor of copper struck me. Its taste clung to my tongue and throat. Peeking through the gap—

I gasped.

The bleeding room was soiled with brownish-red stains. Dried blood was splattered on the walls, caked into the slanted floor. A drain stretched across the far end. Its metal grates had been stained crimson from all the ichor it had collected.

And then I saw him.

The gillie had his back to me, but I recognized the cracked, warped cap. He turned, revealing the same beady stare with a mole underneath the right eye, the puffy lips that moved as he hummed, and the elongated hand.

It was the man from Reishi Temple.

He stepped toward a rolling cart, putting his victim on full display: A fungal girl. She hung upside down by chains in the middle of the space. She writhed and screeched, too little to be any older than six or seven. Her wails filled every corner of the bleeding room … and my mind.

Two mutts were tied up in the corner, their hackles and fungi-tipped tails raised. Blue ropes wrapped around their napes, tugging at the stiff fruiting bodies that sprouted through their caramel coats. They choked themselves with the bonds, knowing I was close.

With the element of surprise gone, I drove the door open. Its wheels grated as I pushed and pushed. I rushed into the room when the door finally gave way.

"NKPD!" I shouted, training my pistol on the killer's cap. Then in Hōpponese: "Under arrest. Hands up!"

The dogs jumped and snapped at me with slobbery muzzles full of sharp fangs. Only their leashes kept them at bay.

"Down," the killer said softly in his language.

In an instant, the hounds sat, their whines strained. The killer then caressed the girl's grimy face with his deformed hand. With the other—his normal hand—he stuffed a dirty ball of fabric into her mouth. He brushed his fingers across a mycoleather apron before picking up a glistening bone saw.

"Drop it," I ordered in Coprinian, the translation escaping me.

The girl caught sight of the instrument and threshed. Her restraints rattled. The killer snatched her by the wrist. He ignored me, pressing the saw's jagged teeth into the pallid skin of the victim's forearm.

"Drop it, *now*!" I roared.

The killer relented. He planted the bone saw on the top tray of the cart, next to an array of tools laid out atop a leather roll. Casually lilting his head, his unkempt hair flopped beneath his gills. He turned to face me. Despite the brightness of his yellow irises, beyond that was emptiness.

The sporesack's face stretched in a rictus, a disturbing expression that thinned his upper lip. In accented Coprinian, he said, "I knew someone would come."

CORNERED

- - - - - - - - -

WALK AWAY FROM the girl!" I demanded in Coprinian. I gestured to his cart. "Push it aside, then put your hands behind your head."

The killer obliged, that creepy smile still plastered on his pudgy face. With his blood-stained boot, he nudged the cart toward the wall. He didn't move—his demeanor was one of unsettling calm, like a predator sussing out its prey's weaknesses.

The dogs growled in the corner, putting me on edge. The girl continued to scream through her gag, and her inverted head was flushed with the extra flow of blood.

"Turn around," I said. "What is your name?"

"Tsutomu," he replied, his back now to me. His hands were beneath his gnarled cap, caressing his mess of moldy black hair.

"Do you think this is a Goddamn game?" I hissed. Taking out my handcuffs, I approached him. "Do. Not. Move." I holstered my pistol and snapped one cuff around Tsutomu's good wrist. As I went for his deformed hand, it slipped from my grasp. With surprising speed, he reached into his apron and whipped out a scalpel.

I stepped backward just as Tsutomu spun, attempting to slash my throat. The scalpel ripped through the air, inches from my skin. He lunged and slashed again. Once, twice. He swung his other wrist, using the handcuff as a flail. I felt a faint gust as the cuff tore past my nose.

Tsutomu recalibrated, adjusting his meager weight and gauging me.

The sick bastard's expression never faltered—his smile was all the more sinister with a deadly weapon in hand.

Wary, I took a few steps back, out into the foul-smelling black of the killing floor. I drew out my gun and took aim. Out of the corner of my eye, I glimpsed a shape scurrying through the shadows.

The killer laughed—a mirthless, throaty sound. He pressed the blade to the girl's throat. Her face bulged in fear. "Are you sure you want to do that? It would be a shame for another child to die by my blade."

Koji tiptoed toward the bleeding room. He looked at me, ready to pounce.

I shook my head side-to-side, as imperceptibly as I could. "That is the last thing I want." Beads of sweat rolled down my back, watching Tsutomu playfully nick the girl's flesh. "So, let's talk."

I had to lure Tsutomu out and give Koji a chance to take him down.

"You would like to talk?" Tsutomu snickered, his smile disappearing. The dogs' low growls became more intense, their hackles heightened again. "I can sense your friend out there."

Shit.

"The girl will die," Tsutomu said with surety, "and then I will kill myself. Or, you could do it for me." He pitched his misshapen cap from side to side, running the flat of the scalpel along the girl's jaw.

I took a step forward. "Don't play coy with me." While Tsutomu was distracted with the victim, Koji's eyes met mine. I twiddled three fingers beneath the grip of my gun and mouthed, *On three.* He caught the motion and nodded. "You've done enough harm, Tsutomu, so just let her go."

"Now, now …" Tsutomu's lifeless stare returned to me. He touched a spindly finger to his button nose. "I realize, I do not know your name."

"Henrietta Hofmann," I said, taking another step. I curled one finger—two remaining. "NKPD Homicide division."

Tsutomu raised both hands. His disfigured hand clapped the palm of the other, the scalpel still in his grip. "Well, congratulations are in order, are they not? But please, detective, do not come any closer."

"Thank you for the applause," I mocked. Second finger—one remaining. "If I'm honest, you had us running in circles for almost two days."

"Well, I cannot take *all* the credit." Tsutomu's grin returned. He held the scalpel up. "But I am not one to divulge the secrets of others."

Third finger.

He thrust the scalpel at the hanging girl. At that same moment, I fired. His hand exploded in a spray of bones and muscle tissue. The blade clanged on the floor, Tsutomu howling at the loss of his functional appendage. Koji burst around the corner into the bleeding room, his teeth bared. He enveloped the killer, trapping his arms and neck in a submission hold.

Koji forced Tsutomu to his knees. "Hofmann, handcuffs."

I rushed over and cuffed the murderous molder, the top half of his right hand now gone. The dogs went wild, their teeth clacking as they snapped at us. Tsutomu looked up at me, grinning and breathing heavily—he reeked of sour fish.

"Stand," I ordered.

Koji lifted Tsutomu off the ground. The killer began to hum again—fucking cocky bastard. I flipped my pistol around and clubbed him in the temple with the corner of the grip.

"Hofmann!" Koji scolded. He supported Tsutomu's unconscious body as it slithered to the floor. "Why did you do that?"

I holstered my gun. "I'd had enough of his bullshit. We need him alive and in the interrogation room, as soon as possible."

Koji flared his nostrils, puffs of inky spores flowing from his gills. "Check on the girl."

I shrugged off Koji's judgmental tone. The girl's eyes were lethargic from the blood pooling in her head. The dogs kept barking—too close for comfort but still restrained—as I cranked the chain gear and lowered her to the floor. Removing my jacket, I placed it beneath her neck, then unwrapped the chains around her frail torso and legs. The saw had cut her forearm, but the wound was shallow and had already clotted.

"Her presence in the fungalnet is fading," Koji noted, examining Tsutomu's vitals. "How is her pulse?"

The girl was limp, but still breathing. "Her heartbeat is slow," I said. "She'll pull through."

Seeing her up close, I recognized her face from the Missing Persons case files. She had a delicate pink cap, a teardrop face, thin lips, and round ears. Satsuki Haru—that was her name.

I let out a long-held sigh. Satsuki had survived Tsutomu's torture. Death had knocked at her door, but she'd avoided that terrible fate.

Memories of Liz resurfaced. The look on her face when she realized she was dying was seared into my mind. I winced. I'd forced her end upon her, and no matter what I said … Words would never suffice. No person should ever face their end so young …

I sniffled and held back tears.

Satsuki was alive—that's what mattered now. We caught the murderer, and he wouldn't be harming anyone ever again.

But something Tsutomu said troubled me: *I cannot take* all *the credit.* He hadn't done this on his own. Could there be someone else? Something bigger at play?

Koji came to my side. He planted a palm on the girl's cap: "Mother Chikyu, protect this young spirit as she hangs in the balance between our world and The Great Beyond."

I glanced at the dogs. Their defensive rage had subsided—they were on their stomachs, paws out, whimpering while fixated upon Tsutomu. Their master.

"What shall we do with the hounds?" Koji asked.

"Leave them," I said dispassionately. "The moment we take their leads off, they'll attack us." It was a harsh truth. There was a slim chance a forensics team and a cleanup crew could make it out here—if they were willing to risk the gangs.

But Koji wasn't having it. He approached the animals, one hand out and gills respiring. Shutting his eyes, he neared them. They sniffed at him, cautious of the stranger getting too close.

Inch by inch, he neared the canines. The fungi on their necks and tails twitched, but their overall body language was calm. He was within a hair's breadth of their muzzles. Simultaneously, he stroked each dog on the snout. He trailed his hands down their napes until his fingers touched their fruiting bodies. Mycelium extended from Koji's fingernails, wrapping around the stems.

All of a sudden, the dogs' eyes rolled back and their bodies convulsed. After a moment, they came back to. They lolled their tongues, nuzzling against Koji. He scratched behind their ears, removing the ropes one by one before nudging the dogs out of the bleeding room.

"Be free," Koji whispered to them. They took off, disappearing into the dark.

Koji stood and scowled at me. He went to Tsutomu, removing a small first aid kit from his jacket. With mycelial dressings, he began to bandage Tsutomu's mangled hand.

"Happy now?" I chided. I scooped Satsuki up, rising to my feet with her cheek pressed against my chest. Draping my trench coat over her tiny frame, I tucked the edges underneath her feet and legs. Her head rolled to the side and exposed her neck. There, carved into the skin atop her jugular, was a small rose tattoo.

My mind fluttered through recollections: The victim on Spirit Island, a patch of skin missing. The child at Reishi Temple, covering his neck. And gangsters, with roses tattooed on their chests.

Kinoko Rose.

"Nameko, we have to go," I said. "You carry Tsutomu. Let's get the Hell out of Riverside."

— — — — — —

I LAID SATSUKI in the passenger seat. She was fast asleep, so I buckled her in and propped her head up with my coat. Unfortunately, Tsutomu had woken up and was giving Koji a hard time.

"Tsutomu, please cooperate," Koji said, struggling to get the gillie killer to sit his ass down.

"Do you want to me hit you on the bloody head again?" I called to Tsutomu.

Tsutomu spat on the dividing window between the front and back seats. "*Bakira gaikamu*!" He waved his bloody, bandaged hand at me. "What else are you willing to subject me to?'

I rapped a knuckle on the glass and grinned. "It's not the first time someone has called me 'dirty foreign scum.' How about we play a game? Let's see what other imaginative obscenities you can come up with, and I'll think of more ways to give you a taste of your own medicine."

Tsutomu banged his knees against the divider. Koji held Tsutomu down, urging him to stop, but the two froze mid-grapple.

I squinted my eyes, observing the strange occurrence. "What is happening? Nameko—"

"Step out of the car, Hofmann," a voice called out in Coprinian. "You, too, Officer Nameko."

I ducked out of the passenger seat and closed the door. Koji left Tsutomu alone in the back of the Metro.

Goddamnit …

More than a dozen gillie gangsters filled the alleyway entrance, their guns pointed at us. Sumi and Dikku stood at the front of the colony, arms crossed and looking far too pleased. They all wore colorful suits and open-collared shirts, a ridiculous contrast to our destitute surroundings.

They bloody well had us cornered, though.

"Good to see you again, *detective*," Dikku sneered, flashing his golden teeth.

"How's your Derby?" I asked.

Dikku glowered at me. "*Shabi*, I'll rip your—"

"That is enough." Sumi stepped forward, staring inside the Metro. "Return Tsutomu and the girl to us and you are free to leave. Unharmed."

"Sumi, Dikku. It's an honor to properly make your acquaintance," I deflected. "Ryo told me so much about you."

Dikku cracked his bulging knuckles. "Where is my sister?"

"Gone," I said.

"Oh, Ryo," Sumi mused. "Her betrayal was … disappointing. But we will find her, and she will receive a fitting punishment." Sumi's Coprinian had the cadence of Hōpponese, but he spoke eloquently. Even when he was talking about retribution against Ryo. "Now, enough stalling. I will not repeat my request again—hand over Tsutomu and the girl."

"I am afraid we cannot do that," Koji replied. Black spores began to trickle from beneath his cap. "I sense your intentions—they betray your words."

They weren't going to let us leave here alive.

Sumi ground his polished mycoleather shoes into the snow. "What a pity." He smoothed some wrinkles on his blue pinstripe suit. "What a pity that you two officers are being so uncooperative, but I am afraid your investigation is at an end. The girl will return to Tsutomu's capable care, so that he may continue his work."

"Work …," I scoffed. "You call killing kids 'work?' And with the rose tattoos on their necks, wouldn't that mean they *work* for you?"

Sumi tensed. He flexed his jaw muscles.

"They know too much," Dikku said in a gravelly growl.

"Indeed, they do," Sumi agreed. He clasped his hands together. "A shame, then, that we will have to kill you both."

"Killing us will not solve anything," Koji piped up in Hōpponese. "The NKPD knows we are here, and they will come after you. They will find your distilleries and end your paltry operation. They will arrest each of you for the murder of two officers and the children."

"Where is the evidence, officer?" Sumi took out brass knuckles and slipped them onto his fingers. "You overestimate the power that the police have in this city. Still, I appreciate your attempt to rile me up. Tell me, how is Hana? I was saddened to hear of your uncle's passing—Shika-ku-*jero* was especially heartbroken."

With a snarl, Koji lunged forward. I rounded the car and caught him in a hug, forcing him to stay back.

"Don't play their games," I warned Koji. I turned to Sumi. "Why do all this? Why kill the children?"

Dikku chuckled, his thick neck throbbing with each guttural laugh. "It's hard to move up in the world, detective." His Coprinian was harsh and stilted.

"My *jiujiu* is correct," Sumi said. "When certain barriers stand in your way, the only options are to turn around, defeated, or break it down." He looked at his fingernails, as if the conversation bored him. "Kinoko Rose has shown us its limits. Its lack of foresight. Dikku and I are planning for a future in this brave new world we call home. Change awaits Neo Kinoko."

A wave of confusion washed over my brain. "You two aren't the leaders of Kinoko Rose?"

Sumi laughed. "Who you see before you are The Stem"—he nodded his chin toward Dikku, then he pounded his own chest with a fist—"and The Veil. Kinoko Rose is far more than you know, detective. But enough of this. Dikku, take care of them."

In a blur, Dikku pulled out a silver-plated pistol and fired twice.

Boom.

BOOM.

I was still alive. Koji was next to me, unscathed.

Two gangsters had crumpled to the ground. Their heads lay at weird angles from the bulk of their mushroom caps. Blood poured from wounds in their foreheads, staining the snow red.

The next moment, chaos broke out. Gunfire rang through the alley. Bright muzzle flashes burst from Kinoko Rose weapons. Two more gangster gillies went down, sprays of spores and gore erupting from their caps and bodies. Sumi and Dikku ran to the alley walls for cover, barking orders at their remaining crew.

"Who's shootin' at us?" one gangster yelled.

"Gray Cap Gang!" another gangster shouted in return. "They're after The Veil and The Stem!"

Too many fucking gangs, too little time.

The assault tore the gangsters' attention away from us. Koji and I had to get out of here, with both Satsuki *and* Tsutomu.

"Nameko," I commanded, "get in the car."

Bullets tore past as I hurried to the driver's side. I opened the door and threw myself into the seat. Koji got in the back, holding Tsutomu down as the murdering bastard blubbered incoherently. Satsuki woke up, startled and screeching.

"Get down!" I warned the others. Koji, Satsuki, and Tsutomu all ducked.

The instant I fired up the engine, the windshield cracked, a hole appearing in its center. The shot had ripped through the divider and embedded into the back seat between Koji and Tsutomu. I put the car in reverse and revved the engine.

"What is going on?" Satsuki cried.

"Kinoko Rose," I told her. "We'll get you out here."

Ahead of us, Dikku's hulking form took up a quarter of the alley's width. Sumi was pressed against the wall. He saw me and snarled, sparks showering off the walls around him where stray bullets ricocheted. More Kinoko Rose gangsters fell to the Gray Caps' assault.

I slammed my foot on the pedal. The Metro lurched backwards, ripping down the alley. All of a sudden, more fungal gangsters appeared, blocking the rear exit. Gray Caps. They opened fire on us, bullets thunking into the car's metal exterior.

There was only one way out for us: Forward.

I shifted into first and floored it, heading straight for Sumi, Dikku, and their gangster goons. Sprays of gunfire peppered the Metro. One shot took out a sideview mirror. Another punctured the windshield and lodged itself in the dashboard.

Dikku didn't move from the middle of the alley, but I sped up regardless. I clipped one gangster in the hip with the front corner of the car. He spun to the side, screaming in agony. Dikku took aim again, but I plowed right into him. The enormous fungal rolled onto the hood and into the windshield—cracks snaked across the glass.

I drifted out onto the street, flinging Dikku through the air. He tumbled into a mycobrick wall, getting up within a matter of seconds, as if he hadn't just been hit by a fucking car.

Three more bullets struck the car. One whizzed past my ear, tearing away a layer of skin. I watched Dikku shrink in the rearview mirror. Blessing God that we'd made it out in one piece, I flew down the snow-packed street.

I pressed play on the tape deck, turning up the volume on "Grave Endings" by Virdi. Its ghostly guitars thrummed along an ethereal, harmonic soundscape. Visibility was shit, but the music helped me focus.

"Everyone alright?" I asked.

"Tsutomu and I are fine," Koji said.

"Help ... me ..."

I turned to Satsuki. She was slumped in her seat, blood blossoming from her upper chest. She was bleeding out before my eyes, just like Elisabeth had all those years ago ... I had to get her out of Riverside and to a hospital. "Nameko!" I called out. "Radio the nearest precinct. Tell them we have a child in need of medical assistance."

I caught Tsutomu in the rearview mirror—his horrible smile had returned. We had to get that piece of shit into custody and out of Kinoko Rose's grasp. Then, it would be time for an interrogation.

So many pieces had been laid atop the table, but it was still unclear how they all fit together. I reached out to Satsuki and put pressure on her gunshot wound. She howled and bawled.

"Stay with us," I told her.

MINDHUNTER

[26] Case File #42-56
NKPD Central Precinct | 7:33 p.m.

- - - - - - - - -

POUNDED MY fist on the interrogation room table, rattling Tsutomu's handcuffs. "Satsuki almost died getting your worthless ass out of Riverside," I hissed, "so *talk*!"

Tsutomu sat back in his chair, his expression impassive. He stroked the wrappings of his ruined hand with the spindly fingers of the other. "The injury she sustained was due to your incompetence and lack of foresight."

Koji leaned against a white padded wall. His arms were crossed and one eyebrow was cocked. "Says the man who was preparing to dismember her."

"That is beside the point," Tsutomu said. "You ask me to spill all my secrets, but did you truly expect it would be so simple?"

I massaged the bridge of my nose. "Either way, you're going to jail for a long time, so why not do some bloody good and tell us what we want to know?"

"Honor, detective." Tsutomu's puffed lips puckered, like he'd eaten something sour. "You may not understand it, your culture being as dishonorable as it is. But for our people, honor is a code bound by blood and spores."

"Your actions taint our codes of honor," Koji said. "Do you believe killing *children* was an honorable act?"

"I did not do it for myself," Tsutomu admitted.

I placed my palms on the table and leaned closer to Tsutomu. "That's hard to believe. I saw the way you appraised Satsuki, like an object for your own sick fantasies. I saw you at Reishi Temple, too, watching that little boy."

"War altered me, awakening dark urges that I had previously suppressed." Tsutomu's lazy gaze drifted around the room, as if he were daydreaming. "But those desires are not what compel my actions. Those children have their purposes, alive or dead. Understand that there are events bigger than I on the horizon. I have simply sacrificed my own morality for the betterment of Neo Kinoko."

I burst from my seat. Its feet scraped along the concrete floor. Reaching across the table, I seized the murderous prick by the collar of his gray prison jumper. "Oh, how righteous of you! And what would this noble endeavor be, exactly?"

Tsutomu's rictus returned. His small eyes scrutinized Koji and me. "Change is afoot."

I laughed. "Change is *always* afoot—that's how the Goddamned world works."

"And it does not justify what you did," Koji added.

Tsutomu inched closer to me. His cap almost grazed my forehead, and his breath still stank of salted fish. "That remains to be seen."

A subtle beep sounded from a speaker on the ceiling.

I let go of Tsutomu's collar and glanced at the one-way mirror to my right. Captain Ridgeway was on the other side, observing us. "Nameko, with me."

As we approached the door, Tsutomu called out: "The fruiting bodies of our labor will soon sprout. All that will be left to decide is which side to choose."

Koji and I left Tsutomu alone, heading into the dim, concrete observation room. There was a small table in there, where audio and video recorders were set up. Ridgeway drummed his fingers on the plastic surface.

"Your tactics aren't working," Ridgeway commented, still watching

Tsutomu through the glass. He coughed into the crook of his elbow.

The foul gillie sat there beaming. He side-eyed the mirror and waved with his disfigured hand, the fingers moving like the claws of a supernatural creature.

I grimaced. "It doesn't help that Koji has no clue what 'good cop, bad cop' means."

"That's not his Goddamned fault," Ridgeway sniped. "He is trained in … other forms of interrogation. Ones that don't involve partners."

I looked at Koji, then Ridgeway. Koji bowed his head in subservience. "What the Hell does that mean?"

Ridgeway turned to me. "You'll find out." He went over to Koji and whispered something in his ear. "Hofmann, I'm not convinced your more traditional approach will get anything of value out of Tsutomu. You'll stay here, while Koji handles things his way."

"*His way?*" I said, shaking my finger at Ridgeway. "I've been a cop for over twenty bloody years. What fucking experience does Nameko have that he can crack this killer on his own?"

"Observe." He snapped his fingers and Koji left the room.

"But captain—" I stopped myself, a chilling memory coming back to haunt me: The morgue. Koji, invading that child's brain. And Jeremy, allowing it to happen.

No … Ridgeway couldn't …

Koji entered the interrogation room. He stood behind Tsutomu, his face unemotional—but I could see the quivering conflict in his eyes.

In a blur of motion, Koji clutched the killer's deformed cap with outstretched hands. He dug his fingers into fungal flesh, causing Tsutomu's eyes to bulge. The killer wailed, a piercing cry that penetrated the mirror. Mycelial strands grew from Koji's veins and fingers, crawling out of his skin with the litheness of a snake.

"No … no … no …," Tsutomu begged, strings of saliva stretching between his lips.

I was horrified. "Captain, please … Don't make him do this."

It was just like the autopsy, and Ridgeway wanted it to happen. How many fucking times had he done this? And why was Koji going along with it?

"Watch, Hofmann. Your new partner is a natural," Ridgeway said, like a proud parent seeing their kid win an award. "What these fungals are capable of, it's miraculous."

But I wasn't proud—I was disgusted.

In the interrogation room, Koji's filaments burrowed into Tsutomu's cap. The mycelium crawled between his gills. They continued, wriggling down the killer's face, entering into his eyes, nose, and mouth. In a matter of seconds, Tsutomu's entire head was blanketed in a bloom of fine white fronds.

Tsutomu screamed hoarse, the sound muted by his mycelial cocoon. Vomit rose up in my throat. Coming face-to-face with the dead was something I'd become accustomed to as a cop, but this …

This was depraved. Unholy.

I couldn't watch it any longer. Not Koji's pained look. Not Ridgeway's delighted smile. I had to stop it.

Without thinking, I ran to the door and swung it open. Ridgeway yelled, but my ears blocked out anything that manipulative bastard had to say. I burst into the interrogation room.

Dear God …

Koji's eyes had rolled up, revealing whites welling with tears. His lips moved but no sound came out. Tsutomu twitched in his seat, his cuffs clattering on the table. I hurried to Koji, trying to tear him away. The mycelium tugged at Tsutomu's head, but the strength of the invasive connection was uncompromising.

The speaker beeped and Ridgeway's voice roared through: "Hofmann, get out of there!"

"No!" I bellowed.

I wouldn't let Koji debase himself with this wretched act. To cater to the whims of his cruel superiors.

Again and again, I wrenched his torso. He wouldn't budge. With each tasking breath, my nose and throat were smothered with cloying scents of sweat, mulch, and must.

"Hofmann, *leave, now*!" Ridgeway warned.

In an instant, the air was sucked from the room. Silence.

A powerful pressure squeezed my brain as the atmosphere rushed back. Koji arced his spine and I was thrown backward. I scurried to the far wall on hands and feet, witnessing streams of spores pour forth from Koji and Tsutomu's throbbing gills—pale from the former, ink black from the latter.

The cramped space flooded with a contrasting swirl of particles. The black-and-white tempest quickened. I shielded my face with my sweater, but the minute molecules swept under my clothing, brushing against my skin. The spores flew into my orifices. I blinked furiously, terrified that now was when my true colonization would begin … Or was I just imagining the threat they posed? Was infection even possible?

Quiet.

No movement. No sensations. Time and space, together in stillness. I pulled down my sweater: A thick soup of spores was suspended in the air like a galaxy, with Koji and Tsutomu at the core.

A few seconds passed. The spores began to emit a faint bioluminescent glow. The green glow flickered, brightening with each heartbeat. Soon enough, the room was bathed in organic illumination.

Koji spoke: "TSUTOMU." His voice took on a frightening omnipresence, as if each spore were an amplifier. "I call upon Kala, The Timekeeper, Goddess of Time and the Unseen, to reveal the hidden truths in your mind. When I ask, *you will speak*!"

As soon as the last word was uttered, reality twisted.

The galaxy of spores churned—a relentless swarm that shifted my perception of space. I felt like I was drowning, choking on liquid spores that flowed through my nostrils and down my throat. A humming chant rose up beneath the hissing cyclone. It thrummed, the bioluminescence matching the song's rhythm.

I stood, enthralled. My body moved of its own accord, step after step into the maelstrom, toward Koji and Tsutomu. Before my conscious mind could register my actions, I placed my right hand atop Koji's.

Then I was gone.

Surrounding me was a black so pure, I was unable to see my own shape. The inky environs began to writhe with living shadows. Distant mycelial blooms and mushroom colonies the size of mountains passed in and out of my vision.

Was I hallucinating? What the fuck was happening?

A vivid scene took shape before me. Inside a rice paddy, a small fungal boy stood up to his knees in water. He cut rice shoots with a curved blade, collecting them in a mycelium basket strapped to his back. In the distance, the slopes of a snow-capped volcano stood out against pink sunset hues.

The boy's familiar face drooped. Despite the sublime landscape, he appeared lonely and despondent. I startled as he looked up, our eyes meeting. Recognition set in.

Koji.

The scene disintegrated, particles swirling until they began to take shape again. A car drove along a road. The forest backdrop came and went, as if in a film, but the car remained constant.

That was the road to my mum and dad's home, just outside of Morellum. And that was *my* car—the silver Benton M4 that I had until …

In my mind, I wanted anything but to be inside that vehicle. The hallucinatory replay reacted to my thoughts, but did the exact opposite of what I desired. The spore projection came apart and reformed into the tacky faux-wood interior that Frederick had chosen.

The version of me in the hallucination drove, with Elisabeth in the passenger seat. Her pop music played on the radio—a mainstream group of pretty boys called the Backyard Bunch.

"Mum, enough!" Elisabeth cried, as if it were real. I nearly choked hearing her whiny teenage voice again. "I know you've been drinking."

"Bloody Hell …," my projection said. She rubbed her forehead, her eyes looking glassy.

"D'you think I can't smell it on your breath, mum?" Elisabeth looked at me—Henrietta. "When are you ever sober these days?"

"That's none of your fucking business, Liz!" Henrietta snapped. Silence. After a pregnant pause, she glanced at Elisabeth. "I … I—"

"I don't know what's going on with you." Elisabeth sighed, her eyebrows furrowing. "Is it dad? Are you two gonna get divorced?"

"No!" Henrietta panicked. "No … No …"

Watching my past self, how could I have known how to tell her? That my job put me on the frontlines every day. That I faced death when most people only faced discomfort. That being a cop had jaded me, ruined me … desensitized me to the horrors of the world. I couldn't explain it to her then, and I doubt I could do it any better now.

But I knew what came next …

Henrietta turned to Elisabeth and held her hand—she took her eyes off the road for a second too long. The blinding headlights of a truck shot around a sharp curve, crossing into the opposite lane. Henrietta reacted with a jerk of the steering wheel. The speed and the angle sent the M4 careening over the side of the road. It flipped and rolled down an embankment, pieces of metal shearing off and evaporating into spores. The car landed on its roof in a field.

The sense memory was visceral. So real—all the colors and textures exactly as I'd remembered them. The chemical smoke in the car as the electronic systems sparked and melted. The suffocating scent of smoke. How it crept into my throat and made me gasp. Cows mooing nearby and the smell of shit.

I forced my mind to avoid the crash, but I couldn't look away—it was human nature to be drawn to disaster, to bathe in the brutality of our brethren.

Henrietta—*me*—crawled out of the shattered car, bloody and reeking of booze. She walked and stumbled, falling into the grass. With clumsy movements, she dragged herself to the other side of the vehicle. For what felt like minutes, Henrietta pulled at the crushed wreckage of the passenger door until she could pry it open. She dragged Elisabeth out as the car burst into flames.

My Liz …

Her perfect face was torn to shreds, her body pierced with shards of metal and glass. Her heartbeat slowed as blood leaked from her wounds. Her lungs waned with every rasping breath.

And there I was: Henrietta Hofmann, a drunken, miserable excuse for a human being. Broken and unsalvageable. Too drenched in her vices to fully grasp what she had just done—what she was responsible for.

I had taken a *life* by getting behind the wheel. My own daughter …

Rain surged down from the Heavens like the tears of angels. Henrietta ran away from the flaming car, collapsing to her knees across the field. She wept, Elisabeth dying in her arms.

I shrieked, unable to bear the pain of reliving this moment …

Henrietta and Elisabeth whispered to each other, but I couldn't bear to listen. Tears fogged my vision as I looked anywhere but at my despicable self. Across the field, where its edge melded with sentient shadows, stood Koji. He smoked a cigarette and watched an alcohol-soaked mother grieving over the child she herself had killed.

He watched me as I watched *myself.*

"The truth is a bitter pill," Koji said, the sound seeming to come from inside my own head, "but remembering is the first step towards acceptance."

The hallucinatory vision erupted in a cloud of spores. Precise details dimmed like the fallible memories we carried inside us over the course of a lifetime—the pain we hid away, hoping to forget rather than confront.

"I'm sorry, Liz …," I said, feeling wet trails run down my spectral face. "I love you."

Everything went dark. I continued to cry, amidst a flurry of sounds and the whipping sting of spores that glimmered and pulsed. Flashes of memories formed in the void, fluttering before me. Frederick's stricken face when I'd told him Elisabeth was gone. Me signing our divorce papers, a pen in one hand and a half-empty bottle of vodka in the other. The night Frederick and me had fought, my drunken ass taking a verbal argument too far by beating the shit out of him. And a week after that, when he'd come to me with an ultimatum.

"I could have you arrested, Hen," he'd said, "but I'll give you a choice instead. Go to prison on assault charges, or leave Coprinia. For good."

My head pounded with the pressures of past mistakes. Frederick's voice in my head, blaming, blaming, blaming.

All of a sudden, Frederick's face morphed into Tsutomu's. The killer's sickening smile grew larger and larger, until it became a grotesque kaleidoscope that ate itself over and over.

"TSUTOMU!" Koji's voice boomed across the mindscape. "Show me your victims! How many have you killed in cold blood?"

A feeling of fear permeated the air with an oppressive density.

Mycelial strands crept ahead of me, coalescing into fifteen children—boys and girls, fungals and half-breeds. Their forms were so small and fragile. The fungals tilted their mushroom-capped heads, and the half-breeds' fruiting bodies bobbed in their hair. Not one of them could be more than ten- or eleven-years-old.

These kids were mental replicas, built from the memories of the monster who murdered them.

An imitation of the interrogation room took shape in the void, surrounded by the children. Koji sat on one side of a table, and Tsutomu on the other.

"Why did you kill them?" Koji asked in Hōpponese, his voice normal again.

Tsutomu sat there, looking at Koji without uttering a word.

"Do not make me ask again," Koji warned.

No answer.

Koji raised his hands and mycelium surged from the shadows. It stabbed at Tsutomu. The killer tried to move but couldn't, just had to endure the sharp filaments puncturing his body without end.

"Stop!" Tsutomu bawled. "I will … Please, stop … I will talk."

"Speak," Koji said with his hands folded on the tabletop.

Tsutomu's words came through weak and wobbly. His torso was riddled with holes that oozed ichor onto his jumpsuit. "They b-brought them to me."

"*Who?*"

"My c-c-cousin," Tsutomu sputtered. "She came to me with Sumi … and Dikku."

"Who is your cousin?" Koji pressed.

Tsutomu bowed his head. "Nikuya Yuki."

Fucking Hell … Sea Dragon Seafood Co.

"Kinoko Rose p-paid me well, and Yuki g-g-gave me access to the slaughterhouse," Tsutomu said. "At first, I delivered the body parts to her, but something happened. They gave me new instructions for how and where to d-d-dispose of specific parts, and …"

"And?"

"To feed the rest to my dogs …"

Demons. All of them.

"Yet why did they ask you to kill these children," Koji said, gesturing to the kids around the table. "What role did they play in all of this? Why *them?*"

"YES," the children said in unison, "WHY US?"

A pause. The air pulsated with anxiety, shadows vibrating and shrinking. It was like the world was closing in. Finally, Tsutomu answered: "Kinoko Rose call them 'rose-runners'—pushers and messengers. Nobody pays much attention to kids, so they can get into places where others can't. They used them for delivering coded messages and orders. All of it was done by hand, untraceable."

"Why the rose tattoos?"

"They pay the kids a pittance, but still more money than they've ever seen. The rose-runners are sworn to secrecy, separated from their families, and the tattoos are a symbol of their allegiance. It is also Kinoko Rose's way of keeping track of them—like brands on cattle."

I felt Koji's anger roiling around the edges of the mindscape, the shadows trashing in response. "Why then were children sent to you for slaughter?"

Tsutomu sighed. "They became a risk, snitched, or simply outgrew their usefulness. Sumi and Dikku are ruthless. They do not treat betrayal lightly."

"But Sumi and Dikku are not the true leaders of Kinoko Rose," Koji said. "Who is?"

"I do not know," Tsutomu replied.

The mindscape clenched like a fist, a claustrophobic pressure building. Sharp fungal tendrils hovered around Tsutomu, ready to impale him.

Once again, mycelium rose from the dark. Koji's voice enveloped the void: "WHO IS?"

"I do not know! No more … please," Tsutomu pleaded.

"A final question: Why do you kill?"

"It gives me *purpose*." Tsutomu's hair-raising smile returned, stretching his face like an elastic. "I indulge in the ritual. It began when I was a teenager: My first kill was an accident. But it fueled something within me, a beast I have been urged to feed ever since. The Spore War, that was a blessing—it gave me free rein to satiate my … desire. Inconspicuously, without inquiry."

"What desire?"

"To watch the light of life in a person's eyes be extinguished."

I'd experienced that extinguishing so many times … It had broken me down, but with this psychopath, it had built him up.

I couldn't take it anymore, how he spoke so blithely about murder. I pushed my mind to be beside Tsutomu. Instantaneously, I was in front of the twisted gillie. I didn't have hands that I could see, so I imagined throttling his throat—and I did. Shadow hands extended from me and strangled the fucking sporesack.

Next thing I knew, the mindscape fractured. The shadows cracked and came apart in a spiraling cascade of spores. Tsutomu's mind shrieked and laughed and cried, a perverted amalgamation of his pain and pleasure.

The illusion broke.

I was in the interrogation room choking Tsutomu, my real hands crushing his windpipe. Koji's mycelium retracted, revealing Tsutomu's beet red face. The bastard's body twitched, and I lavished in it.

Ridgeway pried me off of Tsutomu. My fingers lost purchase and I fell to the floor, crying, "*Fuck you*! *FUCK YOU!*"

The mycelium slinked back into Koji's skin. The killer was unconscious, his face locked in a look of perpetual suffering. Straggling spores floated in the air, but nothing compared to the maelstrom we'd endured.

I had witnessed the true horrors of what fungals were capable of. What Oze had nearly subjected me to.

"Nameko, get yourself cleaned up," Ridgeway said. Then he hauled me off the ground. "Hofmann! You and I, in my office, *right fucking now*."

ACTIONS & REACTIONS

[27] Case File #42-56
NKPD Central Precinct | 8:18 p.m.

- - - - - - - - -

CAPTAIN RIDGEWAY GROANED and pinched the bridge of his thick nose. He held his tiny glasses in his other hand. "Shit, Hofmann," he muttered under his breath. "You're going to give me a bloody heart attack one of these days."

Outside Ridgeway's office, the bullpen was still bustling—even at this hour. Cops and detectives were drenched in fluorescent lights, clearing their workloads before the Fuyu Lantern Festival preoccupied the whole force.

Windsor glared at me from across the room. I flipped him off. In response he mouthed the words, *Eat mushroom dick.*

It was a poor comeback—mushrooms were starting to grow on me.

"What the fuck were you thinking, going into the interrogation room?" Ridgeway scolded. He put his glasses back on, squinting as he observed me. The hard angles of his face looked even sharper in the dim light of his office. The room stank of stale cigar smoke, and the mold patch on the ceiling seemed larger than it was yesterday.

"Trying to prevent Nameko from doing something he'd regret," I shot back.

Ridgeway scoffed. "Are you so bloody dense that you'd believe that was his first time?"

"Of course not, but I see what it's doing to him." I bit my lower lip. "How long has this been going on?"

"A year," Ridgeway admitted.

A whole Goddamned year. What had that done to Koji's psyche?

Ridgeway coughed. "Give me a moment." He raised a fist to his mouth as it turned into a hacking fit. "Fucking mold."

I took the bottle of anti-fungal meds out of my jacket. After what happened with Koji and Tsutomu, I wondered if it even mattered anymore. If I got infected, so be it. I didn't give a shit anymore—I was already an exile in this country, so why live in constant fear? I threw the bottle in Ridgeway's trash can.

Rising from his chair, the captain went to his liquor cabinet and set out two glasses. He paused, giving me a sidelong glance. With a pinched-mouth expression, he put one glass away.

"So sweet that you remember," I joked.

"Shut the fuck up, Hofmann."

He poured himself a generous helping of caramel-colored whisky— McCallister Reserve, from northern Coprinia. Oak barrel-aged, hints of leather. Its intoxicating peat scent reached out to me from across the room.

I scratched the back of my hand. "Is that why Nameko is the only fungal on the force?" I guessed. "You brought him on as some sort of, what? Experiment?"

Ridgeway took a sip, a meaty mitt clutching the comparatively small whisky tumbler. His face wrinkles creased in satisfaction. "I witnessed firsthand what those bloody gillies could do during the war—it was petrifying. But I also realized how it could be used to our advantage. Humans have never been good at reading each other. In our line of work, that means we're pretty fucking terrible at interrogations."

"But why Nameko? Why choose him?"

"He …" Ridgeway sucked in a breath. "Seven years ago, he killed my entire squad—eight of my brothers and sisters in arms—all on his own. He took us by surprise in the dead of night. I managed to escape, but I never forgot his face … or what he did. I found out everything I could about him—it took years for me to track him down."

"Where did you find him?" I asked.

"On a bloody fishing boat in The Docks, working with his uncle." Ridgeway chuckled, swirling his glass. "War changes a man, but going back to normal life, *that* is a jarring experience. I could see that Nameko still had that Devil inside of him. And I could've killed him, taken my revenge, but I had more … constructive plans in mind." The captain put his drink down on the desktop. "The NKPD needed more innovation, and it still does. So, I gave Nameko a choice: Join the NKPD and do as I ask, or I'd go to Hajimari and pay a visit to his father's rice farm."

I stood so fast my chair fell over. "You blackmailed him into a being a fucking slave, Ridgeway!"

"*Sit down*," Ridgeway insisted. "Causing a bloody scene, you are."

Righting my chair, I took a seat. "He's a good person, and no one should have to endure that kind of trauma—especially not as often as he has … It's not right, captain."

"Oh, but the crime statistics disagree. Hundreds of cases have been solved thanks to evidence Nameko provided."

"He's not fucking *chattel*!"

Ridgeway jabbed a finger at me. "Enough, Hofmann! A couple of days with the molder and now you're the morality police? And with your background—I know everything you did to land your ass here. You're a lowly Goddamned detective in a shit heap of a city, so let it go or keep your opinions to yourself."

"Yes, *sir*." Piece of shit.

I wouldn't let this go. Koji didn't deserve what was happening to him. Somehow, I'd figure out a way to help him.

Ridgeway finished the final dregs of his whisky. "Now, you went and caused a bloody mess in Riverside, *and* you got sucked into Nameko's interrogation—tell me something useful came out of this clusterfuck."

I didn't want to see Ridgeway's Goddamned face anymore, but I still had a case to solve.

Laying a folder in front of Ridgeway, I said, "Kinoko Rose and Sea Dragon Seafood Co."

Ridgeway tapped the folder. "Kinoko Rose, those unsavory spore-sacks. You know, CPAN and the NKPD agreed to let them fight over crappy territory like Riverside and South Pines. That way, gangs like Kinoko Rose and the Gray Caps would focus more on killing each other, such that we wouldn't have to deal with them. If we dig too deep, they'll set their sights set on us."

"But they're planning something big, so we'll have to deal with them sooner or later. We can't just brush this aside."

"What exactly are they planning?" Ridgeway asked, pushing his glasses up his nose.

"At the distillery in Mold Town, I saw maps of Neo Kinoko and Fuyu Temple." I opened the folder, spreading out documents. "They're flooding the city with shine. Add to that, the locations where dead bodies have been found is also where protests and riots have occurred. Tsutomu's involvement confirms that Kinoko Rose is behind those killings—Sumi Washizu and Dikku Waru, specifically."

The captain blew a long breath. "Those two … Why did Sumi and Dikku orchestrate the killings?"

"I don't know," I replied. "They told Tsutomu precisely where to dump the bodies and when. They wanted them to be found, for all of this to be public."

Ridgway scratched his cheek. "But why do that?"

"That's what's eating at me." I massaged my forehead, brushing aside stray hairs. "Sumi and Dikku are running illegal *somake* shine distilleries. Vice is investigating them, but we don't know exactly how many. Sumi said something to us in Riverside that I can't wrap my head around: 'Kinoko Rose has shown us its limits. Its lack of foresight. Change awaits Neo Kinoko.'"

"Well, that's fucking ominous, isn't it?"

"Ominous *and* confusing."

"Confusing doesn't instill me with confidence, Hofmann. The festival is tomorrow and the fungals are putting up quite a fuss. Dead and missing children, food shortages, and all that." Ridgeway planted his bulky hands on his desktop. "I want this case cleaned up and put aside. I gave you two days, and time is ticking."

"I understand. At this point, Sumi and Dikku will be difficult to track down, which is why"—I slid a couple of pages toward Ridgeway—"this is our best lead."

Ridgeway adjusted his glasses, reviewing the papers with zealous concentration. He furrowed his bulbous brow and rolled his hand. "Fill me in, detective. What are the connections here?"

"Bue Nikuya and Yuki Nikuya," I said. "The former is the landowner of Buta Meats, where Tsutomu was killing his victims. A location provided to Tsutomu by Yuki, his cousin."

"And who is Yuki?"

"She's the floor manager at Sea Dragon Seafood Co." I tapped the documents. "The very same business that Tsutomu confessed was dumping bodies offshore for Kinoko Rose."

"You're sure about this?" Ridgeway asked. "Their records came back clean."

"Not true. I found a match for the rope attached to the first victim. The rope came from them—their records prove it."

Ridgeway exhaled, his heavyset body deflating a tad. "Regardless, that alone won't be enough for a conviction. But I suppose you can give Sea Dragon one more shakedown." He opened a drawer and pulled out a sheet of paper. "Your warrant was expedited and accepted. Tenable circumstances, what with MacArthur and the government being up my ass every minute of every day." He placed the warrant in front of me.

"Thank you, captain." I picked it up and stood to leave.

"Hofmann, wait. With Tsutomu in custody, we've got our scapegoat. That will go a long way to placate the hopheads before the festival tomorrow. But try to wrap this thing up tonight."

"I will," I said.

Ridgeway worked his thick jaw. "Good, because tomorrow we'll be all hands on deck. NKPD and CPAN will have officers and soldiers patrolling the festival route, from those bloody big trees in Chaga Park all the way to Fuyu Temple. I expect you to do your part, too."

"Yes, captain." I was about to leave, but lingered above the door handle. "What of Satsuki, the girl from the slaughterhouse?"

Ridgeway leaned back in his chair, cradling his muscular stomach. "MacArthur was pleased about that one. Good news helps to ease tensions."

Deep down, I knew that the bureaucratic machine would only use her as a symbol of hope for the fungals. That the police were hard at work.

But how many murdered children never received the justice they deserved? And how many more were still missing? I'd do whatever I could to bring them some semblance of recognition—or retribution.

"Is Missing Persons looking into the disappeared children, at least?" I asked.

"Resources are tight, but the gears are in motion." Ridgeway leaned forward. "Stay focused on your own bloody case, though."

"Of course. Good night."

"The night isn't over yet." He coughed, then cleared his throat. "Put that warrant to good use, and please, don't fuck this up."

"I won't."

I left Ridgeway's office with a clear sense of purpose and the warrant to back it up. Koji and I were going to net ourselves a sea dragon.

ROTTEN

- - - - - - - - -

A HEAVY HAZE hovered low over The Docks. Koji and I approached Sea Dragon Seafood Co. on foot, our path obscured by the gathering snowstorm. I'd opted for a bulkier jacket—a gut feeling that conditions were going to get worse—as well as Koji's scarf. The bloody thing was coming in handy.

"Nameko, you sure you're warm enough?" I said in Coprinian.

Koji chuckled, puffs of condensation escaping his mouth. "You do not know much about fungal biology, do you? One day, I will teach you a thing or two about it. But I am fine, just ..."

"Tired." I could see how much the interrogation had worn him out.

"Yes," Koji agreed, "What happened with Tsutomu ... Your daughter ..."

"I don't want to talk about it," I barked. I couldn't keep reliving what I'd done to Liz. "I'm sorry, I just ..."

Koji held a breath, then said: "I understand."

The unspoken words hung between us as we made our way through the maze of warehouses. We reached a familiar loading bay. Angled winds blew snow across the dock and into the covered space. Three late shift fungals worked beneath blinding lights, hauling small crates into a delivery truck.

"Our warrant only permits us to search the place," I said. "Right now, we're working with *reasonable suspicion*, so no arrest without probable cause. Got it?"

"Of course, Hofmann-*kato*," Koji replied.

"Oh, so we're colleagues now?" I joked, referring to the honorific. "I may not be so opposed to having you around, but I'm still your senior officer. Follow me."

Crossing the loading bay, the workers took notice of us. Their yellow eyes narrowed in suspicion.

"*Zaowa*, we NKPD," I said in Hōpponese, holding up my badge and the warrant.

Koji jumped in with the more complicated details. "We have authorization to search the premises. Where is Nigikuri Yuki?"

One of the workers stepped forward. He was a thickset button, with bulging forearms and a scarred chunk missing from his funnel-shaped mushroom cap. He raised a bushy black eyebrow, eying my badge with skepticism.

"Yuki's in the back," he said in a voice like a busted car engine. He snorted, something awful churning in the back of his throat. Then he spat at my feet.

"Well, fuck you, too," I said in Coprinian. "Seems there's a standard greeting at this place."

Koji patted my back. "Superstitions run deep."

We took the ramp up to the red door and went inside. I tugged the scarf tighter around my neck. Same as yesterday, the interior of Sea Dragon was bloody freezing. Even more so than the looming storm outside.

The warehouse was mostly empty. Some stragglers stretched their hours, stacking boxes and transferring them to walk-in freezers. A couple of janitors swept and mopped up pools of melted ice and rotten fish guts.

Koji's eyes darted around the space, his gills and the fruiting bodies on his shoulders sensing. We made our way to the far end. While we walked, I pulled out my tape recorder. Rewinding the tape, I checked that everything was in working order. Then I hit record and slipped it back into my jacket.

"Useful strategy," Koji commented.

"Something I picked up back in Coprinia. You never know what people might admit when they think no one is paying attention."

We found Yuki sitting atop wooden pallets, reviewing a clipboard with a pen in hand. She was dressed as sharply as the day before, a slim auburn pantsuit, white dress shirt, and beige heels.

"*Zoawa*, Yuki," I said. "Mind if I sit?"

The dense colony of ivory mushrooms atop her skull flinched at the sound of my voice. She audibly groaned at my presence, then perked up when she saw Koji. They bowed to each other.

"I knew you two would be back," she responded in rough-edged Coprinian. "It is not a free country, but it is *your* country. Please, sit."

I planted my buttocks on the coarse pallet, hoping I wouldn't get a splinter. "I had a feeling you spoke my language."

"It helps to do business with the colonizers when you cater to their laziness. Somehow, learning our language is an affront to some people's sense of pride." Yuki slid the pen under the clipboard's metal clasp. "It helps even more to hear things others assume you do not understand. Now, why are you here?"

Pulling out the warrant, I laid it on her clipboard. She read it over. Her face twisted in my direction so fast I thought her slender neck would snap. An agitated expression brought unwelcome lines to her young appearance.

"What is this?" she hissed. "Why are you *really* here?"

"Buta Meats," Koji said.

Making an educated guess, I added: "Your father's signature is still on the property record. Bue Nigikuri, is that corr—"

Yuki growled and lunged at me. I snagged her by the collar of her stupid suit. Spinning her around, I shoved her face into the cold mycocrete floor.

"That was a dumb move, attacking a police officer." I grabbed a handful of the mushroom stems atop her head and squeezed. Yuki yowled. "I'm willing to let that go, *if* you answer my questions."

"Fuck you … *gaigai* whore," Yuki managed through her squished mouth. She tried to spit at me, but ended up choking on her own saliva.

"You missed." I pulled on her stems. "How about you give us some answers?"

Yuki squirmed in an attempt to escape my grasp, but all she succeeded at was smearing her face in a murky puddle. I drove a knee into her back to keep her still, cuffing her wrists. Some employees came over to see what the noise was about, but Koji flashed his badge and waved them off.

"Are you willing to talk, Yuki?" Koji squatted down next to her. "Or do you prefer to listen while I tell you about your father's slaughterhouse?"

Raising her dripping face out of the puddle, she said, "Get me up … and I … I will cooperate!"

"Good." I lifted her off the floor and threw her toward the pallets. Several of the wooden planks snapped as she fell on top of them. She slumped to the floor brushing off splinters. Her disheveled shirt revealed the edges of a chest tattoo.

"What do you know?" Yuki asked.

I squatted, feeling my knees *pop* in complaint—this Goddamned case had worn me down more than middle age. But Koji and I were on the cusp of completing the puzzle, and Yuki sat before us, ready to provide some clarity.

"Bue owned Buta Meats. Is that right?" I asked.

A pregnant pause. "Yes."

"Wonderful. I'll continue." I inched closer to Yuki, taking in the worry of her angled eyes and golden irises. The way her lips spasmed when I talked. "My partner and I, we paid a visit to your father's business earlier today—lovely place. It's a shame it went under. How'd that happen exactly?"

Yuki readjusted, stretching her legs out. "The war. Like everything in this cursed city, the Spore War tore us apart … My father was killed by Coprinian soldiers. His business crumbled. Our lives crumbled …"

"Is that why you decided to help Kinoko Rose?" Koji asked. "To allow Tsutomu to carry out his cruel acts there?"

Yuki gave a weak smile. "So, you know about them?"

"Your cousin is already in custody, and we know what Kinoko Rose is planning." I leaned forward, close enough to smell the apricot blossom perfume wafting from Yuki's skin. "Question is, what is your role in all this? Are you a member of Kinoko Rose?"

No answer.

"*Are you a member of Kinoko Rose*?" I repeated angrily.

Still, no answer. Yuki's gaze hardened. Frustrated, I tore open the top buttons of her shirt, only to find …

Her skin was inked with a flower, but not a rose. The moldy tattoo depicted five white flower petals surrounding a delicate yellow-capped stamen. The flower's lines fluttered, as if touched by wind.

"It is a Hōpponese snow flower," Yuki said. "That is what I am named after. I got it in honor of my father … after he passed."

"I …" I was wrong—Yuki wasn't part of Kinoko Rose. "Then why was Kinoko Rose using your father's slaughter—"

A gun hammer cocked behind me. "She was acting on my behalf. Now, stand up and uncuff my cousin."

Cousin …

I turned to see Iwashi, hand trembling as he held a revolver to my head. Sweat beaded on his pudgy face, thinning hair, and gills. Wet stains spread under the armpits of his gray dress shirt.

I laughed. "I'm so fucking tired of fungals pointing guns at me today."

"That is enough, Iwashi," Koji said, drawing his SIG P26. "Put it down."

"I am not m-messing around." Iwashi stepped towards me, the barrel of the gun between my eyes. "If you shoot me, Hofmann dies."

"So, it was *you*," I murmured. "Tsutomu is your brother?"

"Y-yes," Iwashi stammered.

I had underestimated him. But my mind reeled with the realization of what he had done. "Why did you help Kinoko Rose?"

"It is simple, is it not?" With his free hand, Iwashi opened the top of his beige button-up shirt. On his chest was a rose tattoo. "We f-fight for the future of our country, and Kinoko Rose has given me b-b-brotherhood. They have given me hope."

"They also pay you handsomely," Yuki sniped.

Koji inched closer to Iwashi. "By dumping dead bodies in the ocean. The bodies of *children*."

"Yes," Iwashi admitted callously, "a-a-and to smuggle shine amongst our products—"

"*And* to offer up your uncle's slaughterhouse as the ritual grounds for murder!" I spat in Iwashi's face. "You sick sporesack. Did either of you ever enter into that place? Did you ever *see* what horrors Tsutomu wrought?"

Nothing but silence from both of them.

"Now, now, d-d-detective." Iwashi wiped the spit from his face. He pressed the gun to my forehead, the cool metal digging into my skin. "Bue's business was going to waste. When it was no longer v-v-viable for us to dump bodies offshore, I offered Warizu-*shen* and Waru-*shen* an … alternative. In exchange for money, of course."

"Iwashi," Yuki pleaded, "please, shut up."

"N-no, *you* shut up!" Iwashi screeched. "Your father left that business to *me*! I started Sea Dragon and gave you a job, with the caveat that you f-f-follow my orders. All that you had to do was supervise the business and *stay quiet*. Without m-m-me, you would be nothing."

I clapped, playing to Iwashi's ego. "You've played the game ever so well—I'm honestly quite impressed. What I still don't understand is, why did those fishermen have to die?"

I could see a twinkle of pride in Iwashi's eyes. "They were overzealous," he said. "After they had figured out what they were d-dumping, they hounded me relentlessly. That damned Iroh and his c-c-crew of morally righteous thugs."

Koji's finger hovered over the trigger.

"So, who killed them?" I asked, stringing the information out of Iwashi. "Who carried out the order?"

Iwashi twisted the barrel into my skull, looking at me as if I were dumb. "Sumi and Dikku, of c-c-course. We snuck some of my Kinoko Rose brothers onto the boat, and they took care of the rest out at sea." The bastard snickered. "Serves them r-r-right. There is no room for morals in this city. Not anymore."

Koji ground his teeth. Black spores spilled from his gills.

"But enough chit-chat," Iwashi said. "I am afraid I c-c-cannot let either of you leave here alive."

My eyes went wide. Not from the gun to my face, but from something completely unexpected.

"*Kuta dai*. Cousin." Shut the hells up.

Behind Iwashi, a broken wooden board rose above his head. Yuki swung it down, her wrists still cuffed. The solid beamed clocked Iwashi in the cap with a dull *thunk*. The son of a bitch collapsed to the floor. He groaned, blood pouring from his mushroom head.

"*Ariari do*, Yuki," Koji said. He stood above Iwashi, his pistol aimed at that sad excuse for a gangster.

I took out my tape recorder and waved it around. "Now, you two are under arrest."

Iwashi glared at me, holding his bleeding cap. Then he turned to Yuki. "If I burn, you will b-b-burn with me, cousin."

Fuck this foul fungal. "Nameko, cuff him."

— — — — — —

KOJI AND I stood under cover in the loading bay, in order to avoid the intensifying storm. It choked the ocean in a thick cloud and blanketed the surrounding warehouses. Blue-and-red police lights reflected off the deluge of snowflakes. I rubbed my mittens together, cursing this God-damned weather.

I watched Iwashi and Yuki as they were escorted in handcuffs to separate police cruisers. Their heads and caps were bowed in shame. At least a dozen officers had arrived to pick apart Sea Dragon Seafood Co., unveiling the full extent of Iwashi's operation.

This would be a huge blow to Kinoko Rose's shine smuggling, but … I still felt unsatisfied.

"You okay, Nameko?" I asked.

He had an unlit cigarette between his lips. "Sumi and Dikku ordered my uncle and his crew killed—I cannot help but think Shikaku does not know the truth. My cousin is still out there. *Daigoro* is still out there. I must find them."

"But they could be anywhere," I said. "We caught Tsutomu. Iwashi and Yuki are under arrest. What other leads do we have?"

Koji worked his jaw. "*They killed my* shushu …"

"I'm sorry, Nameko, but we've got nothing until Iwashi is processed and put under questioning. What else can we do about it now?"

"Not a fucking thing," a familiar voice called out.

Captain Ridgeway approached, stepping gingerly across the snow-packed dock. He shook himself off once he was shielded by the over-hanging roof. It was strange to see him out of the precinct—even more so with a heavy wool jacket draped over his hulking frame.

Ridgeway cupped his bare hands and blew into them. "I told you the night wasn't over, Hofmann," he said sardonically, "but you picked a damn good one to close this case."

"Excuse me?" Koji and I said at the same time, in some uncanny moment of interconnectedness.

"The case is closed," Ridgeway said. "Tsutomu is behind bars. Iwashi's operation has been exposed."

"But—"

"But nothing, Hofmann. Windsor will take over from here." Ridgeway waved an arm toward the red door, where Windsor, Morris, and Hughes directed a forensics team and a few officers.

"Those knobheads?" I blurted.

"Look," Ridgeway shifted his stance, offering us a sympathetic look, "you both have done solid work. Feel proud, but you're done here. Get some rest and enjoy the festival tomorrow."

I was *not* done here.

"Sumi and Dikku are still fucking breathing," I snapped. Shikaku was out there, too, and who knows what he was subjecting his son to. "How many more missing children are in those gangsters' clutches? This isn't over!"

"The case is *closed*," Ridgeway warned. "MacArthur wants this cleaned up, today."

"But Iwashi and Kinoko Rose killed Koji's uncle!"

"Hofmann, enough!" Ridgeway thrust his forefinger toward my face. "You're on thin fucking ice, and you're not doing yourself any favors by pissing me off. It's a tragedy, Nameko, and I'm sorry for your loss. Life doesn't make things easy—least of all in this city—but Iwashi *will* face justice."

I understood the implications in Ridgeway's words: *Don't dig any further.*

But my investigative instinct urged me to keep searching, to find out what the Hell Kinoko Rose was up to. There were too many dead. Too many innocents who'd suffered and were *still* suffering.

What would I get from going down that road, though?

I was broken. The fragmented remains of a once-whole woman. One who'd buried herself in booze, killed her daughter, ruined her marriage, and ran her career into the ground. A shell of a woman, wasting away in this Hell called Neo Kinoko.

Koji placed a hand on my shoulder, like a lifeline pulling me back to reality. "It is okay." He wouldn't push back against Ridgeway—the captain had a noose around Koji's neck, and he wouldn't hesitate to tighten it.

Ridgeway cut through the moment like a sharp blade. "Hofmann, am I clear? This ends here."

"Yes," I said. No.

"Excellent. Tomorrow is a big day, so go home. Listen to some of your bloody cassette tapes or whatever it is you do in your spare time." Ridgeway left, disappearing into a wall of falling snow.

"Good night, Nameko," I said, my tone dour.

"But, Hofmann, I—"

"You *nothing*. Like Ridgeway said, tomorrow is a big day. The Fuyu Lantern Festival is for you and your people. Go be with them."

Koji wrung his hands. Surprising me, he put his cigarette away. After opening and closing his mouth a few times, he said, "*Zaowa*, detective. It was an honor working with you." He bowed at the waist.

"Wait," I said as he turned to depart. I bowed in return. "*Ariari do*."

Koji smiled. He walked away into the building blizzard.

I made my way back to my car. The snow was piling up now, reaching past my ankles. Pulling the scarf over my hair, I realized Koji hadn't asked for it back. I made a mental note to return it to him.

The Metro was in the shop, getting repairs after that narrow escape from Rivierside. In the meantime, the NKPD had given me another loaner: A royal blue Roxhall Cadet. It was already coated in a layer of white. I used my sleeve to brush snow off the front and back windshields.

I reached out with the keys in my hands. What the Hell was I going to do now? My mind fired blanks—I'd been thoroughly demoralized. Perhaps a night of *actual* rest would benefit me.

Snow crunched behind me.

A bag was thrown over my head, obscuring my vision. I made to scream, but something blunt and heavy struck me in the skull. Disoriented, I lost my balance. Someone caught me. An agony swept across my brain like hammers striking nails.

Thud.

Another blow, this time to my temple.

Thud.

Blackness.

BOUND &
BROKEN

[29] Case File #42-56
Location: Unknown | Time: Unknown

- - - - - - - - -

THE BAG WAS torn from my head. I shrieked and thrashed. My eyes stung as they adjusted to the blinding brilliance of wherever the Hell I was—the lights intensified the pulsating pangs inside my skull. I squirmed, but I could barely move. Whoever brought me here had stripped me down to my bra and underwear. My legs, wrists, and chest were bound with hairy mycelium.

"Shut up and stay still," a guttural male voice said in Hōpponese.

A fungal.

As my vision came into focus, I saw radiant fungal bulbs hanging from a mycelium ceiling. I was face up on a flat surface. Against my back and legs, I felt something soft and furry ... Mold.

I was strapped to a mold table.

The room I was in reeked of cleaning chemicals and high-proof alcohol. Nearby, I heard muffled conversations, as well as the beeping of heavy machinery. Wherever I was, I knew I was bloody well fucked ...

I'd delved too deep into the greed of this Godforsaken city. Kinoko Rose, Sea Dragon Seafood Co., the NKPD. All of them were corrupt. I was sure CPAN could be added to that list, too.

Now, all that was left was for me to face the consequences of what I'd uncovered. In my relentless search for answers, this was the bitter truth I had to accept—the pill I had to swallow.

Death had always loitered at my doorstep. It was about time I welcomed it into my home.

Two mushroom-headed silhouettes appeared above me. I recognized the round curve and conical warts of Sumi's cap, as well as Dikku's up-turned gills.

"There she is." I cringed at the sound of Sumi's smooth timbre, the way his articulate Coprinian came across as arrogant. "How are you, Hofmann-*jero*?"

"Oh, I'm doing fine," I said with a weak smirk. "Bit of a headache, but it'll pass. Wonderful to see you two dickheads again."

With his fat fingers, Dikku grasped my cheeks. My parched lips cracked as he squeezed. "Say that one more time, meatbag," he warned.

"Enough, *jiujiu*," Sumi said. "Raise the table so she can be intro-duced to our associate."

Dikku placed his hand next to my head. I heard the slither as fungal filaments extended from him. Without any effort, the table moved of its accord, musty mold rustling beneath me.

Had Dikku done that? Commanded the mold itself?

My sense of gravity shifted. The table was nearly upright, at a slight angle. Enough that I could take in the empty room we occupied. The floor and walls were also made of mycelium, with a door on the opposite end. Two openings on one side served as windows, looking out into a large warehouse. Gangsters and workers bustled about: Some filled ce-ramic bottles with shine, others packed those bottles into crates, and forklifts loaded the crates onto transport trucks.

Kinoko Rose's operation was in full swing.

And standing in the doorway, slender hands massaging her pro-truding belly, was Airi. Her hawk-like expression impaled me. She was dressed in a flowing robe of crimson with black trim, contrasting her pearly complexion.

Sumi, The Veil. Dikku, The Stem. And Airi—

"The Gills," Sumi said, his palm outstretched toward her.

"We have met," Airi said, drifting over to me. She cocked her head and looked at me with a mix of curiosity and venom. "How far you have fallen, Detective Hofmann," she said in soft, subdued Coprinian.

"I didn't have much farther left to fall," I joked. "I've burned nearly every bridge I could in my life, so what more do I have to lose?"

"What a sad story," Dikku said, pouting his lips.

Sumi came closer, examining my features. A chill ran down my spine and triggered a wave of goosebumps across my skin. "Your end will come with a whimper, human. You are nothing but an afterthought—a blip in the history of your foul race, and a malignant memory in the lives of those around you. No one will mourn you. Not the NKPD. Not Koji, your ex-husband, nor your *dead daughter*."

"Filthy fucking gillie!" I snarled.

A burst of rage tore through my fatigued body. I tugged at my bindings, the threads of mycelium digging into my wrists. How dare he bring my daughter into this?

Sumi and Kinoko Rose were the types who'd given their species a bad name. Deep down, humans and fungals weren't all that dissimilar. Same despicable desires, same moral decay—just different packaging.

Dikku laughed. "Seems you hit a sore spot, *jiujiu*."

"Enough wasting time," Airi said. "Send in Shikaku and allow me to take care of Hofmann. You two have much to prepare."

"You are correct." Sumi nodded. He sauntered toward me, brushing hairs over my ear. I chomped at his fingers. "It is a shame you will not see the show. The Fuyu Lantern Festival promises to a spectacular occasion."

I spat at Sumi's feet. "Whatever you have planned, I hope it burns to the ground."

He cackled. "Oh, but that is *exactly* what we want to happen. Burn it all down, for a new era for Neo Kinoko is at hand. From those ashes, a new mushroom will bloom, with the three of us atop the cap. Your colonizing coppie kin will regret the day they invaded us."

"Sounds like a half-assed game of succession," I teased. "That's optimistic for a group of middling gangsters smuggling illegal booze. Tsutomu and Iwashi are going to rot in prison. It won't be long before you all join them."

"You underestimate us—"

"You underestimate *me*," I warned.

Sumi's hand shot out, clenching my throat. He dug his fingers into my flesh. My windpipe constricted and I fought for air.

"Do you not see where you are?" Sumi asked. "The position you are in? There is only one path left for you, and that is *death*. Airi will take pleasure in watching you beg as your body is cut to pieces, just like the children whose murders you struggled to solve. Iwashi and Tsutomu were but small players in a larger game. They are of no use to anyone."

He let go. I gasped and coughed. Air flowed into my lungs in ragged wheezes.

Sumi continued: "The festival will be our revenge. CPAN made the mistake of capitulating, even an *inch*—giving us our celebrations, allowing us to practice our religion. Our leader has been shortsighted, submissive. Dikku, Airi, and I, we see that the future is fungal. That it belongs to Kinoko Rose."

The Veil stepped away. Airi swooped in to replace him, bringing the smell of green tea with her. She ran her knuckles across my face, grazing me with the tenderness of a lover. "Your corpse will serve as a message for the Coprinians. Piece by piece, they will know our names."

"How could you be a part of this, Airi?" I asked. "Bringing your own child into this world, all while others *die* for your sick purposes."

"It is about survival, detective. When an animal is backed into a corner, it reverts to its base instincts. As I told you yesterday, we must face the future, head on, as fungals. If a dozen children die to serve the greater good, then they are worthy martyrs."

Her words sickened me. "You're no better than the Coprinians who invaded this country!"

Airi ignored me, vanishing from my sight—she laughed from somewhere in the room. Sumi and Dikku waited by the doorway. A small child ran in, lungs heaving and gills flaring. She bowed to Sumi and held her hand out: A slip of mycopaper lay on her palm. She also had a rose tattoo on her neck.

A rose-runner.

Sumi took the paper and shooed away the child. He unraveled the message and read it, his expression turning serious. "Shikaku is on his way. We leave her in your capable hands, Airi."

"Farewell, detective," Dikku said, blowing me a kiss as he and Sumi exited the room. Airi returned holding a syringe filled with clear liquid. She flicked it. Several droplets fell to the floor.

I trembled. "What is that?"

"Do you know what *somake* means?" Airi asked. "'Soma' refers to the body in its entirety, but separate from the mind and spirit. My people believe in the distinction between the physical and the spiritual. For millennia, *somake* has bridged that gap, grounding the spirit within its physical host. We have gone a step further by … concentrating it. Now, I wonder, how long has it been since you last drank, detective?"

Since I last—Oh, no. No, no, no.

Before I could react, Airi wrapped mycelium around my upper arm and knotted it. She clamped down on my forearm, even as I tried to get loose. I writhed and howled and … felt the sharp pinch as the needle entered my vein.

"Pure shine," Airi said, inspecting the empty syringe. "Only the best for our dear detective."

"Fuck you! Why are you doing this to me?" It would be less than a minute before the effects hit me. Either I'd be immediately drunk, or I'd overdose and die right here.

Shikaku came into the room. "Did I miss it, Airi-*shen*?"

"Not yet," Airi said. "I've only just injected her. Bring me Tsutomu's tools."

I heard metal clinking, then Shikaku was next to Airi with a myco-leather roll unfurled across his palms. Tsutomu's knives, scalpels, saws …

"D-Don't do it!" I begged, fighting my bonds. "P-Please …"

Airi hummed a lullaby as she picked up a saw—the very saw Tsutomu had used on Satsuki ….

"Start with the arm," Shikaku suggested.

Airi bobbed her head in agreement. She held the saw in one hand, and with the other she cradled her belly.

Fucking psychopaths. All of them.

"Think about D-Daigoro …," I said to Shikaku. "Think about … Emiko."

"Do you think I give a shit about either of them?" Shikaku looked at me with scorn plastered across his countenance. "That boy's destiny is sealed. He'll be one of the sparks that'll ignite a revolution."

Airi gripped my shoulder, shoving it into the bed of mold. She tickled my skin with the serrated edge of the saw, lining it up.

I braced myself.

The alcohol worked its way through my system. A potent grogginess settled in. Exhausted, I muttered through shallow breaths, "Bring it … on … *shabi*."

She began to cut.

My bicep was torn apart. I bawled, feeling myself slip into unconsciousness. Nerves fired off non-stop. My brain was barraged by an agonizing sensory overload. Bile rose in my throat and I spewed. Stomach acid lingered at the back of my throat. A coppery scent mixed with the punch of sick as Airi kept sawing.

I was spent.

Eyelids drooping, my head rushed with adrenaline and alcohol. I was ready. These sporesacks could cut me up. I was ready to die …

But the suffering continued … I didn't know for how long. My concept of time was skewed by the shine and the pain. Liz beckoned to me from the afterlife … I ached to reach out to her.

Part of me held on, though … even if I wanted to let go.

All of a sudden, there was yelling out in the warehouse. Something crashed and glass shattered. Shikaku whipped out his pistol. Airi removed the saw from my flesh. Out on the main floor of the warehouse, mayhem broke out. Gangsters and workers argued. More bottles smashed.

"Shikaku, go see what happened," Airi ordered.

Seconds passed. Airi was distracted. My arm throbbed and bled.

"Put the saw down," someone said.

A knife appeared behind Airi's throat. She dropped the tool on the ground.

"Now back away," the voice continued.

Airi withdrew, and behind her …. Oze.

"I am sorry, Airi-*shen*." Oze raised a massive fist and punched Airi in the temple. She went limp, and he eased her to the floor.

Oze rushed over to me. "You will not have long," he whispered, scanning the windows. His broken nose was covered in a hardened paste.

Stunned and intoxicated, I couldn't think straight. "Wh-What's … what's going on? Why are you … here?"

Oze cut at my bindings—they snapped off one by one. "Things are not as they appear, detective. My family—" Shouts rang out from the warehouse. Oze sliced through the final binding, holding me as I fell forward. "You must leave."

"Y-You did that?" I pointed a floppy finger toward the noise.

"The forklift provided a fortuitous distraction," Oze said, "but we cannot waste more time." He wrapped my arm in mycelium bandages, then poured water down my throat. I sputtered, almost choking. My throat was raw and burning, but the water was a blessing.

He pressed a bundle of clothing into my hands. "Get dressed."

I stared at the white robes he'd given me. "Wh-Why?" That was all my drunken ass could manage.

Oze's gaze fell. "I cannot change those who are set in their ways, but I can repent for the sins of my family—and for my own. Please, put the clothes on."

He helped me into the robe, adjusting a sash around my waist. Then he gave me a pair of shoes made from mycelium. I put them on, the threads conforming to my large feet. Airi stirred as she awoke from unconsciousness.

Oze shoved a satchel into my lap. "Gun, knife, food, fresh water. Get out of here while they are still distracted. Head north toward the river and do not look back."

"What about … you?"

"Do not worry about me, detective." Oze's brows furrowed. "I have made my peace, whether my story ends here or I live to see the sun rise. Perhaps I will see my father again." He bowed his cap at the mention of Iroh. "But you must escape. Escape and muster all of the aid you can to Chaga Park and Fuyu Temple—"

Sumi, Dikku, and Shikaku shouted outside the office, berating someone about the forklift. Airi groaned. I flinched at the sudden blast of a gunshot.

Oze dragged me to my feet. He led me to an opening behind the mold table. "Follow this hallway until you reach the final door. It will exit into the far end of the warehouse. After that, you are on your own."

"*Ariari … do.*" I wobbled, barely able to stand.

"Go, please," Oze begged. He prodded me through the door. "Hogosha protect you. Reishi heal you. Now, go!"

I stumbled through a hall made of mycelium. My head spun and I almost fell. I staggered, dim fungal bulbs lighting the way. Dragging myself along the corridor, I used the mycelium as a handhold. I passed storage rooms, offices, and bathrooms. Inch by inch, I made it to the end.

The "final door" was more like a curtain of fungal threads, reaching down to the floor. I parted the threads, peering out into the warehouse. Fungal gangsters scurried about, ordering workers to move faster. I saw crate after crate of decorative bottles being packed onto pallets for distribution. Stacks of boxes were off to the side, filled with mounds of folded white cloths.

I had no idea what they were planning, but Oze was right: I had to escape and warn the NKPD.

Searching through the satchel, I took out the gun … It was a God-damned fungal pistol. But it was better than nothing.

Through unfocused eyes, I scanned the warehouse. Two mycelium doors were on either side of a wide garage. The garage was closed, so the nearest door was my optimal exit. It was unguarded, and the gangsters were occupied. I ran for it.

Halfway to my goal, an animalistic roar reverberated across the warehouse. Dikku. Then Sumi shouted in Hōpponese: "The prisoner has escaped! Find her! Kill her!"

Fuck.

I darted toward the exit on rubbery knees. Someone called out, "She's here! She's here!"

Nearing the exit, I glimpsed a dozen or more gangsters sprinting in my direction. I fired off a few shots, bullets exploding in sprays of spores. The gillies scattered and took cover. I sprinted toward the door, ripping through mycelium and out into the freezing gloom of night.

The white mycelium walls of the encompassing warehouses were engulfed by a wall of white—the blizzard obscured the sky and the very world around me.

I took in my immediate surroundings: A small loading bay, and three trucks parked in front of the garage. I hurried in a random direction, trudging through knee-high snow in nothing but a Hōpponese robe and mycelial booties. Step after step, my clothes got more damp. The cold became an active chill, settling itself in my bone marrow and numbing my skin.

Oze had said north toward the river. Which river? Where the Hell was I?

I kept slogging through a labyrinth of alleys, my body exhausted and my brain soaked in booze for the first time in years. Shouts pursued me. Gunfire and angry gangsters spurred me onward. I fired random shots over my shoulder, knowing my aim was worth shit in my current state.

I pushed myself to the brink of physical exhaustion—the only thing that kept me going was sheer force of will.

Turning a corner, I heard the gurgle of rushing water and howling winds. I'd almost made it.

I crossed an open, unlit street—there were no buildings across the way. Reaching the opposite side, I shambled over an embankment and rolled. My face met icy muck. I crawled to my feet as a clamor echoed behind me.

Shit … I was out of options. In one direction was a vast freezing river. In the other were gangsters who wanted me dead. My only chance of escape would be to risk the water. I wouldn't be able to swim far or I'd freeze, but the river was narrow here—only a few hundred feet to the opposing bank.

That left swimming across to … Old Kinoko.

The silhouette of the bombed-out zone haunted the snowy skies. An irradiated landscape of claw-like remains hugged what I now knew was the Kinoko River. Broken buildings and collapsed towers jutted from the earth in perverted shapes.

The cold had awakened in me a deep instinct for survival. Even with the threat of radiation, Old Kinoko was my only choice.

It was this or die.

Confused cries sounded on the road. Time to move. I stepped through frosted sludge, my shoes slurping with each difficult stride. I made it to the water's edge. Taking a deep breath, I kept going. Every shivering step submerged me deeper in the ice-cold river. I knew I had to take the plunge and get it over with.

"She's down by the river!" a gravely-voiced gangster boomed from the embankment.

It was now or never.

Amidst a hail of gunfire—flashes of pain nipping at my skin in several places—I dove into the Kinoko River.

FALLOUT

[30] Case File #42-56
Old Kinoko (Restricted Zone) | Time: Unknown

- - - - - - - - -

FUCK ME … Somehow, I was alive.

I'd washed ashore across the river, on the fringes of Old Kinoko. The gangsters were a distant memory as I coughed up clay-flavored water. I spat the remnants of grainy silt from my mouth, crawling through icy sludge, algae, and aquatic fungi. My injured arm gave way. The bandage on my bicep was saturated with blood and mud—it seeped through the sleeve of my robe.

I collapsed onto my back, sprawled out and shivering. The satchel Oze had given me dug into my side. My adrenaline wore off, making the blooms of pain across my body more apparent.

The cold suppressed the fact that three bullets had struck me: Two in my right thigh and another in my left ribcage. Glancing shots, I hoped, given I wasn't unconscious.

Regardless, I was in desperate need of medical attention.

My stomach grumbled and my throat was parched. I was a bloody drunken mess, too. The shine permeated my system, leaving me off-kilter. My clothes were soaked and the subzero chill leached into my bones.

Half sunken in the mire, I gazed up at the gray sheet of clouds above. Fast currents of snow swept across my face. I took the water bottle from the satchel and drank small, deliberate sips. Then I ate a rice ball filled with seaweed.

"Thank you … Oze," I mumbled.

I couldn't process how things had panned out. How Goddamned

sideways it had all gone. I went from detective to prisoner to fugitive in a single night. And for whatever reason, Oze had helped me to escape. Not too long ago, he'd nearly subjected me to torture in an alley. But he went against his brethren to set me free. Why?

His words kept repeating in my head: *Things are not as they appear ... The sins of my family.*

What the Hell was he talking about?

But I couldn't dwell on unknowns—I had a mission now: Fuyu Temple. Sumi had said that the festival would be their revenge.

Burn it all down.

Part of me was determined to prove Oze right, to stand up, move, and hurry back to civilization. To warn everyone. But another part of me didn't give a shit. Why not just lay here in this pool of slime and drift away? Wouldn't that be so easy?

But I couldn't go out like that—I wouldn't. Accepting death when I knew I could push through, that would dishonor Liz's memory.

By an invisible force of will I got up on unsteady feet. My knees and back trembled, every joint in my body on the brink of calling it quits. But I was alive, Goddamnit. Drunk and injured, yes, but still functioning.

I had to come up with a plan, before hypothermia set in ... or worse.

Old Kinoko's ruins rose to my left. The bombed-out zone was restricted, patrolled by the military—except along the river. No sane person would willingly enter into that wasteland, especially with the scar of Hogosha Crater irradiating the landscape.

I closed my eyes and tried to remember the layout of the city.

If I followed the river southeast, I would eventually reach Mildew Grove. It was a suburb on the northern outskirts—low-lying houses that gave way to farmland. That way, I could avoid entering into Old Kinoko's unpredictable maze.

The frozen shoreline gave way to a snow-caked bank. It led up to a tall chain link fence topped with barbed wire. In either direction, tangled thickets of skeletal trees and bushes choked the riverside. It'd be difficult to traverse, and swimming farther down the river was a death sentence.

Bloody Hell … The restricted zone was my only path forward.

I had no clue how far I'd have to walk, but if I didn't move now, I'd freeze to death. My toes were already numb, foreshadowing frostbite. I had no idea how cold it really was, but I doubted I could survive the night.

Bitter winds bit at my bare skin as I clambered up the bank. The fence was in poor condition. Most of its tall posts were rusted, bent, or completely broken. There was a section of chain link that had sagged, revealing an opening that I might be able to fit under.

I hobbled over, favoring my uninjured leg. Every step radiated stinging jolts from the bullet wounds. My eyesight was still muddied by the shine, but I made do as best I could in the dark.

There was just enough room for me to squeeze under the fence. I lifted it up and crawled. My joints complained. My wounded leg strained. I scrabbled for purchase on rubble and rocks, pulling myself through to the other side.

I'd entered Old Kinoko.

To my right was a wide street. I got up and limped my way forward. Snowfall had accrued atop the road in a pristine quilt, but it couldn't mask the destruction. On either side, the ruins of mycobrick factories and mycelial structures stuck out of the whiteness, like the warped bones of sunken giants. As always, fungi took advantage of the decay. Dense colonies of fruiting bodies bloomed between crevices. Patches of thick crystallized mold carpeted exposed surfaces. Polypore shelves grew in vertical layers up shattered walls and columns, icicles hanging from their porous underbellies.

I'd heard the stories of this place. Before and during the Spore War, this ward was a smattering of factories, workshops, and businesses—a prime target when an invading army wanted to send a message. But to see the devastation up close was … unnerving.

Errant gales howled along the avenue, kicking up snowflakes that stung my eyes. I kept walking, absorbing the horror of this place.

Fungals had worked and lived here, yet my government had bombed it into oblivion. On purpose. What better way to ensure your enemy's capitulation than to bring annihilation to their doorstep?

I wondered how radioactive Old Kinoko really was. This far from Hogosha Crater, was it livable?

But as much as radiation frightened me, the weather was a more clear and present danger. I had to move faster to stay warm—if I stopped or slowed, I'd die. And no one would ever find my frozen corpse in this Hellish landscape.

Pulling my robe tight around my neck, I continued on.

— — — — — —

WHAT SEEMED LIKE an hour had passed, but I had no way of knowing for sure. The relentless blizzard trapped me in a bubble of isolation. No sounds, save for whistling winds and the crunch of my footsteps.

I became delirious. The inkling that I was being watched or followed made the hairs on my neck stand on end.

My paranoia was only worsened by the shine still poisoning my body. Woozy and fading, I hobbled along barren streets. I traversed piles of icy rubble with raw hands and an ailing stamina. Collapsed structures overgrown with mycelial blooms forced me to crawl through suffocating gaps. Several times, I stumbled upon deep snow, my legs sinking into collapsing pockets.

Time had stripped what the fungals had built, entropy breaking it all down with every passing moment. It had also slipped away from me—each step was a single second in a ceaseless span of agony.

I didn't know where I was. Only the vague hope that I was going in the right direction fueled me.

Barks startled me out of my zombified march. The sounds bounced off my surroundings, amplified by the cavernous carcasses of crumbling buildings. My heart pounded. I rushed beneath the cover of a collapsed balcony.

Images raced through my mind. What kinds of monstrosities could this irradiated environment create? Twisted creatures, mutated by the fallout of Coprinian malice. Then, I remembered Tsutomu's dogs, how they'd symbiotically melded with fungi.

I shuddered to think what horrors this place could produce, or what it could do to me: Cancerous growths and fruiting bodies rendering me a hideous wraith. Colonized, my consciousness no longer in my control. Some alien thing pulling my strings, like the puppet to a marionette.

More likely the bloody cold would kill me first.

Beneath the shadows of the balcony, bioluminescent slime pulsated. Hypnotized, intoxicated, and exhausted, my eyes grew heavy. Sprinkles of snow fell from my head as I startled myself awake. The grease in my disheveled hair had hardened. I broke into maniacal laughter.

How long had it been since I'd slept? I was losing it, physically and mentally. My sense of space and sanity floated away like snowflakes in this fucking storm.

This was where I would die—I was convinced of it.

I'd survived a serial killer *and* gangsters, yet nothing compared to the terrifying power and sublimity of nature.

My laughter subsided, fading into the void. I leaned against a wall. My robed back slid down the rough surface until my ass planted on wet snow and ... something crunched.

Through half-open eyelids, I looked down. Between my legs was a frozen carcass, tiny chunks of frostbitten meat clinging to its mangled skeleton. I shot to my feet, ignoring the stabbing pain in my legs, ribs, and arms.

I ran, remembering my past thoughts: *If I stopped or slowed, I would die*. I had no idea how long I shambled along for, but reality snapped back into focus when I spotted a light in the distance. Its ghostly glow teased me with promise.

Who or what would I find there? Was it worth the risk? I had nothing left and I'd most likely die either way …

Fuck it.

A grim determination welled up inside me. Desperate, I plodded toward the light like a moth to a flame. As I neared, it flickered and danced … Fire. How could that be? Was I hallucinating, or were there people living in Old Kinoko?

I slipped into an alley choked with mushrooms and mold. Fruiting bodies hung down, their stems stiff and crystalline. I ignored a feeling of disgust as I snapped them like icicles. Reaching the end, I peeked around the corner: It was an open plaza, covered in debris. In the middle, a tall torch had been stabbed into the snow.

What was going on?

I heard howls and yips, closer this time. An instinctive fear kicked in, and I turned to leave—to find a safe place to hide. I removed the gun from the satchel, retracing my steps through the mushroom-infested alley. My head swiveled, on the lookout for people or wild animals.

A hand cupped around my mouth, suppressing my gasp. Then a thick arm wrapped around my torso and squeezed me tight.

"Quiet, *human*," they said in Hōpponese.

– – – – – –

I JERKED IN the firm hold of whoever held me. It was a fungal man, judging by the language, their low voice, and their pungent earthy musk.

Buckling my neck backward, I used it as an opportunity to bite his grimy hand. He slapped my mouth. With an awkward spin, I broke from his embrace. I stumbled painfully into the alley and raised my pistol.

"Stay back!" I warned, my voice cracking. "Who … Who are you?"

The hophead held his hands high. He was dressed in a worn-out patchwork of CPAN winter uniforms. Beneath a shaggy cap dripping with jet-black rivulets, his inquisitive yellow eyes darted from me to my gun. He had a bow hooked around one arm. A sword and scabbard hung from his waist.

"Quiet," he repeated, in Coprinian this time. His gills twitched. He lowered his hands, scratching at his beard of bushy black mold. Without a word, he pointed down the street.

More barking, much closer this time.

Keeping my gun focused on the fungal, I inched toward the alley entrance. Down the street, three feral wolves emerged from the swirling mists. Mushrooms grew from their napes and tails, and pale patches of mold plagued their mangy fur. They nipped at each other with snarling jaws full of sharp fangs.

Fucking Hell.

"Listen to me," the fungal said. "Lower your weapon, and I will protect you."

My hand trembled—not from nerves, but from the weight of the gun in my weak grip. "How can I trust you?"

"You cannot," he whispered, "but you can trust your instincts. Either follow me, or be eaten by wolves. The choice is yours. Now please, lower your weapon *and* your voice."

Goddamnit. He had me there.

The button stepped closer to me. He reached out, placing his fingers on the mycelial barrel. I didn't react, just let the pistol sink until it touched my thigh. My gut told me this fungal was the only way I'd survive Old Kinoko.

"What now?" I asked.

"We return to the square and loop around. I know a few shortcuts." He pinched his dirty lips and glanced at the gun. "I warn you, do not use that unless you must. The sound will only attract more wolves."

"Where are you going to take me?"

His stare widened when he noticed the bloodstains all over my body. "To my people."

He unhooked his bow and removed an arrow from a quiver on his back. With soft steps, he crouched and skulked through the corridor. I followed, sharp aches and pinched nerves shocking my system.

The fungal led me deeper into the ruins. We snuck through alleys, narrow side streets, and the crumbling chassis of factories and warehouses. A thick fog had swept in, reducing visibility to a few dozen feet or less. But my guide knew his way around, like the gills on his cap.

Barks and whines echoed nearby. The fungal waved for me to hurry. My cumbersome gait made my hip sore, but I pushed myself as hard as I could.

We left the industrial area behind, entering into what looked like suburbs. Low-lying homes had been flattened by the blast. Their wood frames had decayed, colonized and consumed by fungi. It was like walking through an old graveyard, the tombstones of families long dead.

All of a sudden, the fungal halted. He signaled for me to be quiet, then he pushed me against the wall of a dilapidated house.

A filthy wolf ambled onto the street, not far from where we just stood. Its ears and mushrooms perked up, tilting as they perceived their surroundings. The fungal took his arm off me and nocked an arrow. He pulled the string back, his elbow level with the shaft.

In an instant, the wolf's attention swung to us.

It snarled and dashed, leaping at us with its slobbery teeth bared. In mid-jump, the arrow pierced the animal between its neck and chest. It yelped and fell to the ground with a muted *thud*. Blood pooled, staining the snow.

"We must run," the fungal commanded. "The others will have sensed this one's death." He looped a rope around the wolf's neck and slung it over his back.

I stood there, sickened. Was he planning to eat it?

Frenzied barks broke me from my stupor. The fungal took off, my limping strides making it difficult for me to keep up. Zigzagging through the blast-blown remains of homes, growls and howls taunted us.

We turned a corner and two wolves blocked our path. The fungal nocked another arrow and loosed it before I could even blink. One of the animals crumpled into the snow. The other bared its snarling maw, spittle flying out. Its muscles and fungi tensed as four more wolves encircled us.

I took aim and fired twice. Two wolves died as spore bullets erupted in their heads. The fungal loosed his final two arrows, each hitting their intended targets. One wolf remained.

It crossed the distance in an instant, jumping at me.

In a split-second reaction, I fired, but the Goddamned pistol jammed. The wolf's paws landed on my chest, slamming me into a cushion of snow. I fumbled in my satchel, pulling the knife out. The beast's fangs clacked as it snapped, searching for weak flesh to rend.

Drool dripped on my face, smells of rotten meat and must asphyxiating my nostrils. I wrestled to keep the wolf off of me. It chomped, eyes bulging, paws scratching. Mycelium wormed out of its mouth, the tiny tendrils wriggling in front of my eyes.

Fuck, fuck, fuck.

The foul beast reared its head for a brief moment, enough time for me to plunge my knife into its neck. Blood spurted. The mycelium quivered and flopped, hanging from the dying wolf's mouth. I tossed the abhorrent creature to the side.

Panting, I hauled myself up. I realized now why the fungal hadn't helped me: More than a dozen wolves had surrounded us. Several lay dead already, their ichor dripping from the fungal's sword. I spun around, almost tripping on my weakened legs. Growls sounded in every direction. Stinging gusts nipped at my skin.

"We ... W-We're done for," I said through clattering teeth.

"Have faith," the fungal replied.

His gills twitched as white spores flowed from them. He placed two filthy fingers between his lips and whistled. The high-pitched sound caused the wolf pack to recoil, their hackles raised, fungal-tipped tails between their legs.

A moment later, a whistle sounded in response from within the blizzard.

"Do not move," the fungal commanded.

One of the wolves barked, its neck mushrooms quivering—the pack leader. The quivering spread like a wave, followed by a ripple of growls. The beasts' fungi and ears went taut, snouts wrinkled in salivating snarls. Another bark from the leader and the wolves rushed.

"Do. Not. Move," the fungal repeated.

There was a sudden *whoosh* of air all around me. The snowfall stilled as time seemed to freeze. Arrows flew in from all directions, sinking into each of the remaining wolves. The beasts yowled, collapsing to the ground in gory heaps of twitching flesh and fungi.

I shook. "What the Hell just happened?"

"Faith," the fungal whispered.

"Ogami-*jero*," a female called out in Hōpponese. "Are you safe?"

My guide replied: "I am."

A group of fungals in mismatch winter wear and face coverings materialized from the haze, all armed with bows and arrows. They stopped a few feet short of us. Only one fungal stepped closer, a short female. She approached Ogami, and they bowed to each other.

"Thank you, Yubaba-*shen*."

Removing a scarf from her lower face, Yubaba revealed herself to be an elderly woman. A small smile perked up the edges of her wrinkled mouth, revealing yellowed teeth. Ten pink, cupped mushrooms grew in a staggered stack atop her white-haired head.

Yubaba placed her hands on Ogami's shoulders and chuckled. She patted the wolf tied to his back. "Seventeen wolves—it seems your hunt was successful." Then her dubious golden gaze met mine. "*And* you found a human."

FIRESIDE CHAT

- - - - - - - - -

YOU ARE LUCKY, *gaigai*." Yubaba wrapped a mycofiber blanket over my shoulders, atop the fresh set of patchwork clothes they'd given me. Concern was tattooed across her timeworn countenance—was it for me, or for her people?

We sat on a broken wall that surrounded a two-story estate—the fungals' camp. Its sprawling courtyard was strewn with boulders and covered in snow, a frozen pond occupying one corner. All the trees were long dead, charred from the blast or disintegrated from rot. A shield of fog blocked out the rest of the world as the sun rose in the east.

"I know …" My brain pounded. Weariness washed over me.

"You lost quite a lot of blood," Yubaba noted, "but the bullet wounds only grazed you. That, on the other hand"—she pointed to my arm—"was showing early signs of infection. It would have killed you before long."

Yubaba had stitched up my numerous injuries. "The cold would've killed me first," I muttered.

"Be that as it may. Do not treat your life so carelessly."

I let my eyes wander, preferring not to hear an old woman's critiques. Yubaba's colony had reclaimed and renovated the estate, providing sanctuary for over forty fungals. In the middle of the courtyard, a fire roared beneath a large pavilion, where hopheads roasted mushroom skewers and cubed meat. Most everyone was caught up in busywork. Some cleaned or tended to the fire, while others skinned and carved up the wolves. Lights were on in the house, but Yubaba had refused to let me inside.

It made sense. I was a threat to them—an intruder. Yet another potential colonizer in an ongoing story of oppression.

"Come," Yubaba said.

We crossed the courtyard, our feet crunching on icy snow. She led me by the elbow toward the pavilion. Its columns were made from tightly woven mycelial filaments, with a massive parasol mushroom cap as its roof. I could smell the musk of cooked wolf meat from here.

"Who are you?" I asked, curiosity itching at my brain. "Why are you all living in the restricted zone?"

Yubaba chuckled. "How about you tell me your name first?"

"Henrietta Hofmann. I'm a … detective for the NKPD."

Yubaba's nostrils flared. "A blue? You do not seem the type to be involved in an institution as corruptible as this city's police department. But not everyone is as they appear on the outside." She gestured around the property. "In our case, we are all outcasts, either by choice or by design. Coprinian rule has not been kind to our people."

I knew what it meant to be an outcast.

A dead daughter, a divorce, drunken blackouts, fights, and arrests. One mistake after another and the Morellum higher-ups had gotten fed up with me. When Frederick and his lawyer colleagues arrived with a proposal, it sure as Hell made the bosses happy. They kept framing it as a "promotion," but for me, it was and always would be exile.

"So, Old Kinoko," I said, "and this home—it's a refuge."

Yubaba guided me into the pavilion, settling us down on a polypore bench near the fire. The fungals around us gave me sidelong glances. "The Coprinians fear this place. They know we exist, but they steer clear and will not touch us."

"Except me," I quipped, holding my hands out to the flames.

"Your time here is transient," Yubaba said. "Nor do I sense ill-will from you."

"When did you first come here?" I asked.

The elder folded her hands in her lap, letting out a whistling breath through her flat nose. "Almost two years ago. I was an envoy during the Spore War, tasked with learning the Coprinian language and opening diplomatic channels. Talks fell apart, and many of us envoys were taken prisoner. I escaped, along with several others … Old Kinoko was our only choice." She lit up with a thin smile. "Over the years, we all found one another, forming a self-sustaining colony."

"Why here, though, in this estate? Aren't there better places to settle?"

"Oh, I am sure there are, but this is *home*." Yubaba pointed to a window on the first floor of the house. "That was my childhood room."

I took in the estate, imagining its past grandeur. A courtyard filled with lush gardens, fish swimming in the pond, and intricate stone paths. Mycopaper lanterns hanging from polypore awnings. The walls and trees around the property providing a rare degree of privacy. How times had changed …

"You grew up here?" I asked.

One of the fungals handed Yubaba two skewers. "I did," she said, giving me one stacked with mushroom caps and cubes of meat. "I had nothing but fond memories of this place, until the bomb dropped and it was nearly leveled. There was little left but dust, spores, and the skeleton of a home lost to time."

"But look at what you and your colony have accomplished," I said. The estate was whole again, its mycelium walls and mushroom roofs regrown from the earth itself.

Yubaba nodded, taking a bite of meat. "It took the strength and will of all of us to make that a reality."

My stomach growled. I examined my skewer but hesitated—my mind was conflicted, but my body needed sustenance. The wolf meat stank like wet dog, but I relented and tore off a piece. Its texture was tough and stringy. Each time I chewed my mouth was coated in a greasy film.

Still, food was food, and I was starving.

"How is it that you've all survived here?" I asked between bites.

"We have mushroom farms inside the house, and a garden out here in the spring and summer. We scavenge and make do, surviving on our crops and small game." Yubaba tittered. "The wolves are a rare treat, believe me." She tapped a finger on one of her pink caps. "But the radiation has lessened significantly over the years, and our biology allows us to mitigate most of its effects."

"How is it possible that the radiation is disappearing so fast?" From what I'd heard of nuclear weapons, the effects lasted for decades.

"Mycoremediation," Yubaba replied. "Mushrooms are capable of great healing, from an individual mind to an irradiated landscape—if only we allow them."

What the Hell was mycoremediation?

I looked around the courtyard, at all the fungals contributing to this colony. "Mushrooms *consuming* radiation …"

Yubaba finished her skewer and placed it by her side. "Those who adapt, survive. And fungi are the most adaptive organisms on the planet."

It wasn't an easy thought for me to wrap my mind around.

She turned to me. "Now, it is your turn, Miss Hofmann. Why are *you* here?"

What was I willing to tell her? Sure, she and her people had saved my life, but they were strangers. A colony of vagabonds eking out a life in the wasteland wrought by a nuclear weapon.

Then again, I'd already lost so much. What more was there for me to lose?

The blizzard had waned, but a chill breeze still crept through the camp. The flames writhed around crackling wood and hoof-like fungi. It brought a welcome warmth back to my body. Ogami came over, sitting cross-legged on the mycobrick floor. He sharpened his curved sword with a whetstone.

"It's a long story …," I admitted, ripping the last mushroom from my skewer.

Yubaba smirked. "What is fire for if not the telling of stories?"

"Can I have something to drink first?"

"Here." Ogami passed me a mycoleather waterskin, not even turning in my direction. "Drink."

My throat ached. I drank eagerly, uncaring of the fact that I was sharing it with a fungal. My experiences had nearly broken me, recalibrating my aversions and priorities.

I directed my tale at Yubaba, but I knew others were listening in. I told them about my investigation and the dismembered child on the beach. Ogami perked up as I spoke of The Shelf, Sea Dragon Seafood Co., and the shine distillery. Yubaba leaned forward, absorbing my recollections of Kinoko Rose, Mold Town, and Riverside.

Yubaba was fixated upon me, silent but attentive. Her expression turned to a scowl when I brought up Sumi and Dikku.

I spoke of the second dead child, and the other missing children. How Tsutomu had cut them up and fed them to his dogs. How missing children had been found butchered across Neo Kinoko, and the protests and riots that ensued.

"Kinoko Rose are plotting something for the Fuyu Lantern Festival," I concluded.

Revenge.

A guttural growl rumbled in Yubaba's throat. "Their actions are unforgivable."

Ogami stopped sharpening. "It is a tragedy: Even a most sacred occasion, set to be desecrated by our own people."

I'd seen it myself in Coprinia, how tradition and faith were monopolized and contaminated. Religions tended to stray from their ancient, divine purposes, deformed by the insatiable whims of the greedy—it was a sickness of the modern world.

But maybe these fungals could help.

"Would you join me?" I asked. Many of the fungals avoided my gaze. "Help me to stop Kinoko Rose."

"It is not our fight," Yubaba said, raising her palms up to the sky. "The gods have been forsaken. We sit in the ruins of belief, where bombs and death overwhelm all we once held sacred. What is left for us is *survival*."

"Survival?" I shot from my seat, my frail legs almost giving out. "Do you really think abandoning your brothers and sisters in the city will do you any good?" I trembled as I spoke. "You cower in this corpse of memory while other fungals suffer under the yoke of my nation. Children disappearing and dying … Why hide beneath the veil of radiation instead of facing reality?"

"It is not our fight!" Yubaba's gravelly voice boomed across the courtyard. The wiry muscles and wrinkled skin on her neck tensed. Dark spores swirled from the cream-colored gills of her caps.

The entire colony froze in an unbearable silence, punctuated only by the crackling fire. Dozens of yellow eyes were concentrated on me. Yubaba glared, wearing her emotions on her spores.

Ogami spoke up. "You stand there and judge, yet your people did this to us."

"Yes, but not *me*. I'm trying to stop monsters like Sumi and Dikku from harming more children. From burning this city to the ground. Why am I the only one—"

"No." Yubaba's eyes thinned, her head fungi trembling. "The truth is, you are trying to repent for your own failings. Whatever your sins or transgressions, our people are not helpless. We are *not* foils for your trauma."

Elisabeth.

Was I using this case as a means for personal repentance?

Frederick had meant for my exile to Neo Kinoko to be a prison. In reality, it was a purgatory, where my penitence would be put on trial. Was I destined to destroy it all, just as I'd ruined everything else in my life?

"Do none of you want to come with me?" I implored. "To aid your brothers and sisters. Your children …"

Ogami stood, sheathing his sword. "Understand this. We do not *need* to interfere in Neo Kinoko—we trust that our brothers and sisters will fight for their survival, as we do here in *our* colony."

"That's bullshit," I said, boiling with frustration. "How is that any different from human tribalism?"

No one spoke. I stood before the fire, before the eyes of all the fungals in the camp. My body shook. There was nothing more for me here. I had a duty, to warn the NKPD about Kinoko Rose. To get to the festival and stop them, whatever their plan was.

"I believe it's best that I leave," I said.

"Yes," Yubaba agreed.

"How do I get to Mildew Grove?"

Yubaba took a deep breath. "We will provide you with a guide—a volunteer. They will take you there. But know that the way is heavily guarded by military. The risk falls upon you."

"I understand." I placed a hand on her arm. "*Ariari do*, Yubaba."

"Do not thank me," she said, shrugging me aside with a vexed expression. "You may believe you have the right intentions, but take a moment to understand whether you are doing this for them … or for yourself."

The words struck me. I parted my lips to respond, but stopped.

Yubaba spun around, eying her kin. Her voice boomed: "Does anyone volunteer to guide her to the border?"

Fungals shuffled in their seats. Some got up and walked away.

A minute passed until Ogami stepped forward. He attached his sheath to a mycelium belt and said, "I volunteer."

TUNNELS

[32] Case File #42-56
Old Kinoko (Restricted Zone) | 8:19 a.m.

- - - - - - - - -

THE MORNING AFTER a storm was always a strange experience. The blizzard had pummeled Neo Kinoko, like crumbs being swept off of a table. But now, a paradoxical peace remained in its wake. Too bad my hangover made it difficult for me to appreciate any of it.

I followed Ogami through the ruins of Old Kinoko. He navigated the husks of former homes and businesses with practiced ease, leading me closer to the militarized border with Mildew Grove.

Closer to freedom, and the harsh realities of what lay ahead.

Every step was a struggle, but at least I was warmer. Even though I'd pissed off Yubaba, she'd made sure to outfit me with winter clothing. Her people had gifted me a faded jacket and pants, a multi-colored medley of mycofabrics lined with animal furs. My body ailed me, but I took satisfaction at the *crunch* my new mycoleather boots made in unspoiled snowpack.

After nearly dying at the hands of gangsters and a storm, I was grateful for the small blessings afforded to me by strangers.

The sun had risen into a clear blue sky—its heat was enough to start melting the top layer of powder. Icicles hung from fungal growths and the ruined frames of blasted homes. Around us was a landscape of pure white. Snow blended with mats of frosted mold. Together, they formed an endless swath, like cotton wool.

Ogami paused, signaling for me to wait. A cloud of evaporation filled the air in front of his beard, his gills expanding and contracting like lungs. "It is not much farther," he said in Coprinian.

My body was bandaged in several places, and I'd nearly succumbed to hypothermia and frostbite. Somehow, though, I'd survived—a bloody miracle. But the real challenges had yet to come.

We continued our slog through the snow.

"Move faster," Ogami urged. "This close to the perimeter, we must be wary of patrols."

"Thank you … for volunteering," I said, out of breath.

He scanned our surroundings. "It is nothing."

"Don't be so fucking humble," I retorted. "Your people could've left me and been done with it. You could've killed me or tossed me aside to fend for myself."

Ogami glanced at me over his shoulder. "Given the circumstances, it would have made sense to put you out of your misery. But I know what it is like to be lost. My people and I, we are castaways, rarely worrying about the world beyond our community." He pulled at his beard. "But for us to return, it would surely mean death at the hands of the military. Though my words were harsh, your intentions and morals rang true. I could not leave a fellow warrior to die a dishonorable death."

"What would an honorable death be, then?"

Ogami chuckled. "That is not for me to decide. Whether you succeed or fail, your quest is not over. Fate has yet to reveal its plans for you."

I trailed behind Ogami, his words hanging in the silence. What the Hell *did* fate have in store for me?

Snow fell from the branches of an emaciated corpse of a tree—a bird, taking flight into the cloudless sky. The faint sound of Coprinian voices drifted on the air. I gasped as Ogami tugged me toward a crumbling mycobrick wall.

We waited. The voices grew louder and nearer. I peeked through a crack, spotting two soldiers in rapt conversation. They were well armed, too, with SA-90 rifles hanging from their shoulders.

Seconds passed. Then minutes. I didn't move, keeping my breathing steady. The soldiers' casual chat faded. When Ogami was sure they'd passed, he waved me along.

"How often do patrols come through?" I asked him.

"They rotate in shifts," he said in a terse tone, "with multiple patrols in the area at any given time. But they never venture too deep."

Before I could bother him with another question, he whispered, "Quiet."

We entered into the remnants of a multi-story building made of mycelium. Rimy blooms of mold smothered the walls. Water dripped down from the decaying ceiling. To my surprise, a set of stairs had held together. Ogami bound up them with sure-footed confidence. I followed, wary of every step.

The third floor had almost entirely collapsed, but the second afforded us a wide view of the terrain. Old Kinoko spread out for another mile to the east. There was a stark contrast between its dilapidated, snow-covered latticework and the militarized border.

Multiple layers of barbed-wire fences grew from the border's barren landscape. Running for miles north and south, it separated the restricted zone's destruction from the suburban sprawl of Mildew Grove. Security watchtowers topped with spotlights sprouted up like sentinels along the perimeter.

"There." Ogami pointed ahead. "Do you see the abandoned building with three floors?"

I followed his finger. "The one with the yellow mushroom colonies growing from its windows?"

"Yes," Ogami confirmed. "In that building's basement is a tunnel. It goes beneath CPAN's defenses, to a home on the other side."

"Who made the tunnel? Are there more?"

"Many have helped in the creation of this network. It has taken years of effort and coordination on both sides of the border. Dozens exist, but several have either caved in or been discovered by the military."

"What are they used for?"

"Mostly for smuggling food and supplies, but often—"

"Escapees," I finished.

"Exactly," Ogami said. "Our community grows, month by month. Life under the thumb of your government is not easy—nor is Old Kinoko. But even with its particular challenges, it allows unprecedented freedoms."

"Freedom from oppression."

"Amongst other things."

I was beginning to understand that when a government was willing to occupy and oppress another country, they were just as willing to use those same methods on their own people. Neo Kinoko wasn't free, not for fungals *or* humans.

If I managed to expose Kinoko Rose, what would happen next? Would Neo Kinoko change? Would the fungals still be subjected to squalor and starvation, forced to eat mushrooms and rations in order to live one more miserable day?

A memory of Liz drifted to the forefront of my mind—the way she'd complain about the meals I'd make her. How she hated the way I cooked chicken, or that my steamed veggies were flavorless.

"Think about how many people around the world are starving," I'd say, time and time again.

But, of course, it had nothing to do with the food.

I'd never be able to make up for what I did to her … the life I stole. But if I could save even one more child from Sumi and Dikku, it'd mean my exile to this city wasn't pointless. If I could bring even a single instance of justice to such an unjust place, wouldn't that be worthwhile?

It was obvious there was no redemption for me. Not in the eyes of those around me … Not in this life. But to *save a life*? That was worth sacrificing myself for, even if it went unnoticed. My redemption could be mine alone. An honorable act worthy of Liz's memory.

An honorable act before an honorable death.

Ogami stroked his beard, eying me with curiosity. "You went quiet for some time there."

"It's nothing," I said. "Now, get me over that bloody fence."

— — — — — —

RUN, AND DO not stop," Ogami ordered.

He propelled across the open street, his legs plunging into the snow. I chased after him—my exhausted limbs were reaching their limit. We made it to the other side, ducking into the cover of warped house frames. Ogami was relentless and pressed onward. I had no choice: Either give up and lose my guide, or force myself to keep going.

And so, I ran, following the fungal through the ruins.

"When you enter the tunnel," Ogami said through even breaths, "pace yourself. It is a tight squeeze—several hundred feet from one end to the other."

I panted. "And what … can I … expect on the other … side?"

"Friends."

"That's … it? How do … they know … I'm coming?"

"They are trustworthy," Ogami replied, "and I have warned them of your arrival."

Warned them? Did he mean the fungalnet?

He continued: "Knock three times fast, two times slow, then one final pound with your fist. When they hear this, they will know it is you."

I opened my mouth to reply, but my lungs wheezed. I stopped and held onto the corner of a wall. With each gasping breath, I took in a gulp of frigid air. "I … need … stop."

Ogami halted. He turned and pounced through the snow like a fox, landing next to me. "We must hurry. The patrols are more frequent the closer we are to the border."

"Weak … I'm weak," I complained. "Pause … catch my breath—"

"Hey!" a high-pitched voice yelped in Coprinian.

I snapped to the source of the sound, eyes landing on two soldiers—a man and a woman. They stood a few dozen feet away with wide-eyed expressions.

"Intruders! Halt!" the female soldier bellowed. She raised her rifle and took aim. "Stand up. Hands behind your heads."

Ogami growled. He glared at the soldiers, then at me. Without hesitation, he swept an arm around my waist and hauled me onto his shoulder ... right on top of the little colony that sprouted there. The soldiers clamored in confusion as Ogami took off with me.

With unexpected strength and speed, Ogami carried me through half-collapsed corridors. I could hear his suppressed groans every time I bounced, but he kept at it.

A warning shot rang out. The horizon filled with silhouettes—birds flying off, fleeing danger.

Ogami pushed forward with unstoppable purpose. He took a short-cut, dodging rotting wood beams and mycobrick boulders. A gunshot boomed behind us. Ogami ducked to the side as a bullet whizzed past my head. He hurtled down a series of alleys filled with snow and rubble, intent on outmaneuvering the soldiers.

Chunks of mold, moss, and mycobrick exploded as more shots peppered the walls. Ogami's breathing had taken on a more labored sound. Quick inhales through his nose, long exhales through his mouth.

"Halt!" a soldier cried.

The flash of a rifle's muzzle lit up the alleyway. Ogami dove behind a colony of fruiting bodies. Multiple bullets struck the fungi, sending sprays of mushroom chunks at my face. A stench of sulfur and mulch filled the air.

More shouts came from different directions. Shit ... How many soldiers were after us now?

Ogami readjusted me, tossing me up and slamming my stomach on his shoulder. I coughed.

"You are heavier than you appear," he stated.

Bastard.

He took off again, zig-zagging through partially exposed alleys. Shots ricocheted and sparked on impact. Ogami took a series of quick turns, almost dropping me on the ground. He found his footing and tore through a mycelium door.

Inside, the room was dank. Clouds of spores drifted around, and green bioluminescent fungi provided the only light. The mushrooms grew from the floor and walls, pulsating with a faint glow.

"I carried you," Ogami said. "*Now*, you walk." He put me down and nudged me across the space.

Each step made the moldering wood floor groan, but Ogami was in a hurry. He jostled me down a set of rotting stairs. We descended into a dirt-floored basement—its ceiling was shallow, so I had to duck. More bioluminescent mushrooms and patches of orange mold shrouded the cramped space in an eerie radiance.

I felt a jab in my lower back. "Go," Ogami said.

At the opposite side of the basement, a dense wall of moist gray fungi protruded from the corner. Their slim stems wobbled slightly, a sheen of green flickering on their caps. Ogami bent down. He parted the mushrooms and waved me over. Behind the colony was a trapdoor.

Ogami lifted it, revealing a square hole. Ropes of mycelium clung to the walls of the hole, descending into an abyss.

"Inside," Ogami ordered. "Follow the tunnel until its end, and there, you will find—"

"Friends." I slipped my fingers between his shoulder fungi and squeezed his corded muscles. "*Ariari do*, Ogami-*kato*."

Footsteps drummed on the floor above, followed by a muffled exchange. The soldiers had found us.

Ogami pursed his lips and bowed. "Good luck, Hofmann-*kato*."

I bowed in return. Ogami drew his sword from its sheath. His eyes trailed along the blade's razor-sharp edge. He turned to me, a knowing look in his steadfast gaze.

"Honorable death," I said.

"Honorable death," Ogami repeated. His hands curled around the sword hilt, loving and firm. "Yomi, The Great Persuader, I await your embrace." He touched the blade to the brim of his cap and left. Within moments, he was up the stairs.

"Good luck," I whispered to no one.

Gunfire erupted. Bullets pierced through the floor and embedded into the dirt. I heard Ogami's sword slice through the air with a *swish*. One of the soldiers screamed. The other unloaded automatic rounds across the house.

Silence.

I scurried down the mycelium ladder. Down, below, beyond. Into the darkness and another unknown.

The air thickened as I climbed down. Something cloyed at my nostrils with a combination of rot and rich earth. My grip was unsteady on the chaotic fungal web—the ladder wasn't uniform, I couldn't see shit, and my boots kept slipping.

But deeper I went, until my left foot hit solid ground.

I felt around, grazing packed dirt, damp roots, and wriggling insects. A headache began to thud beneath my skull. I spun, grasping in all directions. Desperation built and my breathing intensified. The tunnel air was somehow both freezing and suffocating. It constricted my throat.

Finally, my fingernail caught on something solid. A thick bundle, like wires or rope or … mycelium.

I used the fungal rope to lead me along. My head bumped into the shrinking ceiling, sprinkling my hair and shoulders with dirt and bugs. The ceiling got lower, to the point where I had to crouch. On hands and knees, I crawled along, fast and frantic. My body rubbed against roots, and slime smeared across my skin. Curtains of mycelium and cobwebs tickled my face.

With every awkward movement, my breathing became more labored. I wheezed. Stars danced in my vision against a backdrop of black.

I could do this.

Up ahead, a spectral glow gave shape to the tunnel—it guided me forward. Hands raw, frozen, and ravaged, I dragged my haggard corpse through the grime and slime. Closer and closer.

The ebb and flow of bioluminescent fruiting bodies filled the path ahead. Spores caught their light, drifting on an invisible current. The fungi's breath-like synchronicity turned the tunnel into a living organism. I timed my breathing to the pulses.

Brightness, inhale. Darkness, exhale.

I pulled myself along, inch by inch. Pushing through the colony, their clammy caps slithered across my forehead and cheeks. My nose was smothered with scents of loam, spices, and … tea?

Surrounded by mushrooms and spores, I eased into their rhythms. They enveloped me—in no way did I feel harm from them. Some of the tension in my body softened, as did the pounding headache.

I could make it to the other side. The fungi were leading me toward a second chance.

BOOM.

The tunnel quaked. A hail of dirt rained down on my head. Clods of earth bounced off the caps of the bulbous mushrooms surrounding me. Chunks got into my eyes, stinging and scratching as I blinked.

There was another *boom* and more of the ceiling shuddered in a shower of soil. The Goddamned soldiers were going to bring this tunnel down on top of me.

I dragged myself through the colony on unsteady forearms. Grasping at stems, I dug my knees into squishy mushrooms and patches of slime. Another concussive discharge rang through the tunnel. My ears popped. The mushrooms around me tensed. A shockwave rushed past, sucking the air from the confined space.

The tunnel trembled … but it didn't stop.

Wedges of dirt broke apart and fell on top of my back and legs. I pulled myself along, pressured by the low rumble of the tunnel's cascading demise. Clouds of dust and spores trailed me. The intertwined roots and mycelium around me quivered.

The bioluminescent colony thinned out. I crawled. The tunnel groaned and growled as its supports gave way. I crawled. The glow of the mushrooms vanished, but the air thinned out. I crawled.

With each painful pull, I was closer to the end. To salvation.

The tunnel's ceiling broke.

Soil and spores filled the space. With interminable determination, I kept going. I pushed my mind and body to persist, my brittle will the only thing that held me together. Through a deluge of dirt and rocks, I dragged. My. Old. Ass. Forward—

—until my head hit a solid wall.

I'd bloody fucking made it.

I searched for a ladder—mycelium, rope, *anything*. My fingers brushed against a bundle of fine hairs. Gripping the mycelial cord, I rose to my feet. Then I climbed.

Nearing the top, lines of light spilled down from the edges of a trap-door. Reaching it, I braced myself and knocked. Three times fast, two times slow. Clenching my fist, I almost punched the hatch I was so God-damned desperate.

Thump.

A moment passed. Footsteps shuffled above. A chain rattled and muffled voices argued. At last, with a creak, the door lifted. The brightness forced me to squint. With a hand over my brow, my vision adjusted to what I realized was candlelight.

In soft Hōpponese, a woman said, "We've been expecting you."

TEATIME

[33] Case File #42-56
Mildew Grove | 10:07 a.m.

- - - - - - - - -

WARM, FLICKERING CANDLELIGHT dimmed to reveal the wrinkled countenances of two elderly fungals: A woman and a man. The portly man offered me a toothless smile. His whole face scrunched up beneath the jumbled layers of red mushrooms atop his head.

"Don't just stare at her, Pom," the woman chastised, smacking him on the rim of one of his caps. "Help her up!"

"*Damitare*," Pom grumbled. He rubbed the spot where he'd been hit. "You don't gotta treat me like that, Moro. Words'll suffice."

Pom reached down to me with a liver-spotted hand. I grabbed ahold and climbed up into yet another musty basement.

All of my muscles ached and protested. I was forced to crouch, the roof only a little over five feet. My disheveled hair got tangled in the vast network of cobwebs and mold above my head. A dusting of spores drifted in front of my face.

The hunchbacked elderly couple, on the other hand, didn't even have to bend—their mushroom caps barely grazed the wood plank ceiling. Moro stared at me through half-moon glasses. Pom's grin stretched from cheek to cheek. They both wore split-toe socks, not minding the fact that we were standing on dirt.

"Welcome to our home," they said in unison. "We are Moro and Pom Poko."

"Ogami ...," I croaked.

I stepped forward—my bent knees almost buckled. I would've collapsed to the floor had Pom and Moro not rushed forward and cradled my armpits.

Moro closed her eyes, looking meditative. The gills on her broad peach-colored cap fluttered. "Ogami ... he is gone. Death and decay, life and growth—he is one with the dirt again, and we will mourn his passing."

A warrior's death. An honorable death. He'd sacrificed himself so that I could escape and ...

Ridgeway—I had to warn him. "Phone," I said in Hōpponese.

"*Kaidono*," Pom said, his grin replaced with a worried expression.

He didn't understand me.

"Take a moment, dear," Moro said. "Let us get you cleaned, dressed, and fed. Then we will talk."

I took in the room, catching my breath after the choking atmosphere of the tunnel. Pom and Moro had sacks of rice rations piled against one wall. Wooden shelves ran along another. They were filled with fruiting bodies of various shapes and colors, which sprouted from blocks of mycelium.

"This way," Moro said, adjusting her glasses.

She and Pom led me to a mycelium stairwell carpeted with powder blue mold. They took their sweet time going up, each step releasing a puff of spores. I didn't even feel the urge to cover my mouth and nose. I was wrecked, likely infected with some kind of fungal-something-or-other, so what was the fucking point anymore?

The two *still* hadn't reached the top of the stairs.

I held back laughter. Here I was, trying to stop whatever Sumi, Dikku, and Airi had in store, and two geriatric fungals were the only people standing in my way.

We emerged from the stairwell into a simple hallway of mycomat floors, dark wood frames, and mycopaper walls. Morning sunlight seeped through a small window to the right.

Moro and Pom turned to me, flattening the wrinkles on their plain white robes. They both had childish grins on their wizened faces, and their puffed cheeks pushed their eyes up into creased arches.

"Phone," I said again in Hōpponese, desperate to get moving. "People in trouble."

"Ogami told us what you intend to do," Moro said. Then she leaned over to Pom—her cap rubbing against his clustered colony—and whispered in his ear.

"I know she wants to help, but what makes her think we have a phone?" Pom blurted. "Don't make sense that a *shinkin* would have one of those stupid things."

Of course, there was no bloody phone …

"Please, dear, do not mind my husband," Moro said, nudging me down the hall with her spindly fingers. "He can't even make sense of the fungalnet, let alone a telephone. Come, we've made you tea."

I cocked my head. Tea? I needed to contact Ridgeway, not settle in and have a fucking tea party. "I need leave. Now."

"You are a mess, dear," she said with the tone of a scolding mother. "You are covered in slime and dirt, and I will not have you sullying my floors. First, you clean up. After, food and tea. Then, we will send you on your way."

"I need go," I urged. "Danger. Fuyu Lantern Festival."

"And what good will you serve in your current state?" Moro rebuked. "Would it not benefit you to at least clean up and eat?"

"I can't! Must go now!"

Moro waved a hand at me. "Bah! Arrogant humans. You act like the heroes out of myth, running into fights headfirst. How can you go about saving others when you can't even take care of yourself? Now, come."

We emerged into a square room. A squat mushroom-cap table sat in the center of the matted floor, with mold cushions surrounding it. Plants and fungi grew along one wall. It was simple and organized, but also inviting—likely Moro's doing.

I was drawn to the sun's rays spilling through open sliding doors. A cold, crisp breeze filled the space. But before I could take another step, Moro tugged at my jacket.

Pom had returned with a stack of folded fabric. A cloth and a roll of bandages were laid on top. "For you."

"Please, dear, get changed," Moro said. "When you come back, tea and snacks will be served."

I glanced at Pom, who stood behind Moro. He nodded and smiled. "You're our guest."

Bloody Hell. Their Hōpponese hospitality was on full display … as well as their elderly stubbornness.

I accepted the clothing from Pom, then bowed as low as my aching body would allow. "*Ariari do.*"

— — — — —

THAT IS MUCH better," Moro said with a clap. The sound echoed across the tea room. She sat on a cushion next to the low table, looking delighted.

I'd cleaned the grime off myself, even rinsing my hair and changed my dressings. Thankfully, none of my stitches had opened up. The robe Pom had given me was heavy, its dark blue fabric weighing on my shoulders. It was a bit snug, too, but it would do.

Pom stared at me from the table, a glint of wetness in his yellow eyes—he'd said the robe had belonged to their son. It wasn't my place to ask what had happened to their boy, but I was familiar with the pained look of a parent who'd outlived their child.

"Please, sit," Moro insisted, gesturing to a cushion across the table from her.

I sat down cross-legged, wincing at the pain in my thigh. The room was fresh, light winter air wafting about. Aromatic steam rose from the spout of a simple ceramic teapot. Through the open door, I heard the scraping of shovels. Fungals must've been braving the outdoors, removing the snow and ice from the sidewalks.

Post-blizzard recovery in Mildew Grove.

Speaking of recovery, a handful of breakfast dishes were laid out across the table: Seaweed rice balls, a rich brown broth with fungi floating in it, pickled vegetables, and sliced mushrooms sprinkled with sesame seeds.

My brows furrowed. I looked at the spread, feeling a pang of guilt. Why did I deserve any of this?

Moro must've picked up on my reaction. She bowed her head and mushroom caps, offering a prayer: "Karu, thank you for this harvest, which we humbly offer to our guest: A friend of fungals, and an exemplar of change in the face of adversity."

I didn't view myself as an exemplar of anything … But Moro was right. I needed a moment of respite before I rushed into anything. Before I faced the real challenges.

"Eat, dear," Moro encouraged.

Pom licked his lips. He reached out for a rice ball. With surprising agility, Moro whacked the top of his hand. Pom groaned in response, massaging his skin and wounded pride.

"Guests first," she chastised. Filling an empty plate, she placed it before me. "Eat." She slid a pair of chopsticks across the table, then winked at me. "It is alright if you would rather use your hands."

I laughed, embracing the warmth of these two and their home. Placing my palms together, I bowed. "I receive this food."

We ate in silence, Moro and Pom with their chopsticks and me with my fingers. I relished every bite I took. Even the sliced mushrooms—which I would've spat out in disgust mere days ago—were tender and flavorful. A feeling of calm washed over me.

A question lingered on the tip of my now satiated tongue. "Tunnel," I said, almost forgetting the word in Hōpponese. "Why help people?"

Pom placed his chopsticks down. "Moro and I've enjoyed a beautiful life together. When you get to be our age you realize, despite the difficulties that life throws at you, nothing's worth doing alone." He laid his hand on the table, and Moro rested hers atop his. "Don't matter if it's your partner, children, neighbors, or community—a life well-lived is one built on *connections*. Who'd we be if we didn't return the favor for all that Mother Chikyu has given us? To help others is a blessing, gifted to those who've received their fill."

"Whether we help our own kind," Moro added, "or humans."

Kindness transcended difference. Community wasn't confined to a single place, nor a single people—if only Sumi and Dikku understood that. But the world wasn't always so black-and-white.

"I need go," I said in their tongue. I had to leave the idealistic optimism of this home behind.

Pom stood and shuffled around the table. He knelt on crooked knees beside me, pouring tea into three ceramic cups. Steam rose in a cloud of floral fragrance. "Before you go," he said.

He distributed the cups and sat back down. I picked mine up, welcoming its heat on my palms. Lifting it to my lips, I let a trickle of hot liquid enter my mouth.

"Bitter," I said. Though I would happily have traded it for a coffee—even the military ration brand.

Moro smiled, then motioned her hand at me. "Drink, dear."

I finished the scalding tea as fast as I could, burning the tip of my tongue. The bitterness swarmed my mouth. Once it dissipated, an aftertaste like citrus and sweet flowers lingered. It coated my tongue and the back of my throat.

"Delicious," I said.

Pom grinned as he sipped his tea. "The tea's my own recipe. Made it using ingredients from the garden …" He gave me a sheepish glance. "And a psychedelic mushroom."

"You fucking *drugged* me?" I cried in Coprinian. I wanted to flip the Goddamned table, or run to the bathroom and purge my system.

"Please, dear," Moro said, "listen."

I placed my clenched fists atop the mushroom table. Taking slow breaths, I steadied myself.

Moro continued: "What lies ahead of you is a complicated path. We thank you for wanting to save our children, but know that you are walking the divide between two opposing cultures. With a mind and spirit as fractured as yours, this drink can help to heal your mind and soul. To unshackle your mind from the constraints of culture, history, and memory. Once you have awakened, you may finally seek freedom from your past in order to enact change in the present."

Pom giggled and wiggled his eyebrows. "It makes for a fun time, too."

"Fuck …" I rubbed the bridge of my nose. These Goddamned hippies really had drugged me—now of all times. I had no idea what I was in for with this tea, but I needed to leave. I had to contact—

"Koji," I exclaimed. "Nameko Koji. Fungalnet."

"I will take care of that," Moro said.

"Fuyu Lantern Festival," I said. "How get there?"

"It starts in Chaga Park," Pom said from behind his cup, "but that's all the way across the city. We don't have a car, and most'll be frozen solid after the blizzard. But I may have something for you." He scuffled across the mats, slipping on boots before going outside.

Across the table, Moro had her eyes closed. White spores began to leak from her gills. Her lips moved but no words escaped. After a minute, she said, "I sense him."

I leaned across the table. "Send message from Henrietta Hofmann. Warn Ridgeway. Kinoko Rose. Fuyu Lantern Festival. *Revenge*."

Moro's eyes twitched and rolled back. The spores streamed out faster, swirling around her head. She inhaled sharply. Holding her breath, she went still for a few seconds. As she exhaled, the spores dissipated and her body relaxed.

"Chaga Park," she said. "That is what I sensed. That is where his intentions are focused."

Then that was my destination.

My thoughts were interrupted when Pom returned. "Come, come."

He led me to the side of their house. The cold nipped at my exposed skin, and crunchy snow piled up to my knees. In the aftermath of the blizzard, the sun shone bright.

"Here you are," Pom said, rolling a bicycle over.

It was powder blue, like the mold on the stairs, with a brown myco-leather saddle seat and a metal basket on the front. Pom dinged a bell on the handlebars, smiling like a child who'd just opened a present.

My entire body slouched. He had to be fucking kidding me … "Me ride that?" I asked.

Pom nodded. "What with the festival today, most roads'll be cleared up by now. If you *gaigai* are good for anything, you sure know how to melt snow."

Oh, God … I hadn't ridden a bike in years. But I was out of options. There was no phone. Even if there was, by the time a squad car made it up to Mildew Heights, it'd be too late. The festival would've already started, Kinoko Rose's plans fulfilled.

I'd have to ride this bloody bike, and fast.

"I put the winter tires on," Pom said, as if that would reassure me. "And remember: Faith guides us, no matter the weather."

I let out a sigh. Faith wasn't going to get me to Chaga Park, but that stupid bicycle just might—so long as the mushroom tea didn't affect me too much.

Pom took me to the front of the house, pushing the bicycle along. The street was mostly cleared of snow, which was piled up into embankments along each side. Moro walked out of the house.

Pom handed me the bike. He eyed me from head to toe, then raised the seat a few inches. "All set."

Pom went to Moro's side. They bowed to me, and I bowed in return.

"May Murio guide you along your journey," Moro said.

I got on the bike, hating how the seat crammed between my ass cheeks. Moro and Pom waved goodbye as I rolled away. I dinged the bell in farewell. The bicycle wobbled at first, but I found my balance. The wind picked up as I went faster.

Setting my sights on the road ahead, I thought about what was to come. Chaga Park. The Fuyu Lantern Festival. Kinoko Rose.

I just prayed that I wasn't too late.

UNDER THE INFLUENCE

[34] Case File #42-56
Mildew Grove | 12:24 p.m.

- - - - - - - - -

I RODE POM'S bicycle through Mildew Grove with a relentless energy, despite the throbbing of my arm wound. Despite the pins and needles piercing my thigh and ribcage. Despite a most wretched hangover and a horrendous headache.

Every push on the bike pedals strained my muscles and joints. It sapped what little stamina I had left. The memories of shine bottles and folded cloths plagued my thoughts. But the image of Sumi and Dikku's wicked grins kept me motivated.

All I wanted was to see their faces as everything they'd worked toward crumbled.

Something terrible was going to happen. I didn't know what, but I had to warn Ridgeway. I had to get to Koji in Chaga Park.

I crossed an icy pedestrian bridge over the Kinoko River. The bicycle almost slid out on an ice patch, but I kept it steady and rode on. Aromas of shit and trash wafted up from the water as I raced south into Sleepless Street.

Reality warped. The river's gurgling flow vibrated in my eardrums. The edges of passing cars and buildings quivered, as if alive and beckoning me to investigate. Films of sweat formed on my skin, tingling when met with the morning chill. The sensation felt oddly pleasant—almost sensual. A warmth blossomed in my core. It spread out from my organs like the sun radiating its heat in the dead of winter.

This had to be an effect of the tea.

Bloody Hell … I was cycling under the influence. What did those ancient fungals do to me?

I picked up the pace as the urban sprawl of Sleepless Street took shape. The area was replete with low-lying buildings—bars, restaurants, nightclubs, teahouses. Half of the businesses were shuttered with mycelium, boarded up, or abandoned and infested with mold.

I pedaled fast, my vision succumbing to distorted motion blur. The occasional fungals had trekked outdoors, now that the storm had passed. The ones I saw were wrapped in simple winter coats, scraping snow from sidewalks. A teenage button glanced at me through a window. Her eyebrows twisted unnaturally and her golden eyes glowed. All of a sudden, her cap morphed into duplicates. I forced myself to look away.

All around, Sleepless Street was awakening from its post-storm slumber, yet nothing was as it seemed.

I struggled to process my sensory inputs. Could I even trust them anymore? I had to get to Chaga Park, to the Fuyu Lantern Festival, and here I was riding a useless fucking bicycle in the snow.

Inklings of hope lingered in my heart, but in my head, I knew it was impossible …

There was no way I would make it on time.

Like fruiting bodies growing from the decayed flesh of a dead animal, those gangsters would take advantage of this ruined city. They would feast upon its remains, reshaping it in their twisted image.

I wouldn't let that happen. But I needed something faster—a car.

There was an NKPD precinct somewhere in Sleepless Street … Precinct … Eight. A web of streets and alleyways wove through my mind. Detailed images formed a mental map, built on the foundation of subconscious memories. Where the Hell was it?

I couldn't rely on myself—I had to ask for help. But everyone in this neighborhood was fungal. I doubted they'd take kindly to a human. Especially not one riding a bloody bicycle in the snow, dressed in tight

Hōpponese robes.

A thought rose to the surface of my consciousness. It said: *Ask and you shall receive.*

Where the Hell had I heard that before? It sounded like a proverb out of the holy texts.

I slowed down in front of a rundown corner store. My knees groaned and the brakes squealed. There was a fungal man out front, smoking a hand-rolled cigarette. He wore old trousers, a sweater, and a smock. His skin was smooth but his expression weary, giving his young demeanor a paradoxical quality. Even more strange was the way his purple cap seemed to drip and slough around the brim.

Was that really happening?

"What are you looking at, *gaikamu*?" he grumbled in Hōpponese. "Can't you see we're closed?"

Mycelium shutters rose halfway up the façade. Even still, I could see how barren it was inside. Near-empty shelves—a fitting reflection of a starving city.

Leaning the bike against a street mushroom, I got off and approached. My limbs felt light, fluid. "*Haowa*," I said. "Where can I find the nearest police station?"

To my surprise, the words flowed from my lips far more confidently than my usual self. Like a linguistical drainpipe had been unclogged.

The fungal looked at me with a skeptical expression, his face melting and reshaping in real time. I tilted my head, as if that would change what I was hallucinating: His stretched jawline, widening nose, and eyes that got closer until they crossed each other and switched sides.

"Police station," I reiterated. "NKPD."

The man murmured under his breath, his lips moving in weird ways that defied gravity. He gripped his shovel tight. With a groan, he lifted the shovel, pointing the flat tip of the blade down the street.

"Four blocks," he said, "then turn left. Two more blocks. You can't miss it."

I sighed in relief. For a moment, I thought he was going to smack me upside the head with that shovel. I bowed and said, "*Ariari do*, *jiujiu*."

The fungal pursed his lips, which contorted into stretched pancakes. "Don't ever call me *jiujiu* again. I am not your brother ... *shimin*." He spat on the snow next to my feet, his hands wringing the shovel's handle.

Now it was time for me to leave.

I bowed again, got on the bicycle, and left. Riding away, the man's slur wouldn't leave my mind: *Shimin*. It taunted me, festering. I wasn't some foreigner here to colonize, like so many of my countrymen. I was an exile here, displaced from my own people just as Coprinia had done to the Hōpponese.

This city and its people, they were reawakening after the chaos of the storm. But Sumi and Dikku wanted that storm to continue—they wanted the chaos to *persist*.

I wouldn't let them.

Captain Ridgeway and Koji were in Chacha Village, and finding them was the first step to stopping those gangsters.

I collected my composure. The very air and I seemed to breathe in tandem, pearlescent waves rippling around me. A surreal lucidity coursed through my mind. Years of stress, anxiety, and trauma had weighed down upon me, but this welling sensation melted all of that away—the exhaustion, the hangover, the aches of age.

I focused on my breathing and rode to Precinct Eight with a resurgence of energy. My tendons and ligaments expanded and contracted, my muscles feeling flexible and strong. Rivulets of sweat ran down my back, but I didn't mind.

Before I knew it, I'd arrived at the Sleepless Street precinct.

It was a brutalist three-story building, all concrete and sharp angles. A garage extended from its left side. Nothing surrounded the structure except empty patches of snow. The nearest neighbors were half a block away on either side. In true colonizer fashion, the police building was like a cancerous growth.

A pair of patrol cops loitered out front, smoking and chatting. One of them—a slim male with a brown handlebar mustache—eyed me with contempt.

"Excuse me," he called out. "Can we help you?"

I ditched the bicycle on a low wall next to the entrance. With long strides, I flew up the steps and past the cops. Mustache said something else to me, but I waltzed inside with no regard for him or his stupid facial hair.

The reception area was simple: Three gray sofas on either side, coffee tables with magazines scattered atop, and fake plants for some half-assed attempt at evoking life in a lifeless place. A receptionist sat behind a long charcoal desk. Her blonde bangs and purple eye shadow made her look like a clown. Then again, it could've just been the effects of the tea.

She smiled at me like an automaton. In a chirpy tone, she said, "Good mor—" She stopped, giving me a once-over. Her expression twisted in confusion, then kept twisting until she became a whirlpool of hair, skin, and makeup.

"Good morning," I parroted.

I heard footsteps behind me—the two cops from outside.

"What's going on here?" Mustache asked. His hand drifted towards the sidearm on his hip. "Who's this homeless lady?"

"Oh, shut the fuck up," I blurted in a moment of unconscious honesty.

Mustache's whole body went taut. The portly cop next to him smirked.

"Is this bitch crazy?" Mustache mumbled.

"Look, ma'am," Portly warned, "I think it's best that you leave."

With a roll of my eyes, I slammed my hands on the counter with a resounding smack. The receptionist gasped and jumped in her seat. The two cops unholstered their pistols and pointed them at me.

"Stand down," Mustache ordered.

"My name is Detective Henrietta Hofmann," I said. "Central precinct's Homicide Division. I'm on an active investigation and I need a vehicle."

Mustache narrowed his eyes. "A detective?"

"Did I misspeak?" I snapped. "Citizens are in danger, so call Captain Ridgeway and get me a Goddamn car!"

— — — — — —

I SHOULD *NOT* be driving right now," I muttered to myself.

A small truck appeared out of nothingness. I swerved out of the way, the front left of the car bumping against a bank of snow. Honks and yells trailed into the background of my perception. Clenching the steering wheel, I willed myself to stay present and aware. I thanked God that the streets had been cleared of snow. It made my hurried, hallucinatory piloting more feasible … and somewhat safer for everyone else on the road.

I just couldn't believe that I'd gotten a cruiser from the Sleepless Street precinct. Ridgeway had given them the green light, and who were they to argue with a captain? But it wouldn't do me any favors to destroy this car.

Shit. Now, I was *driving* under the influence …

My heart tightened. This was the first time since the crash that I'd entered into a vehicle while intoxicated … putting myself and others at risk. But this felt different—mushrooms weren't alcohol. My mind was clear and focused on my goal.

The only issue would be if the hallucinations got worse.

I could tell I was entering the Chacha Village ward by the narrowing of the streets around me. The road shifted from smooth stones to uneven cobbles coated in ice. There were fewer and fewer cars, pedestrians clogging the alleyways and side streets that jutted off from the main avenue. Traditional Hōpponese structures took over, their tapered polypore roofs covered in thick layers of snow. Countless shrines, temples, and spirit gates were nestled between residences.

Ahead, high above the low homes and temples, I saw the towering pines of Chaga Park. The grove was tucked into the middle of the city like an evergreen skystem, its branches punctuated by pockets of white powder.

As I drove closer, the tops of the trees disappeared from my view. I eased onto the brakes. Turning a corner, I came to a stop a block away from the park. Thousands of fungals carried lanterns and wore white robes, ready to celebrate the winter solstice and receive Fuyu's blessing.

A significant police and military presence patrolled the gathering. A barricade of armored trucks blocked off one street. Hundreds of soldiers in gray armor and helmets were lined up next to the trucks, rifles at the ready, awaiting orders. Police cruisers were parked around the perimeter, their blue-and-red lights bathing the scene.

The pulsating rhythm of the flashing lights ensnared my wandering mind. I stared at them for what felt like hours. The illumination was more brilliant and beautiful than I'd ever seen it.

I shook myself from my stoned stupor. Ridgeway and Koji—I had to find them.

Getting out of the car, I scanned the massive colony of Eien pilgrims, marveling at the magic of congregation. Pom was right: Community was everything. Countless living beings, united by a shared culture, religion, and common purpose.

A tingling smile spread across my face. I stared at the sublime majesty of Chaga Park. How colonies of fruiting bodies grew around the trunks in symbiosis. How sunlight filtered through the trees in vivid rays. How nature maintained its roots in a city, despite the encroachment of urban sprawl.

Streams of robed fungals crowded their way into the copse to pray to Karu. Nestled within the trunks and foliage was a shrine dedicated to The Shapeshifter. Fuyu was one of Karu's four servants, so worshippers made offerings to the god before undertaking the pilgrimage to Fuyu Temple.

Fucking Hell … My thoughts drifted again. I had to *focus*.

It took a while, but I found Ridgeway. He was directing a group of officers near the entrance to the park—one of many captains and majors relaying orders to their subordinates.

I slipped into the throng, making my way toward Ridgeway. All around, fungals sang and chanted, cradling their unlit lanterns and flashing devilish red masks. Even in their merriment, I noticed many of them eying the police and soldiers with scorn—in return, the soldiers looked eager to use their weapons.

This festival was on the knife's edge already. Kinoko Rose could easily tip it toward chaos. I prayed it wouldn't come to that.

I brushed aside fungals as I walked. The touch of fabric and fungi on my fingers sent gentle shocks through my nervous system. My hands floated, a drifting extension of my physical form. Festivalgoers gave me odd looks, but I also picked up on hints of recognition in their dazzling golden eyes.

Exiting the colony, I spotted Koji. He leaned against the ridged bark of a gargantuan tree, smoking one of his cheap cigarettes. An apprehensive look had taken over his face, forming worry lines on his forehead.

I ran towards him. The instant he saw me he dropped his death stick. All of his concern washed away. He rushed to meet me, hands gripping my arms. I winced. Picking up on my pain, he removed his hand and examined my injuries, then my entire body.

"Sorry," Koji said, his expression alight with relief, "I thought you were dead."

"And for a moment there, I thought you were going to hug me." I chuckled. "Injured, yes, but it'll take a lot more to kill me."

Koji massaged my uninjured arm, then paused. He tilted his head and leaned forward, so close I could see the textures in his irises swirling. "Are you high?"

I held my tongue. Koji broke into laughter.

"You are!" he exclaimed. "What *happened* to you?"

"It's a long story," I grumbled, "which I'm not going to indulge you in now. But that elderly couple you 'sensed'"—I poked his mushroom cap—"spiked my Goddamned tea. As if that would help me …"

Koji arched his eyebrows, clearly amused. "In truth, they are not wrong. It was common practice for ancient Hōpponese warriors to consume fresh or dried mushrooms before riding into battle. My people have found strength in the conjoining of realities—the union of the spirit world and our own."

"I have no fucking idea what you're going on about, Nameko, but we don't have more time to waste. We need to talk to Ridgeway."

"You are right," Koji agreed, "but be patient. The atmosphere here is tense—there is a great deal of sensory overload, for both humans and fungals. Do not aggravate the captain."

I scoffed. "Yes, sir."

We made our way to Ridgeway, who'd finished his debrief with the officers. When his eyes landed on me, he shouted, "Hofmann! What in the fuck are you wearing?"

"Blending in with the locals, captain. Call it a … camouflage tactic."

"You are full of shit, and you look like shit." Ridgeway approached Koji and me. He dragged us off, away from prying ears. In an aggressive whisper, he continued: "Now, are you going to tell me where you've been?"

"Sir, I—"

"Don't sir me, Hofmann!" Ridgeway spat. "Don't you dare!"

"I was kidnapped … by Kinoko Rose."

"*What?*" Ridgeway stood there, disbelieving. "What happened? Explain everything."

Koji stepped in. "Apologies, captain, but there are more pressing matters at hand."

"Kinoko Rose are planning something for the festival," I said. "Revenge, of some sort. I don't know what exactly, but I witnessed a warehouse filled with crates of *somake* shine."

Ridgeway clenched his teeth. His face distorted, visible vibrations radiating from his head. The captain blew a sharp breath. "Goddamnit, Hofmann … Do you have proof of their plans? Any specifics?"

CPAN made the mistake of capitulating, even an inch.

"I believe they plan to target Fuyu Temple. Will MacArthur have a speech at any point?"

"Yes," Ridgeway said. "He has an address at the temple in about thirty minutes."

Shit …

"My gut tells me that speech is when all Hell will break loose."

Ridgeway took off his glasses and rubbed his nose. "Look, CPAN is watching our asses. If we break protocol now, they're going to get spooked and assume the fungals are stirring up trouble. Wouldn't be long before the soldiers get trigger happy." His eyes darted between Koji and me. "The two of you, go to the temple as fast as possible. I'll do everything I can here to rally the troops and prepare for the worst."

"Thank you," I said.

"Don't thank me yet," Ridgeway chided. "Stop Kinoko Rose."

I nodded. Ridgeway unholstered his own SIG P26 and placed it in my hands. He also gave me his radio. "Nameko," he said, "cover Hofmann's back. I don't know what happened to her, but she looks a bit … peculiar."

Koji hid a grin. Ridgeway glanced at me, then walked away.

"You ready, Nameko?" I asked.

"I am."

I tossed him the car keys. "Good, 'cause I'm in no state to drive."

PILGRIMAGE

- - - - - - - - -

KOJI FLOORED THE police cruiser through Chacha Village. He pressed on the accelerator, and I sank into the passenger seat. My head bounced off the headrest—the car's suspension wasn't holding up against the icy cobblestone road.

He took us away from the pilgrimage route, which hugged a canal all the way to Fuyu Temple and Spirit Island. The streets were emptier here to the south. So much of the population's attention was fixated upon the festival.

"Hofmann," Koji said. I ignored him.

Out of habit, I reached for the glove box—I was desperate to hear some pilzrock. But I stopped with my fingers curled around the latch. "Damn it," I muttered.

The strange sensations that coursed through my head made me crave music. Something loud and atmospheric to match the encroaching madness I felt. Instead, I looked outside. Shrines and homes raced by the car window. They pulsated and rippled in a dazzling display.

Tapping my right foot to no particular rhythm, I drummed on my legs. Maybe impromptu music would help me figure out what Kinoko Rose had planned. Sumi and Dikku had ordered me dead, but I had—

"Henrietta!" Koji burst out, breaking the endless chain of thoughts ricocheting around my head. "Are you okay?"

A pregnant pause. My lips trembled. "I ... survived."

Those were the first words to come out. In truth, I was exhausted

… broken.

The mushroom tea urged me to move my jaw in circles, so I did. But it wasn't enough to distract from the horrifying realities of what I'd succumbed to: Airi injecting me with shine and cutting into my bicep, almost drowning in the Kinoko River, trudging through the blizzard, being attacked by ravenous fungal wolves, crawling through a suffocating tunnel as it collapsed around me …

I shuddered and squeezed my eyes shut. Whether I wanted to or not, those experiences were a part of me. Shapes of light danced on the backs of my eyelids, warped by welling tears.

"Henrietta." Koji spoke softer now. "What happened after the Sea Dragon arrest?"

Biting my bottom lip, I opened my eyes and told him everything.

Koji's jaw clenched. "Shikaku is alive …"

I reached over to him. My fingers interlaced with the fruiting bodies sprouting from his shoulder. Koji shivered. I withdrew, unsure if I'd crossed a personal boundary.

"But thanks to Oze," I said, "so am I. And with your help we can stop them."

"I am sorry, Henrietta," Koji whispered, "for what you went through. If only you had told me, I—"

"If you were there it wouldn't have changed anything. Sumi and Dikku would've killed you, too. But we're here now and we know where they're planning to strike."

Koji grunted. He took a sharp turn, sending me careening into the passenger door. By the scrunched look on his face, I imagined he was thinking of his cousin.

"Nameko?" No response.

In the persisting silence, Koji and I both worked our jaws—him, from anger, and me, from a potent tea. I looked at my hands, how veiny they were, and the grime that had nested under my cracked nails. My fingers seemed to pulsate, oscillating between large and small.

A pleasant clearness washed over me as I remembered how I used to look at Liz this way. I would marvel at how her body grew, seeing biology play out in real time. Counting the freckles on her nose and cheeks. The soft texture of her auburn hair and how I'd brush out the knots every night.

There was so much beauty in children—their innocence and curiosity. The world was open to them, brimming with questions and mysteries … until the responsibilities of adulthood crushed the imagination and the soul, bit by bit.

Elisabeth would never know that. Never know how shit life could be, but also how magic was born from the small, quiet moments. She'd never know …

That's when it hit me.

The pieces assembled in my mushroom-addled brain. I recalled what Emiko had said, about the signal and fungals being drawn to the sites of victims. The gathering mobs. The escalating outrage and sorrow.

The children.

It was always about the children. The dead were meant to send a message. No … *A rallying call.*

"Bloody fucking Hell," I said. "I think I know what they're planning to do."

Koji glanced over at me. "What did you say?"

"I said, I know what Kinoko Rose are planning to do!" Cracking my window open, I sucked in the brisk breeze. It swirled throughout the car and pricked at my face, tugging me back toward a lucid state.

"Drive faster. We need to get to Lantern Shores *before* MacArthur starts his speech."

– – – – – –

BODIES PRESSED AGAINST our car on either side. Koji honked, but the colossal colony of fungal worshippers was too dense. The pilgrimage flooded into the Torotown ward, toward Lantern Shores and Fuyu Temple.

Thousands of Hōpponese, donning their white robes and carrying unlit lanterns, prepared for the darkest night of the year.

"We won't make it through," I said. "Are there any alternate routes to the temple?"

Koji shook his head. He blared the horn again, causing dozens of surrounding hopheads to startle and shoot us sour looks. Through my eyes, their features twisted and distorted, proof that the tea's psychoactive components were still pumping through my system.

Whatever the tea was doing to me, I perceived the bodily effects more now. My appendages and joints felt loose and distant, as if my mind and body were in the slow process of decoupling.

I shook my hands and blinked. The straight lines on the dashboard's digital clock wavered like sound waves. It was 2:47 p.m.—roughly thirteen minutes until MacArthur's speech.

"Nameko, park the car," I commanded, already unbuckling my seatbelt.

"Hofmann—"

"We're wasting time! Park it now, then lead me to the temple."

Koji pursed his lips, the moldy stubble along his jaw shuddering. He pulled over out of the path of pilgrims and turned off the vehicle. Without a moment to lose, I swung the door open and got out. The air was bitter cold, the flush flowing to my cheeks right away. We walked.

"What's the plan?" Koji asked, checking his gun.

I took out Ridgeway's pistol and gave it a quick once-over. Even though it was the same make and model, the gun felt wrong in my hands—the metal was cold and unnatural. "Simple. Find Sumi and Dikku. Stop them."

Koji chuckled. "You are as infuriating as you are surprising, do you know that?"

"I do. Now, let's go."

We skirted the edges of the procession. Low murmurs flowed through the throng, individual prayers that accumulated in a pervading chorus. The street narrowed, causing thousands of fungals to press together. Their myriad caps created a patchwork of varying colors and shapes.

"How will we get through?" I asked Koji.

"We embark on a pilgrimage," he replied.

There was no other way than to join the mass. We held hands, then dove in. In an instant, I was immersed in the stench of spicy sweat and mulch. Crushed together like this, the proximity of bodies was humid and oppressive. Koji and I pushed onward, interrupting prayers, bumping into shoulders, caps, and lanterns.

Chants and shouts and appeals to the gods bombarded me.

My heart raced. I worked my jaw to pull focus away from the feelings of claustrophobia. To get over the constant bombardment of humid, slimy caps slapping my face, or catching in my hair.

"Stay with me," Koji murmured. His hand was drenched in sweat, but he held firm. He had my back, and I had his.

Koji pulled me along through the throng, closer to the outer walls of Fuyu Temple. The walls were a vivid yellow, blooms of lemon-colored mold coating the mycelium foundations beneath. We were funneled into a chokepoint, where spirit gates slowed the progress of the pilgrims.

As we passed under the gate—Koji bowing in recognition of his deities—we came out the other side into a vast courtyard. Its size reminded me of the sports stadiums back in Morellum. And much like the matching jerseys of the Morellum Rangers, Fuyu Temple was awash in a sea of white.

I almost slipped, but Koji kept me upright. Yesterday's snowfall had already been transformed into a slurry of mud and slush by the heat and feet of Eien worshippers. We pressed deeper into the crowd, heading toward the grandiose main temple.

Just by looking at Fuyu Temple, it was clear how important the deity was to the Hōpponese. The structure was a third of the courtyard's width across, with four stories of mycelium and polypore roofs towering above. Like the outer walls, the temple was built from mycelium and adorned with sheets of golden mold. Giant lanterns hung in its open ground floor, and decorative red toadstools sprouted up on either side of a mycobrick balcony.

And standing on that balcony was Duncan MacArthur.

"Neo Kinokans!" his voice boomed in fluent Hōpponese. He stood tall, his posture erect. In one hand, MacArthur held a megaphone, and in the other his trademark pipe. He was surrounded by a retinue of armed guards, along with news cameras and reporters filming the speech live.

"No ... we're too late," I moaned. "It's over, Nameko ... We didn't—"

Koji slapped me. A radiating sting blossomed across my face. Fight-or-flight kicked in, a flood of adrenaline pumping through me. I lifted a hand to strike back, but Koji had already grasped my wrist.

"Come back to me, Hofmann," he hissed. "It is *not* over."

I stared into his amber eyes. His breath was steady and warm, the smell of his cheap cigarettes greeting me. I felt the stickiness of the mud beneath my boots. This was real. Nameko was real. *I was real.*

Like bloody fucking Hell this was over.

"Move your ass, Nameko," I said, gathering my composure. "Let's get closer to the temple."

Koji let go of my wrist and grinned. "Now, there is the Hofmann I have come to respect."

We moved in toward the temple, scanning the crowd. Koji's gills flared as he sensed those around him. Still no sign of Sumi, Dikku, or anyone else from Kinoko Rose.

"Neo Kinokans," MacArthur repeated. "It is my honor to usher in the Fuyu Lantern Festival, a time-honored tradition amongst your noble people."

Agitated murmurs filled the courtyard—no doubt MacArthur's words came across as condescending. And how could they not? Here was a military dictator spouting about how the subjugated were "noble people."

Utter bullshit.

"As our two nations strengthen their bond," MacArthur continued, "it is important for us to uphold the cultural values we each carry. Whether Coprinian or Hōpponese, Neo Kinoko is our home, and our peoples are united through a common goal!"

"What goal?" someone shouted. "Starvation?"

"We're dying!" another voice cried out.

"*Gaikamu* don't give a shit about us!"

The voices rose, more incensed by the second. While they drowned out MacArthur's moment, I kept searching. The number of fungals all around was staggering. Thousands upon thousands of them, each holding their homemade lanterns. Countless buttons also cupped ….

Ceramic bottles, white cloths, and candles.

A grinding noise swarmed my head as I grated my teeth. "Nameko, what are those for?"

Koji leaned in and whispered, "The drink is a tea, meant to satiate the demons who rise from the darkness of winter. The cloth is a personal ward of protection. The candle is a guide in the consuming black, made from the mycowax of the one who holds it. And the lanterns, they rise into the night to keep the demons at bay."

"But those bottles, those cloths …," I muttered.

The warehouse.

That's when I saw them: Eien priests wearing crimson robes wandered through the crowd carrying baskets. They passed out offerings to the worshippers.

I overheard one of the priests: "The demons are on our doorstep, arisen from the shadows. May these offerings serve you in the battle to come."

I ran at the priest and thrust him to the ground. Dozens of ceramic bottles spilled into the mud—the acrid smell of *somake* shine punched my nose. I dug my knee into his chest and held his arms down.

The priest looked shocked, then angry. A crooked smile spread across his pockmarked face. I swore he morphed into a red-masked demon, his eyes aglow with bright flame, horns curling out from beneath his gills.

"Stupid *gaigai* bitch," he spat. "The mushrooms. Will. Rise."

I ripped his robe apart at the chest: A rose tattoo, etched into the top of his sternum. Its lines wriggled, blooms of black mold writhing at the edges. Inky spores flooded from the gangster's gills.

He cackled. "You're too late."

I took out my gun and clocked the gillie bastard across the temple. Then I radioed Ridgeway: "Captain, we need backup. The fungals, they're armed. A revolution is coming."

Somake shine pooled in the mud. Shine, cloth, candle.

Burn it all down.

MacArthur spoke up over the colony. "Do not misunderstand me, *shinkin*! It is our duty to serve the Hōpponese people, and we are working tirelessly to provide for the citizens of this city."

"More like filling your own bellies and pockets!" bellowed an angry agitator.

"I assure you all, we provide for all the citizens of this city *equally*!" MacArthur's attempt to salvage his speech was floundering. He made a hand signal to one of his guards, who spoke into a handheld radio.

"Nameko," I yelled, "it's the priests!"

But Koji was overwhelmed—his gills went wild, spasming as he absorbed the growing disquiet of his kin. I spun, surveying the scene. All around, I saw the crimson robes of Kinoko Rose "priests" mingling in with the festivalgoers. I turned back to MacArthur—he looked frustrated. But above, on the third-floor balcony …

What the fuck?

Sumi, Dikku, and Airi.

They stood with their arms spread and eyes closed, spores trickling from their caps. All of a sudden, the entire crowd writhed and clutched their heads. Koji stood next me, digging his fingernails into his own fungal flesh.

"The … signal …," he managed.

Sumi and the others, *they* were doing this—and I was going to stop them. I grabbed Koji and dragged him through what would soon become a mob. He screamed and lashed out, but I didn't relent. As we neared the temple, Koji's torment lessened.

"Run …," he told me. "I am right … behind you."

Without a word, I let go of him and hastened into the temple. I searched and found a set of stairs in the back—they led up to hallways on each level. I continued to the third floor, but the door was locked. Koji appeared behind me and slammed his full weight into it. Once, twice.

On the second strike, the door rattled loose.

I steadied my gun and dashed inside. Coming face-to-face with …

Hana.

OFFERINGS

[36] Case File #42-56
Torotown | 3:04 p.m.

- - - - - - - - -

S*HUSHU* …" KOJI'S VOICE cracked, confusion falling across his features. His pistol was aimed at Dikku's cap, but his eyes were fixed upon Hana. Shikaku hovered behind her like a shadow.

"Auntie," Koji continued, "what are you doing here? With *them*?"

Kinoko Rose gangsters surrounded us on three sides, making the long room feel even smaller. I counted ten of them, plus Hana, Sumi, Dikku, Airi, and Shikaku. Fifteen in total …

Fuck. We were outnumbered.

Regardless, I had Sumi in my sights. There was no way I'd let that piece of shit walk free again, even if it meant his cronies gunning me down.

"Koji-*dari*," Hana said, taking a few steps toward her nephew, "please, lower your weapon. I will explain."

"Explain?" Koji replied. "I sense nothing but calm from you!"

The crimson Watcher robes Sumi wore bunched up as he crossed his arms. With a venomous grin, he said, "Listen to your auntie. Our elders know best—"

"By the gods, Sumi-*jero*, *kuta dai*!" Spittle flew from Hana's mouth as she told Sumi to shut up. She turned to Koji, her expression shifting from pissed off to placating. "Nephew, please, lower your gun. It does not have to end like this."

I'd had enough of this crap.

"End *how*, exactly?" I interrupted in Hōpponese. Sweat beaded on my palms, dripping down my gun's grip. "Tell us the truth, Hana, or this ends in a bloodbath. Do you want to see your nephew die today?"

Hana approached me, her wrinkled hands raised submissively beside her cap. Her yellow eyes were dull beneath the shadow of her pinched brow. "That is quite enough of the idle threats, detective." Hana studied me, lilting her bulbous head. "Something about you has changed since our last meeting."

I glared at Sumi, Dikku, and Airi. "Finding yourself on Death's door will do that to you. Now talk, old woman. The truth."

Hana cackled. Age lines deepened into crevices around her mouth and eyes, her countenance morphing into something sharp and devilish. "*Old woman*—I like that. If you live past today, you will know soon enough the real effects of age on your mind and body." Sprinkles of dark spores trickled from beneath her cap, and her voice was as rough as a bag of stones. She coughed twice into the sleeve of her dark gray robe. "Still, I am surprised you have not yet figured it out."

Memories trickled back to me, pieces fitting into place: Rose petals on the shrine, Hana holding a flower in the photo with Iroh, shine shipments to The Shelf, the tattoos … And Shikaku, her own son, a gang member.

Oze's words from the warehouse rang clear in my mind: *Things are not as they appear.*

"Kinoko Rose," I whispered. "You—"

"—are The Cap," Koji finished.

Hana's gills flared and contracted. She opened the raised collar of her robe, revealing the moldy lines of a rose tattoo. "It is so, as it has been since the beginning. Kinoko Rose is my creation, my legacy."

Hana, The Cap. Sumi, The Veil. Dikku, The Stem. Airi, The Gills.

Koji's mouth opened and closed several times, words failing to form. His arms slackened, his gills tightening like a fish out of water. Shikaku swept in and took Koji's weapon.

"Sorry, *jiujiu*," Shikaku said. "It's just business."

Hana walked up to her nephew, touching his cheek with thin, bony fingers. "Did your mother never tell you what Iroh's nickname was for me? He taught me how to fish, to hunt, to survive, and so I gifted him the name Skinner. But on our first date, he bought me a single flower—it was all he could afford."

"A rose," Koji whispered.

Hana raised her chin with pride. "I am Kinoko Rose."

"I was so blind …," Koji said. "How did I not sense it?"

"My sister—*your mother*—is the one who blinded you. She obscured the truth from you, and you were all too eager to brush aside the signs that were right in front of you. Family makes you strong, but it can also make you ignorant."

Koji glared at his aunt. Resentment showed in his clenched fists and flared nostrils.

I scoffed, a rough and exhausted sound. "What a lovely story, Hana. You sent us on a wild chase to find Daigoro and Shikaku, meanwhile you've been playing us all along."

"You misunderstand my intentions, detective," Hana said. "Shikaku came back to me, and I am grateful for that, but Daigoro is still missing. No one knows where he is."

Shikaku's eyes darted to his mother, then Koji and I—did Hana not know?

Koji sighed. "I was a fool to ever trust you, *shushu*."

"It has never been about trust," Hana replied coldly. "It has and always will be about the bonds of *family*. Those I raised"—she gestured to Shikaku, then swept an open hand toward Sumi, Dikku, Airi, and the surrounding gangsters—"and those who chose to follow me. Iroh and Oze never wanted to be a part of it, and I respected them for that. It is shameful that Oze chose to free Detective Hofmann from the warehouse, but he will receive a punishment befitting his … indiscretion. Shikaku, on the other hand, has followed the threads that my mycelium has laid. So too will Daigoro, and generations to come. The Spore War …

Your people forced us to cower, but we will cower no longer. We will see MacArthur and his butchers *burn*."

"Auntie ..." Koji looked stricken, drained. "Has there not been enough suffering? Do you wish to add *more* hardship to the lives of our kin?"

"Do you not understand, Koji?" Hana said, her voice firm. Black spores flowed down across her shoulders like a cape, darkening her presence. "We have toiled in the darkness long enough. I witnessed firsthand the devastation the humans wrought during the war. I spent day after day, sending messages and orders to troops through the fungal network—feeling their pain, experiencing over and over the instant the bright flames of fungal lives were extinguished. We fought for survival ... we *still* fight for survival! We will upend the Coprinian boot that seeks to crush us. A new era for Neo Kinoko is at hand."

Hana breathed deep, relaxing her posture. "I want Daigoro back, so that he can carry on our legacy in that new era."

I laughed at her words, hearing her parallel Sumi's remarks from yesterday: *A new era for Neo Kinoko is at hand. A new mushroom will bloom, with the three of us atop the cap.*

Hana scowled at me. She was oblivious to the truth about her grandson—her son had obscured it from her, and like Koji she was too blind to see it.

Scanning the room, I noticed Sumi, Dikku, Airi, and Shikaku were each fixated upon Hana. Their caps quivered and dark particulates signaled that the mood had shifted. Shikaku reached deep into his robes.

Koji glanced at me. I mouthed to him: *Be ready. Get down.*

"A new mushroom will bloom," I mocked. "It's too bad none of your family told you how Iroh really died, or why Daigoro was really taken."

Hana froze. She whirled on me but I kept my pistol trained on Sumi. He was the real danger.

"What did you say?" she hissed.

"A new era for Neo Kinoko is at hand. A new mushroom will bloom,"

I repeated. "But you're wrong—everything you've built will crumble into a pile of ash and spores." I said to Sumi: "Tell her about the children."

Hana spun her neck so fast I heard a *pop*. She swiveled between Sumi and Dikku, whose caps were pulsating with a steady release of inky black spores.

"*Which children?*" Hana demanded.

I tapped my foot, sensing the rising tension in the room. "Where are they, Sumi?"

Shikaku approached his mother. A dark aura surrounded the fungal, like storm clouds writhing in violent winds—a man in conflict with himself and his duty. Hana must've sensed something was amiss. She backed away, but Shikaku closed the gap again.

I mouthed to Koji again: *Wait.*

"I am sorry, mother," Shikaku said. "*Damigami nai*"—bless the gods—"for I have sinned."

The moments that followed rushed by in a flurry of frenzied motion, as if the mushroom tea in my system had warped time. I threw myself to the floor, as did Koji. Shikaku wrapped around his mother's arms, drawing a knife to the saggy folds of her neck.

Gunshots fired, the muzzle flashes creating brilliant explosions of arcing light. Sumi and Dikku shouted harsh commands that were drowned out by the onslaught of noise. Airi cradled her belly and spectated, unmoving. Four gangsters fell in sprays of gore and chitinous chunks—one next to Dikku and three from Hana's personal entourage.

Shuffling backwards like a crab, I hid behind a wooden column at the opposite end of the room. I popped out, took aim, and shot two more gangsters—they fell, crimson rivers leaking from chest wounds.

Koji picked up a pistol from one of the dead gang members, but another descended upon him. There was a deafening *bang*, followed by the biting stench of metal and sulfur. Blood sprayed from the back of the gangster's cap. He collapsed onto the floor next to Koji.

"Nameko, to me!" I ordered.

A bullet ricocheted off the column right above me. Splinters shot past my cheek, cutting lines across my skin. I ignored the pain, laying down suppressing fire as Koji ran to me. He slid around the column, taking cover at my side.

Shikaku had dragged Hana off to the far corner of the room. Sumi and Dikku were each behind their own columns, commanding their two remaining soldiers to kill Hana's final bodyguard. They took down their brother in a brutal execution, peppering his torso and cap with seven shots.

I whispered to Koji: "On my mark, we kill those last two before dealing with the others."

"I will follow you, Hofmann." In that instant, there was a single-mindedness in the way Koji's yellow eyes bored into mine.

I held up my fingers, counting down. Three. Two. One.

We popped out and I pulled the trigger. Bullets flew past us, zipping across the room or striking the wood in showers of sharp fragments. My shot met the flesh beneath a gangster's jaw in a spray of gory mist. His blood settled to the floor, followed by the heavy *thump* of dead bodies—Koji's target was also down.

Silence.

Back behind cover, the ringing of gunfire rattled in my eardrums. MacArthur's booming voice rose up from the festival below, along with the cloying smoke of sandalwood incense. His speech was met with the murmurs of a restless crowd and a rising rhythmic chant.

"It's over, Sumi!" I yelled.

A throaty laugh echoed across the room. "You should have drowned when you jumped in the river, detective!"

Peering around the column, I saw Shikaku haul his teary-eyed mother in front of open sliding doors. A mycofabric rag had been stuffed into her mouth. Shikaku's knife dug into her throat as she groaned and complained.

Dikku and Airi appeared, long ropes wrapped around their shoulders. They dragged four children through the doors. Sumi was next to the kids, waving them along with his gun. There were three girls—Chihiro, Yoshiko, Akemi—who I recognized from the Missing Persons case files.

The final child was a boy: Daigoro.

Hana saw her grandson and writhed. Her neck bled from the pressure of her son's knife.

The four kids were gagged and bound at the wrists. They appeared dirty and starved, bruises and scrapes littering their bodies. Their caps, along with the little fruiting bodies of Akemi, the half-breed, looked limp and dehydrated. CPAN was painted on their chests in red pigment—one letter for each child. And on their necks, little rose tattoos.

Rose-runners. Innocent children who'd been bribed into service … and then tortured.

Dikku and Airi tossed the children onto the ground. The kids wept, eyes bloodshot, bodies heaving. Sumi slid open another set of doors, revealing a balcony. A rush of noise flooded in, clearer than before.

"Let them go!" Koji pleaded.

"I am afraid I cannot do that," Sumi responded. "Do anything to try and stop us, and each of them will die."

My mind raced, flipping through options of how Koji and I could save those kids. Nothing. I was blank.

"You will kill them no matter what we do," Koji said.

Sumi snickered. "And that is the whole point. There is no turning back from our purpose."

Dikku and Airi each had a pistol trained on the kids, who cowered on the floor. Sumi stood in front of Hana, so close the brims of their caps touched.

"Your plan was lacking," Sumi said. "These kids, your *grandson*, are worthy offerings to the future of our nation and Kinoko Rose. They are the sparks that will ignite the fire." Sumi dragged a finger through the blood running down Hana's neck. He held it up and examined it. "You had the right idea: MacArthur and his military must feel the pain we have felt. But you do not understand the meaning of sacrifice. You do not understand what it will take for our people to rise up. They must feel agony, in order to unleash their anger."

Hana wriggled. Her eyes were raw with tears. Shikaku's blade scored her skin, but she didn't seem to care.

"Dikku," Sumi said. "Airi."

The Stem and The Gills unfurled the ropes from their shoulders. Airi handed hers to Sumi, as did Dikku. Sumi approached the children, looping the ropes around each of their necks.

Nooses.

Sumi returned to a trembling Hana. Gray spores flooded from her gills. "I want you to watch," Sumi said into her ear, "as we hang these children before our brethren. As the fungals of Neo Kinoko witness a crime so cruel, they will only see what they want to see. They will focus on MacArthur and CPAN—those who have subjugated us. Our people are armed, and the fires will burn bright. Then, we will take back our city, and from the ashes, we fungals will rise."

One by one, Dikku and Airi led the children onto the balcony. They looped their ropes around a support beam beneath the spongy pores of the fungal awning. Airi returned, one hand on a gun and the other caressing her stomach. Hana's screams were dulled by the mouth gag.

Sumi looked back at me. Our eyes met, and his grin stretched wide—he wanted me to watch, too. "Dikku, it is time."

The children were lifted onto the railing, their dirty little feet wobbling on the wood frame. MacArthur continued his plea to the population below. Those he had oppressed. Those who would turn on him in an instant.

I took a deep breath. "Nameko, take care of your cousin. Leave the rest to me. On one."

MacArthur's speech reached its fulcrum. "Despite our differences, fungals and humans can coexist. The war is in the past, a scar on our shared story. But our focus, our energies, must look towards the *future*!"

"Three," I whispered.

"We are here to build that future together. We are about to enter into a new age of cooperation, where Neo Kinoko and Hōppon, Morellum and Coprinia, will rebuild this city in *our shared image*—as the greatest city this nation has ever known!"

"Two."

"Our future is united, and our future is bright! May Fuyu protect you all in the darkest of nights!"

"One."

I hurtled forward, pistol raised and pointed at Sumi. I fired mid-run. Three shots burst from the gun in quick succession. One struck Sumi's weapon, spraying sparks and shrapnel. The fungal bastard growled. The next shot nearly missed the brim of his cap, and the third buried itself in his right shoulder. He fell back into the wall, a pool of blood darkening his crimson robes.

The report of Koji firing resounded behind me. One of his shots narrowly missed his cousin, who pulled Hana away from the balcony doors.

Dikku glanced in my direction, eyes going wide as I rushed his hulking form. He withdrew his fungal gun and fired. The shot whizzed past my ear. He fired again, but the gun jammed, exploding in his face in a cloud of noxious spores. He coughed and stumbled. I took the opportunity and shot him in the knee, but he didn't go down. I shot him again in the chest.

This was for Ryo.

With a roar, Dikku threw his shredded gun at me. I ducked, but kept running, knowing that gravity would be my only resort with this gargantuan stem of a gillie. I closed the distance, bracing myself—just in time for Dikku to push the first child, Chihiro, over the railing.

"No!" I screamed.

I sprinted into his muscular wall of mass, tackling him with all my might. We smashed through the railing in a burst of broken wood, out toward the sprawling colony of Eien worshippers.

As Dikku fell away from me, I reached out for Chihiro. Succumbing to the sublime weight of gravity, my ears filled with the rush of air, the squealing feedback of MacArthur's megaphone, and the shrieks of anger, confusion, and terror from the crowd below.

LITTLE SPIRITS

- - - - - - - - -

I HELD TIGHT to Chihiro's wispy wrist. Her skin was covered in grime, causing my grip to slip. Fear radiated from her amber eyes—the little orbs were wet with teardrops. The gag still filled her mouth, but her smothered screams came through all too clear. She'd been so close to dying: The rope leading to the noose had barely any slack left.

Spectral particles floated around her cap—dust or spores … yet they swirled and glowed in tandem with the girl's cries. It was as if the little spirits were connected to her. As if they were *alive*.

"I've got you, Chihiro," I said softly in Hōpponese.

My mind whirred with recollections of the case files … She'd disappeared from The Pit almost three months ago. I would do everything I could to get her home, even to a place as destitute as that refugee zone.

Fingers aching, I clung to the corner of the balcony. Sweat collected on my palms. I held onto Chihiro's arm with all the strength my ailing muscles could muster.

I tried to pull myself up but failed, nearly losing my hold on her. She cried and choked on her gag.

Goddamnit …

Jarring shouts reverberated across the temple courtyard. The smoky stench of burning filled the sky. Gunshots boomed and glass bottles shattered, followed by the whoosh of flames. I heard MacArthur barking orders beneath us, his soldiers responding with aggressive warning fire.

The rhythmic chant from before was louder now. The voices of thousands of networked fungals rose up: "WILL YOU KILL US ALL, HERE AND NOW?"

It was a challenge to the established order: How far would CPAN go to maintain their power? How many more innocent deaths would they inflict?

I hoped MacArthur met the fate he deserved.

"Stay with me, Chihiro." I had to focus on getting us out of here alive. My hands were weak, and I struggled to keep the distress out of my voice.

All of sudden, Chihiro removed the noose from her neck with her free hand. She shakily looped the rope around my forearm, then hooked the noose on her wrist.

Smart girl.

Chihiro used the last of her energy to tighten the noose, then went limp. I felt her full weight again, tugging at my burning bicep. The girl's face drooped, eyelids heavy. The light blue, conical mushroom cap atop her head was cracked and dirty, and her pink gills were desiccated. I had to get her to safety. Quick.

I heard a series of growls and groans. I glanced downward … Son of a bitch.

Dikku lay atop the second floor's slanted polypore awning. His thick body had landed on a cushioning layer of snow, but his extra load had caused the roof's supports to buckle. The mushrooms protested as Dikku rolled over, clambering onto his knees. He looked up at us.

An exposed smile twisted his face into something evil. Clouds of dark spores churned about him. The gangster reached inside his jacket, and I heard the threatening whisper as a glistening blade exited its mycoleather sheath.

Dikku stood—the knife between his teeth—and climbed.

Fuck.

I made another attempt to pull Chihiro and myself up—my muscles cramped. I jerked, almost slipping. Another attempt, then another.

"I'm gonna fucking gut you, *gaigai* bitch!" Dikku snarled.

I coughed. Thick, black smoke choked the air. Shrieks and gunfire and crackling fire raged below. Bottles smashed on the front face of the temple, and I felt the heat of flames rise up. In response, bombastic ballistics blared across the courtyard, followed by the gargled cries of dying fungals.

Channeling all my strength, fingers burning with pins and needles, I hauled myself up to the broken banister. My chest rested on the balcony, and there was a chance I could get a leg on top. Stretching my foot out, I felt old muscles cramp. I pushed through the pain until … my boot landed on solid wood.

I leveraged my weight and swung Chihiro. She landed roughly on the balcony, motionless but alive. Free of the extra burden, I clambered up, scratching my face and hands on splintered fragments of wood. I hauled my entire body over the edge and rolled over next to Chihiro.

If I could have, I would've passed out then and there … but Dikku was coming.

I peered over the side: That burly fucking gangster had almost reached us. My gun was gone, so I searched for a weapon. I found a fractured section of wood railing and ripped it off. Getting onto my knees, I swung my makeshift club at Dikku. Three times I missed. On the fourth try, he snatched the club and threw it aside. The force of it made me lose my balance. I wobbled and fell to my side.

One by one, Dikku's thick digits curled around the lip of the balcony.

I struggled to my feet. "Fuck you, *shabi*." I spat on his fingers and crushed them beneath my boot, twisting my toes until bones popped and snapped. The bastard howled. I stomped again and again until he could hold on no longer.

Finally, he let go.

Dikku roared, flailing his brawny arms. He plummeted three stories through the air, down onto the snow-packed courtyard.

I pushed Dikku out of my mind and turned to Chihiro. Her breathing was weak, but that meant she was alive. I rushed to the other children, hoisting them off the railing, then removed their nooses and gags. They bawled and thrashed, trailed by frenzied spores that swirled around their malnourished forms.

I pulled them close, not caring about their unwashed stench of stale piss and sweat. Their bodies and caps convulsed against my chest as they sobbed. Leaning back, I looked at them. I wiped away their tears, smearing clear trails across their filthy faces. "Yoshiko, Akemi, I'll get you out of here. But please—"

That's when I realized I was holding only two kids. Yoshiko, Akemi, and Chihiro … one child was missing.

Daigoro.

I draped Chihiro over my shoulder and led the other children inside.

— — — — — —

STAY BACK, HOFMANN!" Koji warned.

I hurried the kids behind the cover of a collapsed mushroom table. Gently laying Chihiro on the floor, I peered over the cap. Koji was in the middle of the room, his pistol pointed at his cousin. Shikaku had replaced his knife with a gun, pressing it against his mother's temple. The life had drained from Hana's eyes, like she knew what was coming.

An inevitability.

"Nameko, what's going on?" I asked. "Where are Sumi and Daigoro?"

"Sumi took him," he said. "Go. I will remain here to take care of … family business."

Shikaku sneered. "That's rich, cousin—*now* you choose to stay. You abandoned us before! You weren't even there when my father died!"

"That does not excuse you for helping Sumi, Dikku, and Airi in their mad quest!" Koji glanced at me, signaling for me to move.

"I have three kids with me, Nameko," I said, holding the girls close. "I can't put them at risk."

Koji winced. "How could you do this, *jiujiu*? Betraying your own mother ... Willingly handing your son over to die ..."

Shikaku's voice cracked. "You ... you weren't the only one to abandon us, cousin. After my father went to The Great Beyond ..." Wet trails cascaded down his cheeks as he dug the gun barrel into Hana's skin. "You became a ghost, mother. Father's death left a void in your place, and Oze and I were left to grieve alone ... At least we had each other. You tried so hard to remember the man who'd died, but you ended up forgetting those who were still alive ..."

Hana heaved with wracking sobs. Koji stepped forward, lowering his gun. "Shikaku ... Sumi and Dikku, they were the ones who had your father killed. Him and his whole crew."

"You're lying!" Shikaku cried. "Mother treated me like trash my whole life, sending me off to do her dirty work. Sumi and Dikku, they gave me responsibility. They gave me *purpose*. They wouldn't do that to me."

"It's true, Shikaku," I said. "Sumi and Dikku were using Sea Dragon Seafood Co. to dump bodies into the bay, knowing they would wash ashore and be found by fungals. Your father found out about it and rallied his crew to go on strike—to reveal what was going on. That's why Sumi ordered Iwashi to have them killed. To make it look like an accident out at sea."

"Stop lying to me!" Shikaku screamed.

Hana's tears turned into panicked chokes—she hadn't known the truth about Iroh, either.

"They killed your father," Koji reiterated, inching closer to his cousin and aunt. "They twisted your mind into thinking your *son* would be a worthy sacrifice—an offering. And for what?"

Shikaku cocked his head. "A future for our people, cousin."

"And you want Daigoro to *die* for that?" I snapped. "You want to deny him a part in this future you've worked so hard to bring about?"

Shikaku laughed ruefully. "I was never fit to be a father ... and Daigoro should never have been born." He straightened up and sniffled. "Tell Oze I'm sorry."

"Cousin, don't do it," Koji warned.

"Goodbye, mother."

"Shikaku, no!"

Koji raised his weapon and fired at the same moment Shikaku pulled the trigger. The bullet struck Shikaku in the forehead—blood bloomed behind him and he crumpled to the floor. Hana's head exploded out the side, sending skull fragments and brain matter across the room.

The two gunshots echoed for what felt like minutes. Koji fell to his knees, his arms sagging at his side. His body convulsed as he stared at his slaughtered family. Yoshiko and Akemi cried next to me, pawing at my arms. I told them to wait there, then I hurried to Koji's side.

"Nameko," I whispered.

"I-I killed him and ...," he managed to say through lip-trembling whimpers. Gray spores streamed from his gills, like a soundless dirge for the dead.

"I ... I'm sorry, Nameko."

He slowly tilted his head to look at me, his mouth agape and dripping with saliva. His eyes were bloodshot, bubbling and damp. "Daigoro ...," he said. He took out his radio, fumbling the knob to the correct frequency. "S-Sumi took Daigoro ... Leave the children with me and ... I will radio Ridgeway for help."

"Nameko, you can't—"

"*Damitare*, Hofmann!" he bellowed. An energy returned to him. The gray spores had coalesced into a blinding-white halo that crowned his cap.

"Go," he said. "Sumi has taken Daigoro to Spirit Island ... to the shrine of Yomi. He will sacrifice Daigoro to the God of Death and The

Great Beyond, to end my *shushu*'s sporeline with one final, spiteful act."

"How do you know this?"

Koji tapped the shaggy scales on his large mushroom cap. His demeanor had steadied.

The fungalnet—he sensed Sumi's intentions.

I corralled the children and nudged them toward Koji. I laid Chihiro in his outstretched arms. "Officer Nameko will take care of you," I said to the kids. "Stay with him until help arrives, okay?"

Yoshiko snagged my sleeve. Her gills quivered and she spoke weakly: "Don't go … please."

I clutched her small hands in mine, caressing them with my thumbs. A warmth blossomed in my chest—I used to console Elisabeth just like that. "There's something I have to do, but I'll be back soon. Don't worry"—I raised my chin at Koji—"he's a friend and he will protect you."

I kissed Yoshiko on the cap and stood. She obliged, going to Koji's side. "Keep them safe, Nameko."

"I will." He held out a fungal pistol.

I closed his fingers around the weapon, pushing his hand away. "You'll need it more than I will. If *anyone* threatens them—"

"I will blow their fucking brains out," Koji said mockingly.

I chuckled. "You're learning."

"Only from the best," he teased. "Now go. May Heriko guide you on the dark path ahead."

There was no more time to lose. I left the room and sped down the stairs.

— — — — — —

EXITING FUYU TEMPLE, I was plunged into a brutal clash.

Thousands of fungals and hundreds of CPAN soldiers slaughtered one another with fists, guns, and shards of glass. Curtains of fire spread across the temple grounds, sending billowing pillars of acrid smoke into the air. The trampled skeletons of handmade lanterns clung to the mud. Shots rang out, leaving bloodied buttons writhing in the muck.

Crowds choked the exits to the temple grounds—fungals who would rather run away than fight. Either that, or they didn't want to be forced into a revolution. But most remained, holding a united front against the Coprinian oppressors.

Droves of hopheads swarmed their CPAN opponents, pinning them down and enveloping them alive in mycelium. I saw a *somake* cocktail smash on a soldier's back. He screamed, consumed by roiling flame. His comrades retaliated with a firing line that gunned down a colony of fungals.

Ash and spores rained down upon the festival. Clouds of spores clogged the sky, smothering the setting winter sun.

Not far from me, an elderly fungal knelt on the ground, praying amidst the carnage: "Hogosha, Goddess of War, bathe this battlefield in your divine protection."

The revolution had begun. Violence and bloodshed signaled a new era for Neo Kinoko.

Part of me wanted to stay, to somehow alter the outcome of this conflict. But I was just one person—it was more likely that I'd die here.

The one thing I *could* do was save Daigoro.

On weak knees, my bones, muscles, and brain exhausted, I left Fuyu Temple behind. But the cries of death and pain wouldn't go away. They haunted me as my boots landed heavy on the old wooden planks of a pedestrian bridge.

I crossed the threshold onto Spirit Island. Stepping foot on the dark sands, my mind flooded with memories of the dead child. Mere days ago, I'd arrived on this beach, opening a bag to find a dismembered body.

I kept running, noticing an erratic trail of footprints and drops of blood—Daigoro was putting up a fight. They led across the shore, toward the blackness of the forest.

Bloody Hell …. I had no flashlight, no flares. Nothing to light my way in the woods. I had no idea where Yomi's shrine was, either.

Then I remembered the little spirits, the ethereal apparitions around Chihiro's head that I'd likely hallucinated. They couldn't have been real, but the way they'd interacted with her …

I closed my eyes, took deep breaths, and prayed. "Little spirits, come to me. Shine your light upon the dark of night, so that I may see the path ahead." A pregnant pause. "Please."

Moments passed in silence. My senses heightened. The rotten egg smell of decaying seaweed mixed with a salty tang. The soft lapping of waves, rustling the sand as they rose and receded. The cold tickle of the winter breeze as it brushed against my skin.

A faint greenish glow lit up the backs of my eyelids.

I opened my eyes to eddies of bioluminescent spores amassing in the air before me. The river of spirits encircled me, dousing me in a musty scent. I felt them drift through my hair and across my cheeks, taking in my form.

They *were* alive—examining me, caressing me. I'd experienced so many strange things in Hōppon, but this …

I playfully ran my fingers through the spores. "Guide me, little spirits," I said, embracing this close encounter with the inexplicable. "Show me the way to Yomi's shrine, to the sanctuary of the God of Death."

The glimmering cloud of spores became agitated, curving in rapid motions. It gyrated around me, faster and faster, before taking off across the beach. A glowing path flowed toward the forest. I followed.

A spirit gate took shape amongst the intimidating wall of trees. Its faded crimson paint peeled, the wood beams rotting and weighed down by snow. Neglect born from the burdens of a changing world.

I recalled the words Narioyshi spoke, here on this beach: *The spirits here are no longer satiated. They have given up and abandoned us all.*

Sumi intended to satiate one of the old gods—to deliver a sacrifice of blood and innocence to Yomi. I wouldn't let that happen.

The little spirits waited for me, spiraling around the gate. I gazed beyond it, up the stone stairwell that would lead me into the unknown. The spirits must've sensed my readiness, drifting up the moss-covered steps. I approached the gate, running my hand along one of its decaying columns.

It was time.

I stepped through the threshold, following the spores up the stairs. We ascended toward Spirit Island's summit, to save a child deserving of life.

"Heriko, protect me."

WELL OF SOULS

[38] Case File #42-56
Spirit Island | 4:04 p.m.

- - - - - - - - -

I WAS PANTING by the time I reached the top of the stairs. The little spirits lit up the woods in an eerie green glow. The air was noticeably warm and thick beneath the tightly-packed trees, their branches and pine needles slick with condensation. Small treetop creatures skittered above, sending droplets of dew falling onto my head. With every breath I took, I tasted the overpowering sweetness of earth and sap.

Flat stones were laid across the forest floor, providing a path ahead. Crimson splatters dotted the rocks—I followed the glowing cloud of spirits and Sumi's bloody tracks.

Glistening fungi sprouted up along the path—they crept through every available nook and cranny. Ghostly groans, yawns, and cries echoed amongst the boughs, as if the boundaries between reality and a spirit realm were blurring together.

I almost planted my boot on top of the raw corpse of a bird. Its chest cavity was open, revealing cracked ribs and glossy organs. A blanket of web-like mycelium covered half its body. Little fruiting bodies grew out of the mycelium like wriggling fingers, feasting on the bird's rotten remains.

Any normal person would be disgusted by that sight—Hell, just *yesterday* it would've made my mycophobic ass vomit. But it didn't bother me now. This was part of the natural cycle of life.

The spirits led me deeper into the forest. I lumbered in pursuit.

"How much farther?"

The swarm of spores swirled around a pair of tree trunks, rushing back to me. They encircled me like an aggressive squall. Minute flecks stung at my exposed skin, then I lurched forward at the hip.

"What the—"

Those bloody little bastards.

The spirits nudged me again. Apparently, I'd pissed them off, and now they were in a hurry to move me along.

Picking up the pace, we crossed a mossy glade. The sky above was darkening, as the winter solstice bid an early farewell to the sun. The stone path cut through the middle of the open space, a trail of blood spattered along the way. Strange statues rested on the moss—hundreds of stout fungal depictions, none more than a foot tall, skillfully carved from rock.

A scream sounded through the trees.

Daigoro.

I ran in the direction of the noise, leaving my little guardians behind. The trees closed in. The air became dense, harder to inhale. I pumped my arms and legs, boots clapping against slippery, uneven stones.

Another spirit gate was ahead. I sprinted through it, snow-capped stone lanterns lining the path into a small valley. Atop a rocky outcrop—at the peak of a winding stairwell—rose the shrine. Yomi's shrine.

It stood four-stories-tall, a slender, tiered tower of crimson mycelium. Snow had gathered on its polypore mushroom roofs, and the structure was in stark contrast to the gloomy foliage surrounding it.

Daigoro screamed again.

A deeply-rooted instinct kicked in and I raced toward the icy stone steps of the stairwell. Up, up, up. Past dozens more fungal statues that peppered the rocks on either side. Past droplets of Sumi's blood.

Daigoro shrieked and I stopped thinking. Just ran until I reached the shrine's large black door.

I slammed into it with my full momentum, feeling a sharp jolt in my shoulder. The door didn't budge. I scrambled, searching for ways to get in. I settled on clawing at the tall mycopaper windows at the front of the shrine. The chitinous fungal pulp buried itself under my fingernails as I tore it apart.

The windows thinned, and I punched holes in the weak spots. Ripping the holes open, I climbed through.

The main room reeked of sandalwood incense and mold. Its cobweb-littered corners were lit by dozens of candles placed atop fire-resistant fungi. This place was old, neglected.

Across the room, Sumi and Daigoro stood before an altar made of a single, wide mushroom cap. White blooms of mycelium hung from the sides of the cap like a wedding veil. Sumi forced Daigoro onto his knees at knifepoint, like a sacrificial lamb from the old Coprinian holy texts.

The gangster prayed to Yomi, the God of Death. He cut his left hand, drizzling warm blood atop the boy's cap. The exit wound on his left shoulder was still bleeding.

I watched, frozen in horror. Without another moment's hesitation, I raced towards them. "Sumi!" I howled. "Step away from the boy."

Sumi spun to face me. His candlelit features scrunched up in hatred. Pitch black spores poured from his gills, churning around him. "Hofmann …"

The room was larger than I'd expected. Sumi had an instant to ready himself, his knife held steady. Daigoro glanced back at me. The boy took advantage of my distraction—he lunged at Sumi's already bleeding hand and bit down.

Ichor flowed from the gangster's split flesh. Instinctively, he dropped his knife and cradled the wounded appendage. He kicked Daigoro in the stomach, but the boy just smiled.

Blood dripped down Daigoro's chin and stained his teeth. He stood to his full four-foot height. Scowling. Fists clenched.

Defiant.

Sumi scoffed at this, hovering above the boy. He tore off a piece of his robe and wrapped it around his hand. "Don't be a fool, Daigoro. You are just another statistic to her. Do you truly believe that *gaikamu* will save you? That she *cares* about you?"

Daigoro studied me. "Yes."

Then I dove—for the second time in an hour—to tackle some piece of shit hophead gangster.

My shoulder connected with Sumi's midsection, sending him careening into the altar. I landed on top of him in a mangled pile of mushroom chunks and tangled mycelium.

Before the bastard could react, I clocked him in the nose. Streams of ichor flowed from his nostrils. I punched him again and again, my knuckles staining red. Sumi quickly countered—he raised a knee straight into my ribcage. The strike didn't hurt all that much, but it surprised me enough for Sumi to grasp my ponytail.

He yanked me down to the floor, the follicles on my scalp searing with pain. Then he forced my head back. He picked up his fallen blade, preparing to gouge my neck like a fish.

But he'd made a mistake, one that was the downfall of every arrogant man: His legs were wide open.

I swung, my fist connecting with his balls. The gangster groaned and collapsed. His cheek slammed against the ancient wood floor. I fell backwards, landing roughly on my spine. Rolling over, I got up onto all fours, angling my feet so I could launch myself forward. Sumi rose from the smashed altar, his face twisted in a grimace.

"You and Daigoro will die here today," Sumi taunted with a fierce smile. Crusted blood covered his mouth and chin. His face bloomed with purple contusions.

"Death comes for us all. One way or another," I said, echoing Hana's words to Koji in Skinner's Room.

Daigoro had fled to the far wall, fear tattooed on his face. *Run*, I mouthed to him.

Sumi leaned down and plucked his knife from the floor, favoring his uninjured side. "That it does, detective." He ran a finger along the spine of the blade. "But Hana's sporeline ends here, and Kinoko Rose will be mine. Neo Kinoko will. Be. Mine."

With startling speed, Sumi leapt at me. Inky spores spiraled around him, disorienting my sense of space. He stabbed straight and fast, nearly impaling me had I not jumped backwards. Again, he pressed the attack, slashing sideways—I ducked out of the way. The cut tore a diagonal line across my jacket, nicking the skin below my collarbone.

By some stroke of luck, the mushroom tea's lingering effects had left me more aware, more present—the effects existed solely in my mind now. Time had slowed, giving me room to react. Still, Sumi's movements were swift and practiced—too fast even for my enhanced middle-aged mind to handle.

He sliced at me once more. I dodged to the side, pulling a candle-covered mushroom down on him. Flames popped and flickered out. Hot wax flew onto Sumi's robes, causing him to recoil. In that fraction of a second, I sprung. He deftly tossed me aside, nearly gutting me with his blade.

I scurried backward, knocking over more mushrooms and candles. Daigoro banged on the door and cried. He tried to remove the barricade, a heavy wooden bar resting atop metal brackets.

Sweat pooled across my back and dripped from my armpits. A tinge of hopelessness crept into my thoughts. Goddamnit ... How in the Hell could I beat Sumi?

"Give up, Hofmann," Sumi said. "Walk out that door right now and leave Neo Kinoko. I promise I will not harm you."

"Your promises are poison," I spat.

Sumi growled. He dashed forward, vaulting over candles and fungal debris. I scurried backward. My brain was sharp, but my body was languishing—I was unsure of how I could defend myself.

All of a sudden, a *clunk* resounded from the direction of the door: Daigoro had lifted the bar off its brackets. The boy swung the door open and collapsed to the floor. He heaved with heavy sobs.

As soon as the entrance was agape, a powerful gust of glacial wind filled the room. It brought with it the fresh fragrance of evergreen trees and … a swarm of bioluminescent spores.

The little spirits swooped into the shrine, coalescing in a concentrated cloud.

"Daigoro, *run*!" I hoped the boy would heed my warning.

I knew Sumi was bigger and stronger than I was, but I had my spores as backup. All I needed to do was distract Sumi long enough for Daigoro to flee.

Aided by the little spirits, I charged. I hurled a fist at Sumi, going ballistic in my assault. Concurrently, the spirits converged on him. My punch landed on his gills. He yowled in pain. Glowing spores then swarmed his face—he clawed desperately at the shapeless motes.

I set upon him with a rage that I'd suppressed ever since Elisabeth died … Since I killed her.

That knotted anger welled up and released. I barraged Sumi's cap and gills with raw knuckles. Sumi's skin contorted and bones fractured as I rained blow after blow. I dug my fingers into his shoulder, twisting his bullet wound. Adrenaline pumped through my body with a furious intensity. I swung my arms over and over, connecting with his soft gills and stiff skull.

My vision blurred, and the shrine faded away into darkness. Only Sumi and I remained. All of a sudden, a bright flicker of iridescent lights flashed in my eyes, followed by a powerful shock that sent my body into convulsions—

—and dragged me—

—outside of myself. I floated in nothingness. All around, a stink of iron and incense permeated. Wraithlike shadows reached out to me with their churning tentacles. I stared down at a skinny old woman beating a fungal to death, punching his purpling cap into a chitinous pulp.

Was this Hell?

Ghostly forms writhed in the black, dipping in and out of existence. They began to take shape as fractal scenes—half-constructed, breaking apart in agonizing screams. Children cried for help as they were bound and tortured. Scents of gore and antiseptic chemicals. The grating of a saw cutting through flesh and bone. A metallic screech as a car flipped and rolled. Gasoline fumes, frayed wires sparking, the stink of melting plastic—

—*Elisabeth.*

My little girl wept in my arms—not me, but past me. "It's okay, mum," she said weakly, her words repeating in an echoing loop.

I reached out for Liz with invisible appendages, desperate to be close. To feel her and console her and take away the torment of my mistakes. I urged myself forward, whatever insubstantial form I inhabited. So close, I could smell her favorite gum, feel the warmth of her spearmint breath …

"I forgive you," Elisabeth whispered.

And then she froze. Her eyes clouded over. The color drained from her skin. In an instant, she erupted in a burst of fragmented molecules, spreading out into the darkness. All that remained was my past self, drunk and weeping.

I forgive you.

Those three words bored into my brain. Liz had said them that day, offering me a way out the moment before she died. But in my grief, I never forgave myself. Frederick never did, either. But *her* forgiveness was all that mattered … and I'd ignored it.

Why had I wallowed in a despair that she'd freed me from? Why did I waste away my life and my relationships because of a guilt that was entirely *mine*? Was I so egotistical that I could only think of myself?

I was despicable. A rotting remnant of a traumatic past—

The scene of my daughter's death disintegrated into a shower of particles, slowly reforming into Tsutomu's toothy grin. He filled the shadowy void, gigantic and grotesque, as Sumi and I took shape again. I wanted to vomit, seeing that murderer as he took pleasure in my physical body mutilating Sumi.

Was I as much of a monster as Tsutomu? As Sumi?

Tsutomu's laughter filled the void, melding with wails and weeping, accruing into a relentless cacophony. Recollections from different lives fused into a cloud-like dome of inexplicable horror. Memories built from spores. A projection of the underworld, showing death and torture and suffering.

The dome closed in like a curtain, roiling and threatening to crush Sumi and I—the *physical me*. Then, like a flash of lightning, apparitions swirled out of the shadows.

A well of souls birthed from spores, rising from the intangible depths.

They were children—fungals and half-breeds. Their bodies solidified, broken and dismembered. Limbs, caps, and body parts were missing or hung loose like torn fabric, held together by flaps of skin.

As the dome of memories contracted, the children crept closer to Sumi and I. They did not speak, but rather hummed and chanted. The song started out gossamer thin, building in strength to drown out the din of the memory dome.

The spirits of the dead children pulled me away from Sumi, then gathered around him. They placed their hands all over his body ... just like Oze and the fungals had done to me on The Shelf. Their song grew in intensity, mycelium snaking from their phantom fingers. The filaments spread and crawled across Sumi's figure. Under his robes, probing and searching ...

The kids' heads snapped back unnaturally. At that moment, the mycelium pierced Sumi's flesh and entered his ears, mouth, nose, and eye sockets. The kids stared up into the chasm of darkness. Their hands tensed and trembled.

A sudden *boom* sucked all the air and sound from the dome.

Silence, if only for a second.

Then Sumi arced his spine violently, howling in horror. His mouth went wide, releasing a tornado of ashen spores. His eyes bulged, showing bloodshot whites. The children's mycelial network glowed. Light trailed out of Sumi's body, through the fungal threads and into the tiny digits of those he'd tormented.

For what seemed like an eternity, I heard nothing but the anguished screams of a fungal monster.

His life force was drained away by those he hurt—the children whose deaths he caused. Sumi's entire body was consumed by a radiating chrysalis of mycelium.

I was a witness to this ceremony. A spiritual cleansing and demise worthy of the God of Death.

The children's network pulsated in time with a rising brightness, like breaths of light. A sudden burst of blinding whiteness consumed the dark spirit world and—

I panted, my chest rising and falling. I was motionless, straddling Sumi's limp body.

Where was I?

The broken altar. The smell of incense and candle wax. Yomi's shrine. Spirit Island.

But where had I *been*?

Sumi's face was a shattered mess, broken and bloodied. I checked his pulse: Still alive.

My breathing slowed. I stood, feeling a weightlessness pervade my whole body and being. I would leave my ego and my pride behind in that Hellish world. All of the trauma—years of emotional and psychological burden—that was a part of me. The flaws, aggression, grief, and resentment.

For so long, my past consumed me. No longer would I carry that burden.

"Detective," a frail voice said in Hōpponese.

I turned to see Nariyoshi Keisuke—the elderly man from the beach. The one who'd discovered the dead body. He stood in the wide doorway, a twig of an arm curled around Daigoro. A group of twenty or so fungals stood behind him. I approached them.

I left Sumi's unconscious form behind me, approaching Nariyoshi. "Keisuke-*shen*," I replied, bowing deeper than my aching back would've liked.

Nariyoshi placed a bony hand on my shoulder. "Rise, Hofmann. You need not bow to me, nor anyone. Not after what you have done today."

"How'd you know to come? Did you sense him?"

"Your Hōpponese has improved these past couple of days," Nariyoshi joked with a hollow-cheeked smirk. Then his face turned solemn. "But yes, we were drawn here by the boy's pain. Luckily, he found us first, in the forest."

I sighed with relief.

Nariyoshi pointed a crooked finger at Sumi. "That man, he is a *zunoro*"—a curse—"upon our people, but he is just one of many. There is much healing left to do."

"I agree," I said. "And Sumi will rot in a prison cell, as he deserves."

"No." Nariyoshi shook his head. "He is one of ours, and deserves justice in a way only we can mete out. We will punish him in a manner befitting our people and our customs."

"*What?*" I hissed. "He should be tried under Coprinian law!"

"Have you learned nothing? When will humans learn that their systems and institutions do not apply to all beings? Believe me when I say, Sumi will be punished for his crimes, but it will be done *our way*."

"Fine," I relented. "Sumi is yours. But let me take Daigoro to his mother."

Nariyoshi bowed slightly. "If the boy so wishes."

Daigoro tore away from Nariyoshi. He ran to me and hugged my legs. I cupped the back of his head, massaging his moldy black hair. White spores drifted gently from his gills.

"*Ariari do*," he whispered.

I lifted the boy, despite my back muscles objecting. "Let's go."

Nariyoshi and the other fungals parted, making a path for us to pass. I staggered through the door and out into the cold. I paused, turning back to Nariyoshi. "Don't go easy on Sumi."

The elder dipped his head and grizzled cap, closing his eyes as he did so. "Mother Chikyu will guide us. Farewell, Hofmann."

Exhausted, I shambled down the stone steps. Daigoro shivered against my chest. I stared up at the sky, expecting the faint twinkle of stars, or the luminous moon.

I stopped, awestruck.

Standing out against the mauve blanket of twilight were hundreds of floating lanterns. Spirits in the sky, glimmering with bioluminescence. A well of souls rising toward Heaven above.

WORLD OF SLEEPERS

[39] Case File #42-56
Spirit Island | 5:11 p.m.

- - - - - - - - -

BY THE TIME my boots touched sand, Daigoro snored softly. He was nestled in my arms, reminding me of Elisabeth at his age. The way she'd snuggle up in the crook of my armpit when we watched movies. Or her frequent night terrors, where I'd lay awake in her small bed, enveloping her like a cocoon.

I treaded slowly along the blackening beach. The breeze was brisk down here, and the last trickles of sun painted the sky purple. I held the boy tight, wrapping my loosened robes around his body. Exhaustion had consumed me so deeply that I barely took notice of it anymore.

A large colony of fungals had gathered on the shoreline. Getting closer, I saw that hundreds of them had taken off their shoes. They waded into the freezing water, brushing aside sticky seaweed. Groups of kids splashed each other, unworried and unburdened.

A tear rolled down my cheek. It clung to my skin, the chill night air attempting to slow its journey.

I wandered into the throng. The fungals stared at me, confusion washing over their faces. But that expression faded the moment they took in Daigoro, asleep in my embrace. The gentle rise and fall of his lungs matched the contractions of his gills. The fungals seemed to sense it, calming at our presence.

Continuing through the crowd, I stepped into the dark ocean. The shock of immersion was stunning. It didn't matter that my boots were wet, my feet sodden and toes frozen. There was a joy to this moment, these people.

I made my way to the front of the colony, submerged up to my knees. Homemade paper lanterns drifted out into Kinoko Bay, their silhouettes bobbing up and down. Dozens more fungals placed their own handmade creations atop the water. They nudged the lanterns while speaking heartfelt prayers to Fuyu, Heriko, and other Eien deities, fingers resting on the brims of their mushroom caps.

The swarm of floating lanterns glowed with faint flickers of light. The fungals chanted, their eyes closed as they swayed in the waves. Then the lanterns ignited in bioluminescent brilliance—they began to lift off the water's surface. One by one, the lanterns rose, sailing upward like a sea of scintillating, spore-lit beacons.

Fuyu's bright guardians, holding off the demon horde in the dimming twilight.

The sun had finally set in the western sky, a dreamy haze in shades of orange and indigo. I gazed out at the silhouetted skyline of Neo Kinoko—rubble and ruin that projected as much beauty as it did sorrow. Leftovers from The Long War. Memories that couldn't be wiped away.

But at least Neo Kinoko and the fungals had the Mother Mushroom. She was a symbol for them to hold onto—a matriarch who could provide hope for a better future. Mother Chikyu, casting a protective blanket over her damaged city.

The distant, rhythmic *thump* of CPAN helicopters echoed across the bay. I watched as they cut above Spirit Island, heading towards Fuyu Temple and Torotown.

The temple still stood, but its surrounding walls and grounds were littered with smoldering fires. Smoke rose in opaque, gray plumes, and hints of burnt carbon wafted on the winds.

My heart skipped a beat.

Koji …

Surprising the fungals around me, I spun and trudged through twisted bundles of seaweed. My feet and legs tingled with numbness. "*Yisima*," I repeated, splashing those around me with murky seawater. Daigoro, so deep in sleep, barely even stirred.

Once I was back on the beach, I shifted Daigoro onto my left shoulder. That gave me a chance to unclip my radio. "Nameko," I said, "it's Hofmann. Can you read me?"

– – – – – –

NOT EVEN TWO hours had passed since the festival had descended into destruction, but the battle was already over.

Daigoro weighed down my arms as I stood at the edge of the Fuyu Temple grounds. Speechless, heartbroken …

"Dear God," I whispered.

The clash between the fungals and soldiers had left a wasted landscape in its wake—a foul mix of slush, mud, and ichor was smeared across the ruined earth. Weak fires still burned, charring the ground and spewing smoke. Crushed or torn lanterns were strewn about the field. It was an abstract expressionist painting that portrayed a story of conflicting cultures with every violent brushstroke.

I skirted the outer wall towards the temple. Koji still hadn't responded to my bloody radio calls. No one from the NKPD had.

At last, fatigue was setting in, my limbs going numb. With Daigoro in my weakening arms, I couldn't plug my nose and avoid the assault of rancid death. A cloud of spores and smoke hung over the battlefield in a low fog, carrying with it a heavy metallic scent. Hundreds of bloody bodies laid in the mire. The mutilated caps and white Eien robes of fungals stood out, but there were also CPAN soldiers who'd fallen. Some were burnt, their bodies mangled and charred. Others were completely or partially consumed by webs of mycelium.

Pairs of human paramedics trudged clumsily through the mud, wearing hazmat suits with red crosses on the chest. They carried away the corpses one by one.

I'd witnessed death many times in my life, but not on this scale.

Helicopters circled above, then swerved deeper into Torotown—scouring the aftermath for further signs of disobedience. On the far side of Fuyu Temple—where vehicles could gain access—the lights of ambulances and NKPD cruisers strobed, illuminating the night.

I headed in that direction, hoping it was where I'd find Koji and the kids.

"Please, let them be alive," I begged.

A few minutes passed on tired feet. The front of the temple had been scorched by explosive cocktails, and bullet holes riddled its walls. I rounded a corner, entering into a swirl of chaos.

Ambulances were lined up in rows across a walled courtyard, engines idling and ready to leave. Dozens of emergency responders hastened to get the injured loaded up and ready to be rushed to hospitals. Full body bags had been stacked along one side of the enclosure. Pairs of NKPD officers were directing vehicles, and handfuls more stuffed handcuffed fungal dissenters into vans.

I let out a long-held sigh when I finally saw Koji's shaggy cap.

He stood at the rear of an ambulance, talking to a paramedic. A fungal child was loaded on a stretcher in the back of the vehicle—I couldn't tell who it was. Another paramedic sat in the back, examining the child.

The paramedic patted Koji on the arm, then closed the rear doors and got in the driver's seat. The ambulance roared to life and was directed out of the courtyard.

"Nameko," I said as I shambled towards him.

Koji's eyes went wide at the sound of my voice. He ran to my side. "Hofmann! You are alive, you—" His mouth hung open, turning into a disbelieving smile. With shaky, blood-stained hands, he reached out to the boy. "D-Daigoro."

The boy's soft breathing put pressure on my chest. "He's fast asleep … mostly unhurt."

Koji choked up. With the utmost of care, I transferred Daigoro into Koji's familial embrace. I remembered the photo I'd seen of Koji and his father in Danban Diner—he and Daigoro looked so alike. The connection made me laugh, but it came out as a rattling wheeze.

"What is it?" Koji asked.

"Nothing," I responded. "This day has made me appreciate the little things."

He snorted roughly, running his fingers through Daigoro's moldy hair. "I could not agree more."

I paused and swallowed, my throat raw and dehydrated. "The other children, are they okay? Chihiro, Yoshiko, Akemi?"

Koji nodded slowly. "The ambulance that just left took Yoshiko. Chihiro and Akemi were sent off a few minutes earlier. But … you saved Daigoro."

I told Koji about my ascent to the peak of Spirit Island. The fight with Sumi and the spirit children who consumed his twisted soul. And of Nariyoshi's request to deal with Sumi in their own way.

He came closer, concentrating on my eyes. "Your pupils are still dilated."

The tea.

"I cannot thank you enough," Koji continued. "There is goodness in you, and the fighting spirit of Virosa. Sumi will see justice served, but what you saw in the spirit world …" He drifted off, his brows tightening. "There is something strange about you, that you would be capable of witnessing things so uniquely … fungal. I doubt many, if *any*, humans have ever entered into the fungalnet or The Great Beyond."

The Great Beyond?

I couldn't explain what I'd experienced. Couldn't rationalize the surreal nature of it. The memories, the sensations … It was so *real*. But what had I actually seen? Was it the fungalnet? Or could it have been a hallucination from the tea?

"Did Moro and Pom's concoction allow me to do all that?"

Koji grunted, low and slow. "Perhaps."

"But Nameko, I saw Elisabeth again."

"As you did during my interrogation of Tsutomu …"

I shivered, thinking of the invasion of Tsutomu's mind. The way it merged with mine and Koji's. "What do you think it means?"

"It will require further investigation," Koji said, becoming pensive. "The manners by which memories permeate the fungalnet are different from how humans experience and process life … You have stumbled across a most strange enigma, Hofmann."

I bit my lower lip. "If only *this* bloody mystery didn't involve me."

Confused, I crossed my arms. I'd unintentionally turned to face the deathly tableau that had tainted Fuyu Temple's holy grounds.

Koji noticed—his body language spoke volumes. The slight bow of his cap cast his upper face in shadow, his posture hunched, and his tone turned solemn. "Let us go. Ridgeway will want to see you."

Bloody Hell … What now?

Cradling Daigoro, Koji led me through a maze of emergency vehicles and responders. The pained screams of the injured rang out. Dozens of soldiers were loaded on gurneys, their wounds gaping and gory. Ambulances came and went, with NKPD officers managing the flow.

I caught sight of Ridgeway surrounded by a crew of cops.

"Masks on," Ridgeway barked. "Do a final sweep of the temple grounds, and make sure all the dead are accounted for. MacArthur wants specifics, so don't fuck up your numbers. Go!"

The officers saluted Ridgeway before breaking off to carry out their duties.

"Captain," I said.

Ridgeway spun on his heel and cocked an eyebrow. "You're alive. Good."

I touched my forehead in a weak salute. "I thought you'd be happier to see me."

"Ha! Look around, Hofmann," Ridgeway said through bared teeth.

"You were right, but you also failed to stop this fucking massacre from unfolding. Kinoko Rose got their wish: Fungals and humans, at each other's throats." Before I could defend myself, he waved me off. "What was I expecting? A miracle, in *this city*? If we're not careful, it'll be the Goddamned fucking Spore War all over again."

"There is still hope that relations can be mended," Koji added.

"You're a naive optimist, Nameko," Ridgeway spat. He looked tired, the engraved age lines around his mouth and forehead looking deeper than ever. "Over three hundred fungals dead, and hundreds more injured. Thirty-nine Coprinian soldiers, killed in action! Do you really believe either side will take this lightly?"

"No, sir," I said.

Ridgeway cackled. "Again with the 'sir,' Hofmann? You really know how to charm an old man."

"That I do. *Sir*."

"Well, at least we have someone to pin all this on," Ridgeway said. He took off his glasses. Removing a cloth from his jacket, he cleaned a smudge on the lens.

"Who?" I implored.

Sumi was taken by Noriyoshi. Hana was dead. Airi had escaped. So that meant …

"Dikku Waru is alive." The words escaped my mouth, despite my mind disbelieving them.

I glanced at Koji—he looked deflated. Then to Ridgeway, who said, "Severely injured and likely crippled, but the fucking gangster gillie lives."

"*Where is he now*?" I demanded.

Ridgeway pointed across the courtyard. "See for yourself."

Dikku lay unconscious atop a stretcher, mycoleather straps holding him in place. One leg and both arms were bent at unnatural angles. The kneecap of the deformed leg was shattered from the shot I'd fired earlier, and a dark pool of blood spread out from the bullet wound on his chest. A retinue of CPAN soldiers followed behind two paramedics, guns trained on Dikku in case he woke up in an aggressive mood.

I couldn't believe that bastard was alive. It took everything in me not to go over there and end his life.

Another stretcher followed Dikku's, but this one had a body bag on top. Beyond them, Duncan MacArthur stood with his hands behind his back, surrounded by bodyguards. The bastard looked smug—as if he hadn't almost been killed in a riot.

"Who's in the bag?" I asked.

"Hana," Ridgeway replied.

Koji tensed up, and I shot him a look. Why would CPAN take her body?

"I asked to bury her," Koji muttered, "in the traditional ways of my people. She would be returned to the earth from whence she came, consumed by mycelium and continuing the cycle of life and death. But …"

"MacArthur denied his request," Ridgeway finished, scratching his balding scalp.

I worked my jaw. "What are they going to do to her?"

Ridgeway gave me a sideways glance. "Need-to-know basis, and none of us are need-to-know. Hell, maybe they'll prop her up in a public square to set an example for any fungals who cross CPAN again."

In a brief flash of fate, MacArthur's stony stare strayed in my direction. His gaze landed on me. He wouldn't recognize me, but for some reason he didn't look away, either.

I kept my eyes locked on his. There was a man who had ruined a nation, who lorded over a people he didn't understand. I had no clue what he had planned for Dikku or Hana, but I knew one thing: Neo Kinoko was changing, and I doubted he could crush the fungals under his tyrannical boot for much longer.

A soldier rushed up to MacArthur, speaking frantically. Dikku and Hana were stowed into two separate military vans. A minute later, MacArthur and his entourage filed into the vans. They took off in a rumbling convoy.

I squeezed Koji's arm comfortingly. "I'm sorry, Nameko."

Koji bowed his head, his lips touching Daigoro's cap. He whispered a prayer to Hana's grandchild.

After a moment, Ridgeway said: "Go home, both of you." He sighed, his broad chest rising and falling. "Me and a couple others have been put in charge of cleaning up this fucking mess, so I don't want to see your annoying faces no more."

"Yes, captain," I replied.

"And take a few days leave, will you? It's Holy Feast on the twenty-fourth, so celebrate however you can in this Hellhole of a city. Get some fucking rest, too. You still look … off."

The captain walked away without waiting for a response. Typical, but I appreciated his bluntness. Brutal honesty was Ridgeway's style, but the way he'd used Koji had broken my trust in him. Few words that came out of his mouth now weren't blighted by the thought of Koji's blackmailed servitude.

Trust was a bloody hard thing to come by in life—let alone in Neo Kinoko.

Koji nudged me with his shoulder. "Will you be alright?"

"What?"

"The last days have not been easy," Koji said. "Is there anything I can do for you?"

"I … I'll be fine, Nameko." I angled my chin at Daigoro. "Go. Take him home to Emiko."

Koji pursed his lips. He eyed me warily.

"*Ariari do*, Hofmann-*shen*," Koji finally said. He bowed slightly, so as to not wake the boy.

I bowed in return, my midsection complaining all the while. "Thank you, too, Nameko-*kato*."

Koji smiled thinly and left, Daigoro resting safely in his arms. The boy would return to his mother, a whole life ahead of him—even if it was in this "Hellhole of a city." Second chances were rare, and they weren't to be wasted.

Elisabeth's words crept back into the forefront of my mind: *I forgive you.*

If my dying daughter could forgive her drunken wreck of a mother—the woman who took away her opportunity at life—then who else was capable of forgiveness?

In a world of sleepers, forgiveness and acceptance were fragile concepts.

How many of us were just sleepwalking through life, pulled along by the invisible strands of society, culture, and Goddamned expectations? Each day of life plagued us with the weight of guilt and trauma, continuously tearing away tiny pieces of our souls.

Coprinia had wrought its iron will upon the people of Hōppon, but look how that turned out. How many Coprinians had died or wasted their lives bending to the biddings of others?

I'd spent too long squandering my existence, doing the dirty work for powerful pricks while personal guilt consumed me. Perhaps there was a way to make a real difference from inside the NKPD. Rebuilding this post-war city, case by case, person by person.

Perhaps it was time I woke the fuck up.

WINTER HARVEST

[40] Case File #42-56
Kala Commons | 2:03 p.m.

- - - - - - - - -

I SAT ON a wobbly toadstool, holding Ryo's bandaged right hand. An organic thread-like tube trailed down her throat, feeding her nutrients. The shorn skin on her face was raw and puckered, and parts of her apricot-colored cap were peppered with shrapnel scars. Most notably, a network of mycelium and skin cells had begun to fill the gaping hole on her cheek.

I had no idea how long wounds like that would take to heal ... if they ever fully would.

The field hospital Ryo had been placed in was a madhouse. It filled the inside of a large one-story building—similar to a gymnasium or community center—and was packed with mold-cushioned beds and operating tables. The space reeked of must, piss, blood, and antiseptic chemicals. Fungal doctors and nurses tended to fungal patients—mostly refugees and those injured at Fuyu Temple.

A rolling tray with squeaky wheels cruised behind me. Whoever pushed it mumbled to herself in Hōpponese about being overworked. Her high-pitched gripes sounded just on the other side of Ryo's myco-fabric curtains.

No one in this hospital had much privacy.

I was just thankful Ryo was being taken care of by her own people—they had the patience and empathy for one of their kin. And she had the time to properly heal.

The mental scars, on the other hand … those would linger for far longer.

My ass was numb, but I was going to bloody well bear the discomfort. For her. She led Koji and I to the shine distillery in Mold Town. She had put her life on the line in order to escape a dire situation. Four innocent children were saved as a result.

In the three days since the Fuyu Festival, Hartog, Jackson, and their Vice squad had busted nine more Kinoko Rose distilleries around the city. Another was found in Mold Town, with the rest hidden in abandoned warehouses and underground tunnels. One was even discovered in a derelict ship over in The Docks.

Ryo had been the catalyst for this chain reaction.

I had to admit, the fungals were bloody resourceful. But I couldn't get over the fact that Sumi and Dikku were still breathing. Ryo was safe, yes … but for how long?

"Thank you," I whispered to her in Coprinian, massaging the mycelial bandages trailing up her arms.

Ryo stirred.

I almost jumped out of my mushroom stool—the nurses said she hadn't fully woken up since the explosion. Ryo's fingers twitched beneath their dressings. She slowly pried opened her eyelids. The vivid gold of her irises stood out, even when the flesh around was cut up and disfigured.

"H-Hofmann … is that you?" Ryo's ravaged mouth trembled when she spoke.

"*Haowa*," I said in her language.

Her lacerated lips parted in a weak smile. "G-Good afternoon to you, too … d-d-detective."

"I'm glad you're alive."

Ryo managed a feeble laugh, but winced when the pain was too much. "Me too. What … w-what happened?"

I caught Ryo up on the events of the past few days, about the explosion, the fire, and the distilleries. I walked her through Sumi and Dikku's scheme, as well as Tsutomu and the children who he'd murdered on Kinoko Rose's behalf. I told her of the Fuyu Lantern Festival and the clash between fungals and human soldiers. How Koji and I had managed to rescue the children, who were now safe and recovering in a hospital similar to this one ... despite their minds being scrambled by their traumas.

Tears ran down Ryo's cheeks, pooling in the grotesque grooves of her scabbing skin. "S-Sumi and ... my brother. Are they dead?"

I opened my mouth, but my voice stumbled over the words. How could I tell her that the men who'd haunted her were still alive?

Ryo glared at me—I knew I'd taken too long to answer. "You p-promised you would get me away from them ... That I would have a new identity and a w-w-way out of this godsforsaken city!"

I raised my hands reassuringly: "They're not free, Ryo. Sumi was taken by your people, by fungals, to receive his punishment. Dikku was taken into CPAN custody, so I doubt he will be free anytime soon."

Ryo shook her head back and forth, howling in anguish. "They will come for me ... I know they will!"

I stood so fast I almost tore the toadstool's cap from its stem. Slowly, I lowered myself next to Ryo, cupping her burnt face. "I'll take care of you. Once you're healed, I'll get you out of Neo Kinoko. For now, you're safe here—police are posted at every entrance and—"

Spit flew from her mouth: "It does not matter! You do not know them ..." Her teeth were clenched now. "They will find me ... unless they are dead, *they will find me ...*"

Ryo's ragged body shook beneath her bandages. She sobbed silently, her mouth agape and dripping drool. I hugged her tight, trying not to hurt her.

"I will protect you, Ryo," I whispered into her ear. Over and over, while her ruined figure rose and fell with each hopeless gasp.

I didn't want to fill her mind with empty promises, but what was my protection worth? Was I capable of *actually* protecting her? I didn't know how long I held onto Ryo, but I would do my bloody best to honor my vow.

If Sumi or Dikku returned—if they ever tried to lay their hands on her again—I'd bring those fungal fuckers to their knees.

That was a promise I could keep.

– – – – – –

THE SUN WAS setting, basking Reishi Temple's open plaza in an orange quilt of light. I pulled my jacket tight as I limped through the spirit gate. The winter sunsets were beautiful, but not even its warmth could counteract the bitter fucking winds.

The temple bustled with life, unlike the panicked, injured protestors Koji and I had encountered here the week prior.

Wandering into the snow-covered grounds, I perused the dozens of vendors who filled the square—they'd sprouted mushroom tables alongside one of the temple buildings to show off their wares. Bioluminescent fungi and tooth-like icicles hung from the building's polypore roof.

I overheard a squat, elderly fungal with a wide red cap haggling over mycelium scarves.

"I made these *myself*," she said. "You can't put a price on handcrafted goods!"

More practiced voices rang out with the deals. Sellers hawked mycoleather boots and belts, fragrant incense in dozens of scents, vegetables preserved in old jars, mycowax candles, bags of rice, blankets, kids' toys, and more. It was a mishmash of handicrafts and dwindling supplies for a desperate population.

Someone nearby had their radio on—it crackled as the signal came and went. The female radio host discussed a series of protests and fires across Neo Kinoko in response to the events at Fuyu Temple. There'd also been a massive fire in the Riverside ward. It had burned down a swath of the contested gang territory.

Buta Meats.

Had Sumi and Dikku destroyed the evidence before the NKPD could investigate further? Or was it a case of gang warfare gone awry?

"What're ya buyin'?" a middle-aged fungal man asked in lazy, accented Coprinian. He smirked, showing off three missing teeth.

"What're you selling?" I replied in Hōpponese.

The man's yellow eyes went wide. He scratched his slimy mushroom cap and scrambled for ideas, spouting off a list of bargain prices for crap I'd never need. "I have carved wooden statuettes, um, tobacco pipes! What else for the lovely lady?"

"*Yisima*, that's enough. I'm fine." I left him behind, continuing along the stalls.

His bargains turned into curses: "*Bakira shimin*!" Another vendor chastised him for his foul mouth.

I chuckled. I'd rather be a cheap colonizer than a fool for buying his shoddy shit.

One table in particular caught my eye. I stopped, admiring baskets full of plump mushrooms with brown caps and thick stems. A smell akin to cinnamon wafted up from the fungi, along with the sweet scent of evergreen sap—bright green pine twigs had been placed in the baskets as decoration.

"Can I interest you in some *matsutake*, detective?" a woman asked in Hōpponese, although she said the final word in Coprinian.

Detective?

I looked up. "Emiko."

Daigoro's mum stood across the table from me, her arms crossed. Dark bags cradled the undersides of her eyes, and her gills were pallid and dry. Her loose mycofabric pullover hung on her frail body like a coat hanger.

Of course, any mother whose child was missing might look the same. I know I looked like a wreck after Liz died.

Emiko stared at the mushrooms in their baskets, then up at me, then back down. She rubbed her neck. "I … I misjudged you, detective. You

…"

"It's okay," I responded. "You don't owe me anything—not even an apology."

She reached across the table and grabbed my hand. Her grip was tight, her skin cold and clammy. "But you saved my boy! You brought Daigoro back to me, and I … I will be forever grateful for that."

"Like I said, you don't owe me. Just raise him right, and keep him away from people like …"

His father.

I grimaced, but Emiko picked up on it. She leaned forward. "Koji told me what happened to Shikaku. He was a troubled man who caused pain until his end. But he got what he deserved, and Daigoro deserves a life free of his tyranny."

"At least your boy has a mother who loves him."

Emiko's eyes glittered with half-formed tears, her closed lips curving upwards. Gratitude looked awkward on her, but genuine at the same time. She let go of me and filled a mycopaper bag with mushrooms from the baskets.

"… harvested last month, before the snows came …" Emiko mumbled to herself.

In a somewhat forceful gesture, she held the bag out to me. I accepted it, a puff of earthy cinnamon wafting up from inside. Emiko bowed at the waist, beads accruing along her eyelashes.

"*Ariari do*," she whispered, and hurried off.

I squeezed the paper bag again, sniffing the intoxicating mushroom scent. I wondered how I might cook these—perhaps keep it simple with garlic and butter?

"There you are."

I turned to see Koji approaching, Daigoro at his side. The boy looked at me with bright eyes and a devilish smirk. He ran over and hugged my waist. "Hello, Henrietta!"

"Hi there, Daigoro-*bae*." I pulled him close, feeling his cap squish against my stomach.

The boy let go and waved goodbye. He ran off toward a small group of fungal and half-breed kids, who giggled and playfully tapped each other's caps. A few of them held glowing lanterns, same as the ones from the festival.

"You got my message," I said.

"I am here, am I not? How are you healing?"

"The limp is a pain in the ass, but it's the arm that bothers me." I remembered how Airi had cut into me, as if I were a piece of meat. "I appreciate you coming, though. I wanted to see Daigoro before he and Emiko leave town. How is he?"

"He is well," Koji replied. "Content to be with his mother again, and excited to meet my father."

"When do you leave?"

"Ridgeway fast tracked their paperwork to cross the checkpoints—it clears in a week. I will take them to Hajimari at the beginning of the new year."

"Goodbye, Neo Kinoko," I quipped.

"It will be good for them," Koji said, "especially Daigoro. Fresh country air, rice farms, and the slopes of Mount Maitake."

"Sounds beautiful," I replied. "I'd love to visit one day."

"I have no doubt you will." Koji placed a hand on my upper back. "I noticed you and Emiko had a chance to speak."

I snorted. "She … apologized to me. In her own way."

"You saved her son, Hofmann. That is no small thing."

"I know, it's just … Bloody Hell, after all I've witnessed the past few days, even since I arrived in Neo Kinoko …" I cocked an eyebrow and glanced at Koji. "Is there any chance fungals and humans will ever get along?"

Koji paused. "It is a possibility. When first contact takes the form of war and invasion, it does not make relations easy. But there is hope."

"Yeah …" I held my mittens to my mouth and exhaled to warm my skin. "After all the shit we went through, I might just have to start seeing a therapist. I can't even begin to imagine what you experienced during the war."

"No more wearing masks, asking about a fungal's personal life— what has happened to you, Hofmann?" Koji joked. "Is it 'that time of the month,' as you humans are so fond of saying?"

"Piss off." I backhanded him in the chest. The bastard flinched and laughed quietly.

"Your daughter …" Koji's tone turned serious. "She would have been proud of you, for what you have done and who you have become."

What felt like a brick lodged itself in my esophagus. "Thank you. For everything. I wouldn't have—*we* wouldn't have solved this case without one another." I cleared my throat and removed a mitten, reaching inside my jacket. "This is for you."

I placed a beat-up black cassette tape in his palm. He tilted his head, examining it with curiosity.

"It was one of my dad's favorites," I said. "A pilzrock band called The Wyld Kings. The song 'Outlaw Empire' in particular is fucking fantastic."

"I—" Koji stopped.

"I figured you might want to broaden your musical horizons." I pointed out five signatures, written in faded silver marker. "It's even signed by the band."

His face widened with a broad grin. "Thank you, for trusting me." He lifted the cassette tape between finger and thumb. "*And* for this thoughtful gift—though, I do not have anything to play it on."

"How about you come for rides with me in the Metro? We'll blare pilzrock all over Neo Kinoko."

"You got your car back from the shop already?" Koji chortled.

"I did."

"Then yes, I … I would like that. You have got yourself a deal."

I shifted on my feet, slipping the mitten back onto my freezing fingers. As I rubbed my hands together, a genuine question popped into my head: "What have you sensed in the fungalnet since the festival?"

"Disorientation, anguish, vengeance," Koji murmured. "Yet Neo Kinoko is coming back to life."

"Your people have experienced so much tragedy. When will it be enough?"

Koji sighed. "Life is not that simple. But know this, Hofmann: My people are predicated on resilience. We are mushrooms in the midst of a raging tempest. When the storm subsides, we find renewal where others find destruction."

I stood silent, watching the fungals in the plaza talk and haggle and smile.

"What is in the bag?" Koji asked.

I lifted Emiko's gift. "Tonight is Holy Feast. I figured I'd try something new."

"Is that so?"

"Although, I'm not entirely sure how to properly cook it, so I might need some help. Would you care to join me?"

"My first Holy Feast?" Koji said, a smug grin lifting his lips in one corner. "I would like that, but only once you tell me what is inside."

I pushed the lumpy bag into Koji's chest, the paper crinkling. "Call it a winter harvest."

Koji opened it. "It appears you were infected after all."

"Don't even fucking start," I scolded.

My face scrunched up as my mood soured a smidge. Bloody Hell … this city itself was a fungus: It colonized you from the inside out.

"Do not look so blue, Hofmann," Koji said. "Change is not always bad."

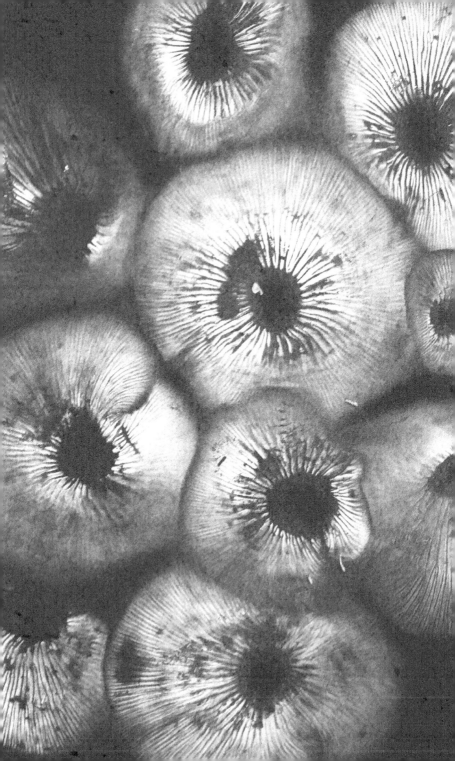

ACKNOWLEDGEMENTS

I'm a weird person, so it was inevitable that I would write a weird book. But the beauty of a project like this is that it made me realize: I didn't have to be alone in my weirdness, and books are not created in isolation. They may be written in isolation, existing within the depths of the author's imagination, but at almost every step along the way, trusted voices and opinions come into play.

I've learned this is especially true for a self-published book. So many people contributed to the dream of making *Mushroom Blues* a reality. To the wild, fantastical, hallucinatory truth that a book I wrote will now be out in the world for people to read. Whether it was someone near and dear in my life, or talented individuals who became a part of this process (professionally or otherwise), you all made this happen—for that, I am forever grateful.

That reality is due in largest part to my wife, Natalia. I am awestruck by the patience she has displayed over the years, for her endless support during my emotional ups-and-downs, and for encouraging this dream of mine to begin with. She formed the sturdy stem for my mushroom cap to rest upon, such that I could pursue this path, and she fueled me when there was little left energy in the tank.

I want to thank my parents and my brothers, who've always supported me as I ventured across the world and explored various creative pursuits. Whether it was tattooing, podcasting, or whatever else I was doing, they've had my back.

To my friends Felix Maspers and Sam Parker, you both saw The Fungalverse take shape from the very beginning. Your friendships and feedback have always been valuable, and I cherish you both. Also, a massive thank you to Viktor Eidhagen, who worked with Felix on the *Mushroom Blues* soundtrack (as the production duo Sporer). You both did an incredible job capturing the vibe of this world through music.

Nicholas Eames, who I've known since I was an immature university student. Seeing you and your career grow has been an inspiration. I'm so blessed to still have you in my life, all these years later, and I'm so glad you don't wear cargo pants anymore.

Peter Hartog and Patricia A. Jackson, the two of you mean the world to me. No one else has taught me more about writing than you, and our critique sessions really put me through the grinder that I needed in order to improve. Thank you, for breaking me down so that I could build myself up.

M. J. Kuhn, you and I have gone through some shit together. Ever since you became my co-host on SFF Addicts, your support has lifted me up through very tough times. Our burgeoning friendship is one I hold dear, and I can't wait to see what the future holds for us.

R.R. Virdi, I'm so thankful you reached out to me on social media and lit the spark for what our friendship has become. You are courageous, hilarious, and full of wisdom. I will never get tired of talking about psychedelic experiences with you.

Krystle Matar, my indie darling. You are the most punk author I know, and it has been an honor getting to know you and learn from you.

I also want to thank Ryan Cahill and Rob J. Hayes, for taking the time towalk me through self-publishing essentials. Dan Stout, who helped me get a critique group off the ground, and has since cheered on my writing. Sarah Chorn, who really helped to tighten up the earlier parts of this story, and showed immense patience. Felix Ortiz, who is an insanely talented artist and the best person I could've collaborated with for the cover of this book—the process of working with you was so smooth. Jonathan Nevair and Frasier Armitage, your feedback on the pre-release version really helped clean up some vital moments. And to the authors who offered blurbs (including Adrian Tchaikovsky, Moses Ose Utomi, Dyrk Ashton and others who I've already mentioned), having your names and words on my book is a privilege.

To David Walters and the FanFiAddict family, you all have changed my life and helped me grow, giving me the confidence to immerse myself in the SFF community. I'm so thankful that FFA was the first book blog I reached out. To The Break Ins, my debut author family on Discord, the encouragement, knowledge, and love you all give me (and each other) is a blessing.

Finally, to all of my friends in the podcasting and SFF communities, to everyone who helped with my book tour, to every guest who's appeared on SFF Addicts, and to every fan who's listened to the podcast, I am blessed to be doing what I do based on your support alone.

Much like the symbiotic mycorrhizal relationship between fungi and trees, people are nothing without the love and sustenance of those around them. I count myself so lucky to have each of you in my corner.

ABOUT THE AUTHOR

ADRIAN M. GIBSON is a Canadian speculative fiction author, podcaster and illustrator (as well as occasional tattoo artist). He was born in Ontario, Canada, but grew up in British Columbia. He studied English Literature and has worked in music journalism, restaurants, tattoo studios, clothing stores and a bevy of odd jobs. In 2021, he created the SFF Addicts podcast, which he co-hosts with fellow author M. J. Kuhn. The two host in-depth interviews with an array of science fiction and fantasy authors, as well as writing masterclasses.

Adrian has a not-so-casual obsession with mushrooms, relishes in the vastness of nature and is a self-proclaimed "child of the mountains." He enjoys cooking, music, video games, politics and science, as well as reading fiction and comic books. He lives in Quito, Ecuador with his wife and sons.

@adrianmgibson | www.adrianmgibson.com | @sffaddictspod | FanFiAddict on YouTube

Photo credit: N. Villafuerte

Weekly podcast featuring interviews and writing masterclasses with your favorite sci-fi & fantasy authors, hosted by Adrian M. Gibson and M.J. Kuhn. New episodes release every Tuesday in both audio and video.

LISTEN OR WATCH NOW!

Check out the official *Mushroom Blues* soundtrack, composed by the Swedish production duo SPORER. Featuring 8 full-length tracks, including:

SIDE A:
1. Fragmented Memories
2. Reawaken Pt. 1
3. Reawaken Pt. 3
4. Mood Hat

SIDE B:
1. Spores In The Snow
2. Rosa Svampen
3. Gargantuan Stem
4. Mushroom Blues (Outro)

LISTEN OR BUY NOW!

Listen to the MUSHROOM BLUES Spotify Playlist

A playlist of songs that inspired the world, story and atmosphere of *Mushroom Blues*. Curated by Adrian, with one song per chapter. Features original music from the book's official soundtrack.

Chapter 1: "First Light" by Brian Eno & Harold Budd

Chapter 2: "Gargantuan Stem" by Sporer (Original Song)

Chapter 3: "Made to Stray" by Mount Kimbie

Chapter 4: "Mood Hat" by Sporer (Original Song)

Chapter 5: "Return of the Fishermen" by Sweatson Klank

Chapter 6: "Ringleader" by Shigeto

Chapter 7: "My Father in Hong Kong 1961" by Gold Panda

Chapter 8: "Floating in Memories" by Moss Garden

Chapter 9: "small talk" by Seb Wildblood

Chapter 10: "Seat" by Yamaoka

Chapter 11: "Rubycon (Part One)" by Tangerine Dream

Chapter 12: "Foreign Parts" by Seb Wildblood

Chapter 13: "DNA" by The Kyoto Connection

Chapter 14: "Rosa Svampen" by Sporer (Original Song)

Chapter 15: "Spore" by Sundial Aeon

Chapter 16: "Nespole" by Floating Points

Chapter 17: "Deep Breathing" by Shigeto

Chapter 18: "Hotaru" by Hatchback

Chapter 19: "Endless Light" by Teen Daze

Chapter 20: "Against the Sky" by Brian Eno & Harold Budd

Chapter 21: "Forgive the Moth" by Gavinco

Chapter 22: "Fragmented Memories" by Sporer (Original Song)

Chapter 23: "Sapphire" by Bonobo

Chapter 24: "Supersede" by Carbon Based Lifeforms

Chapter 25: "Shinjuku Stasis" by 外神田deepspace

Chapter 26: "Interloper" by Carbon Based Lifeforms

Chapter 27: "Suspended Motion" by Gaussian Curve

Chapter 28: "Ono Waterfall" by Folamour

Chapter 29: "Ash & Snow" by Christian Löffler

Chapter 30: "Spores In The Snow" by Sporer (Original Song)

Chapter 31: "Encountered" by Si Matthews

Chapter 32: "Raum" by Tangerine Dream

Chapter 33: "Tea Spirit" by Gavinco

Chapter 34: "Window" by The Album Leaf

Chapter 35: "Migration" by Bonobo

Chapter 36: "Break Well" by Mount Kimbie

Chapter 37: "Reawaken Pt. 1" by Sporer (Original Song)

Chapter 38: "Reawaken Pt. 2" by Sporer (Original Song)

Chapter 39: "World of Sleepers" by Carbon Based Lifeforms

Chapter 40: "Mushroom Blues (Outro)" by Sporer (Original Song)

Scan the QR code below to listen on Spotify:

IMAGE ATTRIBUTION & COPYRIGHT

Printed in France by Amazon
Brétigny-sur-Orge, FR

22682737R00233